3/08

the prodigy

the prodigy

the prodigy

A Novel of Suspense by

Charles Atkins

MIDNIGHT INK
WOODBURY, MINNESOTA

First Edition
First Printing, 2008

Book design and format by Donna Burch
Cover design by Gavin Dayton Duffy
Cover art © 2007 Thinkstock/Woman's Body, and Brand X Pictures/Man's Face
Editing by Connie Hill

Midnight Ink, an imprint of Llewellyn Publications

Library of Congress Cataloging-in-Publication Data:
Atkins, Charles.
    The prodigy : a novel of suspense / by Charles Atkins. — 1st ed.
        p.   cm.
    ISBN: 978-0-7387-1039-6
    I. Title.
PS3551.T533P76   2008
813'.54 — dc22   2007038522

.
Midnight Ink
Llewellyn Publications
2143 Wooddale Drive, Dept. 978-0-7387-1039-6
Woodbury, MN 55125-2989 USA
www.midnightinkbooks.com

Printed in the United States of America

ACKNOWLEDGMENTS

The author wishes to thank the following for their help and encouragement: Al Zuckerman, Barbara Moore, Elizabeth Fitzgerald, Gary Jayson, his family, Lisa Hoffman, Stacey Rubin, Doreen Elnitsky, Colette Anderson, Maya Rock, and Elissa Velez.

ONE

Jimmy startled from a dream; something was wrong. He sniffed, expecting smoke and charred flesh, but smelled only pine-scented polish and the tang of soured milk, like baby vomit floating across a forgotten cup of tea in a Dresden cup.

The phone rang—that's what had pulled him from sleep. Kicking off the mohair throw entangling in his long legs, he belted his robe and stumbled barefoot across the silk Sarouk. The Siamese kitten, who'd been lying in wait, tackled his ankle and wrapped his mewling body around his foot. Jimmy cradled the tiny blue-eyed animal in one hand, hugging him to his chest, as he picked up the receiver.

"Hello?"

It was Ellen, his twin. "What's up, Jimmy? Carrie said you called, said it was urgent."

Fear pulsed, "Something bad happened." He remembered a fragment of his dream, there was a bird, no...two, massive vultures, and a golden-haired child running through a rocky canyon.

1

"What?"

He glanced at his ankle as the red light on his security bracelet pulsed. "Kravitz is dead."

"Oh my God! When?"

"Yesterday, I guess. I got a call from his secretary this morning. I left you a message as soon as I heard. I need another psychiatrist."

"How did he die, Jimmy?"

"I don't know," he heard suspicion in her voice. "I need you to take care of this. I can't wait," anxiety fueled his speech. "You know it's part of the agreement, I need to see a psychiatrist once a week. They have to report to the board monthly. I know who I want." Like an eager child, words blurted out.

"He wasn't that old," Ellen responded slowly, ignoring her brother's urgency. "How did it happen?"

"I don't know...Look, I know who I want. I saw her once, and then she didn't come back; you wouldn't let her. That's who I want. You know I never wanted Kravitz."

He could hear her slow exhalation. "I know...And if I refuse?" Silence.

"Are you there?" she repeated. "Are you sure? This is how it starts. You need to be sure."

"It's not like that," he said, letting the kitten suckle the tip of his baby finger. "If I don't see a shrink this week they can send me back."

"I know," she said. "I spent three years of my life, and a quarter mil in legal fees, working on your release. There are other shrinks. I'll find someone else."

"No. Her. Do this, Ellen."

"Too risky."

Why was she doing this? Anger bubbled, he had to think. "You know," he said, switching tactics, and glancing toward the mahogany doors that led to the foyer with its sweeping staircase that spiraled up the six-story townhouse. "How when we were kids we played Hansel and Gretel. Do you remember?" His voice shifted, the vowels wide, and the S's like the hissing of a snake.

"Of course."

"Do you remember what Hansel and Gretel did?"

"Stop this."

"You do remember…It's interesting how they never found any trace of our dear parents and their poor Latino driver. You'd think after dragging the lake they'd have come up with something."

"They did," she corrected him.

"That's right, I read it in the paper, an Hermés scarf and one of father's shoes. A couple of fashion accessories, Ellen, but no flesh and blood. You know, I'm curious, did mother dig up the rose garden before she died…or did that come after?"

"Jimmy, this is for your own good. You have to know that."

He tried to be patient. "I know that's what you believe…but she's the one, Chicky. You need to get her. Pay her whatever it takes."

She hesitated. "I'm not making promises…I'll let you know."

"Thanks." He blinked, and sensed her uncertainty, her unhappiness. His voice softened, sounding younger, sweeter. "Ellen…"

"Yes."

"I love you."

"I love you too, Jimmy."

He replaced the handset and stroked the purring cat. He looked out at the clutter of sheet music, and bound collections, piled high across the surface of the carved Chippendale secretary. The scores were the piano accompaniments that Dr. Morris Kravitz preferred. There were the Romberg and the Beethoven duos for cello and piano, some easy Vivaldi and books of short pieces in which Kravitz would identify a bit of Teleman or Handel that his clumsy fingers could negotiate on the Bösendorfer concert grand that stood facing an equally spectacular eighteenth-century Italian harpsichord. Jimmy's lip curled as he recalled Kravitz's attempts to conceal his musical mediocrity. "This looks interesting," he'd say, identifying a largo or lento movement with few notes, easy chords, and a minimum of flats and sharps to tax his limited abilities. It had been agony, but now…now it would be different. So why was he frightened? He could still turn back. One call to Ellen, "get someone else." He inhaled deeply, and looked across the expanse of the library. Two stories high, it was lined with glass-fronted mahogany bookcases. The parquet floors, glimpsed between intricate carpets, were deeply patinated from generations of Martin men with pipes and cigars. The French windows leaked filtered light through claret-colored drapes faded to a light rose at their sun-kissed edges. The paintings, bronzes, and marble sculptures were English, French, and Italian, purchased by great-great-grandfather James Cyrus Martin on his art-grab tours through cash-hungry, turn-of-the century Europe.

Yes, Jimmy thought, with Kravitz finally out of the way, things would be different. This would be the first step toward a new life; the life he'd always wanted. Dressed only in his plush robe—a present from Ellen—he put down the protesting kitten and picked up Allegra, his darkly varnished Amati cello, and nestled it between his hairless legs. His mind drifted as he resined his bow and plucked the strings, finding them still in tune from last night. His fingers, trained by a lifetime of daily practice, moved effortlessly through the arpeggios of the first movement of the Bach Unaccompanied Suites. Even the years he'd been forbidden from playing had not dulled his talent; if anything his artistry was sharpened. Once the calluses had reformed on the pads of his fingers, the pain of those years locked away...tortured...had given birth to a passion and urgency in the music. His mind floated. Graceful passages soared through the air as he remembered his dream. He was standing over the kitchen sink and through the window saw two massive birds circling the sky over Mother's rose garden. At first he'd been excited, thinking, *the vultures have returned*, and then he saw a golden-haired child running below them. Only they were no longer in Manhattan, but in a vast canyon. One of the birds—a black-and-white one with a huge wingspan—swooped down upon the fleeing toddler and sank his talons into the flesh of his back. Horrified, Jimmy ran after the bird, only to see its mate dive toward the dangling child as he was carried into the sky. Just as a mid-air collision seemed inevitable, the black-and-white vulture dropped the boy. Jimmy raced toward the toddler, certain that the fall meant death. He did not want to find a dead child; how would he explain it? They'd blame him. Still, he had to see.

The boy was alive. He was quiet, almost calm. He couldn't have been more than three, with apple-blush cheeks, liquid blue eyes, and a shock of thatch-gold hair. He had the face of the perfect American toddler, the one that got plastered on baby food jars, or on milk cartons that carried the tragic whiff of abduction and murder.

The boy looked at him, "I want to go home," he said.

"Where do you live?" Jimmy asked, wondering how it was that a child so young could speak so clearly.

"You know."

As he passed seamlessly into the second movement of the Bach, Jimmy focused on the child's face. He saw something familiar, something he couldn't place. As the connection crystallized, the moon-faced grandfather-clock chimed. Halfway through its pronouncement, the doorbell rang.

Jimmy blinked and stared at the clock as it struck ten. An hour had passed, sometimes much more than that would slip away, sometimes days, and sometimes weeks. Getting up, he let the folds of his robe cover his legs as he placed the priceless cello into its rosewood cradle. He loosened the strings of his gold-and-ivory-tipped bow, picked up the kitten and went to the front door. He knew who it was, but peered through the fisheye anyway, affording him a distorted vision of Gramercy Park and the hundred-fifty-year-old Gingko tree out front. A caramel-colored face smiled up at him; the man lifted a brown-paper shopping bag.

"Sounding good, man," Hector said as Jimmy opened the door.

"Thank you."

"You know, I get here early just to hear you play. I didn't think I liked all that classical music, but I've got to tell you I've bought some CDs since getting to know you." Hector looked past Jimmy up the sweeping expanse of the staircase that rose like a twisted spine through the Italianate townhouse. "I even bought one of yours."

"They're hard to find," Jimmy answered, wondering how long this conversation with his puppy-eager, court-mandated case manager would last. "Everything back then was on vinyl."

"You know, I could transfer them to CDs."

"Thanks, but that's a part of my life that's over. No need to bring it back." But as he said that, he tasted the long-forgotten feel of stepping across a concert stage, making his way into the spotlight, nodding to the conductor, feeling the applause. What would it be like, to have that again, to have that with her?

"It seems a pity," Hector replied. "I mean you could really do something with it. Although I guess money really isn't your problem."

"No," Jimmy agreed.

"Well," Hector put down the grocery bag and pulled a plastic box out of his backpack. "I guess you'll be wanting these."

"I guess I will." Jimmy set Fred on the table, picked up the bag and led Hector—who even after three months still gawked at the mansion—back toward the kitchen.

Jimmy opened the polished-chrome refrigerator, pulled out a milk carton and stared at it—no picture of a blond-haired child, just the chart of nutritional benefits. He watched as Hector counted out his medication—900 milligrams of lithium, and 3 of Risperdal—and dropped them into a tiny plastic cup.

Jimmy took the pills and swigged them back with milk. He sat and opened his mouth so that Hector could inspect. He lifted his tongue and moved it from side to side.

"Looks good," Hector replied, in a chatty tone. "So we need to find you a new psychiatrist. It's sad. I liked Dr. Kravitz."

"Me too," Jimmy said, "but I think I've already found a replacement."

"No kidding, that's great, man. Who did you get?"

"I don't know for certain, but I'll let you know as soon as I find out."

Hector eyed Jimmy warily, "You know it's got to be somebody that the board approves."

"I know. I'm trying to get someone who already works for the department. I met her once when I was in Croton, so I don't think there should be a problem."

"A woman psychiatrist? You think they'll go for that...I mean with what you...sorry, man. I shouldn't say shit like that, it was a long time ago. Right?"

"Right," Jimmy glanced up at the clock, wondering when Hector would leave.

"Maybe I know her."

"Maybe," Jimmy stared at his ankle bracelet as it winked its fifteen-second reminder.

"You don't want to say?" Hector persisted.

"I can't see the point. If she agrees, then I'll tell you."

"Oh, come on, man. What's the big secret?"

Jimmy looked at the eager smile on his aide's face. "Dr. Barrett Conyors."

Hector whistled, "Hot shit!"

"You know her?" Jimmy asked, surprised by the response.

"Who doesn't? They call her in for all the hard cases. She's one very smart lady. And..." Hector smiled, "she's not hard to look at either. You think she'll take over for Dr. Kravitz?"

"I hope so," he said, finding that Hector's response triggered a mixture of emotions, pride that she was so highly esteemed and fear that he was getting into something that might go bad. Still, the memory of her beautiful face and stormy gray eyes called to him. Fate had brought her to him in the hospital. He'd recognized her immediately; she was the one, the only one.

"I hope you're right," Hector said. "But if it doesn't work, let me know. You know we can't let too much time go by…So, you want me to pick you up anything for this afternoon or tomorrow?"

Jimmy heard the eagerness in his youthful voice, like feeding time at the zoo. "Sure," he reached into his pocket and felt the sandpaper rasp of hundred-dollar bills. He glanced at the refrigerator. "Just some milk, a T-bone steak—have them trim the fat—some frozen macaroni-and-cheese, some kind of fish for Fred—maybe wild salmon—not the farmed kind—but make sure they take out the bones—and if it's not too much trouble, you could stop by Fisher's and get me an A string."

"Pirastro Eudoxa, right?"

"That's right," Jimmy said, pleased that Hector had remembered the correct brand of cello string. He pulled out three one-hundred dollar bills, two of them he'd ironed together to where they looked and felt like a single piece of currency—an honest mistake. "Just keep the change for your trouble," he said, well aware that the total amount would have been covered by a little more than a hundred dollars.

"No problem," Hector wadded the bills into the pocket of his chinos. "You sure you don't want anything else?"

Jimmy thought about saying, *my freedom*, but even things said in jest had a way of getting distorted and magnified into something that could hurt him. "I'm all set." Without further talk, he led Hector back through the banquet hall that could seat forty, the Victorian side parlor, and finally, the foyer.

"Our boy's doing well," Hector remarked as Fred lunged for his ankle.

Jimmy paused, not certain what Hector was referring to.

"The cat, man."

"Right."

"He's getting big. I was a little worried they weren't going to let you keep him. Or that he wouldn't make it. He was pretty sick when we found him."

Jimmy froze, sensing that a trick was about to be played on him. *Don't let them take Fred.*

The aide kept talking, unaware of the mounting panic surging in Jimmy; *don't let them take my kitty.*

"I'm glad they let you keep him. You need somebody in a place like this. It's an awesome crib, but I'd go out of my mind without some people around."

Jimmy pressed his lips into a smile. "It's better like this. I can deal with animals, it's people that give me a hard time."

"I hear you," Hector replied. "I'll see you at five, then."

Jimmy opened the door, clutching the purring kitten and keeping his face hidden in the shadows. He watched as Hector bounced down the eight brownstone stairs and walked across the street to where he'd chained his bicycle to the cast-iron spokes of the fence that encircled Gramercy Park. Not for the first time, Jimmy noted how the tips of the fence were like spearheads. He wondered if that was intentional, an added reminder to outsiders that they were not welcome inside the private park. He locked the heavy oak door and watched through the fisheye as Hector liberated his bicycle and pedaled away.

To Jimmy, this twice-daily ritual had achieved a dance-like quality. As Hector vanished, Jimmy retraced his steps to the kitchen. Turning on the faucet he observed the silvery flash of water as it landed on stainless steel and swirled clockwise down the drain. He stuck two well-calloused fingers down his throat. The pills, protected from his gastric juices by the milk bath, found their way easily out of his stomach and into the sink. He grabbed the hose and chased the undissolved medications down the drain.

He stared out the kitchen window onto the devastated remains of Mother's rose garden. Beyond that, completely hidden by trees and brambles, stood the two-story carriage house that Ellen had cleared of its tenants prior to Jimmy's release from Croton. Growing up, it's where mother's chauffeurs had lived. He looked at the gnarled vines, and realized that this was the scene that had started his dream. Great things would soon happen in that building. He hummed the opening bars of Chopin's *Revolutionary Étude*—the piece she'd played all those years ago. Closing his eyes he heard the dizzying passages. His breath quickened as he pictured her. She was dressed in a cheap, homemade, blue velvet dress with white lace at the collar and at the hem. He remembered how she'd crossed the stage and sat to play, her thin legs barely reaching the pedals, her eyes intense, and then the music…unlike anything he'd ever heard before…or since. And then he saw the woman who'd come to visit him that one time at Croton, her eyes filled with compassion and love. Her voice, tinged with the soft Southern vowels of his childhood nanny. His chest tightened, and he felt a fierce longing. Lost in the moment, he didn't hear the phone until the answering machine picked up on the sixth ring.

He listened as Ellen's voice spoke over the message. "Jimmy, pick up."

He grabbed for the receiver, "Hi, Ellen."

"Well," his sister did not sound happy. "Here's the deal…"

TWO

DR. BARRETT CONYORS GLANCED anxiously over the head of her chain-shackled patient at the wire-fronted prison clock in the cement wall. It was nearly four and it had been one hell of a day. If traffic was good—and that was a big if—she could be parked back in Manhattan by six. It was her mother's birthday and she would not be late. But there was still the matter at hand to be gotten through, and she'd been dreading this for weeks. Her gray-blue eyes looked Charlie straight on, as she ran a hand through short-cropped hair.

"What is it, Doc?" he asked. "You got a date?"

"Nice try." She leaned forward, the sleeves of her navy suit—bought on final markdown at Loehman's—touched the scarred wood surface of the bolted-down table.

"Then what? You're going to tell me something bad, aren't you?"

She met Charlie's gaze. Over the past eighteen months he'd cleaned up nicely. Not at all the bedraggled and wild-eyed madman who'd been captured—in part thanks to her—in a cave-like stretch of abandoned tunnel near the East 33rd Street station. Now, his beard, shot through with streaks of white, was trimmed and his thick coarse-gray hair had been cut and neatly parted. If it weren't for the hospital-issue jumpsuit and the chain attached at his waist, his wrists, and his ankles, he might have passed for a professor.

"You know what this is about, Charlie."

"Time's up, huh?" his arms strained against his shackles.

"You got it in one."

"What's the verdict?"

She hated this part; it made her stomach churn. She knew that Charlie Rohr, like others in his family, suffered with serious mental illness. In his case, the voices inside his head and bizarre delusions gave him a diagnosis of schizophrenia. Bad enough, but through some horrible collision of genetics and upbringing, Charlie Rohr was also a murderous sociopath. For nearly five years he'd preyed on transvestite prostitutes on the West Side. His victims were members of a population prone to bad things, but Charlie's psychotic flourishes had pushed him onto the police radar. And when he mistook a "partying" city official, who was out for the night in drag, for one of his usual victims, Barrett—a forensic psychiatrist—had been called in as a consultant to profile the killer. Some tabloid reporter had dubbed Charlie the Caravaggio killer, after the renaissance painter who had created images that were both glorious and horrifying, most notably Saint Sebastian crucified and shot through with arrows—just like Charlie's victims. Only instead of arrows, he used knitting needles with which he'd blind and pierce.

14

"The judge isn't buying the insanity plea," she told him bluntly.

"Because of you?" Charlie asked.

"It's a tough standard, Charlie. And all along you knew your actions were wrong."

"That's not true. It was the voice of God. I was just following the word of God. I was his angel. I am…" he stopped himself.

Barrett was startled by an intensity in his dark eyes that she'd not seen in months. She recognized that no matter how good he looked, or how rational he sounded in brief moments, beneath his veneer of sanity lurked a psychosis never fully dampened by the medication.

"You hid your crimes, Charlie," she said softly, wondering if there was any way to do this with kindness. "You covered your tracks. If you want a not guilty by reason of insanity ruling you can't do those things."

"But you said I'm sick. Aren't you the one who keeps telling me that I have schizophrenia," his voice swelled and his words spilled fast. "Aren't you the one who tells me that it's a biologic condition? That I was born with it. This isn't my fault. I'm sick. I need to be in a hospital." He glared at her accusingly, "I took your pills!"

"I know," despite his shackles, she edged back. "It's the law, Charlie. You know what's going on now; you didn't before. You're going to have to stand trial."

And there it was, the essential kernel of their relationship hung in the air.

"You must feel real good about this," he said. "You've done your job. That's what this is about. You were here to get my craziness under control so that they can send me to the chair. I'm competent to stand trial; isn't that what you call it?"

"Yes."

"So let me get this straight. You're a doctor, right?"

"Yes."

"I thought doctors weren't supposed to kill their patients. You made me better so that I can fry."

"This is my job, Charlie," she replied, hating the canned sound of her answer.

"Did you know that the Nazis put doctors in charge of the concentration camps? Just following orders? Well, fuck you, Dr. Conyors!"

Barrett pushed away—under normal circumstances she would already have been out of there. She didn't put up with this kind of language from anyone. But Charlie had reason. While she'd repeatedly told him the rules, that there was no confidentiality and that her alliance was to the State of New York and the preservation of public safety, she was also his psychiatrist. And for the last eighteen months she'd worked hard to get his voices under control...so that he could stand trial. He was correct; he could get the death penalty—in addition to the prostitutes and the councilman, he'd killed a cop with a crowbar—at the very least he'd get life without the possibility of parole.

"So now what?" His words spat between clenched teeth.

"You'll leave here, she said, her body tense. "You'll go to a behavioral health unit in a maximum security facility while you await trial."

"When?"

"Today," she said, knowing that there were two marshals just outside, ready to transport.

"And my lawyer?"

"She knows." What she omitted was the request from Charlie's chicken-shit public defender that Barrett be the one to break the news.

"Then we're done," he said.

She wanted to tell him that she was sorry. But what good would that do? Sure she was sorry, sorry that he had to have schizophrenia and sorry that he was tormented by voices that told him to do horrible things. "Goodbye, Charlie." Barrett stood and walked back to the door of the interview room—she wanted out. She looked through the wire-mesh window and saw the two marshals—a twenty-something man and a stocky Latina woman—whose job it was to transport Charlie from Croton State, where he'd lived since his arrest, to a maximum security prison.

She tapped on the door and tried not to think about what she'd just done. Charlie was crazy, but stupid he wasn't and he'd honed in on her dilemma. Doctors weren't supposed to hurt their patients, and that's exactly what she'd made possible. Because of her, Charlie could get death. "What have you done, Barrett?" she muttered. And not for the first time she wondered if this was any kind of work for a psychiatrist, any kind of work for her.

She stepped through the door and stood back as the marshals and the guard entered the interview room.

As the Croton guard unlocked Charlie's shackles her gaze landed on something that shouldn't have been. She wasn't the only one to see it, and what happened next took on a horrifying slow-motion quality. The younger of the two marshals had somehow made it through security with his sidearm—a severe breach of policy.

In the split second that she realized the potential for disaster, Charlie's shackles clicked open, and the previously docile patient leapt at the inexperienced officer. Barrett stood transfixed as Charlie's sinuous fingers liberated the weapon from its holster. The marshal, realizing too late, grabbed for his gun. A shot exploded in the cement-and-metal room. The marshal, who looked like he could have just graduated from high school, clutched at his throat. There was a wet sucking noise as bright red blood gurgled between his fingers and he sank to the floor.

Charlie's gaze darted around the room; he pointed the gun first at the guard—an old-timer—then at the female marshal. Like an uprooted carnival wheel his gun hand spun around, as he tried to think.

He saw Barrett through the open door. "You see what you did, doctor! All your fault. I don't want to fry!"

"Don't do this, Charlie." Barrett tried to hold his attention, but almost telepathically she knew what he intended. "Don't do it."

"And why not, *doctor*?" His voice softened and his eyes fixed on hers. Never breaking their gaze, his gun hand came up to the side of his head and he lodged the barrel against his ear. Words spilled fast from his mouth, at first she couldn't hear, but then, "...I shall not want. He maketh me to lie down in still waters, he leadeth me by the way. Yea, though I walk through valley of the shadow of death I shall fear no evil." His eyes burned into hers, his lips kept moving. He squeezed the trigger, and mainlined a ball of burning lead into his brain; there was little blood as his head jerked, his knees buckled and he fell to the floor.

"No!" Barrett screamed as her nostrils filled with the bitter smell of singed flesh and hair. Her ears rang with the gun's reverberation and the hoarse screams of the elderly guard. She moved slowly toward Charlie and felt something stick to the bottom of her low-heeled pump. She looked at a puddle of something oily and dark. She turned. The marshal Charlie had shot stared back at her. Tears tracked down his clean-shaven face; he tried to speak, no words, just a froth of pink blood that dribbled from his lips.

"Call a code!" Barrett shouted to the guard. Even as the words left her mouth she realized where she was. Croton Forensic was a hospital all right, but the only kind of doctors wandering the halls were shrinks like her. Not exactly what you needed for a direct hit to the carotid artery.

The white-haired guard, who was counting the months until his retirement, was having trouble standing. His arthritic knees shook beneath his gray polyester uniform. "You mean a code yellow?" he gasped, clutching at his chest.

"Whatever. Just get an ambulance and paramedics as fast as you can. You…" she turned to the female marshal, "go with him." The dark-haired woman nodded mutely, shell-shocked and eager to flee. Barrett turned her attention back to the injured officer. "It's going to be okay, just hang on, we're going to get you help."

The young man tried to speak.

"Don't," she knelt down and put her hand over his. She pressed in against the side of his neck to stem the massive seepage.

His brown eyes blinked as he struggled against the blood loss and encroaching shock.

"Hang on," she whispered as his hand lost strength. "Just hang on." His body went limp. She checked his damaged neck, and then jammed her hand back down. His liquid pulse throbbed against her palm; with each beat she felt it weaken. She watched his chest waiting to see the rise and fall; it didn't come. He'd stopped breathing and it would be a matter of seconds before he'd go into full cardiac arrest. Keeping her hand clamped to his neck she eased him down flat onto the cement floor. She pinched his nose shut, sealed her lips over his and attempted to breathe into his lungs. She felt resistance as her air didn't make it past his throat. She repositioned his head, feeling his ever-weakening pulse against the flat of her hand. She broadened her stance and heard the unmistakable rip of her skirt. She pressed her full lips against his open mouth, tasting blood and the salt of his saliva; no air went in. As seconds passed, she felt him slipping away. She tried a third time and a fourth. She pushed his head back, hoping to open the airway, but still nothing. Her fingers felt tiny crackles beneath the clammy surface of his upper chest. She looked down at his neck and saw that his Adam's apple and windpipe had twisted toward the left. It took her brain a panicked moment to register the reality; he'd dropped a lung. She'd seen this before as an intern, even performed the procedure once. Only then, she'd been surrounded and supervised by emergency room doctors and trauma nurses, with all of the latest equipment, and years of experience.

She looked around, her eyes wide. She needed help, and there was none. Everything was bolted to the floor. She needed a chest tube. She patted her inside breast pocket and found a ballpoint pen. Biting down on the tip she pulled out the ink cartridge and then bit off the nub on the other end.

The man's pulse was barely palpable. Holding tight to his neck, she ripped his shirt open with her other hand; a button hit her below the eye as another pinged against the floor. She flinched slightly, eyeballed his rib cage, and grasping the plastic pen casing, placed its tapered end against the flesh an inch below and a palm's-breadth lateral to his right nipple. Using all her strength, and praying that the plastic wouldn't shatter, she pressed in, tearing through skin and muscle as she jammed a bloody path between his ribs and the membranous casing that surrounded his lungs. Seconds ticked by as she worked at her gory task, it seemed like hours, and she wondered if all she were doing was defacing the body of a dying man. In reality, it was just over a minute before a moist sputtering sound rewarded her efforts, as blood and air escaped from the deputy's chest.

Leaning over, she again attempted to breathe into him, and this time the air passed through his mouth and expanded his lungs. Between bloody breaths she clamped down on the pen, knowing that to not do so would cause his lungs to again collapse. At least his pulse was still pumping, weakly, but still there.

When the paramedics finally arrived, she felt a tremendous wave of relief, as they stomped in with their bright-orange field kits and oxygen tanks strapped to a gurney. They quickly replaced her makeshift chest tube with the real thing, hooking it to a vacuum seal in an attempt to stabilize the critically wounded marshal's chest.

"Tension pneumothorax," one of the medics commented, as he strapped a pressure bandage onto the man's neck, letting Barrett have her hand back. "That's quite a pickup. You a doc?"

"Yes," Barrett rolled back on her heels, not caring that she was perched in a pool of blood. She started as her gaze met Charlie's open eyes; even in death they held his accusation.

"Emergency room?" the medic asked.

"Huh?"

"Are you an emergency room doctor?"

"Psychiatrist," she pulled her gaze off Charlie.

"No shit."

She stood to help the paramedics slide the marshal onto the wooden backboard.

"No shit," she answered dully, as they hoisted him onto the stretcher and beat a hasty retreat.

———

Two hours later, and still badly shaken, Barrett pressed down with a new ballpoint through quadruplicate carbonless forms attempting to put what had just happened into a sequence. They had sent the guard home, leaving her as the only witness to fill out the paperwork. There would be hell to pay on this one. How did they let the kid into the facility with a firearm? She tried not to think about that, just like she resisted the urge to call the hospital—yet again—to get a status report on the wounded officer, Corey Williams, aged twenty-two. He'd be in surgery for hours; at least he was still alive. But Charlie, her patient, was dead. She kept seeing his eyes, and hearing his accusations. "Doctors aren't supposed to kill their patients..."

Alone in the guard's grungy office, she tried to focus on the stupid little check boxes. The instructions were clear—"leave no blanks." Much as she detested filling out forms, she knew that what found its way into the medical record became history. As a forensic psychiatrist, this was especially true. It's what she was taught and it's how she instructed her medical students and residents. "If it's not in the record, it didn't happen."

She signed her note, and entered a second one into Charlie Rohr's chart. A tear slid off her cheek and splattered on the blue-lined paper.

Her pager—set on vibrate—buzzed against her hip. She looked at the display—it was her home number.

She dialed; her fingers felt numb.

"Barrett?" her sister picked up on the first ring.

"Justine."

"Where are you, girl?…What's wrong?"

"Don't ask."

"You're still at work, aren't you?"

"Uh huh," Barrett signed her note.

"We have reservations for seven," her younger sister reminded her.

"I'm still at Croton."

"Barrett…if I didn't know you better I'd say you were avoiding coming home."

"I'm sorry," she struggled to keep her voice steady. "You would not believe the day I've had."

"Well, we still love you. So what's the plan?"

"I'm just getting finished. I can be out the door in five minutes. So give me an hour and a half. Okay?"

"Wait a minute…Hold on, Mom wants to talk to you."

"Hi, sweetheart," a strong, south-of-Atlanta Georgia accent, like being tucked into bed, floated across the line.

Barrett glanced at the shredded seam of her skirt, "I'm so sorry, Mom. I wanted this to be a good birthday."

"Just stop right there. You'll get home when you get home."

"But, it's your birthday."

"Don't remind me…and don't worry. So what's wrong?"

"It's nothing," she said, seeing Charlie's wide-eyed stare as he mouthed Psalm 23 and pulled the trigger. "I love you, Mom."

"I know you do."

After she hung up, Barrett closed the chart and handed it off to the records clerk. As she passed through the security check and retrieved her briefcase and pocketbook, she asked the guard in the booth, "So what happened?" Her voice was shaky.

The silver-haired old-timer shrugged his shoulders. "I just got on."

"I'm not saying it was your fault. I just want to know how it happened. Why didn't his gun get picked up by the metal detector? Not to mention that there are signs everywhere telling officers to surrender their weapons before entering."

"He was young, Dr. Conyors—maybe he couldn't read."

Barrett looked through the bulletproof window. There was something in the man's expression, indifference…contempt. Many of the guards had been here for decades—just like the patients. They were institutionalized and resistant to change. Psychiatrists were viewed as patient-coddlers, and a woman psychiatrist, well that was just wrong.

She stared him down, "Someone didn't do their job, and because of it, my patient is dead and a twenty-two-year-old law officer might not live through the night."

The guard said nothing as he slid the sign-out clipboard beneath the opening in the window.

Barrett found her name two pages back and logged out. She needed to get out of there. What made this even worse was that she'd been on a committee appointed by the Croton superintendent to develop a policy on firearms four years ago. That committee had been formed following another incident, one that had left two guards wounded and a patient and his wife dead in a murder-suicide. The instrument of destruction had been a guard's Ruger Speed Six.

At the time, she'd visited every forensic hospital in New England. When they'd wrapped up the study it was clear—Croton was years behind in allowing its aging force of guards to carry firearms into patient areas. What she hadn't counted on was the powerful resistance to the new policy. She had no doubt that the rosy-cheeked deputy had been waved through with a nudge and a wink, his firearm clearly visible from the guard's observation booth. It would stretch out into a long investigation, and as typically happened, if it stayed out of the papers—and it would—whoever was responsible would get off with a wrist slap.

Dusk was falling on the warm late-April night as she retrieved her two-year-old leased Saab 9-3 convertible from the physician's lot. With trembling fingers she undid the latches and opened the top. Pushing eighty, she cranked up a Neville Brothers CD, needing the feel of speed and wind as it whipped through her hair. An hour and fifteen minutes later she pulled off the Henry Hudson and headed east on 28th. She signaled left and took the ramp to the underground garage that cost her $1,000 a month.

From there it was just a block's walk to her one-bedroom co-op between 8th and 9th Avenue. Her body felt tight and she wished that she could cancel dinner. Just have a shot or two of whiskey and soak in the tub. But as she got off the elevator on the fourth floor and saw a band of light spilling from her condo, she tensed.

Adrenalin pumped at the sound of a man's voice. She pushed open the door and saw her husband, Ralph, dressed in his concert tux, ensconced on their cream-colored sofa. "What are you doing here?" she asked, feeling the room spin. She did not want to see him, her anger still too hot.

"Barrett, what happened?" A look of concern crossed his face.

Justine, her long hair up, appeared from behind the galley kitchen, she stared at her sister. "Jesus! Are you okay?"

Barrett caught her reflection in the chrome-framed mirror next to the door. What she saw was a tall, dark-haired woman in a crumpled navy suit with a bloodstained linen shirt, torn and stained panty hose, and a jagged tear up the side of her skirt.

Justine went to her, "You okay?"

"What's he doing here?" Barrett asked, trying to avoid Ralph's worried gaze. "And where's Mom?"

"I couldn't stop him. And Mom decided we're having fried chicken and biscuits. She went to D'Agostinos."

Barrett turned to Ralph, avoiding his rich brown eyes. "Please leave," she said, while a part of her so wanted him to hold her.

"We have to talk, Barrett. I don't know what to say." He lowered his voice, "I'm sorry. It was a mistake."

"Look," she said, noticing how his jet-black hair was starting to turn silver around his sideburns, and that his smile still made something inside of her go weak. "I thought we agreed…" she needed to stay strong, to not give in. "I need time."

"I know. I just came to pick up some stuff before the concert."

Barrett found it hard to speak. It had been less than two weeks since she'd come home in the middle of a Wednesday afternoon with the news that her research, on the classification of sociopaths into those who could be safely brought back into the community and those who needed to be indefinitely locked up, had been accepted for publication in the prestigious *American Journal of Medicine*. They'd even suggested that, with a little more work, they'd publish her groundbreaking work as a book. Ralph—the principal trombonist for the Manhattan symphony—had no rehearsal on Wednesdays, so she had wanted to celebrate. What she hadn't expected was to find him with Carol Gartner—a woman she considered her friend—naked in their bed.

Barrett looked at her sister, needing the anchor of her closeness. "Please go, Ralph."

Justine stood by her sister, "You should leave."

Barrett felt the tears; her throat tightened, and she couldn't speak.

"I'll go," he said. "But we have to talk. I don't want us to be over, Barrett. I'll do whatever you want." His full lips softened into a smile, dimples formed.

Damn him, she thought, wishing she could be angrier. As he turned to go, she realized he hadn't taken anything, that he'd come here just to talk, to try and make things better. But how do you do that? How do you erase the image of Carol's blond curls matted with sweat on your own pillow? How could she trust him? And why did she want to stop him from leaving? To feel his warmth against her, the velvet of his smooth olive skin. *Damn him!*

She stared at the open door as Ralph's footsteps grew fainter. She felt numb as Justine came from behind and hugged her. They listened as the outer door opened, closed, and then opened again.

High heels clicked on the hallway tiles, there was a rustle of plastic bags, and then Ruth Conyors, who, from a distance, could have passed for Barrett and Justine's older sister, appeared in the doorway. Her auburn hair—once natural and now from a bottle—was pinned up; large gold hoops accented her long neck and still-firm jaw line, which she had passed on to her daughters.

"Sweet Jesus! What happened, Barrett?" Ruth's Georgia accent still as strong as the day she left the state.

"It's nothing," Barrett, said. "Let me get changed and then we can go out."

"Don't be ridiculous," Ruth said. "Was that Ralph?"

Justine nodded.

"Is someone going to tell me what's going on?" Ruth asked.

"I feel sick," Barrett sank onto the roughly woven pale-cotton upholstery; she stopped herself. "Look at this," she turned around to show them the bloodied-back of her ruined skirt, "it's all over my car. I should have changed, but I just wanted to get home."

Ruth deposited her bags on the galley kitchen counter that opened into the living area, which contained a small dining nook, a couch, two stuffed chairs, and a massive Mason and Hamlin piano that had been a gift from Barrett's beloved mentor, Sophie.

Ruth looked at her two beautiful daughters, both of them doctors, Justine just finishing her training as a surgeon, and Barrett with her odd choice to work with mentally ill criminals. "Are you hurt?"

"I don't think so."

"You're covered in blood. What happened?"

"It's not mine," Barrett shook her head. "I'm not hurt."

"But someone is."

"I don't want to talk about it…someone got careless and because of it…" She couldn't speak for a moment. "Because of it, my patient is dead. He killed himself, and I watched him do it."

"Oh, Barrett. I'm so sorry."

Feeling as though her head were about to explode, she ripped off her skirt and bloodied slip, and sank onto the sofa, unable to stop the convulsive sobs that shook her.

Justine silently sat beside her and cradled her head against her neck. "It's going to be okay," she said smoothing her sister's silky hair.

Barrett wiped her nose with the back of her hand. "Why did Ralph have to be here? This day was awful enough. Why? Why did he have to do this? Why wasn't I enough? Why?" Tears flowed.

Ruth, busying herself in the kitchen, felt her daughter's heartache, as she pulled down a saucepan and emptied in a bottle of peanut oil. *Conyors women*, she thought, *have bitter luck with men.*

"It's not your fault," Justine said.

"No, it never is." Ruth mouthed, as she rinsed the chicken parts, and assembled her breading—flour, salt, pepper, paprika, oregano, and two whisked egg yolks. Leaving that in a glass bowl, she scooped out Bisquick and threw together biscuit batter. She pictured her own father, a man her girls had never met, who'd died from cirrhosis, who was sweet as pie when sober, and the devil when liquored, which was the usual state of affairs after two in the afternoon. And as daughters will do, Ruth had found a man just like him—Barrett and Justine's daddy—a good-ole-boy sheriff in Pike County, Georgia, whom she'd married at the ripe age of sixteen.

"You have to be strong, Barrett," she said, letting her voice carry, as the oil heated and started to crackle.

"I don't feel strong, Mama." She couldn't look at either one of them. "…this wasn't the first time with Ralph."

"You never told me," Justine said.

"I didn't want to hear what you'd say. He swore it would never happen again. I wanted to believe him." She tried to slow her breathing. "I work with people who lie to me constantly; I expect it. If someone's facing hard time, if someone's a sociopath, you expect it. But Ralph's my husband…I loved him so much. I still do…it would have been better if he'd just hit me. Just hauled off and belted me."

"Don't say that!" Ruth said, feeling her cheeks burn, as she turned the oven knob to preheat. "Don't ever say that!"

"I'm sorry, it's just then everything would be clear. I'd know he was a bastard."

"It's okay," Justine whispered.

"It's not," Barrett said. "And I can't help thinking that this is my fault. Maybe I didn't pay enough attention to him, or…"

"Or what?" Justine prompted.

"Or maybe all that stuff you don't want to believe is true. That men can't take having a woman make more money, or be more successful…All through high school I felt like I had to hide my grades if I ever wanted a boy to look at me. And then you become an adult and you think that stuff doesn't matter anymore, but it does, doesn't it? I know it bothers him…" She put her hands to her face, and thought of all the little warning signs she didn't want to see. Like the fact that she hid her pay stubs, or how half the time she wouldn't even tell him when she'd had an article published, or the time she had to cancel a vacation to testify in an important case and he'd accused her of caring more about her job than him.

Ruth dropped a drumstick into the oil, her ears attuned to the pitch of the sizzle. "It's more than that," she said. "Men get angry when they find that their women are strong. Like it's not our place to do for ourselves. And fools that we are, we believe it."

Barrett and Justine waited for more, their childhood filled with snippets of how they'd come to New York. Barrett had been seven, Justine three, but twenty-five years ago, Ruth Conyors, her eyes blackened and her ribs bruised, had taken her two babies, a 1964 Chevy station wagon, and the clothing on their backs, left unincorporated Williamson, Georgia, and driven north in the dead of night.

"Barrett, you get cleaned up, and Justine, you make a salad, and somewhere I know you've got a bottle. I think for my forty-eighth birthday what I really want is fried chicken, biscuits, bourbon, and a night with my girls."

As the savory smells of Mama's biscuits and chicken filled the condo, Barrett retreated to the bathroom. She unclasped her bra and stepped out of her panties, picked them up, and tossed them into the wastebasket. No way were the reddish-brown stains ever coming out and she didn't need any souvenirs. The Armani suit was also a lost cause, and that was a problem. She had had three suitable-for-court suits; it would have to be replaced. And right now, money was a huge issue. She could talk about man problems with her mother and sister, but she'd sworn that she'd never let them know how tight things were. About the nights she lay awake obsessing over bills that came with a crushing regularity. And if she and Ralph split…Damn. Would she even be able to make the mortgage—$3500 a month? That plus helping Justine with her school loans—$750 a month, her Mama's health insurance—$600 a month, her own school loans—$528, the parking garage, car payments, insurance, utilities. Yeah, doctors make good money, but even earning 150K a year at the clinic, not having Ralph's 75K from the orchestra; no way. No fucking way; it didn't add up.

She stepped into the shower, letting the first cool spray wash over her. As it warmed up she reached for the soap; she froze as her hand connected with the clear amber bar, with its fragrance of orange blossom and lemon zest, a gift, a remembrance of their honeymoon hotel in St. Martin. Ralph had tracked down its man-ufacturer and every birthday and Christmas, without fail, in ad-dition to whatever else he got her, there would be boxes of citrus soap. That was until this past year when he'd learned that the company was discontinuing the line, and for her thirty-second birth-day he had bought up every box that he could find, knowing that there would be no more. She held the bar to her nose, as her eyes fell on his soap. Like hers, his white bar of Dove held a piece of their history. When one day she had jokingly summed up all she had learned in her dermatology rotation as a medical student—"tanned skin is damaged skin, and always use a moisturizing soap." They'd laughed, but his Irish Spring soon disappeared, replaced by the Dove. She touched his soap and turned it over, there was a soft black hair embedded in its milky surface. Holding the two bars together, she pictured his tall naked body. How many times had she felt his strong arms encircling her in the shower? She couldn't recall the last time they'd made love, a few weeks, maybe two months; there was a time it had been every day. And what about the family they'd planned? At thirty-two, the clock was ticking. She longed for a child, maybe two, but not without a father, not with-out Ralph. He'd been the man she'd waited for, the one who loved her for her. Now she wondered if that was true. She knew that men found her attractive, but before Ralph she'd always had the feeling that something about her wasn't quite right, that there were parts she had to hide, like her intelligence and her ambition.

Through the steam she conjured his full lips, the softness of his kiss, the hardness of his body, and his warmth as they'd lie spooned together before falling asleep. She gasped at the memory. So what that he'd cheated—lots of men did. For a moment she let herself believe that, but then she pictured Carol, with Barrett's sheets clutched tight across her large, naked breasts.

Gripping the two bars of soap, she sank down and hugged her knees, letting the spray wash over her back. It was hard to breathe and she felt a pain inside her belly. She gritted her teeth so that Justine and her mother wouldn't hear the scream that wanted to fly from her lips. She thought about Ralph, and then about the young marshal—who was probably still in surgery—and then she pictured Charlie's eyes as he stared into hers, and mouthed a prayer she'd said every night as a child before going to bed. Had he done the same, knelt by the bed with his mother? And then she saw him pull the trigger, the shot, the crack of bone, the smell of burnt flesh…and she clutched her soaps tighter, rocked and sobbed.

THREE

Two days later, Barrett stared at a mountain of undictated charts on her state-issue, gray steel desk. This wasn't like her. Normally she stayed on top of her paperwork, but this whole week had been strange.

She dragged the first file off the top; it landed with a thump. She undid the elastic band that held together two sealed manila envelopes, which contained copies of past evaluations. The evaluee—a euphemism for the prisoners who passed through the 34th Street Forensic Evaluation Center—was Monica Harris, a thirty-four-year-old woman who'd stabbed her live-in boyfriend. It was a bread-and-butter case for the state-funded and university-affiliated center that handled the bulk of psychiatric forensic evaluations for the city of New York. But for Barrett, it was the kind of case that hit home. Ms. Harris had bounced in and out of various sectors of the New York State health and welfare system since she was ten. She'd first come to the attention of the Department of Youth Services when a fourth-grade teacher had noted bruises on her arms. From there her story involved an abusive father and a stepfather who'd raped her. After a couple years she was removed from her heroin-addicted mother's custody. Over the next four years she was placed in eight foster homes, until she ran away at sixteen. Her case was reopened as an adult when she tried to hang herself in the Ninth Precinct lockup after being arrested on possession of narcotics and prostitution. The charges were nollied on the condition that she attend court-mandated psychiatric treatment.

From there, she worked as a prostitute, and went through a string of boyfriends who got her pregnant and beat her up, not necessarily in that order. She'd had three children, all of them removed from her custody, and two months ago had been arrested for attacking one Melvin Jones with a steak knife.

For Barrett, Monica's case stirred up eerie emotions and memories. Like the night her father tracked them down to the tiny apartment over the music store. His fists pounding on the security door. The fear in her mother's eyes, Justine crying, Sophie and Max shouting that they were calling the cops. And Barrett, eight years old, shrieking at the door as it started to break, "Go away! Go away!" The sirens, the red-and-blue lights flashing through the window. Terrified of being taken from her mother. Of wishing he would just die.

To Barrett, this Monica Harris carried the scent of what could have happened if her mother had not run from her father. The night they fled was still crisp in her mind. She was in the front seat, Justine asleep between them, as they drove, stopping only for gas, eating Wonder Bread and peanut butter sandwiches slapped together at a truck stop with a white plastic knife. Her mother barely speaking, her raccoon eyes fixed on the road. Twenty hours of driving, and the acrid smell of burning oil, until the engine seized in lower Manhattan. With two small children, a ruined station wagon, and fifteen dollars in a ripped K-Mart purse, Ruth Conyors' life could have gone many ways.

For Monica Harris, it had gone all wrong, and now the court needed two questions answered. Could she stand trial for her crime, or was her mental illness so severe that she was not competent to go before a judge and jury? If that was answered in the affirmative the next big question, and the one that could get parlayed into a not guilty by reason of insanity plea (NGRI) was: As a result of her mental illness could she understand right from wrong?

Barrett's task was to write up a ten-to-twenty-page report that detailed Monica's history and pull together her evaluation. She'd talk about Monica's recurrent depression, intermittent paranoia, and severe post-traumatic stress disorder. She'd mention Monica's borderline personality disorder and how that caused her emotions to cycle uncontrollably. But aside from all that, at the time she stabbed Melvin Jones, even though it was in the heat-of-the-moment, Monica did know that it was wrong, and her case would fall apart. The judge would determine that she had the ability to choose a non-criminal method for dealing with her boyfriend—such as a restraining order—and as long as she could take part in her defense, she'd stand trial. Monica wouldn't go to a hospital; she'd serve time.

"Shit," Barrett muttered, feeling heaviness in her body and a resistance to the work that lay ahead. She pictured Monica, dressed in hospital-issue pajamas, rubber-soled slippers, and a thin cotton robe. Her blond hair had grown skunk roots and her eyes were amazingly pale, as though the color had been drained from them.

At first, all she'd wanted from Barrett was a cigarette. As the hours had passed the thin woman who'd stabbed her boyfriend, and sometimes pimp, laid out a story that was a roller-coaster ride of how a life gets twisted into something not worth living. Her raspy voice had dulled as she spoke about the rapes and the beatings and how every so often a rage exploded inside, and if there was a knife, or a gun, or a bottle of pills, someone would get hurt. Usually it was herself, sometimes someone else; this time it was Melvin. She wasn't sorry, but said she would be if it would help her case. "Melvin is a piece of shit," she'd told Barrett. "He had it coming. I should have killed the bastard."

Barrett stared at her dictating machine. "Just do it," she clicked on the machine. She needed to work, to try and stop her thoughts from racing back over her unraveling life. She saw Ralph's panicked face, as she walked in on him and Carol in bed—her bed. She heard Monica's cigarette-cured voice, "I should have killed the bastard."

The tape whirred quietly as Barrett—using what she called her *New York* voice— laid down Monica's history, each of the arrests, suicide attempts, rapes, betrayals, beatings, the failed tries to get off drugs, to go to school, and to be a mother, only to have each of her children taken away.

She was halfway through when the phone rang.

"Barrett, it's Anton." Her boss's nasal Boston accent greeted her.

"What's up?"

"I got some records on the Martin case, do you want me to bring them down?"

"Absolutely," Barrett perked at the one potential bright spot on her horizon. "And Anton, I really appreciate your thinking of me. I can use the extra bucks."

"Don't mention it."

———

Anton Fielding, medical director for the forensic center, hung up the receiver and stared out the windows of his ninth-floor corner office. He pushed his thinning gray bangs back against his scalp, and wondered why he hadn't told her the truth. What difference would it make? She'd find out on her own. There wasn't keeping much back from the good Dr. Conyors. His gaze fell on the recent edition of *Psychiatry and the Law Review*. Wherever he looked, there she was with another article on the classification of socio-paths, or taxonomy of stalkers, or.... He was happy for her; at least that's what he said in public. But the truth was, he was facing fifty and had just been turned down for tenure—for the second time. He had one shot left. His last interview had left a bitter taste, as the committee had drifted away from him and onto his *protégé*. He'd smiled and didn't let them see how much pain he was in as they talked about his *"nice little papers"* but that they didn't *"quite make the cut for a full professorship, maybe next year." "And how come Dr. Conyors wasn't on the tenure track?"* The answer to that was obvious, but not the sort of thing you bring up in a room of tight-assed academics. You had to make a living, and for the extreme honor of being on the tenure track you got paid forty thousand less a year. Barrett Conyors was no fool. Before long, she'd take her pages-long bibliography and parlay it into a juicy faculty position at Columbia or Cornell. At least that's what he'd do.

He leaned across his desk and picked up an eight-inch-thick binder. He hated himself for this stomach-churning jealousy. Barrett had bailed him out of more than one tough case. She never complained and she loved her work. She'd even asked him if he wanted to work with her on the development of her sociopathy scale and classification system. At the time he'd declined, citing that his own research consumed all available time. And now…in two weeks her groundbreaking paper, "An Outcomes-Based Classification of Sociopathy and its Ramifications for Recidivism" was slated for *The American Journal of Medicine.* It was bad enough that her work would revolutionize the way everyone evaluated sociopaths, but that she'd had the audacity to send a forensic paper to one of the largest and most prestigious journals, and that they'd accepted it…Why couldn't he have swallowed his damn pride and taken her up on her offer? Even if he weren't the first author, he'd still have gotten his name added to dozens of subsequent publications. "Idiot," he muttered, closing the door behind him and shaking the handle to ensure it was locked. "Idiot."

———

A knock at the door interrupted Barrett's nearly completed dictation. "It's open," she shouted. Balancing one of Monica's files in her lap, she turned to see Anton's smiling face. "Thank you," she said, noticing the voluminous manila-covered chart wedged under his arm.

"This is only a fraction of it," he admitted. "But I figured next time you're at Croton, you can go through the microfiche and read to your heart's content."

"He was there for eighteen years," she said. "Did you know I interviewed him—or at least tried to—when I was doing my fellowship? I wanted to use him as a test case."

"What happened?"

"His sister happened. I was working on an analysis of antisocial and criminal behavior and I thought he'd add an interesting twist; his case was fascinating. So I met with him the one time, had him sign a consent to be a test subject, and two days later I get a call from Dean Werther."

"Really?" Anton asked. "Not a good sign."

"It wasn't. Apparently, Jimmy Martin has a twin sister and she called, threatening lawsuits. Said I was causing irreparable psychological damage by interviewing her brother."

"That's a stretch," Anton commented, pushing aside stacks of papers to clear a spot for the file on Barrett's desk and then sitting down.

"Stretch or no, Werther told me that I was to cease-and-desist any and all contact with Jimmy Martin. I think his exact words were, 'this may be bullshit, but bullshit plus a $500-an-hour attorney equals years of litigation hell'. Which is why this surprised me."

Barrett dragged the chart toward her and opened it. She looked at Anton. "And how did he ever get hooked up with Morris Kravitz? I didn't think forensic work was his bag."

Anton chuckled, "I shouldn't say this, because Morris was a great guy, but he'd go wherever the money was, and as you're about to find out, Jimmy Martin can afford the best."

"I'm surprised the forensic review board would have allowed Kravitz to be his psychiatrist. He's not trained to handle the monitoring part."

Anton shifted position and looked out through Barrett's single grime-smeared window at a pair of pigeons roosting on the ledge. "Maybe they couldn't get anyone else."

"Please," Barrett replied sarcastically, "with his kind of money? I'm surprised they weren't lined up. And Anton…"

"Yes?"

"I appreciate your throwing my name in like this. I don't really want to talk about it, but…it looks like Ralph and I…shit!"

"What?"

"It's not good," she admitted, finding the words hard to get out.

"I'm sorry."

"Me too," she forced the corners of her lips into a smile. "He's staying at his mom's till we figure things out. Anyway, thanks for thinking of me. Because I'm going to need the money."

"Don't mention it," he stood.

Barrett looked up at him, she considered Anton a friend, but even so it felt odd telling him about Ralph. The worst part though, had been last Sunday dinner at her mother's apartment over what used to be Sophie and Max's used bookstore—but was now a Korean deli—on the Bowery. Up till then, she hadn't even told Justine. So when Ruth had innocently asked, "Where's Ralph?" the whole mess had tumbled out.

"So how *did* Kravitz get to work with Martin?" she asked, wanting to change the subject.

"I don't know."

"It's just odd…do you know how he died?"

"Hypoglycemic shock, he was diabetic."

"He wasn't that old, was he?"

"Fifties."

"And it just happened."

"Saturday, I think."

"Interesting," she flipped through the chart until she came to a copy of James Cyrus Martin IV's conditional release agreement. She turned to the page of stipulations and ran her finger down the bulleted terms that outlined the do's-and-don'ts for his return to the community.

"Anyway, I'll leave you to it," Anton commented.

"Right," she said, not looking up, and barely registering the sound of her office door closing behind him.

She found what she was looking for halfway down the second page. Under the heading of *"Psychiatric Supervision,"* it stated, *"Releasee is to meet at least weekly with a board-appointed psychiatrist."* Farther down it spelled out the responsibilities for the psychiatrist that included monthly reports back to the forensic review board, random drug screens, oversight of medication, and appropriate monitoring of same.

She leaned back and watched as a mottled pigeon awkwardly flapped its wings and banked up against the guano-stained brick of the adjacent building. Anton had approached her on Tuesday morning—the day after Charlie Rohr shot himself—with taking over Martin's case. When he'd told her that she could pretty much name her fee, it had felt like a gift. Amazing how quickly it all happened. She'd see Jimmy tomorrow—Thursday—and by her doing that, his chart would reflect total compliance; he wouldn't miss a single week of meeting with a psychiatrist.

She worked her way backward through the conditional release agreement. Most of it was boilerplate legalese that she'd read a thousand times before, a laundry list of all the rules that Jimmy Martin had to follow if he wanted to stay out of the maximum-security hospital—required at all times to wear an electronic monitoring device and if he intended to travel farther than a quarter-mile radius from his home, he needed written permission. All his medications were to be supervised and any "significant changes" in his drug regimen had to be approved by the review board.

The main thing that struck her as odd was that Kravitz had gone to the patient's home for their sessions. Barrett provided psychiatric coverage for other releasees in mid-Manhattan, but they all came to her office—usually in the company of their parole officer or case manager, This would be a first and it didn't sit right. She'd told Anton that the only way she'd take the case was if Martin agreed to a police escort. Apparently, that was no big deal. She'd gotten an affirmative response in under half an hour.

She flipped to the front of the chart and fanned the pages in search of a typed summary. She pictured the obese and twitching blond man she'd interviewed when she was still in training. Scanning through the documents, she remembered why she'd found his case intriguing. Jimmy Martin had spent well over a decade at Croton following his arrest at age eighteen in the apartment of a young violinist from South Carolina, Nicole Foster. Ms. Foster, along with her bass player fiancé, had been brutally and sadistically butchered. Immediately following Jimmy's arrest he had a psychotic break and was deemed incompetent to stand trial, and eventually found not guilty by reason of insanity. Beyond that was the curious twist that the murders were actually committed by a second man, Mason Carter, who subsequently hung himself in prison prior to being tried. Also odd was Jimmy's consistent assertion that he'd never touched the murder victims, which was corroborated by a lack of physical evidence linking him to the mutilated bodies. What was clear, however, was that Jimmy had been fixated on Nicole Foster, and had been stalking her. The prosecution also had strong evidence that money had passed between him and the murderer. At his arraignment, Carter had alleged that he'd been hired by Martin to scare away Ms. Foster's fiancé, and that in the heat of the moment, things had gotten out of control. Key pieces of that were never confirmed, and within days Carter was found slumped down in his cell with a sheet knotted around his neck.

For the next half hour Barrett gleaned whatever she could from the forensic center's records. It was a creepy case, but she found a comfort in the work, not having to think about Ralph or Charlie Rohr. She scanned Kravitz's weekly notes. Clearly, he was no forensic psychiatrist and she found little insight into Jimmy Martin's internal world. Still, it felt good to be immersed in the unknown of a new case.

The phone rang. Without looking up, she picked up.

"Dr. Conyors?" her secretary's breathy voice asked.

"Yes, Marla."

"There's an Ellen Martin on the phone for you."

"Is something wrong, Marla?" Barrett asked, noting a tremor in her voice.

"No. Do you want to take it? Or should I tell her you're not in?"

"Put her through." Barrett listened as the line clicked, and wondered if her lucrative gig might be about to disappear.

"Hello, Dr. Conyors?" The voice was husky, the syllables crisp.

"Yes."

"I understand you've agreed to work with my brother; I was hoping we could have a chance to chat first. I suppose I should start by letting you know that I'm Jimmy's conservator, so you won't need a release to talk with me."

"Of course," Barrett said, having already scanned the paperwork giving Ellen Martin responsibility for handling Jimmy's finances and treatment.

"Did you know that I met your brother one time before?" Barrett asked.

There was a slight hesitation, "Yes, I'm aware of that, and I suppose I should explain why I didn't want you interviewing my brother back then."

"No need."

"No, it's actually pretty complicated. Is there any way I could get an hour or two of your time? This may be presumptuous, but I know you have to see him tomorrow…could I buy you dinner?"

"Tonight?"

"If you're able, there's a lot to tell."

Barrett weighed the pros and cons. Ellen Martin, as Jimmy's conservator, could be a powerful ally in the treatment. Beyond that, it was clear from the record that Ellen had been instrumental in securing Jimmy's release. But it was unusual, and a bit beyond the norm to have a meal with a patient's family, still…she'd get a lot more insight out of the sister than Kravitz's bone-dry notes. "What time?"

"Fantastic, how's seven?"

FOUR

IT WAS DUSK, THE air warm and spring sweet as Barrett cut through Bryant Park and headed west. Since Ellen Martin's call, she'd plowed through her work, and realized that several things about this case had her intrigued. The fact that she'd be getting $750 a pop for meeting with Jimmy Martin didn't hurt. Beyond the money, she was hooked, loving the challenge of the unsolved mystery. Of the four people in that bloody apartment eighteen years ago, only Jimmy was still alive. In reading through the chart, the impression the Croton doctors had was that Jimmy was a victim. Sure, he'd been stalking the girl, but the actual murders had been committed by Mason Carter—a previously convicted sex offender. Their conclusion had been that Jimmy was just in the wrong place at the wrong time.

Something about that didn't jibe—starting with Carter's allegation that Jimmy had paid him. Admittedly, Carter would say all sorts of things if he thought it would lessen his sentence, but why was he there? It seemed statistically unlikely that Nicole Foster—a talented violinist from Charleston—would be the object of two stalkers. Plus, the detectives and the prosecution had built an argument that traced twenty thousand in cash found on Carter back to a series of withdrawals made by Jimmy Martin. If Martin hadn't wound up at Croton—declared too crazy to stand trial—he would have faced accessory to murder, possibly more. As it was, the whole case and definitive investigation got short-circuited by Carter's suicide and Jimmy's not guilty by reason of insanity plea.

Mulling this over, she arrived at Siam Garden, the Chelsea restaurant Ellen Martin had suggested. She pushed through the dark glass outer door, and scanned the mostly empty, candle-lit interior.

A smiling Asian hostess in a turquoise silk sheath dress approached. "Dr. Conyors?"

"Yes."

"Your party is waiting. This way, please." The hostess led Ellen back toward a curtained alcove. The hostess pulled back a richly embroidered drape covered with gilt elephants and monkeys, and led Barrett into a cozy private dining room, the walls and ceiling hung with garnet-colored silk. In the center stood a carved teak table with two leather club chairs, one of them occupied by a tall blond woman in a beautifully draped black suit, holding a martini glass.

The woman stood as Barrett entered. "Dr. Conyors, thank you for meeting at such short notice."

"Don't mention it," she said, taking Ellen Martin's extended and perfectly manicured hand.

"What are you drinking?"

Barrett's first response was to say *nothing,* but between the openness of Ellen Martin's china-white smile, and the nest-like comfort of the room, she was lulled. "What are you having?"

"Grey-Goose martini with Jalapeno-stuffed olives."

"Sounds good," she said to the hostess, who stood by silently.

"Another for me," Ellen said. "So, come, sit…you must be wondering what the hell you've gotten yourself into."

Barrett smiled as she sank into the glove-soft chair. She looked at Ellen, with her symmetrical blond hairdo that cut off crisply beneath her ears, and was sculpted around the back of her head, like a high-fashion helmet. Her skin was flawless and glowed pink in the reflected light from the candles and the hanging silks. She was striking, but the squareness of her jaw gave a masculine cast to her features. "Have we met before?" Barrett asked, finding something both familiar and forgotten in Ellen's clear blue eyes.

Ellen looked back. "I don't think so," she said slowly. "But now that you mention it, you do look familiar…odd."

"It'll come to us," Barrett said.

"You're not from around here, though, are you?" Ellen asked. "There's something in your voice…"

"No," Barrett admitted. "Late in the day I sound more like my mother's Georgia."

"So is this very strange?" Ellen asked. "Meeting like this with a family member?"

"Yes and no. As your brother's conservator it's not so strange. I think it's a good idea that we try to stay on the same page."

"I'm so glad to hear you say that." Ellen looked up as a waitress entered with their drinks and menus.

Barrett took a first sip of the icy cocktail, and savored the tang of pepper and the cool bite of vodka.

"How adventuresome are you?" Ellen asked.

"Excuse me?"

"With food?"

"Pretty much anything."

"This place does a wonderful banquet, they just keep bringing things until you can't move, sound good?"

"Sounds wonderful," Barrett agreed, letting Ellen order.

Once the waitress was out of earshot, Ellen leaned forward. A gold and topaz necklace dangled and refracted the candlelight. "I feel like there's so much I need to tell you. I almost don't know where to start."

"Does your brother know we're meeting?"

"I haven't told Jimmy yet, but it won't matter to him. He's so used to my arranging things that it wouldn't surprise him." She took a long sip of her drink, "Sometimes I think half my life is spent trying to keep my brother out of trouble."

"You arranged his release from Croton."

"Yes, but not without a lot of effort…and expense. To be honest, I think that's what finally tipped things, the fact that we're paying for everything."

Barrett kept quiet, while making a series of observations about the woman, from the absence of a wedding ring, to her poise and ease in what might have been an uncomfortable meeting. She wondered why someone as attractive and articulate as Ellen was single and what it was that caused her to spend so much time advocating for her brother. And she couldn't help but admire the subdued richness of the woman's clothing and jewelry. Her own seasons' past, off-the-rack navy Donna Karan suit felt graceless in comparison. "They were reluctant to release him." Barrett finally commented.

"That's putting it mildly, all of which made no sense, considering they never actually proved my brother had done anything. The breaking and entering was the only thing solid, everything else was circumstantial. If I'd known what I now know, I would never have let my parents do that to him. If he'd gone to trial he'd have gotten what, a few months? Maybe less, but not eighteen years. It was so unfair."

"You were young." Barrett offered, not wanting to argue that the charges might have gone all the way to murder one.

"We were eighteen. My brother was only eighteen when they put him in that hell hole!"

The curtain slid back and the waitress deftly slid platters of an assortment of steamed, roasted, and fried dumplings onto the center of the table. Pointing to each, she described the fillings, identified three varieties of dipping sauce, poured green tea, and left.

Barrett skewered a roast-pork-and-water-chestnut dumpling with her fork, and while savoring the crunch and soothing peanut flavor, tried to draw Ellen out. "In reading the chart," she said, "it sounds like your brother had a psychotic break at the time of the arrest."

"He did, but even so, he could have gone to trial. My parents were dead set against that."

"Because?"

"Publicity." She fished an olive from her drink. "They didn't want the Martin name dragged through the press. The papers did a number on him anyway. But as time went on…" She shook her head, and took a deep breath.

To Barrett, it appeared that Ellen was close to tears. "What is it?"

"I thought this was going to be easier, but I guess if you're going to be working with Jimmy you'll find all this stuff out sooner or later. Our parents were not good people," she stated bluntly. "As an adult, I can sit back and say they should never have had children…I hold them directly responsible for what happened to Jimmy."

Intrigued, Barrett waited.

Ellen looked at her, "They wanted Jimmy locked away forever. When I was twenty-one, I tried to hire a lawyer to review his case, my father blocked me, said it was none of my business."

"Why would he do that?"

Ellen gave a bitter laugh, "You don't know how hard I've tried to come up with rational explanations for the things my father did; it's useless. One minute he'd shower us with gifts, and the next…" She stopped and reached back for the curtain, "excuse me, but I'm going to need more liquor to get through this." She signaled for the waitress with her empty glass and then turned back to Barrett. "I think my father was clinically insane, and mother wasn't much better."

"Insane how?"

"Erratic, paranoid, addicted to pain pills…sadistic. You need more?"

"Toward you?"

"Yes. But mostly toward Jimmy; he got the worst of it."

"Physical abuse?"

"Yes, but that's nothing compared with the way he'd play with our minds. Our childhood was like some gruesome fairy tale. If anyone had known what was going on in that house…we should have been taken out of there. All of which is easy to say, but when you're a kid, you think the stuff your parents do is normal. You have no way of knowing how sick it is. And to an outsider, things probably looked pretty good. Our family is very wealthy and has been connected in New York society for over a hundred years. My great-great grandfather was one of the founders of the Knicker-bocker Club. And a couple years back I gifted our Newport cottage to the Historical Society; it's now a museum. People see our kind of wealth and privilege and can't imagine children being tortured inside such a beautiful home."

"Was there sexual abuse?" Barrett gently asked, while thinking of her own financial straits, and wondering what it might be like to donate a mansion, or to own an oceanfront mansion and call it a *cottage*.

Ellen paused as the waitress reappeared with drinks and fresh delicacies. As the curtain closed behind her, she resumed, "Yes, and I don't know how much. We were both exposed to my mother's indiscretions. She had a string of chauffeurs who were little more than male prostitutes. She and father slept in different rooms…different worlds, actually. I often wonder how they managed to conceive the two of us. When we were kids, and this is pretty sick, we'd sometimes spy on her in the carriage house. We used to think it was funny. Now, it just makes me sad."

"There's more, isn't there?"

"Tons, but there's stuff I can't remember. I even went to a therapist a few times to try and get the memories back; it made things worse, like I was about to fall apart. So I stopped going, figured my brain knew what was best for me by just blocking stuff out. You see," she said catching Barrett's eye, "work is my therapy...But back to your question...I don't think my father molested me...I don't think so. But he did stuff to Jimmy."

"From what age?"

"Young...you asked me why my parents didn't want Jimmy going to trial?"

"Yes."

"I think the real reason is they were petrified of what would happen if any of this came out. In their twisted way they decided better to lock their son away, than for people to know what kind of sick fucks they were!" Ellen looked up, "I'm sorry, I hadn't intended to get into all of this. I've never told this stuff to anyone...it can't go anywhere."

"Of course," Barrett said, finding herself with a newfound sympathy for Jimmy Martin, and his elegant sister.

Ellen reached down and grabbed a crispy duck roll. "So Jimmy ends up spending half his life locked up, and I take over the company after my parents' death. Although fortunately for the shareholders, I got father to let me handle much of the business prior to the accident."

"How long ago was that?" Barrett, asked, recalling something in the chart about an off-site supervised visit when Jimmy was allowed to attend a funeral.

"Three years," Ellen said.

"And that's how you were able to get him out?"

Ellen looked up, and gave Barrett a questioning look.

"I mean," Barrett said, "with your parents dead you were able to work on getting your brother out."

"Yes," she said, "I took over, had the lawyers make me his legal conservator, and lobbied for his release. He's my only family…unless you count a few second cousins who're licking their chops over the fact that neither Jimmy nor I will ever have kids."

"Because?"

"Boy, you're good at this," Ellen commented. "I used to think that after what my parents did to us, there was no way in hell I'd ever reproduce—that I'd never take that risk. But when I turned thirty I…shit! I'm sorry…" Ellen swigged her cocktail, "When I was thirty, my thinking shifted and I found myself really wanting to have a child. After all of those years of throwing myself into work; I began to think—what for? And all I could focus on was that I wanted a child." Ellen glanced at Barrett. "Does this make any sense, or have I had one too many?"

Barrett met her gaze, "No, it makes perfect sense."

"I thought that maybe if I had a child, I'd get it right. And give this kid all of the love we never had, raise a little person that could take over the business—or not—if they didn't want to…but then I started to get all sorts of weird symptoms…headaches, hot flashes." Her mouth twisted in a wistful smile. "I guess you can figure where this is going?"

Barrett nodded.

"Early menopause," Ellen shrugged. "Apparently it runs in the family. As for Jimmy, I don't see him as the marrying type. I'd also be worried with him around kids."

"Has he ever done anything like that?"

"Pedophilia?" Ellen asked, "God, I hope not. But I'm a realist. I know my brother has problems. I don't think having him around kids is a good idea."

"How has he dealt with being out? After eighteen years that's quite a transition."

"Yes and no. He's not really free, is he?"

"No," Barrett agreed, having read through the stringent rules confining him.

"Certainly he's happier, and he's playing cello again, and considering his time away from it, he sounds great."

"Cello?" Barrett perked, remembering some mention of it in the histories.

"Yes, music is probably the only thing that kept us halfway sane growing up."

"You play, as well?"

"I did…very little now…piano. Jimmy was always the star. My brother was a child prodigy. My playing was more in the range of competent accompanist."

"Did you do competitions?" she asked, flashing on an old memory of two beautiful blond children, the boy on cello, his sister on piano.

"Yes," Ellen met her gaze, and smiled. "That's where we know each other, isn't it?"

"Oh my, God. That's it!" But the three-hundred-pound Jimmy that Barrett had seen that one time at Croton bore no resemblance to the cherubic blond boy who invariably took first prize in the music competitions that had been such a major part of her childhood.

"You play piano, don't you?" Ellen asked.

"Yes, but like you, it's hard to find the time to practice."

"But you were good. You won some competitions, didn't you?"

Barrett's cheeks flushed.

"…yet you went into medicine. You could have had a concert career."

"Long story, and not terribly interesting. Was that what Jimmy wanted to do?"

"Yes, and I think a part of him wonders if it's too late now. He had a recording contract, and the horrible irony is that two days before his arrest he won the Dubrovnik cello competition."

"Really! That's impressive."

"I know, and the one thing that gave him any comfort—his music—was taken away for eighteen years. I think more than the things father did to him, or some of the horrible stuff that happened at Croton, not having his cello broke him."

Barrett resisted the urge to reach across the table and take Ellen's hand, to try and comfort her. "You really love him."

"I do," she stated, struggling to keep her emotions in check. "I guess for me it boils down to there are two loves in my life, Martin Industries, which my father nearly ran into the ground, and my brother." Draining her drink, she added, "In a way they're kind of similar, they both need a lot of work, but they both have incredible potential."

———

Two hours later, Barrett parted with Ellen outside the restaurant.

"Can I give you a lift,?   Ellen asked, easing into the backseat of a waiting black Lincoln.

58

"No, thanks."

She was about to say more when Ellen added, "I'm so happy that you decided to work with Jimmy. I've got a good feeling about this, and who knows," she said, harking back to one of their many topics of discussion, "maybe cello playing can be his way back. I guess it comes down to whether or not he's still good enough for the concert stage."

Barrett watched as the limo pulled away. Her head felt light, but good. Three cocktails and a sumptuous meal had been what the doctor ordered. And the conversation, she had to admit, was one of the most interesting ever. She hadn't come prepared to like Ellen Martin, but there was something heroic about the CEO who had endured and overcome the horrors of her childhood, and was now in the driver's seat of a Fortune 500 corporation that ran the gamut from high-rise real estate to breakfast cereal. And their joint history of having done the kiddie concert circuit was an odd connection. Piano playing for Barrett had been the ticket to many things, but fifteen years ago she had turned down a full Juilliard scholarship to pursue medicine. As she had reminisced with Ellen about the weird world of child prodigies, she discovered that her childhood dream of one day playing major concert halls still smoldered. So many memories, the warmth of the spotlight, of walking toward the conductor, of her feet making first contact with the pedals, her fingers poised over the keys, her wrists in perfect alignment, Sophie's Polish accent reminding her to breathe.

Lost in thought, she wandered the four blocks north to her condo. There had been other parts of the conversation, however, that had left Barrett unsettled. As always, when hearing stories about cruelty to children, her heart went out to the victims—to Ellen and Jimmy. But her life in forensics, and her research into the development of sociopaths, had shown that children who've had those experiences never leave them behind. She saw it in Ellen, as she had talked about what the abuse had done to her, and how she had sublimated those feelings into funding a charitable foundation that aided battered women and their children. Her ears had perked when Ellen mentioned her spotty memory and brief stab at therapy. Maybe it was nothing, but it carried the diagnostic whiff of a traumatized child who walls off bad periods of time, maybe to recover the memories as an adult, and maybe not. But for Jimmy, who by Ellen's account had endured far worse, she suspected that his coping had not been so adaptive. There were clinical terms for it, reaction formation, identification with the aggressor, but it came down to a couple of things; abused children grow up to either become the exact opposite of their abusers—such as Ellen—or, as was more common in men, they turned into their abusers, perpetuating the cycle.

She glanced at her watch, and was surprised to see that it was after ten. Normally she'd push herself to the kung fu studio for a workout, but Sifu Henry Li closed up around eleven, so there'd be little point. As she rounded her block, her eyes fell on a familiar man's silhouette on her front stoop. Her heart quickened, as she approached. At least he hadn't keyed into the condo.

He stood as she approached. "Barrett."

"What are you doing here, Ralph?" And realizing the hour she added, "and how long have you been here?"

"I called out sick," he said, with a half smile. "I'm not sure that was a lie. I miss you so much, Barrett. I'm not sleeping, I'm not eating."

She saw sincerity in his eyes, he seemed so unhappy. "Ralph."

"Barrett, there's got to be something I can do to make this right."

"I don't know, Ralph," she admitted, feeling a tingle up her spine as he took her hand.

"Please," he brought her fingers to his lips, his coarse stubble against her knuckles, his warm breath on her skin. "Can't we talk?"

Her knees felt weak, *it has to be the alcohol,* she told herself as her mouth, seemingly disconnected from her better senses, said, "Okay, you can come up, but just for five minutes."

"Thank you." He followed her up the stairs.

She felt his every footfall as they rounded the landings, and then, outside their condo door, his presence close, his hand on the small of her back, a gesture so familiar, and so missed. She fumbled with the key.

"Here," his hands on hers, steadying them, twisting the knob.

The warm smell of home washed over them. She turned toward him, struggling for resolve, wanting to say, *"just five minutes."* But before the words could come, his deep-brown eyes were on hers, his expression sad…tender. He was pleading, wanting another chance. And in that moment, Barrett surrendered. She didn't care, the ache in her chest and tightness in her throat cried for relief.

"Okay," she whispered, as his arms wrapped around her, drawing her in.

The touch of his full lips on hers was electric. She pressed against him, needing to feel his length against hers. She closed her eyes, and felt the floor give way, as he swept her up, and carried her toward the bedroom. A tiny voice tried to remind her that she was mad at him, that he'd betrayed her with another woman…again. In that moment, she didn't care, she was floating in his arms, and then on the soft down of their quilted comforter. Her hands snaked under his shirt, feeling his hard muscles, the flatness of his belly. She grabbed at his belt and pulled him toward her.

"Thank you," he mouthed, his lips finding hers, his musician's hands quickly working at the buttons of her blouse. "I love you," his mouth on hers. "I love you."

Two hours later, Barrett lay flat in bed, her thoughts dreamy. Ralph was fast asleep, exhausted from their lovemaking that had ended in the shower. *"Getting clean and getting dirty all at the same time,"* he'd whispered while holding her tight under the spray.

Now, the sound of his breathing and the sweet, soapy smell of him were like a soothing drug. She gently touched the smooth skin of his back. *Why?* she thought. *Why did you have to do that?*—thinking simultaneously of his infidelity with Carol and the beauty of what they'd just shared. She rolled away and swung her long legs over the side of the bed. She picked up his button-down shirt, threw it on and moved quietly toward the door, closing it behind her. Padding silently across the living room, she sat down at her piano. With her left foot damping down on the soft pedal, she let her fingers fall on the keys, and without preparation drifted into a Chopin Nocturne, letting the vibrations of the wistful music fill her. As that ended—perhaps fueled by the conversation with

Ellen—she launched into the *Revolutionary Étude*, amazed that her fingers remembered. Images of Sophie and recitals long past flashed before her, as dizzying runs spilled from the Mason and Hamlin. She pictured the Martin twins—so beautiful—a pair of blond angels sparkling in the spotlights. *How sad*, she thought, moving seamlessly from Chopin to Erik Satie's dreamy *Trois Gymnopédies*, and wondering—hoping—that she'd be able to help the tortured child—now a man—that Ellen Martin had described.

———

Two miles away, on the Upper East Side, Ellen Martin's limo pulled into the garage of the Georgian townhouse that had belonged to her great-great grandfather, James Cyrus Martin. She felt exhilarated and realized that despite her initial reticence, Jimmy had finally gotten it right. Barrett Conyors was perfect. She was beautiful—even though she tried to play that down with her ill-fitting suit and near absence of make-up. Her intelligence was impossible to deny—which gave Ellen pause—and she'd been more than modest about her skill as a pianist. And the accent she tried to hide…just like Nicole…just like Maylene all those many years ago. A whiff of something dangerous from her past bubbled up; and she felt the shiver of a very bad thing that, try as she might, she could not remember.

As the chauffeur held the door, Ellen's mind raced through all that had to be done. Jimmy might have made the right selection, but as she well knew, his talents did not extend far beyond his cello. She could almost hear her father's hissing voice, *"Chicky's the one that makes things happen."*

Yes, she thought, punching in the code to let her into the house. She had many plans to make and they'd have to be very careful—Dr. Conyors would not be easily led—but after their dinner, she knew that it would be worth the effort.

FIVE

JIMMY'S POWERFUL FINGERS ATTACKED the Allegro with razor-sharp precision, while Ellen's soaring accompaniment spilled from the stereo; it was a recording of their Carnegie Hall debut at the age of twelve. He glanced up at the massive Bösendorfer and imagined Ellen there, instead of Fred the cat curled in a ball, watching him.

His blond bangs fell across his face, as his bow hand arced and plunged, pulling soulful phrases from his eighteenth-century cello. One with the music, the room slipped away and a fantasy emerged, fueled by the heartbreaking melodies of the only piece Chopin ever wrote for cello. He felt the heat of the lights as the vibrations filled his body. He'd be in tails and the woman at the piano was no longer his sister. She was Barrett, dressed in black satin with a single strand of lustrous pearls encircling her throat. Her gray eyes would sparkle as she'd challenge him to ever-greater virtuosity. He'd look up, and there she'd be, loving him, wanting him.

For half an hour he ran from movement to movement, the allegro moderato, the scherzo, the mournful largo, and the release of the finale. As he drew the final chord across the strings his head sagged, and he imagined a stunned silence in the auditorium, and then the first tentative applause, which would blossom and explode into a standing ovation. There'd be shouts for an encore, and with sweat dripping down his face he'd turn to his beautiful Barrett. Their eyes would lock and the emotion would be more powerful than words.

The turntable skipped and the needle scratched. Startled, Jimmy put down his cello and switched off the player. He gingerly lifted the decades-old vinyl and replaced it in its sleeve. He ran the tips of his long fingers over the photograph on the front. In the picture, he was facing forward and Ellen, in profile, was looking at him. He traced the outline of her cheek. He'd been hard with her on the telephone, he knew that she meant well, but in the end, she'd see he was right. "Chicky." His raspy voice whispered Ellen's childhood nickname.

He put the album away and looked at his cello, feeling a familiar emptiness. He glanced at his bracelet as it sparked its fifteen-second reminder. The urge to go out was fierce. His tongue flicked at his bottom lip as he thought of the cool night air, and pictured her building, knowing which windows were hers, knowing the lock on the security door was broken. He pictured the black and white tile of her downstairs hallway, the worn treads on the wooden steps, the creak of his weight, as he moved closer toward her…

He walked to the fiberglass cello case Ellen had had custom made in Sweden, its velvet interior perfectly fitted to contain the Amati that Father had purchased at Sotheby's. He reached in and released a hidden catch in the bottom. A panel clicked open and he retrieved another one of Ellen's gifts—an electronic key. Sitting on the edge of a damask sofa he crossed his bracelet-encircled ankle over his left knee. Aiming the metal key at the release, he waited for the red light. Quickly inserting it, he depressed the catch, nothing happened. He tried again, and still nothing. The light blinked. He pulled out the key and wiped the magnetic strip against his pants. He checked the lithium battery, but knew that it was still good; he'd just replaced it. He waited for the light and reinserted it. Jamming his thumb hard against the button, he strained to hear the sound of the catch, the sound of freedom. "Come on," he pressed it again and again, carelessly ignoring the flash of red. Ellen had warned him not to release the security bracelet when it was transmitting; if he did so, a malfunction reading would occur and within minutes a monitor from the forensic center would come knocking at his door. "Come on." He took the key out and, holding it under the light, examined its every surface. Sweat beaded his forehead, his breath quickened as he tried a third time—it still wouldn't work. Ignoring Ellen's warning, he pushed it in and out. Frustration mounted, rage surged, and before he could think, he hurled the key across the room. "Shit!"

The cat leapt from his perch and raced under a table as Jimmy watched the malfunctioning key fly through the air. For a moment he thought it would land safely on the rug, instead, it cracked against the white-marble fireplace.

"No!" He ran over and looked down. The plastic casing had shattered, revealing its complicated electronic guts. He picked up the biggest piece, tears welling.

A familiar voice whispered in his ear, *"Stupid boy. Such a stupid boy."*

"No," he tried to block out Father's voice.

"Never could take care of your things, could you? Perhaps Jimbo needs a visit?"

"No, no, no."

"I think you do," and then laughter.

Jimmy's knees buckled, and he dropped the ruined key. He jammed his hands over his ears, knowing it wouldn't help. "Go away," he tried to shut out the laughter. "You're dead, you're dead."

"Do I sound dead?"

"Leave me alone."

"I don't think so. You have to pay, Jimbo."

"What do you want?"

"You know…"

Jimmy shuddered. He smelled whiskey on the back of his neck, and his chest squeezed as though he were being pressed down hard against his mattress. "No," he sobbed, feeling father's clammy fingers pull down the back of his pajamas.

"Yes, yes, yes" the voice whispered, the words slurry and moist.

"No!" Jimmy shouted, clawing his way back toward reality. "You're not here, you're dead, you're dead!" He focused on the piano, and his cello, he looked across at the mahogany ladder that could be wheeled across the two-story-high bookshelves. "Go away!"

Father's laughter echoed in his ears, as he stood on shaky legs and backed away from the fireplace. "Go away!"

The laughter faded, but wouldn't stop. Jimmy tried to slow his breathing; his heart pounded. Desperate for comfort, he picked up a dog-eared program from a long-ago recital. It was from the Manhattan Prodigy series. With trembling fingers he opened it, stopping briefly on the glossy black-and-white headshots of himself and Ellen, two gifted teenagers who for their last three years in the program had monopolized the coveted last spot. He flipped back through the pages, passing through ever-smaller photos until he came to the one that he needed. It was that of a nine-year-old girl, with gleaming dark-brown hair and almond-shaped eyes, who had stolen the show when she had erupted with a brilliant execution of Chopin's jaw-dropping "Revolutionary" Étude; a piece that not even Ellen could handle. He stared at the picture, remembering the gawky girl who had played with fierce intensity. She'd worn an ill-fitting velvet dress and her face—her beautiful face—seemed lit by some internal light. It's a face he'd seen one other time, only then the gawky girl had blossomed into the most magnificent creature, like a fairy tale princess. She'd come to him in the hospital; she'd had such compassion, as though she could see his pain, could know it, could make it go away. And then the miracle happened; in that hell hole, on that day; he'd felt love spark to life. And with that came a certainty that what he felt, she did as well. He saw it in her eyes, a desire and a longing for him. And through the long years that followed he knew that she'd be there. And now…

"Barrett Conyors," he whispered, reading the name beneath the photograph. The laughter subsided; it was going to be okay.

He put the program down and walked to the fireplace. Dropping to the hearth, he gathered the pieces of his shattered key. Satisfied that he had them all, he straightened and headed toward the kitchen with Fred mewing at his heels. He unlatched the back door and took a deep breath of evening air. Careful not to let the cat out, he stepped into the walled courtyard. In front of him was a weathered marble fountain, no longer functional, but filled with rainwater and muck; a swarm of newly hatched mosquitoes swirled over its surface. Above him soared a dense canopy of hundred-year-old evergreens, a Japanese maple, and exotic specimen trees that had started to unfurl their spring foliage. To his right lay the ruined remains of Mother's garden. She had loved her roses, spending hours pruning and spraying them, picking off Japanese beetles and crushing them in her fingers.

"And now she's buried under them," Father whispered.

"So are you." Jimmy spat back.

"Details, details."

He stood still and looked around. Supposedly, they'd both perished in a car accident three years ago, along with a twenty-something Latino chauffeur. When he was first told, it didn't take him long to figure it out. Starting with the fact that Mother and Father rarely went anywhere together.

"Accident my ass," Father hissed.

Jimmy stared at the sprouting weeds, and tangled remnants of once-carefully tended arbors. When they were little, he and Ellen had a game of make-believe; they called it Hansel and Gretel. Only, in their game it wasn't just the witch that went into the oven. Depending on the day, and who they were mad at, it could be just about anyone, Jimmy's cello teacher, a piano-playing rival of Ellen's—but mostly they'd fantasized about pushing Father and then Mother into the oven, and having their beloved Southern nanny, Maylene, take care of them.

When the social worker at Croton had broken the news, Jimmy had asked for the details, to see the newspaper clippings, to go to the funeral. They'd all assumed it was a healthy grief reaction, and he was granted permission to attend, albeit accompanied by two guards. But Jimmy had read between the headlines, and had observed how easily Ellen took over as CEO for Martin Industries. No bodies were found in the submerged BMW sedan, just a scarf, a shoe, and a chauffeur's cap, everything else presumably washed away in the swift currents of the Hudson.

Perhaps one day he'd do a bit of digging, but now, other desires took precedence. He walked past the fountain and entered the dense thicket of ivy, weeds, and bramble that created a dark tunnel. Moving by feel, his hand found the cool surface of the brownstone carriage house, constructed of the same material as the mansion. Opening a small wooden door he entered a world that the review board knew nothing about. Still well within the range of his bracelet, this was his special retreat.

He stepped into the darkened hall that ran the length of the building. To his right was the garage, which housed a 1952 Rolls Royce Silver Shadow, a maroon Jaguar XKE, a Ford panel van to which Ellen had made a variety of modifications, including the installation of a 340 horsepower V-8 engine, and a yellow cab—the most anonymous vehicle one could have in Manhattan.

He looked through the garage to the front door, and wistfully noted the dark outline of his black leather car coat hanging from its hook. There'd be no going out tonight, at least not to where he wanted. If he strayed beyond his range—about a block in any direction—they'd come after him, and… "No," he shut his eyes, and tried to block out the smell of pine disinfectant, and Croton's ever-present stench of body fluids.

He climbed the twisting stairs to the second-floor quarters, which Ellen had converted into a large loft space. It was first accessed through a narrow antechamber that contained his computer and a row of security monitors that would warn him if anyone approached the house, or rang the bell, a necessary precaution as it would not go well if Hector—or anyone else from the board—came calling and he wasn't in. The ceiling of both the security booth and the large room were covered with dark acoustic tiles, the walls—also black—she'd paneled with a sound-absorbent polymer; once the door of the security booth was closed, both rooms became entirely soundproof. He'd told her that he wanted to use the carriage house as a recording studio. But that was not entirely correct. And in the weeks since his release, he'd arranged for contractors to begin the next phase of construction. Several unopened boxes with additional monitors and sound equipment were stacked above and beneath the counter of the security room, and a massive deadbolt had been recently affixed to the steel-reinforced door that separated the two rooms.

As he'd done, almost every day since leaving Croton, he typed in Barrett Conyors' name, and stayed until dawn, rereading her articles, learning what he could about her sister's surgical program, seeing what workmen had filed permits for repairs to her mother's building, even getting the orchestra-seating chart to know exactly where her husband, Ralph Best, sat. He found it interesting that she'd never taken his name; obviously, she was waiting for someone else. At times, it amazed him how much he could discover about her through the Internet. Most of the web had been blocked to him while at Croton, as he'd spend hours in the library earning 33 cents an hour, supposedly doing clerical work, but actually learning what he could about his Barrett, and trying to maintain finger dexterity by typing. Those snippets of information were powerful messages; she was leaving a trail for him to follow, just like the bread crumbs that had led Hansel and Gretel back to safety.

SIX

ARMED WITH HER KENNETH Cole briefcase and dressed in a light-weight black wool suit, Barrett strode quickly from the Forensic Evaluation Center on East 34th to Gramercy Park. Her emotions were all over the place, and had little to do with this first meeting with Jimmy Martin. Ralph had stayed the night, and waking next to him had felt so right. He had pulled out all the stops, and had even said the one thing she'd desperately wanted to hear, *"Barrett, I think it's time we had a kid."* Still, she'd told him that she wanted more time to think things over; she couldn't trust him, and if one night of fabulous and reckless sex was going to undo the damage, she'd have to give that some careful thought.

She took a couple deep breaths and turned onto Gramercy Park North. She stopped; it was beautiful. In front of her was the iron-gated park, its symmetrically laid-out perennial beds were thick with mottled patches of yellow and white crocus and narcissus. The hundred-year-old fruit trees and specimen trees were ablaze with pink and white blossoms that perfumed the air. Behind her, the noise of Manhattan dropped away, as though this were a different city, one that had become fixed in the late 1800s. The Victorian hotels and Italian style townhouses with wrought-iron galleries spoke of an elegance and gentility removed from the bustling fervor of the outside streets.

She pulled out a scrap of paper with Jimmy Martin's address and headed toward the south side of the park. Midway down the block she saw two men standing by a dark blue sedan parked in the shade of a budding Gingko tree. Her pulse quickened.

"Ed," she called out. "Detective Hobbs?"

The taller of the two, with closely cropped salt-and-pepper hair, turned. "Barrett, it's good to see you."

"You too," she offered her hand, but found herself swept up into a more gratifying bear hug with Ed's bushy moustache tickling the side of her neck.

The other man, who was leaning against their car, drolly noted, "I take it you two know each other."

Barrett stepped back; something didn't make sense. "What are you doing here?" she asked. And then followed up with a whispered, "Are you undercover?"

"No," he shook his head, "what you see is what you get. You asked for an escort and here we are."

"But detectives? You? They send deputy chiefs for…"

His hazel eyes met hers briefly, and then looked away, "Not anymore."

"What happened?" she asked, sensing sadness in the man with whom she'd spent many fine hours in the past. The last case he'd called her in on was Charlie Rohr. But that was two years ago. There'd been numerous times when she'd thought about calling him, maybe going out to lunch. But when she had those thoughts they were usually followed by the realization that she and this tall, married detective had a chemistry that felt as if it could go far beyond tracking serial killers.

"It's a long dull story," he said.

"Maybe you'll tell me."

"Maybe. So this is the perp's house?"

Barrett checked the numbers, and gazed up at the looming mansion. She stepped back to get the entire effect; it was a lovely building from its ivy-covered wrought-iron porches, to the carved cherub heads that stared out from above the imposing front door and from beneath each of the shuttered French windows.

"Nice crib," Ed commented.

"He has the whole building to himself," she stated.

"I have two rooms and a bathtub in my kitchen," Ed replied, "and I can barely afford that."

"Don't you still live in Queens?"

"I did; now I don't."

"But…"

He shook his head. "Enough about me."

His partner joined them, "Ed is a fine example of why you shouldn't piss off your boss. So, do I get an introduction to the beautiful lady?"

Barrett rolled her eyes, as she mentally noted that Ed's partner would probably hit three hundred pounds and lose the rest of his thinning red hair before the age of thirty.

"Dr. Barrett Conyors, Officer Bryan Cassidy."

They shook. "So how do you guys know each other?" Cassidy asked.

"We worked a couple cases. Barrett is the best profiler I've ever met," Ed stated. "By the way, I heard about Charlie Rohr...I heard you were there. I'm sorry."

"It was pretty awful," the bloody scene played in her head. "The idiots let someone in with a firearm."

"You're lucky to be alive."

"I hadn't even thought about that," she said, looking up at a cherub and feeling an unpleasant sensation as its eyes appeared to be watching her. "I don't know if cops get it the same way, but all of my bad cases kind of follow me around. I know I'm going to be seeing Charlie Rohr for a very long time."

"You think his family will sue?" Ed asked.

"No idea. They didn't want anything to do with Charlie while he was alive, but there's a damn good case to be made against the state, so you never know. It wouldn't surprise me."

"Why is that name familiar?" Bryan asked.

"The Caravaggio killer," Hobbs replied.

Cassidy smiled, "The guy with the knitting needles who liked girls with something extra."

"That's right. Barrett did the profile. If it hadn't been for her he'd still be out there."

"I thought you didn't believe in profiling," Bryan commented.

"I don't," Ed said, but then added, "I believe in her."

"Oh, please," Barrett brushed away the compliment, yet clearly enjoyed Ed's admiration. As she recalled, that had been mutual.

But what the hell was the deputy chief of detectives doing here? If he wasn't putting Jimmy under surveillance, it made no sense. And why was he living in Manhattan, what had happened to his wife and kids? "I wondered why you hadn't called me," she said.

His head cocked slightly.

"For a case," she added.

"Can we talk about that later?"

"Sure…"she looked at her watch, and felt a growing apprehension, standing in front of the Martin townhouse, feeling it tower over them. "I guess it's time to head in."

"You wearing a wire?" he asked.

"No."

"Don't you think you should?"

"I don't usually tape my patients without their knowledge."

"This is different and you know it."

"True, but still." She smiled, glad that he was taller than she was, and why no wedding band? While Ralph had no difficulty carrying through on his lustful thoughts, Barrett's would-be infidelities had always stayed between her ears. Although, back when she and Hobbs had spent long hours unraveling the inner world of Charlie Rohr, she'd wondered what it would be like to be wrapped in the powerful arms of the no-nonsense detective.

"Think about that wire," Hobbs said.

"You'll be there," she reminded him.

"I'd rather be listening in."

"I'm not hearing this," Cassidy remarked.

"Enough," Barrett hefted her briefcase, let a car pass, and then crossed the street and walked up the broad granite steps. As she approached, she caught the mournful sound of a cello spilling from the house. With her hand on the antique fox-head doorknocker she paused. She assumed it was a recording, probably Brahms. A clock chimed the hour from inside the house; she knocked and the cello playing stopped.

The towering mahogany door swung in and a tall blond man with pale-blue eyes greeted her. At first she thought he was the butler, but realized a servant wouldn't be dressed in belted chinos and a white oxford button-down shirt. A Siamese kitten batted at his ankles, drawing her attention to the unmistakable red-blink of a security bracelet.

"Dr. Conyors?" the man said, his voice pleasant and deep.

"Yes," Barrett answered, feeling a blast of cool air spill over her as gooseflesh popped on her arms.

He stepped back into the dark, marble-floored foyer. "I don't know if you remember me, but we met once when I was in the hospital." He extended his hand.

"I remember, but you look different," she said, shaking his hand, noting the strength of his grasp and that he was wearing musky cologne. *Had she been mistaken? This couldn't be the same guy.* At the same time her eyes were pulled in a dozen directions as she started to grasp the grandeur of the house. Even in the dimly lit foyer, it was hard not to gawk at the majestic sweep of the spiral staircase, or the beautiful inlaid marble on the floor, or the carved wood paneling and columns, and the artwork…like being in a museum.

The plainclothes cops trailed in after her.

"That's right," Jimmy said, watching as they entered, "you requested an escort. At least they're not in uniform."

To Barrett's ear, it was a reproach. "As you said, it's what I requested."

"Never mind," his tone conciliatory. "The kitchen is to the right, past the parlor and through the dining hall," he directed them, as though they were a pair of in-the-way servants who needed to be gotten from underfoot. "There are some deli sandwiches on the table. I'd offer you something other than soda, but I can't have anything stronger in the house."

"We could stay here," Hobbs offered, looking Jimmy straight in the eye.

Jimmy held the detective's stare and then turned to Barrett. "Is that necessary?"

"No," she said, "it'll be fine. Where would you like to meet?"

"I thought the library would be best."

"You're sure you don't want us out here?" Hobbs asked.

"No," she met Ed's gaze, thankful for his concern. "So where's the library?" she asked, trying not to be intimidated by Jimmy's environs.

"This way," and turning his back on the detectives, he picked up the Siamese cat and strode across the foyer to a pair of paneled doors with bronze handles in the form of North Wind heads. He pushed them open and Barrett got her first glimpse of the cavernous, book-lined room.

"Wow!" she muttered, as she followed him into the two-story library. She immediately noted the cello and wooden music stand positioned next to a concert-grand piano. "That was you playing," she stated.

"Yes."

"You sounded wonderful. Brahms?"

"The E Minor. You like Brahms?"

"Very much," she admitted, barraged with information. This was not the man she remembered. Her one interaction with Jimmy Martin had been with a hulking and obese patient, whose hands shook and whose eyes were barely visible beneath folds of fat.

"The piano part is beautiful," he commented. "I have it out…if you'd like to play."

She stopped in front of a pair of oxblood leather-upholstered club chairs arranged around a carved marble fireplace, with Grecian women on the sides and an open-mouthed gargoyle in the center. "That's not why I'm here," she replied curtly, wondering how it was that he had assumed she could play. *Had he and Ellen talked? Maybe she'd told him about their shared past.*

"I'm sorry," he said, "it's just that Dr. Kravitz liked to play duets."

Barrett stood behind a leather chair, "We should talk about that."

"If that's what you'd like." He sank into a leather chair, stroked the cat and watched her intently as she sat across from him.

"Before we start," Barrett began, slightly unnerved by the two pairs of startling blue eyes that followed her every movement, "we need to be clear about a few things."

"Yes?"

"First, because you're under a forensic board release agreement, what we talk about is not confidential. Even though you're footing the bill, I am expected to make a full report back to the board every month."

"I understand."

"Also, if I find that you've violated any of the conditions of your release, I am obliged by law to report that."

Jimmy stiffened, "Yes."

"Just so long as you understand this from the beginning. Do you have any questions?"

"No."

"Good," Barrett regretted her sternness, but experience had taught her that it was best to clarify up front. Forensic psychiatry was different from therapy. While Jimmy was her patient, her loyalty belonged to the State of New York and toward preserving public safety. "I was sorry to hear about Dr. Kravitz," she continued, having gotten through her disclaimer.

"He wasn't a very good pianist," Jimmy remarked. "But it's odd, I'd gotten used to him being here. This is exactly when we'd meet."

"Would he play the Brahms with you?"

"Too hard. We'd play other things, mostly the kind of stuff I did when I was a little kid."

"You've played a long time?"

"My whole life. But they wouldn't let me at Croton."

"I can't help but notice how different you look from that one time we met. It must have been what, three years ago?"

"But I remember you," he blurted, his tone almost like a child's. "You seemed very nice, not like all of the others. That's why I asked for you."

His information startled her. "You asked for me?"

"Yes, you didn't know?"

"No," she admitted, wondering why Anton hadn't told her.

"Does that matter?"

"No," she wondered if she'd misinterpreted what Anton had said, and why hadn't Ellen mentioned it? "But what you were saying about Dr. Kravitz…that the two of you played music. Do you miss him?"

"I only knew him for a few months. He visited me at Croton once it was clear they were going to let me out. And then he started seeing me here every Thursday. At first, we'd sit and talk…like this, but every time he came he'd go over to the piano. I could see he wanted to play, and so one day I offered; it made the time go by."

"Don't you think that's odd?" she asked.

"I don't know. Before Croton I never had anything to do with psychiatrists, and now I must have met over a hundred. Some of them were very strange. I don't think Kravitz playing duets with me would even make it into the top ten of weird. Like your coming here; is this normal?"

"Not really," she admitted, feeling his eyes boring into hers.

"But you're here, anyway—albeit with cops in my kitchen. That's kind of how things go for me."

"I don't understand."

"I've had a strange life, starting right at the beginning. I don't think people even realize that kind of thing until they're much older, but when you look back, you can see how it is you got to be the way you are. Do you know what I mean?"

"I think so, but can you be more specific?" she asked, wondering whether his story would match up with Ellen's. "What made your childhood strange?"

He grunted, "What didn't? It was like living in quicksand, where anything solid could suddenly slip away and you'd be left struggling just to keep alive."

"And your sister?"

"Right…" He looked down at Fred who lay curled and purring in his lap. "She was the only thing I could grab onto. We had each other."

"Even when you were in the hospital she looked after you, didn't she?"

"Yes. They wouldn't have let me out if it weren't for her. As far as my parents were concerned, I could have stayed there forever."

"You know that she didn't want me to interview you when you were in Croton."

"Yes."

"Why was that?" Barrett asked, comparing his responses to the sister's, and to what actually had happened.

"She thought you might make it harder for me to get out."

"How is that?" she asked, watching for subtle physical and verbal cues that could reveal the presence of lies.

"It's like you said, whatever we talk about isn't confidential. And things have a way of getting twisted in the retelling. You weren't the only one who wanted to use me as a…a test subject."

"You were going to say something else," she prompted.

He gently wiped a bit of sleep from out of the corner of the cat's eye. "A guinea pig."

She smiled back, "It's a beautiful cat."

"His name's Fred."

"Why Fred?"

"Frederic Chopin."

She stopped herself from blurting that Chopin was her favorite composer. "How old is he?"

"The vet thinks he's about six months old."

"You don't know?"

"My case manager found him in the garbage one morning as he was coming with my medication. He was with two other kittens and they were both dead. He brought him over and I fed him with an eye dropper. He was so tiny and for a while I didn't know if he would live or not." He stroked the cat under the chin, "But he's getting to be quite the fat little thing."

"I can't get over how different you look," Barrett said, noting how gentle he was with the kitten, and that Jimmy Martin was a good-looking man.

"I was huge," he admitted. "It's what that place does to you."

"What do you mean?"

His expression darkened, "I try not to think about that."

"You were very young when you went into the hospital."

"I was eighteen," his breath caught.

"Do you remember much about what got you arrested?"

"Do we have to talk about that?"

"Yes," she urged, sensing a shift in Jimmy, something different in the eyes, the voice, the posture.

"Dr. Kravitz didn't make me."

"I'm not him, Jimmy. I'm going to need to know how you think about your crime; it's part of my job."

"I don't think about it. I was out of my mind."

"And you're not now?"

"No, that's behind me."

"You were found in Nicole Foster's apartment."

"Please don't do this," he rubbed the sides of his head, pushing his carefully brushed silky blond hair into tangled twirls.

"We're going to have to talk about it sometime, Jimmy."

"Why? I want to forget! You don't know how many times I've been asked these questions. I don't remember, and yes, I feel terrible. If I could have it all come undone I would, but I can't. If I could have those years of my life back, you can't imagine what that would be worth to me."

"What about Nicole Foster's life?" Barrett asked, wondering if Jimmy's remorse was real or feigned.

"Of course," he said, but not convincingly, "I feel terrible for what happened to her...and her boyfriend, their families." He glanced up at Barrett, his eyes pleading. "Couldn't we play the Brahms instead?"

"No." She wondered at the fear in his eyes.

"Why not?" he blinked and started to rock in his chair. Fred startled, jumped from Jimmy's lap and ran beneath a couch.

"Okay," she eased back, "we'll talk about something else. How did you manage to lose so much weight?"

Jimmy's breathing slowed and he sat still, "Once I knew they were going to let me out of that place, I pretty much stopped eating, and tried to exercise as much as I could. They'd let me take walks on the grounds and so I'd go for hours and hours. I lost a hundred and twenty pounds."

"That's impressive." Barrett studied him, generating a quick differential of how and why he could have changed so dramatically. "Losing weight can be quite challenging for someone who's on the medications you're taking."

His head shot up.

"Are you taking your medication?" she asked.

"Yes," he answered too quickly. His pale eyes narrowed.

"Are you?" she persisted, noticing that the strong lithium tremor he'd had in the hospital was absent.

"I said, yes."

"You know I have to check, and I can tell you that you don't look like someone who's taking medication."

"What are you trying to do to me?" he spat out.

Barrett tensed. "I'm not trying to do anything, Jimmy, but let's be clear. Part of your release agreement is that you'll take all prescribed medications and that you won't miss a single dose without a very good reason."

He started to rock again, "You don't know what it's like."

"That's true, I don't. But I do know that you were found not guilty by reason of insanity for a very serious crime."

"I never touched her," he interrupted.

"That's what all the reports say," she agreed, trying to keep her voice neutral and professional. She reminded herself that Hobbs was in the other room, and wondered what exactly it was that was making her skin crawl. "Jimmy, you never stood trial for whatever role you played in those murders. Instead, the court determined that because of your mental illness you couldn't be tried; you went to Croton. Now, because of this, and I know that I'm not telling you anything new, you must follow—to the letter—your release agreement. Do we understand each other?"

"Yes."

"Good. Now let me ask you again; are you taking your medication?"

His nostrils flared, "Yes, Dr. Conyors, I'm taking all of my medication."

"Good. Then I'll have them draw levels in the morning."

He said nothing, but she could see the rage behind his eyes.

The grandfather clock clicked as the gears for the hour mechanism engaged and the chimes resonated heavily through the room. It was five o'clock.

"We need to stop," she said.

"Of course," he replied.

Barrett uncrossed her legs and stood on shaky knees. Her thoughts were troubled by the competing bits of what she referred to as jagged data—things that didn't fit.

"Aren't you forgetting something?" he asked, still seated.

"What?"

He reached across the small eagle-footed Federal table and opened the drawer. He pulled out a linen envelope and getting to his feet, handed it to her. "Your payment."

Feeling his eyes on her, she took the envelope and pocketed it unopened. There was something contemptuous in the way he gave it to her, like a john paying a prostitute.

"This time is good for you?" she asked.

"Yes."

"Then same time next week."

He nodded, his jaw set through clenched teeth.

Through the library's open door she saw Hobbs and Cassidy waiting for her in the foyer.

Without a word, Jimmy strode past them to the front door. He opened it, and keeping to the shadows he watched with hooded eyes as Dr. Barrett Conyors and her policemen left.

SEVEN

Barrett felt rattled as she walked away from Ed Hobbs and from Jimmy Martin's opulent townhouse. With each step she rehashed the hour, thinking back over the pieces that didn't fit. Almost without thought, she pulled out her cell and dialed the forensic center.

"Give me the surveillance team," she said, wondering why she felt so jangled.

A woman came on the line, and Barrett told her, "I want to get some blood drawn on James Martin…today, and send it stat. Get me a lithium level, basic electrolytes, drug-screen, Risperdal level, and you may as well check his liver, thyroid, and renal function at the same time."

The woman read back her order; Barrett thanked her and hung up.

Nearing First Avenue, she noticed a sickly tingle in the tips of her fingers, and a mounting nausea. It took her a split-second to realize what was happening, and by then the sensations had leapfrogged to her feet, her throat. Her pulse sped, its beats ringing in her ears. Her thoughts skidded to a stop and she clutched her chest. This couldn't be happening; it had been years since the last one. She felt herself slipping out of her body and wondered if perhaps her therapist had been wrong all those years ago, and that perhaps this *could* kill her. It felt as though it were happening to someone else, as though she weren't there, standing on the corner of First and 21st Street.

"Barrett," a man's voice called to her.

She turned and saw Hobbs running toward her. Could he see what was happening?

He stopped, not at all winded by his jog. "I was thinking that maybe we could get some coffee, or something?"

"You're not on the clock?" she managed to ask, wondering if her voice betrayed what was happening inside.

"Nah, Bryan can take care of the vehicle. I'm just doing this to pick up some overtime." He looked at her, his eyes searching. "You okay?"

"Not great," she admitted. "I'm having a panic attack."

"Can I help? You need a paper bag?"

"It'll pass," she said, more as a reminder to herself. "They always pass, the bitch is I haven't had one since I was a resident."

"You think it had something to do with our boy, James?"

"Could be," she agreed, noting that her palpitations had begun to subside. "Here," she offered him the underside of her hand, "feel my pulse."

Ed took her wrist, "Like a rabbit," he commented.

"That's what I can't stand," she tried to slow her breath. "It's such a paralyzing feeling. The funny thing is," she started to walk, "I never get them when I'm in the middle of a crisis; they always come after. Like in medical school, I'd finish some horrible exam and fifteen minutes later I'd be holed up in the bathroom wondering if I was going to die or not."

"But you said you haven't had them in a while."

"I know. I saw a therapist about them, and I'm pretty good at making them go away. I trained myself to where I can stop them before they take over."

"Until now," he commented.

"Lucky me, but it's going."

"Greek diner?" he asked, looking across the street at a restaurant with a pink and purple neon sign that read *Acropolis Restaurant—open 24 hours.*

"Sure," she said, wondering if maybe she should just take the rest of the day off.

He held the door for her, "When do you have to be back at the office?"

"I just have some paperwork. I might blow it off," she confessed, as a dark-haired waitress with heavy crescents of blue eye shadow led them back to a corner booth.

They were handed thick plastic menus, which promised everything from eggs and bacon to stuffed lobster tails. They both ordered coffee and a bagel and cream cheese.

After the waitress left, Barrett looked at Hobbs, and noted his worried expression. "It's almost gone," she admitted. "They never last long; I thought I was done with them."

"My wife used to get them," he offered.

"Used to?" Barrett asked, trying not to focus on his ringless finger.

"Maybe still does, we don't talk much. They put her on some pills, Xanax or something." He looked at her, "But you and I haven't talked in a while, have we?"

"No," she said, noting the fine lines around his deep-brown eyes, the furrows etched in his brow; those seemed new.

He gave a bitter laugh as the waitress set down their coffee. "Not a good year."

"Is that why you're on the babysitting patrol?"

He sipped and nodded.

"You don't have to, Ed," she offered, but felt curious as hell, and touched by his sadness.

"I'll give you the abridged version. And if I start to sound like a perp, just kick me."

"That bad?"

"Not good. You might have seen some of it in the papers."

"I don't read them...too much like work."

"Just as well. Not long after the Charlie Rohr thing, I got a heads up that one of my men was taking bribes from a smut dealer. I did what I thought I was supposed to do, because God help you if you point the finger and you haven't done everything by the book. So I made a report to Internal and the next thing you know it blossomed into one hell of a conspiracy. Some good men—or at least I thought they were good—got kicked off the force, or re-signed. And I, as their incompetent supervisor, was strongly urged to follow."

"I'm so sorry, Ed." She resisted the impulse to touch his arm.

"Not your fault, and that, as they say, was the start of the deluge. Margaret couldn't take it, and she wasn't about to stick with a proven loser. We signed papers a couple months ago. I get Alice and Becky on weekends and half the holidays. That is if I keep up with child support and alimony. So I let them bust me down to grade three detective, while I try to figure out what comes next. I guess I'm lucky they kept me at all. And you?" he looked up, plastering on a smile. "Please tell me that you're still moving forward brilliantly."

Barrett spread cream cheese onto her bagel, "Or...we could turn this into a twisted game of *I Can Top That*."

"What do you mean?"

"Well, at least work's going okay; at least I think it is."

"And Ralph?"

"I don't know," she heard her words resonate in the space between them.

"Really?"

She put down the uneaten bagel, "I don't know why it feels like I did something wrong, but I caught Ralph cheating. God, that sounds like something from a country western song."

"You're sure."

"Yes, I'm sure," she snapped, sounding harsher than intended. "I came home to find him in bed with somebody I considered a friend."

"Ouch! You don't have kids, do you?"

"No," she stared at the speckled Formica tabletop.

"You want kids?"

"You giving some away?" she tried to make a joke, but he'd honed right in on the issue. "It's so fucked up. Yes, I want kids, and the funny thing is we've been talking about it. So why the hell did he do this? My eggs don't have all that many years to go and I don't want to be some forty-five-year-old woman with no husband and a Down's Syndrome baby…It's like you get up one morning and everything's the way it's supposed to be, and twenty-four hours later it's all different. And then I start looking back, and maybe things haven't been okay for a while, and maybe I've been walking around with a paper bag on my head. He says he's 'sorry,' says 'he loves me, wants to get back together.' I have no clue what I'm supposed to do."

"No wonder you're having panic attacks," Hobbs offered. "Jimmy was just the straw that pushed you over."

"You're right," she met his gaze. "And that's a whole other can of worms."

"What do you mean?"

"You know his case?"

"Not much," Ed admitted. "I read through his arrest report, pulled up the court files, and even looked at his release agreement, but it doesn't give you a strong feel for him as a person."

"I'd forgotten," Barrett said, remembering Ed's intelligence and attention to detail.

"Forgotten what?"

"What it was like to work with you."

"Those were some fun cases," he agreed.

"I guess, if you think that looking at pictures of people with knitting needles sticking out of their eyes is fun." She smiled, "I can't really talk to most people about what I do. But the sick thing is if it weren't for work, I'd be losing it. But back to Jimmy, it sounds like you've got as much information as I have. Even going through volumes of evaluations and a summary from his last psychiatrist, there's hardly anything."

"The one who just died," Ed inserted.

"Right, Morris Kravitz…any chance you could track down his death certificate?"

"Not a problem, why? You think Jimmy had something to do with that?"

"Just curious. You know the strangest thing—I have no clue who was in that room with me."

"What do you mean?" he asked.

"When we first worked together you gave me a piece of advice that I've used ever since."

"Really? What was it?"

"You said something about 'jagged data,' about things that don't fit," she said. "And that *jagged data* needs extra consideration—because if it doesn't fit, there's a reason."

"So what does that have to do with Master James?"

"Nothing fits," she sipped her coffee.

"You going to tell me?"

"Where to start? I almost don't want to tell you about this first thing, so I'll go with that." She chuckled, "Somewhere deep down I have a soft spot for Freud."

"You've lost me."

"Resistance, there's something that doesn't want to come out, so that's probably the first thing that needs to…and it makes no sense. My boss—Anton—gave me Jimmy's case, and it felt like he was doing me a favor."

"Some favor."

"No, it really is. This is off-the-clock work, and Jimmy is paying big bucks for door-to-door shrink delivery."

"And?"

"Well, Jimmy said that he asked for me specifically."

"Why you?" Ed leaned forward, the banter gone, his expression worried.

"I interviewed him a single time when he was at Croton. I was still a resident and I was working on some research on stalking. I guess he must have liked me. Although his sister sure didn't." Barrett looked at Ed, "She threatened to sue the medical school, me, and anyone else her lawyers could think of if I didn't leave her brother alone."

"Why would she care?"

"You know she took me out to dinner last night?"

"Because?" letting his voice trail.

"She's his conservator. Arranged for his release. So I asked her, and she said she was trying to protect him."

"Did she tell you why he wanted to meet with you?"

"No, and that feels jagged, too. Why wouldn't she?"

"So what are your options?" he asked.

"About which piece?"

"Why he wants you?"

"I don't know. I don't think I'm so wonderful that after a single visit someone is going to pick me out from all available psychiatrists."

Ed traced a finger around the rim of his cup. "There's an obvious reason."

"Which is?"

"Look in the mirror, Barrett. Maybe the boy has a crush."

She shuddered, "Don't even go there."

"Hey, you want to make the jagged pieces smooth, you got to roll them through the possibilities. And common things are common.

Look at it this way, here you've got an inmate living what? Eight, nine years in a maximum security hospital."

"Longer—by the time I saw him, it would have been fourteen or so."

"You think he's straight?"

"He's something. Do I think he likes girls? In some fashion and based on what happened to Nicole Foster, I'm not certain that breathing is a prerequisite."

"Nice. So you've got a perp who's spent eighteen years in the nut house and in comes this hot, twenty-something psychiatrist who's all concerned about his welfare. I bet he can remember everything you wore that day. He probably spent nights…"

"Stop right there."

"Tears on his pillow," Ed chortled.

"Are all men pigs?" Barrett asked.

"It's the hormones."

"I thought that was the PMS defense."

"Same idea, different sex."

"What if he picked me because I was the only name he could think of?"

Ed's head cocked slightly as he mulled her suggestion, "Second choice at best."

"Why?"

"How many shrinks would he have seen at Croton over the years?"

"Good point. There would have been dozens. But if *your* answer is the right one, and he's got some sort of crush, why didn't he ask for me at the time of his release?"

"Don't know. Maybe he did. Maybe something changed between then and now. You said his sister didn't want you to see him at Croton, and now she's taking you out to dinner, maybe she had something to do with it."

"All of which leads me back to the beginning. Who the hell is he and what makes him go? You know that music we heard outside his place?"

"Yes."

"It was him."

"He's good," Ed admitted.

"Really good. Like concert-stage good."

"Seriously?"

"I think so. In another life that was where I was heading."

"Music?"

"Yeah, I've played piano ever since I was little." As she spoke, she pictured Sophie, and the back room of the used bookstore where she'd have her daily lessons, and would then spend hours practicing.

"No kidding. Why'd you switch? Leave that and become a shrink?"

"It's funny, but when I was applying for medical school that was the question I always got asked. Not, 'Why do you want to be a doctor?' or 'How do you feel about working with sick people?' It was always something about music."

"So what's the answer?"

"You know, I had a lot of pat answers. And looking back, it's the hardest thing I've ever done. I had this amazing piano teacher." She looked up at Hobbs, "This is boring, isn't it?"

"Hell, no," he said. "Let me hear this. Who's this teacher?"

"She was incredible, both of them…Sophie and Max. They're both gone now. They kind of adopted us, my mother, sister, and me. We landed on their doorstep and they just happened to have an empty apartment over their bookstore; my mom still lives there.…I don't want to go into the details, but when I was real little we had to get out of Georgia in a hurry and these two Polish refugees we'd never met let us stay with them. I don't think they even charged rent for the first year, and every day when mom was out working they'd look after us in the store, and somehow I started fooling around with this big old piano in the back, and Sophie decided that I had some talent. She was a concert pianist in Poland, both she and Max were Jewish; their families killed by the Nazis, but they survived and came to New York. Some of the stories they'd tell…just amazing." Her eyes misted.

"They sound like good people."

"You have no idea. And the way she taught…every piece of music was a story, every composer laying down his life in the notes and the melodies. I became obsessed with playing, and I got really good. So she started entering me into these competitions, and we'd go together, and my mom and sister would be in the audience. And you see, I've got this little competitive streak."

"No kidding."

"I know; it's really bad."

"It's not; it's cute."

It felt like flirting, and Barrett wondered how Ralph would feel if the shoe were on the other foot.

"So how'd you do?" Hobbs asked. "Although I think I know."

"At first, not so good, but it just made me determined. The first time I won, the look on Sophie's face, and seeing how proud my mother was; I was hooked. And as I got better, music became this wonderful world where I'd lose myself for hours."

"I'd like to hear you sometime."

"I don't play much anymore…at least not in front of people," she said, feeling a familiar pang.

"So why did you switch? It sounds like something you really loved."

"I had to be practical. Although I never told my mother this, or Sophie."

"I don't get it," Hobbs said.

"My mom's spent her entire life taking care of me and Justine, she was a waitress forever, and now she tends bar. She has no benefits, and I had to beg her not to take out a mortgage on her apartment—Sophie and Max left it to her—she wanted the money to help pay for college for us…Very few make money as concert pianists. It's an incredible risk, and the further I got with the competitions, I knew there would always be people better than me. Medicine was a sure thing; it meant that at least one of us would have a steady income. So instead of Juilliard, I went premed."

"That must have hurt."

"Yeah…and that's another odd thing with Jimmy."

"Yes?"

"You know when I said I'd met him only the one time, it's not true. I'd actually seen him and his sister growing up. They were four years older than me, and very much the stars of the competition circuit. They were these two ethereal blond twins who would make the most amazing music. I made the connection with Ellen, we kind of recognized each other, but didn't know from where.

When I interviewed him at Croton, I would never have put it together."

"Why not?"

"He was huge, grotesque. He told me that he's lost over a hundred pounds since then. There's no way I would have ever connected the beautiful boy I saw playing the cello with the man I met at Croton. And it's not just the weight, but the younger Jimmy was dazzling."

"Poor guy."

"Why do you say that?"

"I've been to Croton," Ed commented. "It's not that different from prison, and pretty boys in prison have real problems."

"I hadn't considered that. Maybe that's why he gained the weight."

"It's been known. Doesn't necessarily make the problem go away, but it might decrease it."

"And here I'd just written it off to the medication. Which, by the way, I don't think he's taking. So all of this could wind up being for nothing. If he's not taking his pills, I have to report that to the board, and chances are they'll lock him up."

"Goodbye, golden goose…although, everything you're telling me is that the man is not stupid."

"True."

"But if he's really this brilliant cello-playing prodigy, then I don't think he's going down without a fight. That is unless getting shower-raped in prison is how he gets his jollies. And one thing *you* taught me is that the minute you have a sociopath with an IQ above 120, you've got a serious predator on your hands."

"Also true," she said, remembering the feral and dangerous look in Jimmy's eyes.

"I don't like you being in that room alone with him. Any chance I could talk you into having someone else take his case?"

"No."

"Then you've got to wear a wire."

"You think you can get a warrant for one?"

He leaned across and whispered, "I wasn't going to try."

EIGHT

GRABBING THE BANISTER, JIMMY raced up two flights of stairs and ran into Mother's room. Peering through Brussels lace, he glared down at Barrett Conyors as she conversed with the two cops. They were talking in front of what was obviously an unmarked police car, as if the neighbors didn't have enough to talk about. His pulse raced as he devoured details of the woman who'd just interrogated him. She was more perfect than he'd remembered, from her swan-like throat and pointed chin to the high arch of her brows and the willowy grace of her body that not even her off-the-rack suit could conceal. But it was her eyes that held him, dark and stormy gray. *Why*, he pouted, *did she have to be like that?*

"No," he told himself, knowing that she loved him. "She's just doing her job." But Dr. Kravitz had been doing his job, at least the job that Jimmy and Ellen had wanted him to do. Ellen had warned him, not about Barrett, but about all the shrinks who would do whatever they could to see him locked up again. They'd pick at his brain until there was nothing left, and then throw him back into stinking Croton where the others would come for him, wanting to use him like a twenty-dollar whore.

He stared at Barrett as she laughed with the cops. "What are you saying?" he needed to know. She was laughing. What words were coming out of her painted lips? She looked back at the house, but he knew she couldn't see him. He lifted up the lid of the window seat and pulled out a pair of binoculars. He focused on her as she hid her eyes behind rimless sunglasses.

"So pretty," he murmured, wondering what it would feel like to stroke her cheek or to touch her hair. Like a princess, like Sleeping Beauty. He blinked.

"*Mustn't touch, Jimbo,*" Father's voice chided. "*Mustn't ever, ever touch.*"

"Shut up." He saw Dr. Conyors was saying something to the taller guy with the moustache. Jimmy focused on him, wanting him gone, wishing that he wouldn't talk with Barrett. "What are you saying?"

She was turning away now, heading east, probably back to her office. He watched as she stopped and pulled out a tiny cell phone. He needed to know who was on the other end.

She clicked it closed, and was nearly out of view when the tall cop called out to her. Even through the closed windows, Jimmy could hear him use her first name. Such disrespect, surely she'd ignore him, or at the very least inform him that she was to be referred to as doctor. But that's not what happened. She just turned and smiled as the dark-suited man jogged toward her. He waved back to his partner, and to Jimmy's horror, he and Dr. Conyors walked off together and disappeared from view.

"No!"

"*Stupid boy,*" Father needled in his ear. "*Such a stupid boy. But don't worry, she'll see you get nicely tucked away.*"

"Shut up!" Jimmy shouted into Mother's empty boudoir.

"*What's the matter? Can't deal with a little competition?*"

"She doesn't like him. How could she?"

"*I bet he has a nice big cock. Perhaps if you asked him, he'd show it to you.*"

"Shut up, shut up, shut up."

Father's voice sang inside his head. "*Stupid boy, stupid boy. Jimbo is a stupid boy.*"

Jimmy pictured Ellen, she'd know what to do; she always did. He had to think, to plan. He had to find a way to get through this. Dr. Conyors had caught him off guard; she knew that he wasn't taking the medication.

"*But if she loved you, Jimbo, why would she care?*"

As always, Father found the thing that hurt most. "She loves me," he said, but felt a horrible uncertainty.

"*She'll send you back.*"

Jimmy turned frantic. That couldn't happen. He couldn't go back to Croton; he'd never survive. Needing to calm himself, he tried to retrieve his earlier fantasy of he and Barrett on stage. They'd make music, he'd take her in his arms, his lips would find hers, and love's first kiss; it would be perfect.

Father's hissing laughter surrounded him, fueling his fear. "*You wouldn't know what to do with her. Mustn't touch. Mustn't ever touch.*"

She'd said she was going to check his blood; she'd know that he'd not been taking his pills. She didn't trust him.

Now he almost regretted what had happened to Dr. Kravitz—what he'd done. Not that he felt remorse, but a sort of dull reflection of that emotion. Kravitz too had wanted to check his blood.

He ran down to the kitchen and into the pantry. There, surrounded by glass-fronted cabinets filled with priceless dinner services, sterling silver tureens, and the Bennington ironstone that Mother had purchased during a Vermont retreat with one of her drivers, he reached up and into a pink-and-gold Meissen teapot. His long fingers fished inside and pulled out a handful of blue and white pills. Selecting four rhomboid-shaped lithium and three tiny white Risperdal, he poured himself a glass of water, and one by one swallowed his emergency stash. Her threat was now a hollow one; by the time Hector arrived in the morning his lithium level would be normal.

He stared out the back window, still trying to calm himself, watching a crow hop on the edge of the muck-filled fountain. And suddenly, he realized what she was doing. It was obvious; she was testing him, wanting him to prove his love. She was a prize worth fighting for, and she knew it. Like the fairy tales Maylene would read to him in her warm Southern drawl, like Snow White and Sleeping Beauty waiting for the prince who could prove himself worthy of love's first kiss. It had to be earned, had to be fought for.

He headed out the back door, through the courtyard and into the carriage house. In the sound-proofed upstairs, he went to the phone, and used a line that the review board did not know existed. The entire world of the carriage house had been concealed from them. The phone lines, the cable for the computer were all registered through a subsidiary of Martin Industries. The board had never thought to ask if the fabulous mansion in Gramercy was connected to a separate property. After all, the carriage house had its own 19th Street address, and why tell them more than they demanded to know. The psychiatric review board had total control over his life—at least it was supposed to. They could tap his phone, search his home, and had explicit directions to audit any computer in his house.

He dialed Ellen's direct office number—she didn't like him to do that, but he had to.

She picked up on the third ring.

"Ellen."

"What's the matter?" she asked, keying in to his anxiety.

"It didn't go right."

She paused, "What do you mean, Jimmy?"

"She's testing me. I need you to help me."

"I see...Were you careful?"

"I don't know. I think so," he felt lost and exposed. "Help me, Ellen."

"I like her, Jimmy," Ellen said, as she carefully chose her words. "But one slip and you're back there. You have to listen to me. She's much smarter than the other one. You're certain that you want to go through with this?"

"I have to see her," he said, barreling over his sister's caution. "I need to get inside, to know what she's doing. You have to help me."

"And you'll do as I say?"

He pictured Ellen in Father's old office. He hadn't been there since his release, but could easily imagine how all traces of dear old dad had been replaced with slick Italian modern. "Yes."

"And Father? Can you control him? Can you keep him from fucking things up again?"

"Yes, yes, please…and I need you to bring me a new key for my bracelet, the old one broke."

"You're not being careful," she said. "What happened to the old one? And I don't *have to* do anything. What if I refuse? I've done enough."

"No," he said, suddenly mad at her, she shouldn't play with him like this; it wasn't nice. "If I go down, this time you'll come with me. I know what you did. I've been in the basement. I know everything."

"You're bluffing, Jimmy."

He said nothing, sensing her uncertainty, knowing that he was right; she'd played Hansel and Gretel without him. He waited, letting the seconds stretch into a full minute of silence.

Finally, she spoke, "No sense arguing. There's work to be done. But keep Father out of this, Jimmy."

"I'll try, Ellen. Shit!" His eye caught a movement in the front door monitor.

"What is it?"

"It's Hector and he's with someone at the door. I've got to go." Without saying goodbye, he raced down the stairs. There was no mistaking the persistent clang of the doorbell.

As he cleared the dining hall he heard the added banging of the brass door knocker.

"Coming!" he shouted, wanting the noise to stop, frightened by this unexpected intrusion. "I'm coming." He peered through the glass fisheye and saw his case worker and a young black woman he'd never met.

"Jimmy, man," Hector said, as the door opened, "what took you so long?"

"I was taking a nap," he said letting them in. "Why are you here?" he asked, trying to keep his tone neutral, while seething at this violation of his privacy.

"Doctor's orders," Hector said, as Fred sniffed at the woman's ankles.

"What a pretty kitty," she said, setting her heavy shoulder pack on the floor.

"I don't understand," Jimmy was freaking. "What orders?"

"Dr. Conyors asked for some bloodwork, said it couldn't wait. This is Veronica."

"Hi," she picked up Fred and scratched the side of his head with her forefinger.

"Now?" Jimmy frantically wondered if the lithium and Risperdal he'd swallowed after the session had had enough time to make it into his bloodstream. He tried to control his breathing, to not let them see how freaked out he was.

"That's the order. Do it in the kitchen?"

"Sure," he said, trying to think of a way to buy time.

"Just show me where to set up," Veronica cheerfully went on, setting down Fred and hefting her bag. "Just three tubes and then we'll be out of here. God," she said, looking around and gushing as Jimmy slowly led them back through the immense front hall,

"What a fantastic house! Hector says you've got it all to yourself. Man, I'd kill for a place like this!"

NINE

AFTER LEAVING HOBBS, BARRETT returned to the office and her paperwork. She'd promised herself to be out of there no later than six, which would give her time to run home, get in an hour on the piano, wolf down supper, and make it to kung fu by eight.

She was also hoping to hear from the lab, to know if her gravy train with Jimmy was about to get derailed. With that plan, she clicked the hand control for the dictaphone. Halfway through her report on a mentally retarded man who'd shoplifted cheap toys from department stores, the phone rang. Hoping it would be the lab, she picked up.

"Dr. Conyors," Marla whispered, "there's an Ellen Martin here who's insisting that she needs to see you right away."

"What's she doing here? ... Never mind." Barrett could easily imagine that Jimmy had called his twin right after the session; clearly she'd struck a chord. "Marla, give me a couple minutes, then send her down."

There was a pause on the line, "... Very good, doctor."

Barrett scanned her desk and locked away any confidential material. She then opened her door and looked down the hall as Ellen, dressed in a dark-green suit, with a gorgeous amber and gold necklace around her throat, quickly approached.

"Dr. Conyors," she said, closing the distance, "I'm so sorry to interrupt this way, but I got a call from Jimmy, and he's freaking out."

"Come in," Barrett stepped back to let Ellen into her modest office. "Please, sit down."

"Thank you," Ellen said, clutching a russet-colored bag in her lap. "And thank you for seeing me on absolutely no notice. I'm so sorry. I was heading downtown when the call came; I had the driver double back. I've been parked outside…I know," she said, catching Barrett's eye, "I must sound like a stalker, but it seems like half my life is spent looking after Jimmy. Could you tell me what he did?"

"I don't think he's been taking his meds," Barrett said, not wanting to prolong this. "I have to check. I sent the lab out to do bloodwork."

"I could just kill him," Ellen said, exasperated. "He knows the rules. What happens if the results come back and you're right?"

"It's not good," Barrett admitted.

"They'll send him back, won't they?"

"Probably."

"Shit! I'm sorry, it's just. Damn! What if I talked to him, read him the riot act, told him you'd be checking every week? Every day if you want. Would that work?"

"It might, but it's not my decision. Any time a rule gets broken, it goes to the board. They have the final say."

"When will you know…about whether he's been taking them?"

"I should get the results this afternoon."

"Could you do me a favor," Ellen said, clicking open her pocketbook and pulling out her business card. "Call me when you get them. Here, let me give you my cell number."

As Barrett reached for the card, she noticed that Ellen's hand was trembling. "Are you okay?"

Ellen shook her head, struggling to keep her emotions in check. She looked at Barrett, her mouth contorted. "No," and then the tears came. "I can't believe this is happening," Ellen sobbed, her shoulders heaving. "I'm so sorry." She tried to speak, but her throat choked as she looked away, her eyes obscured by her perfectly coiffed blond bob.

Barrett watched, helpless in the face of Ellen's sorrow, and wishing there was something she could do. She pushed the tissue box across the surface of the desk, "Could I get you some water?"

Ellen nodded, trying to regain her composure.

Barrett stood, "I'll be right back," and leaving the door open, she headed to the vending machine.

———

Ellen counted to three, turned her head to be certain that she was unobserved, and reaching into her Prada bag pulled out a digital bug—a kind produced by *Klift*, a German subsidiary of Martin Industries that in addition to their pricey brushed-nickel kitchen appliances, manufactured munitions and high-tech surveillance equipment. It was this latter business, and its vast potential in third-world markets, that had fueled Ellen's surreptitious stock acquisition and eventual takeover of *Klift* eight years earlier. One unanticipated perk had been this easy access to the latest in surveillance equipment, which she'd used on numerous occasions to monitor the activity of competitors. Now, moving fast, she peeled off the double-sided tape and stuck the tissue-thin device to the bottom of Barrett's phone, where it appeared to be just another inspection label. Her pulse never quickened, even as she caught the sound of Barrett's return.

Clutching a wadded tissue, she dabbed her eyes, and turned as Dr. Conyors reentered the tiny office. "Thank you," she said, reaching for the blue-plastic bottle of chilled water. "I don't know what came over me…actually I do," she admitted, while again taking stock of Barrett. "I know my brother is mentally ill…I wish to God he weren't," she spoke slowly, wanting Barrett to see how filled with emotion she was. She took a careful sip of water, "He wants to have a normal life, but he doesn't have a clue how to get that. I'd like to see him have that chance." With tears tracking down her cheeks, she met Barrett's gaze, "Is that too much to ask for?"

"No, it isn't." Barrett held eye contact, "But we both know the rules."

Ellen nodded, took a deep breath and stood. "I should be going…thank you. And Dr. Conyors?"

"Yes."

"I will make damn certain my brother is taking all of his pills."

"Good," Barrett said, as Ellen reached for her hand.

"Thank you," and turning toward the door, Ellen felt the giddy light-headed glow of success, like closing a deal, or getting the inside jump on a juicy IPO. Dr. Barrett Conyors had all the right stuff, and before too long, she and little Jimmy would have everything their hearts desired... or at least she would.

—

Barrett felt rattled, confused, and a little sad after Ellen's impromptu visit. She knew checking Jimmy's bloodwork was the right thing, but after all the work that Ellen had put into getting her brother released, it was a shame. "Not your fault," she told herself, picturing the tall blond man, and remembering how being with him had left her frightened and uncertain. She took a deep breath, and turned back to her earlier dictation. A knock came at the door.

"Yes?"

Anton's balding pate appeared. "Hey Barrett, glad I caught you. You got the Anderson report done?"

"Excuse me," she said, glancing at her stack of cases still to be completed.

"Please tell me it's done." His tone nasal and anxious.

"Not likely, the hearing's not for another week."

"It got moved up. I just got a call from the D.A. They need the report like yesterday. Any chance you could fax it to them tonight?"

"I haven't started it," she said, realizing that not only wasn't it started, but it was an extremely complex evaluation involving a twenty-three-year-old man who'd gone into the copy shop that had just fired him, and point blank shot to death his ex-boss and two coworkers. It was high profile, and messy, not the kind of thing that could be dashed off in an hour or two.

"I don't know what to say, Barrett. I need you to do this, sorry."

She saw her plans for the night evaporate. "Okay. I'll do it." There was no way out. "But they're not going to get it till the morning."

"You're a life saver," he turned back toward the door.

"Anton?"

"What?"

She wanted to ask why he hadn't told her that Jimmy Martin had requested her, but as the question formed…"nothing."

As he left, she wondered why she'd held back. Something about him seemed off, it had for a while, a certain jumpiness and tentative quality. And his springing this late-afternoon bombshell—something wasn't right.

———

Four hours later, Barrett felt fried as she clicked the mouse on the print key for her fourth and final draft of the Anderson evaluation. It was nine-thirty. She hadn't eaten since her bagel with Hobbs, and as the pages spilled out, she hunted for the assistant D.A.'s fax number.

She grabbed the completed report, thought about proofing it once more, but couldn't stand to go through it again. She grabbed a pen and signed and dated the last page. Stepping out of her office, she headed toward the deserted receptionist's desk. As she fed pages through the fax, she glanced out the windows that faced 1st Avenue. This day had seemed endless, and the thought of returning to her empty condo made her frown. Ralph would be finishing soon with the evening's performance. What would happen if she called him? "No," but maybe if he called her—but she sure as hell wouldn't wait for it. She glanced at the clock, realized that she might still be able to get in a workout. Maybe Justine would be there.

With that promising thought, she grabbed her original from the paper tray—she'd FedEx it to the D.A. in the morning—and headed back to her office.

She pulled her gym bag out of the closet and stripped off her work clothes, hanging up the suit and folding the raw-silk blouse into the knapsack. She noted how many of her clothes had found their way here. Soon all she'd have to do was figure out a way to move a bed in and she'd never have to go home.

She strapped on a black sports bra and a clean pair of sweats. She laced up her Nikes and checked to make sure she'd remembered her kung-fu slippers.

Closing the door behind her, she rattled the knob to make sure it was locked. Then, jogging down seven flights, she headed into the cool spring evening. Pressing against the brick siding of the forensic center, she did a couple deep hamstring stretches, and then sprinted south in the direction of Sifu Li's 17th Street Dojo.

As she ran against traffic, the lights of the swerving cabs and the signs for restaurants and Korean delis blurred into a whir of color as her feet pounded a steady rhythm on the sidewalk. As she jogged, she thought about Ralph, and last night's lovemaking. And that ever since she'd caught him with Carol, in a weird act of rebellion—or maybe fatalism—she'd stopped the pill. And last night he certainly hadn't been using condoms. She was midway through her cycle—just about time to ovulate. *What if ... ?*

She ran faster and forced herself to think about something else. She replayed her meeting with Jimmy and the coffee with Hobbs. It felt like flirting. Or was that just conversation? And what the hell was she doing thinking about how his eyes twinkled when he laughed, or how strong his hands looked?

"Not good," she grunted as she pushed herself into a muscle-burning sprint for the remaining blocks, timing her pace to the changing streetlights and keeping a wary eye open to the threat of an unseen bicyclist or red light-running cab.

With sweat beading her forehead, she arrived at the basement studio and walked down the cement stairs. As she'd often done, she paused to read the small plaque beneath the eyehole. It read: *"Fear does not dwell in the present. It lives in the past and the future."*

She pushed the door open. The first person she saw was Justine in a navy leotard and matching sweats. Her sister smiled and waved.

She waved back, and then her mood hit rock. "Shit!" There, in the back of the room, was the person she least wanted to see—Carol Gartner, in a tie-dyed purple body stocking with her curly blond hair held back in a ponytail and her large breasts barely contained inside her skin-tight top.

Barrett stayed in the doorway and contemplated her options. She was about to leave when a man's eager voice called out, "Barrett!"

In spite of her turmoil, she smiled as a short Chinese man in a button-down white shirt and crisply pressed black pants approached her. An unfiltered Camel dangled from the side of his smiling mouth. "I was hoping you would be here tonight," he said, and then added under his breath, "too boring when you're not around." He attempted eye contact.

Barrett avoided his gaze, but Henry Li would not be thwarted. He took her wrist in his hand and his fingers touched down lightly on her pulses. "You are troubled," he whispered. "Your energy is not smooth. You come to see me and I'll give you some needles that will help."

"I will," she said without conviction. And much as a part of her wanted to be far away from Carol Gartner, a stronger part wasn't about to run.

"Barrett does not lie well," the Sifu added. "See me."

She nodded. Normally, the thought of a visit to Sifu's Mott Street medical practice would enthuse her. On several occasions she'd gone down there for his electrically enhanced acupuncture needles and found them helpful for various strains, aches, and pulls, although she usually gave a pass to his tissue-paper-wrapped packages of herbs. Nothing against them, but Barrett would have had to be at death's door to take even an aspirin.

She kicked off her running shoes, unzipped her knapsack, and slipped on her rubber-soled kung-fu slippers. She took up a position in the back, and after a few stretches sank into the pigeon-toed Wing Chun slow form. She turned her focus inward, blocking out the large mirror that gave a clear view of the dozen or so students in the room, including the all-purple Carol Gartner and her buoyant, surgically enhanced breasts.

For the next forty-five minutes Barrett stayed rooted to her square of the wood floor. With her knees touching she sank into the challenging position. Her arms moved slowly through the series of blocks and punches, all performed at a speed that would make her appear immobile to a casual observer. Sweat dripped from her elbows and tracked down her back and between her breasts. When she broke from the form, she felt energy coursing up from the soles of her feet.

Justine tapped her on the shoulder and the two women assumed combat stance for the footwork drill. Along with the rest of the Dojo, they shuffled on flat feet back and forth across the floor taking turns punching and blocking.

For Barrett, who'd been doing martial arts ever since she was in junior high, Sifu Li's studio and Wing Chun were an essential part of her existence. The form had been developed three hundred years ago by the Buddhist nun, Ng Mui. The movements were efficient and well-suited for Barrett, who preferred speed and finesse to brute force and physical strength.

As her feet slid across the floor her eye caught Carol's purple silhouette in her periphery. Her thoughts wandered and Justine's palm slipped past her block.

"Gotcha," Justine whispered as she advanced on her sister.

"Yeah," Barrett pulled herself back into the exercise. *What did he see in her? Was it just sex? Was it those breasts?* Barrett inventoried her own body; she was lean and tall, her breasts a full "B", firm and symmetrical. But unlike Carol, Barrett rarely dressed to draw attention. Maybe that was a mistake…at least with Ralph. But that wasn't it, and she knew it. Her problems with Ralph had nothing to do with how she looked. It went deeper.

"Gotcha again."

Sifu came over to the sisters, and positioning himself perpendicular, he shuffled alongside them.

"Barrett not focused, very bad."

She nodded and reapplied herself to the exercise.

"Better," Sifu nodded. "But Barrett still not in room. Where is Barrett?"

"She's in the room," Barrett hissed, taking her turn in the forward attack.

"I don't think so," Sifu commented, as he touched Justine lightly on the shoulder and took her place across from Barrett.

Sifu's birdlike arms began by deftly blocking Barrett's punches. When they reached the wall, they reversed positions and he fired blows, his hands shooting out with blinding speed, as he searched for weaknesses in her defense.

"I no see Ralph in morning class," Sifu commented as they switched again.

"No," Barrett replied, her tightly clenched fists punching at her teacher.

"Ah," he answered. "I did not see. I am very sorry." At the edge of the room he stopped and bowed to Barrett. She returned the courtesy. The wiry Chinese doctor clapped his hands.

"Barrett in center," he instructed. "Peter," he pointed at a tall sweat-drenched soap opera actor, "you go first."

The handsome man grinned as he took up a position across from Barrett. "Watch the face."

She returned his remark with a predatory smile as she assumed a catlike offensive. Trying to use his greater reach to advantage, he attacked with a series of rabbit-fast punches. Unfortunately for him, by the time they would have landed on their target, she had dropped to the floor and swept his legs out from underneath him. In less than fifteen seconds he was flat on his back, with her fist planted squarely over his Adam's apple. Sifu clapped and Barrett released the actor.

"Next victim," Sifu chortled, pointing his finger at Carol.

Barrett shook her head no and stepped away from the center of the room.

"Interesting," Sifu commented, looking first at Barrett and then at the honey-blond restaurant manager, who also seemed reluctant to enter the ring. "No?" he asked, never having encountered this particular scenario.

The two women glared at each other across the room. "Oh, why not?" Barrett stepped back into the center. She cocked an eyebrow and lifted her hands into a starting pose.

Carol accepted the challenge. The two women bowed stiffly and began to spar. On a good day, Carol was no match for Barrett. But the psychiatrist usually took this into account, having assumed the roll of Sifu's second in command. But today Barrett was not interested in furthering Carol's development as a martial artist.

As the blond woman attempted to pierce Barrett's guard, Barrett whispered, "Why?"

"Nothing personal," Carol replied, trying to twist her hand free from Barrett's imprisoning cross block.

Barrett stepped back and looked at her opponent. She deftly broke through Carol's defense and placed two fingers on either side of her throat.

"Oh," Sifu Li remarked, clapping his hand, "she dead."

"Nothing personal?" Barrett whispered, staring into the woman's eyes.

Carol shook her head nervously, "It wasn't," she whispered. "It just happened. Maybe he had a reason. Men who stray usually do. This morning he was telling me…"

Barrett dropped her attack and stared. "This morning?" It was as though Carol had slammed a fist into her gut. "This morning?"

Carol stepped back, "I should leave." She quickly bowed to Sifu, ran to the edge of the room, grabbed her bag, threw on her coat and fled the studio.

Barrett stood motionless, watching Carol's retreat in the mirror. *This morning*, he'd made love to her and then gone to see Carol. It wasn't a one-time thing. She felt the floor shift, and her vision cloud. All of his words had been lies.

"Breathe, Barrett." Sifu's hand on her shoulder. "Okay," he said turning to the dozen or so students, "class over."

———

Afterward, Justine walked uptown with her.

"What just happened in there?" she asked.

"What?" Barrett replied, trying to keep her rage and sadness to herself.

"With Carol."

"That's who Ralph…" She couldn't get the words out.

"You're kidding. I didn't know," she said, not needing Barrett to finish the thought. "I'm so sorry…why would she show up?"

"Yeah, well apparently she doesn't think it's such a big deal."

"That's cold."

"I can't think…It's like *up* is *down* and no one bothered to tell me. Maybe it's normal for married men to screw around. It is, isn't it? They say that over 50 percent of marriages involve infidelity."

"And over 50 percent of marriages end in divorce," Justine added. "Think there's a connection?"

"She said it's my fault."

"That's bull."

"Said he wasn't getting what he needed at home."

"What?"

"She's right. No matter how much Ralph says he supports me and my career, he doesn't. I think he thinks he should. But deep down…no. There are all these little cracks about how much I work, how I'm never around, how there's never any food in the house. And…I think he's still seeing her."

"Oh, Barrett."

"I wanted to believe him. Shit, shit, shit. It's over. My marriage is over."

"Let me stay with you." Justine offered, as they came to the 23rd Street subway station.

"No," Barrett said, as Justine hugged her, neither woman caring that they were drenched in sweat.

"Let me stay. We could talk…or not, watch some TV."

"I'll be okay," Barrett stepped back, noticing tears in her sister's eyes.

"I could kill him for doing this to you," Justine whispered.

"I'll be okay," she repeated, wanting to be alone. "Now get out of here, you've got to be at the hospital at the crack of dawn and I don't want you to be anything less than brilliant."

"I can be brilliant and spend the night at your place."

Barrett hesitated, hugged Justine again. "Please, go."

"You're sure? It's no problem."

"Go."

Justine kissed Barrett's cheek, "I love you, sis…call me later."

"Okay," and Barrett watched as her sister vanished into the rumbling station. Alone on the street, she trudged west. She felt the simple band of gold on her finger, and found its touch repulsive. She twisted it off, scraping the knuckle. She fought back the impulse to hurl it down the street, and instead dropped it into a zipped compartment in her bag. And then there was the issue of money. It seemed unreal. At least she'd still get the money from Jimmy; she'd been wrong about him. The lab had called her a little before six with the news that while his lithium level was low, he was taking it. It had surprised her, and she wondered if maybe she'd scared him into swallowing some pills the minute she'd left; it was possible. And while she was thoroughly creeped out by him, she so needed this money.

She stopped by a well-lit ATM on the corner of 23rd and 6th, and retrieved Jimmy's envelope from the compartment where she'd just tossed her wedding ring. She slit it open. Inside, was a business check signed by Ellen Martin. "Great," she muttered, wondering just what they were playing at, because instead of the agreed upon $750, the check was for $3000.

She stared at it, letting her eyes rake over the amount—dismayed that it was wrong, but needing the cash. She stood still, then pulled out her wallet, put her card into the slot, and walked through the security door. She filled out a deposit slip. "This is not good," she muttered, as she punched in her pin, pressed the key for *deposit* and watched the envelope get sucked away.

TEN

JIMMY CROSSED HIS LEGS and leaned back in the darkness, a large yellow legal pad perched on his lap, his right hand at the ready with a pen. On the black wall of the unfinished studio a flat-screen monitor sparked to life and the digital recording that Ellen had dropped through the mail slot of the carriage house began to play. The first image was of a street sign on the corner of 27th Street and 7th. From there the camera—positioned at waist height—moved down the block, coming to a stop outside her building. With jerky movement, it went up the outside steps of Barrett's building. A click, and the security door pushed open.

The scene shifted to a tile-walled stairwell and to a pair of men's rubber-soled shoes on worn marble steps. The video grew dark from a missing light on the third-floor landing, then another door and a hallway, and then a gloved hand inserted a pick into the first of two locks. The cylinders clicked, the door opened, and the camera was inside.

Enthralled, Jimmy turned the player to a slower speed, needing to catch every detail. He had a chilling sliver of fear as he wondered what would have happened if Ellen were discovered in Barrett's co-op.

Writing fast, he took in the arrangement of the furniture; the framed black-and-white photographs of Jazz players, the near-total absence of color as though someone had been afraid of anything more vibrant than beige upholstery, eggshell walls, and a muddy burnt ocher trim.

The camera panned across the living room, focusing on an ebonized grand piano. Ellen's gloved hand opened up the bench, affording Jimmy a view of Barrett Conyors' most-played repertoire. One by one she held up the titles for him to read; he was pleased to see annotated and dog-eared Schubert, Beethoven, Rachmaninoff, and four volumes of Chopin's etudes, nocturnes, polonaises, and waltzes—all of them used to where the spines were broken, and if not handled carefully, the pages would fall out. Most of these he already had—leftovers from Ellen.

When the camera focused on the keyboard, he could tell from the wear marks on the ivories that she still played. There was no dust—and straining, he could hear those long-ago notes as a nine-year-old Barrett attacked the *Revolutionary Étude* with mesmerizing precision and artistry; she'd stolen the show. He remembered how Ellen had been furious; no way would she share the limelight with anyone other than her brother. He was only thirteen, but Jimmy now knew that his passion for Barrett had been born on that stage.

As the camera resumed its tour, Jimmy winced at the sight of a deep splintered gash in the piano's outer edge. She deserved better, although he appreciated her choice of the 1920s Mason and Hamlin. It displayed a knowledge lost on those more interested in the snob appeal of Steinways, Baldwins, and of course, the crème de la crème, the Bösendorfer. The damage disturbed him, like untended wounds. Had it been at the hands of loutish and uncaring movers? Or was that the only way she could afford the instrument? Perhaps he could have it repaired.

Behind the piano, on an Ikea shelving unit, was a small grouping of framed photographs. He looked at her mother and sister, as they smiled out at him. Next to that was a picture of an older couple in front of the building where she grew up, and where he knew her mother still lived. The woman, whose silver hair was in a bun, was Sophie Gluck, Barrett's piano teacher, whose pre-war recordings he'd purchased on eBay.

He then looked at a posed graduation picture of Justine Conyors in a dark green gown and tasseled cap. And then a wedding photo with Barrett in white silk, wrapped in the arms of her husband. The camera zoomed in, and Jimmy stared into the eyes of the concert-trombonist—Ralph Best. Bile rose as he saw the plain gold band on his finger.

The camera then shifted to a picture of Barrett as a little girl sitting beside her teacher. They peered over the top of a piano—the same one in her condo—smiling, as though sharing a secret. Jimmy couldn't help but think back on his own experiences with music teachers. They'd all been "the best," but none had been allowed to continue with him. Father would say he *needed to take from them what they could give, and then move on.* Now, Jimmy realized that Father's reasons had less to do with furthering his skills as a cellist, and more with concern that Jimmy would confide in one of these artists who came to the home. They'd taught him how to finger and score a sonata, create subtlety and precision with his bow hand, and had helped him hone a razor-sharp intonation. But none had ever stayed long enough to become his friend, and during all of the lessons, Father had been close, listening…watching.

The last photograph was of the two sisters together with their arms around each other, and Justine's head on Barrett's shoulder. The camera lingered, affording him the chance to study their differences; where Justine's face was a cheeky reflection of her mother's; Barrett's had a finer structure, with almost Asian cheekbones, full lips, and those glorious almond eyes.

As Ellen continued her camera tour, Jimmy stayed glued to the screen, taking notes on the yellow pad, scribbling details. He pictured Ellen moving through Barrett's condo. He was certain that she'd have been disguised, dressed as a man, her hair hidden under a dark wig, identical to one he kept stuffed in the pocket of the leather coat in the carriage house.

His attention was pulled away by the ringing of a telephone. He glanced anxiously at the security monitors and then realized it came from the speakers. The scene canted violently, as Ellen put the camera down, and answered her cell. He strained to hear.

"Yes?" Ellen answered.

"And?"

"Good, so he is the taking the medication."

"I see…what does it mean if it's low?"

"Yes…will that have to be reported to the board?"

"That is good news, Dr. Conyors. Thank you for calling."

A palpable relief washed over him. The pills had had enough time. He hated having to take them, the way they made his hands shake and filled him with surging anxiety. But she needed him to prove his love and so he'd take them.

Ellen again picked up the camera, "Happy?" she said, looking into the lens. "You need to be more careful, little brother. That was too close."

She was right. He needed to listen to her, to not make mistakes. Ellen had always been the strong one, the smart one. She'd been born an hour before him, and at over seven pounds, while Jimmy spent three weeks in neonatal intensive care. Years later Mother would casually inform them that there'd been a third baby, smaller even than Jimmy and born dead.

The camera drifted back toward the telephone on the coffee table. The images blurred as Ellen's latex-gloved hands peeled off the backing on a bug and stuck it to the bottom of the phone. Jimmy's heart quickened, "Thank you."

From there, he viewed the galley kitchen with its painted white cabinets and deep red Fiestaware dishes. He jotted down the brands of cereal, made note of the spices in her rack, and on her collection of ruby glass stemware. And then he was in her bedroom, the walls hung with more photographs of jazz musicians. Her bed unmade, the comforter thrown back as though she'd had an uneasy night. Ellen's hand turned back the edge of the duvet, revealing its tag. Jimmy wrote down the designer's name and then the scene blurred as Ellen affixed a second listening device to the bedside phone.

He could hardly contain his excitement. Each added detail brought her closer. He leaned forward as Ellen entered the first of two closets, and went slowly through the suits—some still in plastic dry cleaning bags. Above her work clothes were shelves of neatly stacked sweats and T-shirts. On the floor were three pairs of low-healed pumps—black, navy, and off-white—four pairs of running shoes in varying degrees of deterioration, and a pile of a dozen or more identical black Chinese slippers—the kind that sell for a few bucks on Mott Street.

The second closet was nearly empty, and contained only a bit of men's clothing.

"Interesting," Ellen whispered.

"Yes," Jimmy said, wondering why Ralph Best had so few clothes. At the very least he expected to see a couple of tuxedos—the mainstay of any symphony member. There weren't any, almost as though…as though he'd moved out.

Hope surged.

The camera shifted to a pair of bureaus—his and hers.

"Open them," he mouthed, as Ellen systematically went through Barrett's clothes, and then Ralph Best's half-empty drawers. "Oh, yes," he moaned as he looked over the assortment of silk, lace and cotton underwear. All the colors, the lush browns, corals, purples, and blacks.

"*She's not yours,*" a voice spat back at him.

Jimmy's head swiveled. He peered into the darkness and for a moment saw a shadowy form that might have been Father lurking in the doorway.

"I'm not listening to you," he answered, hating the medication-induced sluggishness that made it so hard to shut out Father.

"*She's too good for a stupid boy like you. Too pretty. Too smart. She'll send you back, Jimbo.*"

"Shut up."

Jimmy tried to watch the video, but Father—as he always did—had pushed his button. Jimmy switched on a table lamp as the screen cut to black. He looked at the bandage in the crook of his elbow and yanked it off. Still visible was the angry red puncture mark where that silly girl had drawn his blood.

"She'll trick you, Jimbo, and then it's back to all of your little friends, and who's going to save you then? They'll come in the middle of the night, that's what you like best. Think of all the fun and games."

"No," Jimmy fought against the voice's powerful pull. He knew that she loved him. Father wanted him to fail. The blood draw had been a test, nothing more. And he'd passed, but a woman like Barrett Conyors had to be fought for—like a princess. She wanted him to win her over, to fight for her, to be worthy of her.

And then it hit. The answer came to him with brilliant clarity. The thing that bound them together, the one thing that would prove without doubt his love, his sincerity, was music. He should have seen this sooner; it was the final piece.

Unable to contain his excitement he was off the couch and dialing information. He wondered if Arthur—his old agent/manager—was even still in the business. Within minutes, he was connected.

"Jimmy? Boychick?" Arthur's Caldwell's Brooklyn twang sounded strong and vital. "It's good to hear your voice. How the hell are you?"

"Good. Real good, Arthur. You're still in the business, yes?"

"Never better, got some real good talent," and he proceeded to rattle off the names of top-classical performers in his stable. "So are you playing?"

"Yes, and that's why I'm calling. Any chance you'd still represent me?"

There was a heavy pause, "What are you thinking?"

"I think it's time to get back on stage, start small, maybe something at the Weill auditorium," he said, mentioning the elegant and intimate Carnegie Hall space where he and Ellen had performed multiple times in the past.

"What kind of program?" Arthur asked.

"All romantic, Chopin, Debussy, Brahms."

"Nice, a night of love. It's what you did best."

"I still do. You interested? I'll cover all the costs, but I need you to do the booking and the arrangements."

"Do you want it recorded?"

"Yes."

"And your sister will be your accompanist?"

"No."

"Who then?"

Jimmy hesitated, "Let's just say, to be announced."

Arthur chuckled, "You got someone special in mind?"

"Yes, very special."

ELEVEN

BARRETT TRIED NOT TO think about her last visit to this particular Croton interview room. The blood had been scrubbed from the floor, the young deputy had survived, but Charlie Rohr was dead. And now she faced a manacled Walker Green. "So the voices told you to abduct these women?" Barrett asked, her tone deadpan.

"It was awful doc, you gotta believe me, hearing voices is a terrible thing."

Barrett stared across the interview table at the handcuffed man. Green—her perp of the day—had been brought to the Croton facility to determine "A," whether or not he was competent to stand trial and "B," if he would make the cut for a not guilty by reason of insanity plea.

"Tell me about the voices," she instructed, skeptical that he was in fact hearing any.

"What do you want to know?"

"Man or woman's?"

Walker's muddy brown eyes narrowed. He shifted in his chair, "Do I have to wear these?" he raised his shackles. "The other doctor didn't make me."

"Not my decision," she told him. "My understanding is you had an altercation with one of the guards last night."

"I didn't do nothing," he whined.

"About the voices. Do you recognize them? Are they people you know?"

"Hey, I've gone through this before. Why do I have to keep talking about this over and over?"

"Because," she said leaning forward in her chair and not backing down from his stare, "your lawyer is trying to convince the judge that you're not fit to go on trial for kidnapping, raping, and murdering three women—at least three we know of. In order for the court to do that they've asked for two separate forensic evaluations and a six-month period of observation. You don't have to answer any of my questions, that's your right."

"You married?" he asked.

"None of your business."

His thin lips split open to reveal a tobacco-yellow leer, "That means no. No ring, no husband. You a dyke? I ain't got nothing against dykes. Hell, bring in a friend and we can make a sandwich."

Repulsed, Barrett stood, "If you don't want to talk to me you don't have to." She pushed her chair back, retrieved her digital recorder and signaled to the guard.

"Don't go," Walker pleaded. "I was only playing. Geez, some people can't take a joke. What do you want to know?"

She waved the guard away. "Start with the voices?"

"Okay, it's only one voice and it's a man's."

"Do you recognize it?"

"What do you mean?"

"Is it someone you know?"

"It's the devil."

"Really? What makes you think that?"

"Stuff it says, and how he says it. Like real grumbly and low."

"Does it come from inside your head or outside?"

"Outside, like someone talking to me."

Barrett began to reevaluate her first impressions of Walker, maybe he really was psychotic. She watched his facial expressions as he talked. There was none of the emotional blunting common in schizophrenia and he didn't appear manic. His speech had rhythm and a normal-enough variation for her to put another tick in the I-think-he's-lying column. "So they come from outside your head. Is that all the time?"

He paused, about to say one thing, and then changed his mind, "No, sometimes they're in my head."

And right there, she had him. He'd done a halfway decent job up until then, at least Walker had done some basic research. She asked some more questions about the voices, but by the time she'd exhausted the topic she'd convinced herself that his psychotic symptoms were feigned.

"I want to talk about the women now," she said. "Let's start with the first one," she glanced at the yellow legal pad where she'd scribbled a few notes from his chart. "Valerie Blake, how did you meet her?"

"You sure I can't take these off, they're hurting my wrists." He put his hands on the table. "It's getting all red; it's hard to think with them on."

"Not my decision," she repeated, in no mood for a repeat of Charlie Rohr. Not to mention that those hands had strangled a woman and left her for dead less than three months ago. That had been Green's undoing; one of his victims had survived.

"No harm in asking."

"I guess not, so tell me about Valerie Blake?"

"Which one was she? I'm not good with names."

"How many have there been?" she asked.

"Just the three."

"So no more women will come forward and make accusations?"

"I don't know. It's like someone else is inside of me when I do these things."

"You can't remember?"

"That's right, I get amnesia."

Barrett suppressed a groan, as this guy added a second twist to try and distance himself from guilt—not only pretending to be crazy, but now he wanted to throw amnesia into the mix. "What attracts you to these women?"

He smiled. "Something in the way they look at me. You know, like they're better than me. Like the way you're looking at me now."

Gooseflesh raised beneath her freshly starched-and-pressed blouse. "Did Valerie Blake look at you that way?"

"Yeah, like she was superior or something, wouldn't even talk to me. I bought her drinks and she wouldn't even talk to me. Rude like," his breathing deepened and his voice drifted. "Some women need to be taken down a peg or two."

"How do you do that?"

"I've got ways."

"So you met her in a bar?"

"Yeah, it was one of those snooty places on the Upper East Side, everyone in their fucking expensive clothes drinking fifteen-dollar martinis."

"So you bought her a drink?"

"Right, I had the bartender bring it over to her. Told him to tell her who it was from."

"What happened?"

"She looked at me and made this face like she'd tasted something bad. But she took the drink."

"Did you go over to her?"

"What's the point?"

"Then what happened?"

"I bought her another, maybe four or five, and she just kept sucking them down while all these bozos tried to hit on her. I mean for seventy-five bucks you can get a decent whore on Third Avenue."

"Why didn't you?"

"You crazy? You know what kind of diseases are out there, stuff that'll make your dick fall off. No, I like them clean. I like them in suits and I like what they've got on underneath, not that cheap shit, but like the stuff from the good stores. They keep it all hidden away, like they're these ice princesses on the surface, but underneath they're all looking for the same thing."

"What's that?"

"A good fuck."

"So you bought her a few drinks, and then…"

"I could see that she was feeling pretty good, so I went over to her. Figured I'd introduce myself."

"And?"

He shook his head. "She told me she wasn't interested."

Barrett watched as the tips of his fingers curled into fists. "How did that feel?"

"How do you think? That's when the voice started."

"What did it say?"

"Take her."

"How did you do that?"

"It's not hard. I told her that I understood and just to show there were no hard feelings I bought her another drink—one of those stupid things that looks like a martini but has orange slices and weird shit in it. She was pretty loose by then and the voice told me to put something in her drink. There was so much crap floating around in there I nearly spilled it. She called me clumsy. Here I'm buying her drinks and all she does is insult me like I'm some fucking lowlife."

"What did you put in the drink?"

"I don't know, the voice bought it."

"Right, what was it?"

"It was blue. Like I said, I didn't know what was going on, like there was someone else controlling my body."

"And then?"

"Then she got real tired, and the rest as they say is history."

"Nice try," Barrett said. "What happened?"

"You want the details?"

"It's my job."

"Hell of a job."

She waited and watched. His eyes glistened as he thought back.

"I helped her out of the bar and walked her down the street to my van, dropped her in back and then headed out of the city to a place I have on the shore."

"You'd done this before," she stated.

"What makes you say that, doc?"

"Call it a hunch."

He chuckled, but neither confirmed nor denied her speculation. "I just do what the voice tells me."

"What was it telling you?"

"She needed to be taught a lesson."

"How did you do that?"

He leaned into the table, "Slowly, doc. I did it slowly. Bit by bit waiting for her to wake up. It's important that they know what's happening. The lesson has to stick, otherwise what good is it? They need to feel every piece of clothing being cut off their body, feel the knife decide whether to go through fabric or flesh. They have to feel my fingers, my tongue, and my cock in all the places they don't want. You can't rush it. I have to see it in their eyes."

"See what?" Barrett tried to mask her revulsion, to not think about the terror Valerie Blake must have felt in the last moments of her life.

"That they know who's the boss."

She didn't need any more. It was clear that Walker Green's crimes had been carefully planned and executed. His psychotic sham was transparent and would never hold up; it was interesting that the court had requested two separate evaluations, but that was often the defense strategy. Get two forensic experts to disagree and it would essentially cancel out both reports. That would leave the determination to the judge and jury, and in a case like Walker's that might up his chances for avoiding prison. He'd have to improve his act, but a few more months in Croton might make that possible. She'd have to do what she could to see that didn't happen.

She spent another hour with him, letting him regale her with accounts of his crimes—all at the command of his bogus voice. She turned off her recorder and was about to call in the guard, when something Walker said caught her attention.

"There's a lot of us out there."

"What do you mean?" she asked, suddenly thinking of Jimmy and wondering if this creep had some real insight to offer.

"You know, guys who like to be in control."

"But they don't drug women, force them into vans, and rape them."

"That's what you think, you're a shrink, and people aren't all that different."

"You think so?"

"I know it. I may not have your education but I've been around. Guys act one way around women, try to come off all smooth and caring, but we're still cavemen inside. Like in the cartoons where you club some chick over the head and drag her off to your cave. And once you've done that, you can't go back."

"So it's natural, what you did?"

"It is. Why would God make us like this if it weren't okay?"

"When you masturbate is that what you think about?" she asked, clicking the recorder back on.

"All the time, but so do most guys."

"You think that's true?"

"Swear to God, all I did was cross a line. It's not that far from fantasy to flesh—just a few short steps, a couple knockout drops, and a place to go. Easy as pie." He laughed, "Cherry pie."

"How old were you when it stopped being a fantasy?"

He opened his mouth and then shut it. He shook his head and clicked his tongue against the roof of his mouth. "Just these chickies, doc. Loose lips sink ships."

"Right," she gathered up her pad and stuffed her recorder into her jacket pocket.

"You coming back to see me?" he asked.

"Probably not, unless you've got more to tell me."

"There's always more," he looked in her direction, but more through her than at her. "Then again, after a while, it's all the same."

———

Barrett passed through the security checks and exited the razorwire perimeter of Croton. She hiked across the park-like grounds that surrounded the forensic hospital, which was part of a tenthousand-acre complex that had once comprised one of New York State's largest mental institutions. She thought about the interview. In many ways it was typical of sexual sadists; an old story, and a central theme in her research and soon-to-be published book. A line gets crossed and then another and another, "Better than heroin," he'd said, and a hard habit to break.

She thought about Ralph and the line that he had crossed. And then she thought about her father. What little she remembered from Georgia and her first seven years of life in a five-room farm-house that had belonged to her grandfather, was filled with images of her father's red and angry face, her mother sending her to her room, and the awful sounds of the fights and the beatings.

She looked up at the weathered-brick facade of Gunther Hall. It was an imposing structure that a century ago had been the very first building for the then New York Hospital for the Insane. Spread over valuable Westchester acreage, it had embraced the moral treatment—a belief that hard work, fresh air, and religious devotion could free a person from mental illness. That of course hadn't lasted long and what followed was the addition of building after building until in the 1950s Croton housed nearly 30,000 patients—the snake-pit era, with insulin-shock therapy, wet wraps, and Thorazine doled out in gram-high doses that left the sick folk drooling and shuffling through endless days and years. Then deinstitutionalization and they were released into the community, and buildings like Gunther Hall were either left derelict or transformed into administrative offices for state employees displaced from their previous jobs.

She went up to the second-floor office she'd commandeered. It was nicer than what she had in Manhattan, and over the years she'd made raids on the basement where wonderful old oak, wal-nut, and mahogany desks, chairs, barrister bookcases, and the like had been stored and forgotten as, one-by-one, buildings shut down and began their crumbling deterioration.

Through her window she had a view of rolling green hills, distant mansions, and the dip in the green countryside through which the Hudson River meandered on its way toward New York City. It was nearly six and the pre-dusk light splashed the landscape with a rose-colored wash.

She inserted a disc into the computer and decided to get a quick start on Green's report. As the screen flashed to life, a buzzing sound intruded. Reaching down she grabbed her vibrating pager; she didn't recognize the number in the display. She dialed.

"Barrett?" Justine's excited voice bubbled into her ear.

"What's up?"

"I got in!"

"What?"

"Harrison picked me. I can't believe it!"

"That's wonderful," Barrett said. "Have you told Mom?"

"Not yet, you're the first. You know, he's never picked a woman. I'll be the first."

"You totally deserve it," Barrett said, thrilled for her sister, and keeping her less-gracious thoughts hidden. Justine had just been accepted into a highly competitive surgical fellowship, in which she'd be chief resident. An incredible honor, and her sister's greatest wish. It also meant that for another two years, Justine would be working at a salary too low to support herself, and as Barrett had been doing for Justine since leaving her own residency, she'd be helping out to the tune of a grand a month.

Her other line rang, and the red light flashed. "Hold on, Justine, I've got another call." She pressed the button for the other line.

"Barrett?"

It was Ralph, and she immediately regretted picking up. He'd been leaving messages on her home machine, asking why she wasn't calling back, pleading. She'd not returned them, still too furious.

"Barrett?" he repeated.

"Yes," her throat went dry. "What do you want, Ralph?"

"What happened?" he asked, his voice hollow. "I thought after the other night…"

Her pent up-rage exploded, "And then what happened in the morning, Ralph? Did you go straight from me to her?"

"What are you talking about?"

"Don't do this, I can't take the lying. Just tell the truth…for once. I saw Carol."

"So? I swear to God, Barrett, I've not seen her…"

"Since when, Ralph? Let me make sure I've got your story straight."

"Since the day you walked in on us. I've not seen her."

"Interesting, because her story's different."

"You've got to believe me, the last I spoke to her was last week. I didn't see her, it was over the phone. I told her I was sorry, that there was no way we could see each other. Barrett, you've got to believe me, it was only sex, it was wrong, and it was stupid. You're the only one who matters. I love you."

Competing thoughts battered away. She remembered something Sophie had once said…"*When someone starts a sentence with, 'you got to believe me,' you probably shouldn't.*" "So what day did you call her?"

"It was after I left our place."

Barrett hesitated; Carol hadn't exactly said she'd *seen* Ralph; just that they'd spoken. It's possible she'd leapt to the wrong conclusion. "So what do you want?"

"You sound so cold…it's you…and us, that's what I want."

He sounded sincere, vulnerable; her resolve wavered. "I can't take the lies Ralph. I just can't."

"Can we get together and talk."

"…When?" she asked, feeling her resolve soften.

"Tonight…please. I could meet you after work."

"Okay, I'll meet you at D'Emilio's," she said, naming the corner bistro and their favorite, let's-not-cook-tonight restaurant.

There was a pause. "Barrett…I love you so much. The other night made me realize what a complete idiot I've been. I can't lose you. Whatever you want me to do, just tell me. I don't want to lose you."

"We'll talk," she said, wondering if talk would again lead to the bedroom, and would that be enough to make her forget, or at least blind her for a time. But that still wouldn't do a damn thing for why he'd cheated in the first place.

"I love you, Barrett."

She said nothing, feeling his words swim in the back of her head, how easy it would be to say, *I love you too, Ralph,* but she didn't. Instead, "I have to go, Ralph, 10:30?"

"I'll be there."

She heard the disappointment in his voice, he'd wanted her to say it. She thought how easy those words came to his lips; did he mean them? He sounded sincere, but what sincere words had gotten Carol into their bed?

She felt lightheaded. Her gaze drifted to the flashing light on the telephone. She pressed the other line, having forgotten about Justine. "Sorry about that," she said.

"What happened? Where'd you go?"

"It was Ralph."

"Oh…what did he want?"

"Everything. He said that he hasn't seen Carol again."

"But I thought you said…"

"I know, I might have jumped to a wrong conclusion. I don't know. I don't know what to believe. He says that he loves me and that he'll do anything I want."

"Do you still love him?" Justine asked.

"Yes…but I don't know if that's enough. Love is supposed to make everything better; it doesn't."

"What are you going to do?"

"I told him I'd meet him for drinks after he gets off."

"Are you going to take him back?"

"I don't know. I miss him so much." She thought about their great night together, and then the scene of opening the bedroom door, and seeing Carol, and then Ralph, naked. "I can't stand feeling this way. It's not just my husband being unfaithful…Ralph is the only man I've ever felt like I could just be myself with…that I didn't have to try and be someone different. And now I think I was wrong; I'm not who he wants, or what he wants..."

"Look Barrett, I'm getting paged. We can talk later, okay?"

"Sure…" and then remembering why her sister had called, "and Justine, congratulations. It's fantastic news."

She hung up and pressed her hands against the sides of her face. It was hard to think. And she hated the fact that one of the things that kept popping through her mind was money. Justine's call, while great news, made things worse. Although, the Martin case, if it were to continue, would certainly help. It was a big *if*, and Jimmy's low lithium level, and the overpayment—which she should never have deposited—weren't helping.

She picked up the stylus for her Palm Pilot and punched up Jimmy's name. Twinges of panic quickened her pulse. She took several slow breaths and forced her fingers to dial. He picked up after the fifth ring.

"Hello?"

"Mr. Martin? It's Dr. Conyors."

"Yes?"

"Your sister told you that your bloodwork came back?"

"She said it was okay."

Barrett paused. "It was low."

"But that's still okay."

She heard his anxiety. "I won't report it, if that's what you're wondering. But I will redraw…frequently. So I suggest you don't play with your pills. I need to talk to you about my fee. The check was for four times the amount. I expect to be paid for each session, no more, no less."

"I didn't write it. Ellen did. If there's a mistake, it wasn't mine."

"I'll call her," Barrett said. "But Jimmy, no games. The same goes for Ellen, and I will talk with her. You need to take your medicine and do everything according to your release agreement. If you don't, they'll pull you back."

"No!"

"Then take this as a warning."

"I can't go back," his voice went flat, "I'll kill myself. Please. You don't know what it was like."

"Calm down. I'll talk to Ellen and we'll get through this."

"Okay."

It seemed as though she were talking with a frightened child.

"Dr. Conyors…"

"Yes?"

"I can't go back."

"That's entirely in your hands, Jimmy. And Jimmy?"

"Yes."

"I'm real good at knowing when someone is telling a lie. Don't do it."

After she hung up she wondered what Hobbs' take would be on all of this: the low lab value, Ellen's overpayment, her gut telling her that something was very wrong. Thinking about the detective helped quiet her racing thoughts. After all, there was nothing concrete. Her certainty that Jimmy had not been taking his medication was shot down by the results of the bloodwork, and the check could be a misunderstanding. Maybe Ellen thought she had to pay for Barrett's time at dinner; that was probably the answer, and thinking about the extra money, Barrett wondered if maybe that was okay. It still felt wrong, almost like a bribe, but for what purpose?

She stared out the window, the countryside now colored in a palette of evening gray. She glanced at her watch and then stuffed her tape recorder and notes on Walker Green into her briefcase. She had wanted to review Jimmy's files in the basement archives, but somehow the time had slipped away, and now it was too late.

TWELVE

A PIERCING PAIN SHOT behind Jimmy's eyes as he thought back through his conversation with Dr. Conyors. She'd sounded cross, disappointed.

"She'll send you back, Jimbo," Father whispered, the voice stronger since he'd restarted the medication. The pills were supposed to make voices decrease; they made it worse. *"She's waiting for you, Jimbo, she's going to lock the door and throw away the key."*

"No!" Seated at his computer in the carriage house, he stared at the screen that displayed date-stamped files for Barrett's calls. First, he replayed his phone conversation with her. When he got to the part about the check, it didn't quite make sense. He played it back a second and third time. Her words ran through his head.

"She took the money, Jimbo." The voice reminded him.

Jimmy stopped, waiting for more. What Father gave with one hand usually came with the other balled into a fist. Like his beautiful cello. Eight years old and already considered a prodigy when Father made the extravagant purchase. But that same day other things happened, bad things, things that crept up in the middle of the night and... "Maylene," he whispered, conjuring up a beautiful dark-skinned face with soft loving eyes. The face of the only person—other than Ellen—who'd ever loved him.

"She took the money, Jimbo. She took the money."

"Yes," Jimmy said aloud.

"Not according to Hoyle, is it, Jimbo?"

"No," he answered, suspicious of the voice's newfound helpfulness. "She should have ripped it up."

Jimmy pondered this. Morris Kravitz had been easy. Dr. Kravitz loved his money, and that blond wife of his had had no difficulty in spending it. And with the others, the guards, and the other patients, subtle, and not-so-subtle gifts were how he'd survived those long years in Croton. With Barrett, his beautiful Barrett, it had to be different. He wanted her to have everything. All the things she deserved, but couldn't afford.

He pressed the button for her home phone, and a series of files popped up on the screen, each one gave time, date, and the caller's number.

He played the first. A man's deep voice came in. "Barrett, please call me back. We have to talk...I'm sorry. Whatever it is, I'm sorry."

Jimmy smiled, and clicked on the next. Again, it was her husband, Ralph. Obviously things weren't going well. The timing couldn't have been better.

But the next stopped him cold, "Barrett, I must sound desperate leaving all these messages. I just wanted to say how glad I am we cleared things up. I'm really looking forward to seeing you tonight...I love you, babe. Always have, always will."

Jimmy's hands shook.

Father sang, *"Her boyfriend's back and you're going to be in trouble."*

He pressed the button to hear the final message. It was another man. "Barrett, you there? I guess I'll try you at the office."

He recognized the voice, the detective who'd run after her. Why was he calling?

"She's playing games, Jimbo."

"No!" Jimmy replied, as his anger surfaced. "It's a test." He pictured the detective, like so many other men who'd questioned him for hours on end, trying to trick him, trying to lock him away. It had happened once, it could happen again. Bile rose in his throat.

He stood on shaky legs. Barrett was testing him. Her phone call, the husband, the detective, all tests. Just like the competitions when they were children, each performance clearing the way to the next and then the next. Each prize bigger, each audience more adoring. He didn't doubt that she loved him, but she needed him to prove himself.

He clicked on the last message—the detective again.

"Barrett, it's Hobbs. Guess you're not there, either. Give me a call. I got the thing we talked about. I really think you should wear it…give me a call."

"What the hell?" Jimmy hissed. "Wear what?"

"Fun and games, Jimbo," Father whispered. *"Fun and games."*

———

Perched on the toilet in the carriage house, Jimmy steadied the new key with both hands, hating the way the lithium made them shake. The pills had to go, but for now, he would take them for her. She had to look as though she was doing her job.

Bending over, he waited for the red light and then plunged the electromagnetic device into the latch of his ankle bracelet. He held his breath, and for an agonizing moment heard nothing. And then it clicked, and the padded metal shifted on his ankle. He gingerly separated the halves, freeing his leg. He stood and looked at his reflection. He wore a dark human-hair wig and a pair of tinted glasses that enhanced his night vision. Dressed in a black leather car coat and jeans, he felt pumped as he bounded down the stairs.

He entered the garage, and headed toward the parked yellow cab with the darkly tinted windows. Anywhere other than New York, it would stick out like a sore thumb, but here it was anonymous and perfect. He turned over the eight-cylinder engine, and looked up at a pair of black-and-white television monitors mounted to the left of the bay doors. They afforded him a panoramic view of the street outside. When it was clear that there were no pedestrians in visual range on 19th Street, he hit the button. The door slid open, and he was out.

He cracked the window, savoring the cool night against his cheek.

He glanced at the time, signaled, and turned up Madison, timing the lights, as one of Mother's chauffeur's had taught him. He pictured Barrett, and began to hum the opening bars of the *Revolutionary Étude*. He could see her beautiful lips, hear the traces of a Southern accent, calling to him, wanting him to prove himself. He would do this for her. He would pass this test.

THIRTEEN

BACK AT WORK ON Tuesday morning, it was all Barrett could do to keep from screaming. Why had she believed him? She'd waited over two hours at the bar in D'Emilio's, thinking that maybe the symphony got out late, or that they had to play multiple encores, or that he couldn't get a cab. All the while the hands on the clock had inched around and around. Several times, she'd gotten up from her corner table and circled the bar and the back dining room, just in case he'd shown and hadn't seen her, sitting at their usual table in a clingy black-knit dress—Ralph's favorite. Throughout her wait, men had approached, wondering if she wanted company. She'd smiled and told them she was waiting for her husband. One had been bold enough to ask why no ring. She'd forgotten it, the gold band still in a pocket of her gym bag. It had been almost one a.m. when she'd finally left. She'd felt numb and doubted whether she'd sleep at all. She'd thought of calling Ralph's mom's house, where he'd been staying. Maybe he just forgot? But no, standing her up for two-and-a-half hours without as much as a phone call was not an accident. It was deliberate and cruel. She'd angrily taken out her vintage jet earrings—a birthday gift from Sophie and Max—and left her dress crumpled on the bathroom floor. When she'd hit the bed, she'd tried not to think about him, about wanting him there with her. She'd hugged her pillow tight and cried. And when she'd finally drifted off, it was to a world of twisted dreams, one swirling into the next, the alarm finally pulling her from a crashing wave of black spiders that had surged out from under the lid of a grand piano.

And now, even work seemed too much of an effort. She wondered if others could tell how furious she was, how confused. But no one had said anything, other than Anton, with an off-handed, *"Rough night, last night?"*

Marla intruded over the intercom, "Dr. Conyors, it's the D.A.'s office on line one."

"Thanks," she pressed the flashing button.

"Barrett, it's Jim O'Malley."

"What's up?" she asked, picturing the late-twenties assistant D.A. with his close-cropped red hair and ghost-white complexion.

"I wanted to discuss your report on Todd Anderson."

"Not my best work," she admitted, thinking back to her rush job.

"It's fine, but before we go into the hearing I wanted to ask…"

She didn't let him finish, "I thought that was last week."

"No…it's Thursday."

"They changed the date again?"

"No…it's not changed at all, at least as far as I'm aware."

"Okay, Jim…something's strange. Anton told me last week that you needed it right away."

"That didn't come from me, Barrett. You know I'd call you myself for something like that."

"Right…maybe someone else on your team?"

"Not likely. Not without my knowing."

"Then what the…"

"Something wrong, Barrett?"

"I don't know," she admitted, trying to fathom Anton's motive. She finished her conversation with the detail-oriented attorney, giving him the additional insight he sought into the mind of the copy store killer.

She hung up and stared at her cold Dunkin Donut's coffee. Her first thought was to call Anton, but she stopped herself. Last Thursday—her first meeting with Martin—was a big ball of weirdness, and Anton's funky behavior was a part of it.

She sipped the stale coffee and dialed the twenty-four-hour hotline for the forensic center. "Has the rest of Jimmy Martin's labwork come back?" she asked.

"I'll get his chart."

Barrett waited, and pictured Ellen and Jimmy as children. He still played wonderfully, and she had a twinge of guilt, knowing that the medications would weaken his abilities on the cello.

The woman came back on the line, "The Risperdal level isn't back, but the prolactin is."

"And?"

"It's normal."

"Thanks," Barrett said, about to hang up. "Wait a minute, could you do me a favor and go back and give me all of his lithium levels?"

"From when?"

"Back to Croton, at least a couple year's worth. And especially any done since his release."

"I'll see what I have."

Barrett heard the rustle of paper over the line.

That's interesting."

"What?" Barrett asked.

"I'm going back all the way and he hasn't had any since his release. The set you ordered was the only one. I can give you the old ones."

"Great," Barrett scrambled for a pencil and piece of paper.

The woman read off the results, all of them within the normal range.

"You're certain there are none since he got out?" Barrett asked. "Kravitz didn't order any?"

"Not that I see."

"And he's been on lithium all that time?" Something didn't add up.

"That's what it says."

"Any chance there's an old prolactin level somewhere in his chart?"

"Let me look. I've got one that's six years old—you want it?"

"Sure."

"It's really high," the woman said. "What does that mean?"

"It means he was taking his medication. Prolactin is a hormone that nursing mothers secrete. A lot of the antipsychotic medications make it go up. That's why some people get breast enlargement—both men and women."

"So *that's* why they check it."

"Pretty much. Can you tell if he was on the same medications he's on now, when that level was taken?"

"You're pushing it, but I'll try…no…I can't tell. The order sheets don't go back that far."

"Thanks anyway," Barrett said.

"But, wait a minute," the woman paused.

"What?"

"This is odd, about two weeks ago a set of bloodwork *was* ordered by Dr. Kravitz."

Barrett perked up, "Where are the results?"

"I don't know…unless…"

"What?"

"That must be it. Two weeks ago our phlebotomist got sideswiped by a hit-and-run taxi."

"She was carrying his blood?"

"Definitely. The cops were more concerned about that than anything else. There was a ton of OSHA paperwork to fill out. They even got the guys in the white paper suits from HazMat. I think your man's blood may have been dumped on the street. So what's this all about? You think he might have stopped his medication?" the woman asked.

"I can't say for certain."

"If you want I could call up to Croton and get them to retrieve his record."

"I already tried," Barrett said. "The whole thing is on microfilm and I was told there's no way to get in until Monday."

"God bless the state."

"Exactly," and they hung up.

Barrett sipped bitter coffee as her stomach churned. Coincidence? Not likely. And for the one set of bloodwork that Kravitz ordered to wind up shattered in a freak accident gave her a chill. And why the hell hadn't Kravitz checked before? Why did he wait? It's the first thing he should have done. Anton had hinted that Morris Kravitz was greedy; he hadn't said a thing about incompetent.

She started to pace.

She grabbed the phone and called the medical examiner's office. She gave them her state identification number and asked them to pull a copy of Morris Kravitz's death certificate. "Could you fax me a copy?" she asked.

She hung up and waited. Five minutes later her machine emitted an electronic squeal. She watched as the state seal of New York rolled out followed by the two-page document. The box for *natural causes*, had been checked off. The narrative stated that he died from *"cardiac arrest secondary to complications of a preexisting diabetic condition and acute hypoglycemic shock."*

Under next of kin it listed Sheila Kravitz, his wife. There was a phone number and a notation that Mrs. Kravitz had been informed of the medical examiner's findings.

Barrett looked at the number. She dialed.

A tired-sounding woman picked up, "Hello?"

"Mrs. Kravitz?"

"Yes?"

"My name is Barrett Conyors and I'm a psychiatrist working with one of your husband's clients. I was wondering if it might be possible for me to stop by some time when it's convenient and ask you a couple of questions."

"I wouldn't know about my husband's patients," she said, a slight reproach in her voice. "He didn't talk about them."

"Of course not," Barrett said, wondering what she hoped to gain by meeting with this woman. "It's just that I'm struggling a bit with this patient and was hoping that you might be able to give me some insight into how your husband worked."

Sheila Kravitz lowered her voice, "This is about that Croton patient, isn't it?"

"Yes." Barrett felt a tingling along the backs of her arms, "Why?"

There was silence on the other end.

"Mrs. Kravitz?"

"You said you were working with him? With the Croton patient?"

"Yes, I'm a forensic psychiatrist."

"I don't know that I have anything to tell you. You're not trying to sue my husband's estate or anything like that?"

"No, I just wanted to ask a couple of questions."

"I'll be leaving town soon. But I suppose if you wanted to come by this afternoon I could see you for a few minutes."

Barrett got her street address, reassured her that she had no ulterior motive, and thanked her.

Then she punched Anton's line. She knew she should have called him sooner, as soon as she had suspected that Jimmy wasn't taking his medications, or the minute after she'd opened her envelope with the big check. The review board was very specific about how psychiatrists, case managers, and anyone else interacting with the releasees were supposed to respond. You didn't need to catch someone red-handed, all it took was a suspicion of wrongdoing.

"Anton," she started, "we've got to talk."

"What's up, Barrett?" he sounded annoyed.

"It's about Jimmy Martin. I don't think he's been taking his medication and I'm pretty sure he tried to bribe me."

"What's the evidence?"

Barrett ran through her first meeting with Jimmy. She told him about the lack of a lithium tremor.

"A lot of people don't get a tremor," Anton replied curtly.

"When he was at Croton, he had a marked tremor, Anton. And his prolactin level is now normal—it used to be sky high. I think I need to contact the review board, but I thought I'd run it by you first."

"As part of the board, Barrett, I can tell you they're not going to do anything. What have you got to go on? He's not shaking? Maybe his body acclimated or maybe he's under a lot less stress so you can't see it anymore. Same thing goes for the prolactin, it can normalize in people who've been taking meds as long as he has; you know that."

"Anton, Morris Kravitz never checked his lithium level. Were you aware of that?"

"I wasn't. But that just speaks to Kravitz's sloppiness, you can't hold that against Martin. It's not his fault his shrink wasn't doing his job. I hate to say it, Barrett, but this case has you scared. Jimmy Martin spent eighteen years in Croton and has only been out a few months—and he's been squeaky clean. The stuff you're rattling off seems more about you and less about him."

Barrett held the phone to her ear, dumbfounded by Anton's stance. Was she overreacting?

"Have you considered that maybe you should get some clinical supervision?" he continued. "Lord knows Martin's paying enough for you to get a few hours with somebody to get your head straight around this."

"I don't know what to say," Barrett commented, feeling betrayed and a little foolish. Why was he talking to her like this? Like she didn't know what she was doing.

"Well, I appreciate your call. But I'd caution you against contacting the board. You have to be careful that it doesn't appear like you're deliberately trying to come up with something to get Martin violated back to Croton."

"That's not what I'm doing."

"I didn't say that. But if you were to bring what you just told me to the rest of the board, it wouldn't look good."

She thought of more she could bring up, but as she ticked through the pieces that didn't fit she imagined Anton batting each of them away as products of her over-active imagination.

"Was there anything else?" he asked.

"No…it's just your response surprises me."

"How's that?"

Barrett thought back to the inconsistency in Anton telling her that Jimmy's case was a gift as opposed to Jimmy having specifically asked for her. "Never mind," she said.

"You know, if you want to unload this case…I could arrange that."

"It's okay," she forced a brightness into her voice, "I'll be fine. This has been helpful."

"I'm glad," he said, but sounding wary, and then hung up.

Was he right? From the way he spoke, it was almost as though she were paranoid. He'd probably freak if he knew she'd just called Kravitz's widow, or if she'd gone into the coincidence around the accident that prevented Jimmy's one-and-only set of bloodwork from making it to the lab. Weird.

She pulled out her PDA and looked up Hobbs' cell number. When he picked up on the second ring, she felt a rush of relief at the sound of his voice. "You busy?" she asked.

"Always. So what's up?"

"I need a favor." And she felt like adding, *and a friend.*

"Shoot. If I can do it, I will."

"It's very strange, and if you say no, I'll understand…Any chance I could get you to tag along on a field trip to see the widow Kravitz."

Ed hesitated, "Kravitz…Martin's shrink, the one who died. The one whose death certificate I was supposed to pull for you. Forgive me, but I totally blanked on that one."

"No problem, I already got it. So, are you up for it?"

"Sure. I've got night duty, so as long as we're done by eight, just tell me where and when."

FOURTEEN

JIMMY DREW THE BOW hard and fast across the cello. Throaty arpeggios leapt forth, his fingers landing with precision. He fought against the growing haze of the pills; he'd take them a bit longer. Still jazzed from last night's outing, he felt the pieces slip into place. Barrett's love, like a beacon, was calling him home.

The music soared, filling the space with Bach's godly perfection. His breath deepened as he pictured the tall man with the trombone case, crossing the street, not looking—careless.

He pressed harder, pushing the tempo faster, nudging the adagio into an allegro, and then a scherzo, the notes blurring, his fingers flying spider-like over the strings. He pictured the auditorium where they'd play, the beautiful and intimate setting where he'd often given recitals with Ellen. It was the smallest of the three rooms at Carnegie Hall—the Weill. Arthur had done as instructed, the hall was rented, and the date was set.

He reached the end of the movement, and without stopping, soared into the opening of the Brahms E minor. He could hear her playing in the background. She'd be dressed in black, pearls at her throat. And after, when the music stopped, he'd put down his cello and take her hand. Applause would engulf them as she'd gracefully rise from the bench. He'd turn to her, and she to him. In his mind's eye he saw her beautiful lips form the word, "yes," and then—

"Ain't going to happen, Jimbo." Father's voice cackled.

Jimmy's head whipped around, his bow faltered and screeched as his fingers missed notes.

"She doesn't love you, Jimbo."

He tried to ignore the heckling. Father was scared. She would save him, and he would love her always, they'd have children, and Ellen would be their aunt, and they'd spend endless nights playing music by the fire and Father would be forever banished.

"Fat chance. The only way you'll ever get her, Jimbo, is if you tie her up and drug her."

"No!" Jimmy stopped playing, hearing the last sour note fade. Father was wrong, but sometimes there was truth in what he said. He cocked his head to the side, wondering if the voice would say more.

"She doesn't love you."

That wasn't true. It was just he had to complete the tests, like a knight or Prince Charming from Maylene's stories. Father was trying to distract him. To make him fail.

Jimmy caught a whiff of stale whisky and tobacco. Adrenalin surged and his pulse quickened. He put down the cello, and looked around the empty library.

"You're not here," Jimmy said. "You're dead."

"You can't kill me."

"You're dead. You're pathetic."

"*She'll never love you,*" Father persisted, his voice high-pitched and whiny.

"You can't touch me."

"*It's the pills.*"

"No," Jimmy said, not about to give in, savoring this newfound strength, "if it were the pills you would have disappeared at Croton, but you didn't. You made my life hell."

"*Just trying to be of service,*" Father replied. "*At least you were popular.*"

"She loves me," Jimmy said. "We're going to be married."

"*Fat chance, Jimbo. Fat chance.*" He was laughing, "*She just wants to lock you up. Hey fellas, Jimbo's back in town.*"

"Shut up!" Father was wrong, but had he missed something? He ran out to the carriage house, and checked the taps on her phone lines. He listened and what he heard was frightening. What the hell was prolactin? Is that why he'd grown breasts at Croton? He'd thought that just came with all the weight. What was she doing? Why was she doing this to him? Checking labs, asking questions?

"*Give us a little kiss, Jimbo,*" Father's cackle seemed to fill the room.

"Go away." Then her call to the medical examiner followed by the one with Sheila Kravitz. But what could she tell Barrett, what could she know?

"*She'll find something,*" Father chuckled. "*And won't that be special?*" he started to sing, "*Jimbo's back in town. Jimbo's back in town.*"

Jimmy focused on the recordings; the one with the detective stopped him cold. He was flirting with her. He played their conversation back several times, listening to the lightness in her tone.

Father changed tunes, *"Her boyfriend's back and you're going to be in trouble…"*

Something was wrong, several somethings. First off, Jimmy had requested plainclothes police. He didn't want the neighbors to see patrolmen coming in and out. But plainclothes didn't mean detective. So why a pair of detectives? And it was obvious that Dr. Conyors had a previous connection with this Hobbs. But what would she be doing flirting with a cop? She talked to him like an equal, like a friend.

Father interjected, *"Like a lover. Like a hot and tasty cop lover with a big fat night stick that…"*

"Shut up!" Jimmy screamed, struggling against a paralyzing fear.

He clicked on the Internet, and began to search. Starting with the police department's web site he retrieved Edward Hobbs' badge number, date of hire, and rank. "Interesting," he muttered finding a glitch in the database where there were two entries for Hobbs' name and badge number. He clicked on the second, "shit!" he muttered. That couldn't be right. How was it possible for someone to go from being a Deputy Chief of Detectives down to a Detective Third Grade? Was it all part of an elaborate scheme to get him sent back to Croton? Anxiety flared, but the date of Hobbs' demotion was over a year ago. Even he could tell that the timing was off. Still, the thought of having the once Deputy Chief wandering around his home and romancing Dr. Conyors made him furious. He switched databases and hacked past the firewall security and into internal investigations. He double-clicked on the icon for *Disciplinary Actions and Outcomes*. In the search field he entered Hobbs' badge number. The screen flashed once as it pulled up a 200-page disciplinary file on Detective First Grade Edward Hobbs.

"My, my, my," Jimmy commented, as he opened the file and started to read. And just like the husband, he now realized that Hobbs would be a test that he could pass easily.

FIFTEEN

BARRETT AND HOBBS WALKED down the carpeted hallway, checking door numbers as they went. Between apartments were groupings of fussy French gilt tables and chairs and crystal-dripping mirrors with lighted brass wall sconces.

"Shrinks make good money," Ed commented, as they neared their destination.

"They can."

"How much do you think apartments go for in a building like this?"

"To buy or rent?" she asked, as they engaged in a favorite New York pastime—*How Much Does That Apartment Go For?*

"Your choice."

"I'd say, to rent, a closet-sized studio is over two grand."

"And to buy?"

"Same apartment...half a mil, maybe three quarters."

Before they could work their way up through one, two, and three bedrooms they arrived at the door to Morris and Sheila Kravitz's apartment.

Barrett was raising her hand to knock as the door opened.

Sheila Kravitz, a woman seemingly in her early thirties with over-processed ash-blond hair greeted them. A cigarette dangled from the corner of her mouth, and her eyes were red-rimmed, even in the dim light. "The doorman called me," she said, as she led them down a long hall. "You have to forgive the mess, but the movers are coming tomorrow and I'm trying to get things as organized as possible."

"You're leaving town," Ed commented.

"And you are?" she asked.

"Detective Hobbs."

"Figures." Sheila turned and looked at Barrett, "You didn't say anything about bringing a cop."

"He's a friend," Barrett said.

"I suppose it doesn't matter. I don't really understand why you're here. But in a way I've been expecting someone. You know I told Morris a long time ago that the money didn't matter." She then stacked three half-packed boxes on the edge of the couch, clearing a space for Barrett and Hobbs. "I guess you'd say he wasn't a very secure man."

"You miss him," Barrett commented, trying to draw a bead on Sheila's elliptical statements.

"You have no idea."

"What did you mean by the money didn't matter much?" Barrett asked.

Sheila straightened up and pushed a wisp of straw-dry hair back from her face. "This," she raised her hands and turned around. "All of this," pointing toward a killer view of the Hudson to the west and a spacious deck, where small evergreens and trailing ivy had been neatly planted, facing east. "If you asked Morris he'd probably make some weird joke about needing it for me, or doing it for me—it didn't matter to me. It's bad enough when everyone around you thinks that you're a gold digger, but when you get it from the man you love…"

"The money had something to do with Jimmy Martin?" Barrett asked.

"That's the Croton man, isn't it?"

Barrett nodded.

"So that was his name. Morris was very good at not talking about his patients. It's one of the first things that drew me to him."

"Where did you meet?" Barrett asked.

"It's a complete cliché. I was a psychiatric nurse at Silver Glenn. He was rounding on patients, and his wife had died, and…the rest was a rather short but sweet time." She looked down at an overstuffed Queen Anne wing chair she'd excavated from a pile of clothing. Her shoulders sagged, she looked at Barrett. "I thought it was cute at first, the way he liked to bring me gifts. I told him it wasn't necessary, but he liked doing it. It got to the point where I had to be careful when we walked down the street, because if there was something in a shop window that I admired, the next thing you know his credit card would be out, and nothing I could say would stop him."

"This has something to do with Jimmy Martin?" Barrett asked, wondering how she could gently reel in Sheila's reminiscence.

"Everything to do with it. Morris had a very good practice. His patients loved him. It's not like we needed more money, at least I didn't."

"What changed?"

"This," she said. "I guess I wasn't clear. What a surprise, I hardly make sense to myself anymore, I can't imagine what it must be like for someone else. This apartment. Do you have any idea what eight rooms in this building go for?"

"No clue," Barrett cut Ed a look.

"I didn't know until he...died...just how much. It's obscene. That's why he was so excited when he got the job through the clinic."

"Do you know who contacted him?" Barrett asked.

"I do, come to think of it. It was an Anton somebody."

"Anton Fielding," Barrett said.

"That's right, Morris had been his supervisor years ago when Anton was a resident. I guess that he thought that Morris would be a good match. It is a little odd though."

"What is?"

"As far as I know that's the only forensic client that Morris had. I wonder why...I guess now it doesn't matter." Sheila finally sat— she looked across at Barrett and Hobbs, her expression troubled. "There's something I don't know, isn't there?"

"Some things don't add up," Barrett admitted. "I'm seeing Jimmy Martin now, and there were some irregularities I'm trying to resolve."

"That involved Morris?"

"Maybe. I mean you were…are…a psychiatric nurse. What would you think of someone who was on lithium and didn't have their level checked?"

"Either ignorance or incompetence."

"Right. Did your husband have many patients on medication?"

"Who doesn't? And when I worked with him at Silver Glenn you *know* all of those patients were on a truckload of pills."

"Was he thorough? Would he check levels and do all of that?"

"Of course. Why? What are you getting at?"

"Jimmy Martin was on lithium and your husband never checked his level."

"That doesn't make sense," Sheila said. "Are you sure?"

"The only time he checked it—or attempted to check it—was right before his death."

"What do you mean *attempted*?"

"The bloodwork never made it to the lab."

Hobbs leaned forward and rested his elbows on his knees. "Mrs. Kravitz," he began softly, "I was wondering if you could tell us what happened the night your husband died?"

Sheila looked up from her lap and into Hobbs' hazel eyes. "They said it was natural causes."

"What happened that night?" Ed urged.

"That's the part that makes no sense. We were having such a good time. We'd been out with friends. He'd been laughing and joking, and he always took care of himself. You know that he was a diabetic, don't you?"

Hobbs nodded.

"I never thought about it much. We'd been together for almost seven years and I'd never seen him have any trouble with his sugars. Whenever we'd go out he'd just give himself a little short-acting insulin to cover a bigger dinner and a couple drinks. He wasn't one to overdo it. But I should have known something was different—he wasn't acting right."

"How so?" Ed urged.

"On the cab ride home he kept saying how tired he was. Considering he'd been up since six in the morning and had a full day ahead of him, I didn't think much about it."

"And then?"

Sheila closed her eyes tightly and gripped the edges of her chair. She tried to speak, but was overwhelmed with tears.

"It's okay," Barrett fished a tissue out of her pocketbook. "Take your time."

"And then the alarm rang, and I didn't hear him getting up. He was always the first one up. He brought me coffee in bed every single day, and then he'd kiss me. But he didn't get up and I rolled over because I knew he liked to get up early and…he was dead. He was cold. I called 911 and they told me to give him CPR…but he was cold. I did it anyway. I couldn't really think, and now that's *all* I think about is the feeling of his cold lips and the sound of bones cracking in his chest as I tried to give him CPR." She shook her head, and reached for a pack of cigarettes lying on top of a half-packed box. "They did an autopsy," she said, lighting up and taking a deep first drag. "They said that he'd had a massive coronary brought on by low blood sugar. There wasn't anything they thought suspicious. Hell, death by insulin and the first person they'd be pointing fingers at would be the wife, especially if she's twenty years younger…that's not why you're…"

"No," Hobbs interjected. "And I have to say how sorry we are for the loss you've suffered."

Sheila looked at the burning cigarette. She sniffled and tears squeezed from her eyes. "I wasn't going to do this today," she said. "I wanted just one day or even a few hours where I wouldn't feel like a total wreck."

"It doesn't work that way," Barrett advised, "you know that."

"The funny thing is, I do. It's just different when you know something and when you're in the middle of it."

"True…Sheila, you said that in all the years you knew Morris he never had a problem with his blood sugars."

"That's right, he was very careful."

"But that night something happened. When you went out, did he not eat or drink as much as usual?"

"Hardly, if anything I would have thought his sugars would have been high."

"Any chance he could have taken the wrong amount of insulin, or even the wrong type?"

"Morris had a whole assembly line for doing his syringes. I've still got all his bottles in the refrigerator. You'd think that's something I would have thrown out, but I don't know if it's the wastefulness of that, or on some weird level I'm still waiting for him to come through the door."

"Could we see them?" Hobbs asked.

"If you'd like," Sheila stubbed out her cigarette and led them down the hall into a black-and-white, eat-in kitchen. She opened the brushed-chrome Sub Zero and reached inside.

"Wait a minute," Hobbs stopped her.

"What is it?" Sheila asked, holding onto the door.

"Has anyone handled the bottles since your husband's death?"

"Probably…I think the EMTs might have. No, on second thought they asked for the bottles and I guess with everything else they just forgot about them."

Hobbs pulled two pairs of sealed latex gloves from the inner pocket of his leather coat. He handed one to Barrett. "You never know," he shrugged.

Sheila stood back as Barrett looked in the refrigerator. It was mostly empty, but carefully arranged inside the cheese container was a half-used metal-and-rubber capped glass bottle of insulin, and several more still in their boxes. Next to these were seven thin syringes already drawn up with medication.

"How far ahead would he prepare his injections?" Barrett asked.

"He did it weekly, every Sunday during *60 Minutes.*"

"So he would have taken his evening dose before going out on Thursday, is that correct?" she asked.

"Right."

"He took it twice a day?"

"Yes, why?"

"Well, if he drew it up on Sunday there should only be six syringes left for the week, and there are seven here."

"No," Sheila said, "that's right. It's like I said, he knew we were going out so he drew up a larger dose."

"He wouldn't have just added to what was already there?"

"I guess not," Sheila said. "But now I'm not certain, like I said, he took care of it himself."

"That's strange," Barrett said, reaching a gloved hand into the cheese container.

"What?" Hobbs asked, standing next to her.

"Look at that," Barrett held up a small insulin bottle. "Look at the cap."

"That's not how it's supposed to be?" Hobbs asked.

"No, the metal is all bent, almost like somebody took it off and then put it back on." She took out an unopened box, pulled out a fresh bottle and compared them. "I think this has been tampered with." She turned them upside down, and watched how the clear liquid moved inside the tiny bottles. She read the labels, "These are both supposed to be the same type of insulin, but their viscosity is visibly different."

Hobbs produced an evidence bag from his jacket.

Barrett looked at him, "What else do you keep in there?"

"Guys don't get pocketbooks, so I get my dry cleaner to sew extra pockets into all my coats."

"You must have been a Boy Scout."

"All the way to Eagle." He unzipped the plastic bag and held it open as Barrett dropped in the tampered bottle and its mate.

"Do you have some way to keep those cold?" she asked, looking first at Hobbs and then at Sheila. "Insulin denatures if it's not chilled."

"There's ice in the freezer," Sheila offered. "and there's an old thermos around here someplace. I don't think I packed it. But what's this all about? The coroner said natural causes. The two of you are acting like it's…like someone killed him."

Hobbs spoke, "Ms. Kravitz, in all likelihood it's exactly as you say, but we have some suspicions that we'd like to put to rest. I will need you to sign for anything we take away as potential evidence."

Barrett watched as Hobbs retrieved a small stack of preprinted forms from his coat of many pockets and had Sheila Kravitz sign.

"So what do you think?" Barrett asked, as they rode down in the elevator.

"I think you think somebody did in the good doctor," Hobbs jiggled the ice-filled blue-and-white thermos.

"And you?" Barrett faced him as the car came to an air-cushioned stop and the wood-paneled doors slid open.

"Something isn't right," he admitted. "You feel like walking this over to the precinct with me?" he asked. "I'll get the guys in the lab to take a look at them."

"Sure, I could use the exercise…and of course the company."

"Of course," he laughed. "And I've got a little present for you."

"Really?"

"Yup, so you can't say I never got you anything."

"Like Sheila…You know," Barrett commented, "she's not what I had expected."

"In what way?"

"Fairly traumatized by her husband's death. I can't imagine waking up and finding someone you love dead."

"You think that's why she's moving? I wish we'd asked," Hobbs remarked.

"Why?"

"Well, getting back to things that don't fit, why is she moving? She kept saying how she didn't need all the things he got for her, and I'm thinking the apartment was high on the list. But is she leaving because it's too big, or she can't deal with the memories, or maybe Dr. Kravitz was living a bit beyond his means."

"I'd take number three," Barrett offered.

"Agreed. So the next question is…what was going on with Morris Kravitz and James Cyrus Martin?"

"Good question. I keep coming back to that damn bloodwork. Even a first-year resident knows that it's got to be checked. It's the first thing you do with a new patient on lithium. Every so often you come upon a real old-timer who doesn't think it's necessary. There used to be this school of thought that the way you could tell a patient's level was by how much they shook."

"Charming."

"Yes, psychiatry has a long and distinguished past. It makes you wonder about some of the stuff we do now and what future generations will say about our ignorance and barbarism…but I digress."

"You do," he steered them across an intersection in the direction of his precinct. "So let's think on reasons why a psychiatrist would neglect to check bloodwork."

"Basically, Sheila pegged it. Number one would be ignorance. I'd follow that up with sloppiness, there are some hacks who see so many patients that they just forget or don't care."

"What else? Neither of those fit."

Barrett stopped beside a Korean grocer's flower display. "I know another reason. He wouldn't check…if he knew that the patient wasn't taking the medication."

"That's the spirit," Hobbs picked up a bunch of purple iris and another of half-opened yellow crocus.

"What are you doing?" she asked.

"Nothing," he handed the flowers to the grocer and paid him. "So if he knew that Jimmy wasn't taking the pills, why didn't he report it?"

"Because that would be the end of a very tidy piece of change."

"Exactly," Hobbs handed the freshly wrapped bouquet to Barrett.

"Thank you," she said, admiring the contrasting yellow and purple blooms, and a bit confused as to how she was supposed to respond. Feeling flushed, opting to say little, she tried to focus on Dr. Kravitz. "But then why would he suddenly order bloodwork if he knew that Jimmy wasn't taking his pills?"

"Something changed," Hobbs remarked. "Hold onto that thought, and I'll be right back."

Barrett watched as Hobbs took the stairs to the brick-fronted precinct station two at a time. She sat on a bench beneath a Ginkgo tree, holding her paper-wrapped blooms and mulling over what he'd said. It was the only answer that made sense. Morris Kravitz must have had some deal with Jimmy and then two weeks before his death something changed. He knew that Jimmy wasn't taking his pills, and they'd been colluding, so then why suddenly order bloodwork? It didn't fit. Lost in thought, she startled at Hobbs' voice.

"Blackmail," the detective commented.

"What?"

"Maybe Kravitz wanted more money, so he started putting the screws to Jimmy. You said that even slight violations could get him sent back to Croton. Not taking medication would fit that, yes?"

"Yes, but…" She tried to focus, to not think about the sun twinkling in Hobbs' hazel eyes, or the bouquet of spice-sweet blooms. "Once the results came back it would be out of Kravitz's hands and he'd lose his golden goose. It's got to be something else."

"Okay, try this on for size…maybe Jimmy had told Kravitz that he wanted another shrink…like you. What would Kravitz have done then?"

"I don't know. If he needed the money that badly I imagine he'd try to talk him out of it," she said, as they headed off in the direction of her co-op.

"And if that didn't work?"

"Then I guess he's screwed, and in more ways than one. Because not only is he losing his best-paying customer, but his shoddy work is about to get exposed. So maybe…maybe he figured that he'd either scare Jimmy into staying with him, or at least try to cover up for what he should have been doing all along."

"Still a little rough," Hobbs commented, "but I think it's as close as we're going to get without more data. But if it's right, then it gets very hairy."

"I know," she said, "we're looking at a hit-and-run where the blood is lost and…"

"And a dead psychiatrist with a young wife and a Park Avenue apartment that he couldn't really afford."

"Do you always finish people's sentences?" she asked.

"Not usually," he admitted. "It's a bit of déjà vu, isn't it?"

"Yes…you know there's something I've been wanting to ask you, and you don't have to answer if you don't want."

"Shoot."

"This is a pretty big coincidence—your showing up at Jimmy's house the way you did. Is it a coincidence?"

"No, I saw your name and pulled a few strings to get the assignment."

"I'm glad you did," she looked up at her building. "Well, this is me," she said, not wanting their walk to end.

"Before I forget," he reached into an outer pocket. "I got a wire for you. I could give it to you here, if you like. Have you ever worn one?"

"No, and just the idea of it makes me pretty nervous. You want to come up and show me what I'm supposed to do with it?"

"Sure," he said, following her inside.

Neither one spoke as they rode up six floors and walked down the hall to her apartment.

Ed watched as she unlocked the door. "You know you should get better cylinders for those locks," he commented.

"I was planning to get them changed...."

"Good idea. The ones you've got now are easy to pick."

As she opened the door, she asked, "What about the ones at the Kravitz apartment—easy or hard?"

"Easy, but at least they have a doorman and you don't."

"Great...can I get you something to eat? Or drink?"

"I'm good," he stood in the doorway taking in Barrett's surroundings. "Interesting."

She took her flowers into the galley kitchen and poured water into a crystal vase, "What's interesting?" She glanced at the answering machine and saw the red light flashing with new messages.

"Your apartment."

"Interesting how?"

"Don't get me wrong, it's very nice, it's just..."

"Not me?"

"Right. It's not what I expected."

"My husband…Ralph did the decorating. Everything has to be very clean, very modern. I like things with color. I guess you pick your battles in a marriage."

"Interesting choice of words."

"Look, you," Barrett placed the flowers on a coffee table and walked up to Hobbs, "if you keep using the word *interesting* instead of the more appropriate *fucked up* or this *woman is out of her gourd* I will hit you."

"I forgot that."

"What?"

"Your temper," he laughed.

Barrett found herself staring deeply into Ed's eyes, noticing flecks of green and rich amber. In the close space she smelled the hint of his aftershave and wondered if he'd put it on for her benefit.

"Do you know how beautiful you are?" he whispered.

She barely heard the words, but rather felt them as they fell from his lips. She wondered what his moustache would feel like. "I can't do this," she said.

"Okay, I understand, I just came up here to show you the wire."

"Right," she tried to pull back, but at the same time didn't want to let the moment pass.

"It's easy," he said, "and I'll be able to hear every word."

"I'm glad."

"It'll be like having you inside my head."

"What are we doing?" she asked, noticing the dryness in her mouth.

"I don't know. But I very much want to kiss you."

Barrett could hear all the reasons why she shouldn't clamor at her brain. She looked into his eyes and nodded slightly. She felt his hand gently touch her cheek, she felt the heat of his body as it pulsed through the opening in his leather coat, and then came the brush of his moustache, so much softer than she'd expected. And as she closed her eyes and his lips met hers, all of the reasons why she shouldn't be doing this left her and she surrendered into the sweetness of a perfect first kiss.

———

Closing the door behind Hobbs, Barrett felt lightheaded and confused. She'd just kissed a man who wasn't her husband. Of course, Ralph had done far worse, and then the anger returned. He'd never shown up, just left her sitting without even a message. She saw the blinking on the answering machine. At least one of them was probably Ralph, what would the excuse be, and how much more of this could she take?

She pressed the *play messages* button. A mechanical voice gave the time "ten forty-five AM." Then, a woman's voice—Ralph's mom, Celia. "Hi Barrett, I'm just calling because I know Ralph was planning to see you last night…I was wondering if he was still there…I guess not. If you see him, I got a call that he's supposed to be at a morning rehearsal…oh, well. Bye."

Barrett's first thought was that Ralph had probably met up with someone else, or maybe Carol, and had forgotten about the early rehearsal. The second message quickly dampened that thought, "Hello, this is Veronica Durst at Mount Sinai Hospital. I need to speak with a family member of Ralph Best. Please call," and she left a number.

"Shit!" Barrett quickly dialed. She'd not even considered that Ralph had gotten sick, and that's why he hadn't shown. "Shit."

The phone picked up, "Morgue."

Barrett's stomach lurched, she couldn't comprehend. Had she misdialed? "This is Barrett Conyors, I was left a message about my husband, Ralph Best."

She heard the slow intake of breath, "Mrs. Conyors, I'm afraid I have some very bad news, we're going to need you to come down."

SIXTEEN

THURSDAY CAME, AND BARRETT—against everyone's advice— had gone to work. She'd needed to escape from the phone that wouldn't stop ringing, as news of Ralph's death circulated. All the members of the orchestra wanted "to touch base," "to express their grief," "to tell her what a sweet man Ralph was." In the end, she'd handed the phone to Justine and her mom, and when they'd finally left, she'd unhooked the ringer.

It was too hard to believe, going to the morgue late Tuesday, the white oilcloth cover being pulled back. "*Is this your husband?*" They'd cleaned up his face, but even so she saw the abrasions of where he'd been dragged on the asphalt. "Yes, it's him," unable to move, the moment frozen forever. He'd been on his way to meet her, to tell her that he was sorry and that he loved her. They might have worked it out and put together a plan to get their marriage back on track, and to talk about children. She was ready; was he? "*This could never happen again,*" she'd say. He would have agreed, and while she'd find it hard ever to trust him fully, she would have taken him back.

After identifying him, and signing her name to several documents, her first call had been to her mother. After that she lost track—the last thirty-six hours fused into a series of terrible tasks. The call to Ralph's mother. "Celia, Ralph is dead." The police coming to their condo, needing a statement. "No, we haven't found the driver. It was hit and run, a taxi ran a red light. Many witnesses, but none of them said more than it was a yellow cab, its windows dark. No one got the plate or medallion numbers."

And now, to finish off her day, she was in Jimmy Martin's museum of a house dressed in gray and wearing a gift from Hobbs—a gold floral lapel pin with a synthetic sapphire in the center. When he'd given it to her—after their kiss—she'd been impressed at what nice equipment the police department provided. His response was that the detective bureau had crappy surveillance stuff and that he'd bought it from a security supply store. She'd thought about their kiss as she'd put it on, it seemed so long ago, but it was just a couple days. *Your husband's killed, you kissed Hobbs*—nothing seemed real.

"Is that a new suit?" Jimmy asked, ignoring the kitten who butted his head against his master's leg. His hair was slicked back, and he was dressed in a white, open-necked polo shirt and jeans.

"It is," she answered, trying to focus, but just wanting to get through this.

"It's a good color for you."

"Thank you," she replied, wondering if his observations on her Donna Karan had any hidden messages, like, *nice suit, did you buy it with the extra money I stuffed into your check?* She looked carefully at Jimmy. He appeared different, quieter, and he was holding his hands together in his lap. "So how's your week been?" she asked.

"Okay, I guess…did you get the rest of my bloodwork back?" He was anxious.

"Most of it."

"And…"

"And your lithium level was on the low side, but your kidneys and thyroid seem fine. I still haven't gotten back your Risperdal level, but I imagine that will be fine, as well."

"They took a lot of blood. You weren't just checking drug levels, were you?"

"I told you I wasn't. Part of the reason you check blood is to prevent some of the potentially toxic effects of lithium." She looked at his hands; he had a fine tremor.

"I had a doctor once tell me that all medicine is poison."

"I suppose in high-enough doses that could be true."

"Even aspirin can kill you," he offered, glancing up and then looking away.

"It could." What was he getting at?

"So you could be prescribing something for one of your patients and it could be killing him."

"I try not to do that," she answered, wondering if she should just cut the session short.

"I wasn't saying…"

"Look Jimmy, I know you don't want to take the pills, I even think I know some of the reasons, but right now you don't have a choice. You could tell me why you don't want to take them. I'm not saying that I'll change them, but at least I'll get a sense of where you're coming from."

He blinked and laughed deeply; he squared his shoulders and edged forward.

Fred's blue eyes darted nervously, the kitten's back arched and he scampered under a sofa.

Barrett too flinched at the abrupt shift in her patient.

"Where to start?" He shot his trembling hands into the space between their chairs. "A strong vibrato is all well and good, but this gets to be a problem." His eyes narrowed to slits and his voice was breathy as though the words were being squeezed from his chest.

"It affects your playing," she commented, pressing back into her chair, her mouth dry, feeling unprepared to deal with this.

"It does. Any chance I could entice you into a duet or two?"

"That's not why I'm here. Tell me more about you and the medication."

"This is such an old story," he replied, putting his hands down. "If you're not a freak before you take the pills, they turn you into one."

"What do you mean?"

"Remember what he…I…used to look like?"

"Yes, we discussed that last week."

"Well most of that was because of the pills. The first thing they had me on was Mellaril and I finally convinced them to stop it because it made me grow breasts. Which I was having enough problems without having them turn me into a woman."

"What kind of problems?"

He lunged forward in his chair.

Barrett tensed, fearing he might attack.

He stood and looked at her with a perplexed expression. "I want to show you something," he walked over to a bank of bookcases, opened a glass door and took out a double-sided brass picture frame. "This was me," he handed it to Barrett.

Barrett felt the cool metal as she looked into the brilliant blue eyes of an adolescent Jimmy. To say he was beautiful would miss the mark. The photographer had caught him with a ray of light that cut across wheat-blond hair, cornflower-blue eyes, and flawless skin. It was an angel's face. The frame was hinged, and on the other side was the matching portrait of Ellen. She too was lovely, but where Jimmy's features were delicate and feline, hers had a squarer, almost masculine, cast.

"I was seventeen in that picture. I didn't look much different from that when I went into Croton…" he stood behind his chair and stared at Barrett. "Can you imagine what happens to boys who look like that in places like Croton?"

"It couldn't have been easy."

Jimmy sank back into his chair. He retrieved his pictures from Barrett and put them in his lap. "*Easy?*…there aren't words to cover it."

"What happened?"

"How did we get here?"

"You were telling me reasons why you didn't like the pills, and how the Mellaril gave you gynecomastia." She heard the words leave her mouth. She sounded canned, and resisted the urge to look at her watch.

"Breasts…that's right. Even when I gained all that weight they still came after me."

"You were raped?"

"Yes."

"Did you report it?"

"I'm surprised," he said.

"About?"

"I would have thought you'd already know this. Unless you're playing some kind of game where you want to see if the story I tell is the same one in the record. Which is it, Dr. Conyors? Is this a game?"

"No. I've been meaning to go back through your Croton records, but they're archived on microfilm and I haven't had the chance."

"Good. I would hate to think that you'd play games around something like this. To come into my house and ask me about things best left alone."

"You don't have to talk about this."

"I don't, do I...but then what will go into your report? How will you label me? Do I become *resistant* or is the term *noncompliant*? Either way, I hold few cards. It's funny—not haha—but sad how, if I'd gone to regular jail, I would have gotten out much sooner and there'd be none of this constant surveillance. But we were too young to know what was going on."

"We?"

"Ellen and I."

"What did she have to do with your going to Croton?"

"Nothing, but if she'd known...it would have been different."

"Interesting...It's not easy to successfully argue a not guilty by reason of insanity defense. There has to be clear and convincing evidence for a judge to even allow it to be presented."

"Look around you," he said. "Things go differently if you have money."

"So you think you purchased that defense?"

"Well, let's say that my parents were not eager to have their son's face plastered all over the dailies. It was more…palatable for me to be crazy."

"So they were the ones who pushed for the defense."

"Yes…although I freely admit that I wasn't in my best frame of mind at the time."

"You heard voices."

"I did."

"Do you still?"

He paused, "At times."

"Inside or outside your head?"

"Outside."

"Do you recognize the voices?"

"Usually."

"Who are they?"

He scratched his head, "I have the feeling I shouldn't be telling you all of this."

"Why?"

"Because it always ends up hurting me when I let people know this stuff."

"Jimmy, I've known hundreds of people who hear voices. What you're telling me now…it's okay. Do you recognize the voices?"

"It's usually the same one…my father."

"What kind of things does he say?" she asked, trying to brush aside intrusive images of Ralph. *The refrigerated drawer sliding open, the official asking, "Is that your husband?"*

Jimmy cocked his head to the side.

"Can you hear him now?" Barrett asked.

"No. He's been quieter the past few days. Can't say that I miss him."

"Why's that?"

"Well…boy, this an interesting one. How do I even begin to tell you about my father? And the funny thing is, I want to tell you." His eyes burned with intensity, "I'd like you to understand, and that hasn't been true before."

"You've never told other psychiatrists or social workers about your father?" she asked, observing the mercurial shifts in his posture, voice, and attitude. And realizing that she wasn't up to the challenge of the session; she shouldn't have come.

"I suppose I have, but not really. I mean, you learn what to say and what not to say. And more importantly, *how* to say it."

"It sounds like you didn't get along with your father."

He inhaled deeply, letting the air hiss between his front teeth. "Sometimes I got along great with Father. You've seen my cello," he turned in his chair and looked at the gleaming instrument perched in its cradle next to the piano.

"It's lovely."

"Father got me that. He bought it at auction and paid nearly a quarter of a million dollars; it's worth much more than that now."

"Impressive," she commented, glancing at his cello, the piano that was well over a hundred grand, the intricately carved antique furniture, oil paintings and sculptures and realized that she was sitting in a room with furnishings that totaled in the millions.

"The night he bought it for me, he came into my room and sodomized me; it wasn't the first time and it wasn't the last. For the longest time I couldn't remember that he'd done those things to me, but lately it's been coming back. Just a few weeks ago I was playing the Brahms E Minor and I remembered that birthday; I was eight."

"You have flashbacks?" she asked.

"Doesn't everybody?" he tried to smile.

"I'm really sorry, Jimmy." Her own grief resonating with his, her tears dangerously close.

"It's not your fault, and just because my father couldn't keep his dick in his pants, it's not like the end of the world."

"Where was your mother?"

"I think I told you the first time you came here, that I did not have a normal childhood. Mother had her own…issues."

"Such as?"

"She and Father were kind of like an arranged marriage. I'm not even convinced that they had sex together. Did you know they were second cousins?"

"So you don't think your father was your biological father?"

"God only knows. I don't think she could stand to have him touch her."

"It sounds like a nightmare, the kind of thing no child should ever have to endure; it's amazing you made it through."

"I had Ellen. We had each other and that's all there was to it." And then, in a voice almost too soft to hear, "Hansel and Gretel."

"Did your father molest her, as well?"

"No. He never did. I seemed to be the sole focus of his attention. And the funny thing is, it made Ellen jealous."

"Really?"

"Yeah, isn't that strange? I would have given anything to have those footsteps pass by my room, but they never did." He glanced

195

over his shoulder, "I can still hear them coming down the hallway. This dull rhythmic thud getting closer and louder, that's why I don't sleep in that room anymore."

"Where do you sleep?"

He smiled, "This *is* sick…in Mother's room, because I know there's no way in hell he's going there."

"Both of your parents died while you were in Croton. How did you deal with that?" she asked.

"I was glad."

"Do you think about them much?"

"As far as I'm concerned Father never really left, and Mother…what can I say," he shrugged his shoulder, "her legacy lives on."

"What do you mean by that?"

"Nothing really," he looked down at the pictures in his lap.

"You were going to say something about her."

"Boy, you really want the gory details. I'm not sure we have time, the hour must be nearly up."

"There's time," she said.

"Great…Mother had a thing for the hired help. Father did too, but his taste ran more toward the paperboy—but that's another story. I know this sounds strange, but you have to remember, I thought this was normal. Mother liked to play games with the drivers and the gardeners. You'd think she would have had the sense to conduct her affairs somewhere else."

"So you knew?"

"We'd watch," he admitted, looking her dead on.

"You and Ellen," his gaze making her squirm, his voice now back to the wheezing hiss.

"Right, through little holes in the wall. And to give you the full impact of life in the Martin house…she knew we were there."

Barrett found it hard to breathe.

"It's true," he said. "I can see by your expression you don't believe me. And no, she never waved and said, *'hi kids,'* but sometimes she'd look straight at us, at these two little holes in the wall, and she'd smile, like she was putting on a show just for us."

"Would you get aroused?" she asked, finding her bearings, and wondering if this wasn't a clue to what had happened in Nicole Foster's apartment.

"Yes."

"How old would you have been?"

"Young, very young. So young…five or six," he blinked and his voice grew soft and airy, almost childlike.

The cat meowed and his blue eyes peeked out from beneath the couch.

"Can you remember more of your childhood?" she urged, wondering—as she often did—how so much evil could be visited upon a small child.

"It's funny that you ask."

"Why?"

"Well, that's been a lot of what I've been finding in the past few months…since I left the hospital."

"What's that?"

"There's big chunks of growing up that I can't remember. Like the day father gave me Allegra."

"Allegra?"

"My cello; she has a name. It was only recently that I remembered what happened that night. I remember him giving me the cello, but the rest of that day is a total blank. I know something happened, something bad. And to be honest, there are entire years of my life that are missing. If you ask me what I was doing in fifth and sixth grade, other than playing cello, which I assume I was doing, I have no clue. In fact, a lot of the time I was at Croton, I had no memory of what Father had done—and it went on for a very long time. It's odd the way your mind plays tricks like that."

"It's not uncommon," Barrett said. "A lot of times we block out traumatic memories; it's a way of defending against them."

"Interesting," he said, his eyes gazed into hers.

They both fell silent as the grandfather clock's chiming mechanism engaged. The hour struck five.

Jimmy blinked three times and looked down at the pictures in his lap. He picked them up and placed them on the table.

"I suppose you'll be checking more bloodwork," he said, his tone accusatory.

"I will," she acknowledged.

"One has to be so careful with medication," he stood. "It's all poison in the wrong amount. Do you take medication? What about your family? Any of them take pills? Here we spent all this time talking about the Martin family and what about yours? Your mommy and your daddy, brothers, sisters…I bet you have a sister, don't you?" He grinned, caught her eye and winked.

Barrett froze. Her fingers tingled and she noted that the cat had again hidden itself.

"I suppose I shouldn't ask," he looked down and opened the table drawer. A sealed envelope lay inside. A twisted smile played across his dark lips. "But that's right…we already paid you for this week. I guess this will have to wait. Unless you wanted to take it now? It doesn't matter to me. I certainly wouldn't tell."

"I'm leaving," she said, praying that her limbs would follow her mind's command.

"Of course," he slammed the drawer shut. "Time's up. Although, you shouldn't be too hard on Dr. Kravitz."

Barrett turned. "What are you talking about?"

"I'm just saying, you shouldn't be too hard on him. Who knew he was such a sick man? I guess it's really true, that you have to live every day as though it might be your very last."

"Why would you think I was hard on him?" she desperately wanted to get out of there, but something in his remark stopped her. She racked her brain. Had she said anything in front of him to disparage Kravitz? How could he know her concerns about Kravitz's shoddy treatment? And what were all these cracks about her family?

"Just a hunch, Dr. Conyors. That sounds so formal. Could I call you Barrett?"

"No," she shot back with more vehemence than she'd intended.

His smile curled into a sneer. "Of course not, what was I thinking? But I'm forgetting my manners," and he bounded past her and flung open the heavy library doors.

Detectives Hobbs and Cassidy had left the kitchen and were waiting in the foyer.

"Ah yes," Jimmy quipped. "Your dark-suited escorts. I hope you enjoyed the donuts. I understand they're popular with police. You should let me know if you have a favorite." He glared at Hobbs, as he opened the front door to let them out. "You know, Detective Hobbs, there's something familiar about your face…as though I've seen it before. I'm just trying to remember where."

Halfway out, Hobbs turned and looked back at Jimmy, "What are you getting at?"

"I think what they did to those children is criminal," Jimmy giggled. "Don't you?" The color drained from Hobbs' face.

"I'm sure you've told her all about that?" Jimmy hissed, and then shut the door.

———

"What was that?" Barrett asked, her pulse racing. She waited for Ed to join her at the bottom of Jimmy's front steps, not wanting him to know how close she was to a full-blown panic attack.

"It's nothing," Hobbs answered. "Let's get out of here."

"You sure?" she persisted, wondering if her voice was even close to normal.

"I should be asking you that. He's playing games," Hobbs said. "Bryan," he called out to his partner. "I'm going to walk the doctor home; I'll see you in the morning."

The younger man smiled and gave a mock salute.

"He's a good kid," Ed commented, looking at the sidewalk in front of him. "How are you holding up? I can't believe you came today. You shouldn't be here. You need to take some time…"

"Don't. That's all everyone's saying, but I need to keep moving. So I'm okay, I guess…Are you going to tell me what happened back there?" she asked, hoping that if she focused on Ed, it would help calm her down.

"Let's get out of here."

Barrett waited for Ed to speak; he didn't. As her anxiety eased, she realized that Ed was struggling with his own demon. They walked west, putting blocks between themselves and the Martin townhouse. "It can't have been that donut crack," she finally said, as they waited for the light to change in front of the Flatiron building.

"He knows stuff," Hobbs said.

"What stuff?"

"This isn't easy, Barrett."

"What?"

"Do you have any idea how hard it is to get bumped down the way I did?"

"No," she admitted. "And I had the impression it wasn't something you wanted to discuss."

"You got that right."

"Did he say something about that?" she asked.

"I think so. So let me just get it out on the table. When I was deputy chief, I found out that one of my detectives was on the take. It was a man I respected and someone who'd helped me get to where I was. In fact, he was the one who first recommended me for the bureau—he wrote my letter. So I had a choice, either report him, or give him the 'if I ever catch you again' speech. I went for the second, because I trusted him. But it goes to show that you never truly know someone."

"What happened?"

"I didn't do my job. Bottom line, I didn't follow up. I assumed because he was my friend, or I thought he was, that what he'd done couldn't be anything more than turning a blind eye to some backroom prostitution or to guys getting their rocks off in an unlicensed peep show. I was wrong. And when I did find out, and I did report it…it didn't go well. I'm surprised they even gave me the option to stay. I didn't do my job. It hit the papers and was very ugly."

"I'm so sorry, Ed."

"Not your fault."

"And Jimmy knows."

"He must. And that sob story he gave you about his childhood is just his way of trying to pull you in."

"You don't think it's true."

"It probably is. Freaks like that have to come from somewhere. I just wouldn't take it at face value."

"I don't," she said.

They walked the remaining blocks in an uncomfortable silence. When they got to her building, she turned to look up at the lights in her condo. She imagined her mother inside, manning the phone, baking a sweet potato casserole, doing the things that needed to be done when… "I don't want to go up."

"Is there anything I can do?"

"I don't think so. I just wish I didn't feel so frightened. It's like everything is coming undone. I never wanted Ralph dead," she said, voicing a horrible sense of guilt.

"Of course not."

"When I caught him with Carol, I could have killed him, killed them both. Oh, shit!"

"What is it?"

"I told you about the hit-and-run…you know where the blood-work that Kravitz ordered landed on the street."

"Yes?"

"The phlebotomist was hit by a cab…" she said, wondering if he'd see it, and wondering why she hadn't.

"Jesus!"

"Right. Lots of cabs in New York, how many hit and runs?"

"Barrett…listen to me. You need to get someone else to take Martin's case. Even better, I'd like to see you get out of town for a couple of weeks until we can figure what's going on."

"I can't," her voice was flat. How easy it would be to follow his advice, but then what? Where would she go? Who'd take care of the bills, and if Jimmy had anything to do with Ralph's death, why would he stop there? Hobbs had said, *"He knew stuff."* Stuff about her, about her family…"I can't."

"Why the hell not?"

"It's too much like running," she said. "I can't do that."

"He's up to something bad, Barrett. Every bone in my body feels it."

"I know. He's like a cancer that everything he touches just shrivels and dies."

"I couldn't stand to see you get hurt," he said.

"I'll be careful…and I've got you there to look after me."

"He knows that," Hobbs said. "That's why he's trying to get to me."

"So what's his motive?"

"Jealousy. He wants to clear the playing field. Look what happened with the Foster girl. Something snaps when she tells him she's engaged. A few days later, she and her boyfriend are both dead."

"That was eighteen years ago," she said, but he was right. And for the first time, she got a whiff of what made Jimmy Martin tick. She felt the ground shift and nausea swell. "Why didn't I see this?"

"What?" Hobbs asked.

"He had an erotomanic attachment to Nicole Foster."

"What's that?"

"It's a delusion. A false belief that the person you're attracted to is also in love with you. It's pretty common, especially with stalkers. And because it's a delusion, no amount of reasoning or evidence to the contrary will make you believe anything else."

"So what would have happened when she told him she was engaged? That's pretty compelling evidence that you're not the one."

"I know, and when erotomaniacs turn violent they often go after people around the one they love. Like boyfriends."

Hobbs said nothing, his expression filled with concern.

"Like husbands," Barrett gasped. This was all her fault. "Oh, God!" she started to dry heave.

Hobbs gently patted her back and waited for her to regain control. "Did you get your locks changed?" He asked.

"No."

"Do it." He shook his head and looked at her. "Barrett, you need to get away from here."

"No."

"This is not good."

"I'll be okay," she said. "At least I know what I'm dealing with."

"You're not making sense. If what you're telling me adds up, and I think it does, Martin could be behind your husband's death."

"I think he is," she replied dully. "He has to be locked up, and he can't ever come out again. I have to make sure that happens."

SEVENTEEN

She slept little, her mind racing from Ralph to Jimmy, to guilt over her attraction to Hobbs. And how could she hang onto the condo without Ralph's income to help with the mortgage? And then scolding herself for being mercenary. She'd picture Ralph, and remember the feel of him next to her in bed, and the tears would start. It was a horrible night, and what little sleep came was twisted with dreams, where she'd be running for her life, and then wake in a panic, not certain what—or who—was chasing her.

As she dressed, she thought about Hobbs' warnings. Jimmy Martin was bad news, and if he had an erotomanic fixation on her, nothing short of incarceration or death would stop him. She thought about other times when she'd encountered violent erotomaniacs—always her advice to the target was "have no contact." So why wouldn't she take her own advice?

Pumping herself with black coffee, she'd headed toward the office, needing the daily grind, the time to plow through Martin's records, to find the thing that had been missed, the thing that would get him sent back to Croton.

"Marla," she pressed down on the intercom, "my schedule's all messed up, what do I have this morning?"

"What are you doing here?" the clinic secretary asked.

Not again, Barrett thought, tired of everyone telling her she should stay home, take some time off. "Excuse me? I thought I worked here."

"God," the wispy voiced secretary sighed, "both you and Dr. Fielding forgot you're expected at Croton for a provisional release hearing on client GF."

"Shit!" Barrett flipped open her date book; there was nothing there. Then she remembered an e-mail a couple weeks back. "I didn't think they'd scheduled it."

"Tell it to the judge."

"What time was I supposed to be there?"

"Ten."

"I have other appointments this afternoon."

"I'll cancel them." Marla said.

"There's no way I'll make it. My car's on the other side of town and it's an hour's drive—and that's speeding."

Barrett turned as a sharp knock came.

Dr. Fielding's carefully arranged combed-over pate peeped through the opening. He grinned sheepishly, "We screwed up."

"Someone did," Barrett replied. "Can you give me a ride?"

"Of course, I was going to ask if you wanted one."

"See," Marla said over the phone, "it all works out. And I get stuck calling both of your appointments for the afternoon and telling them that their wise-and-wonderful psychiatrists can't keep their dates straight."

"Thanks, Marla."

"Thanks are cheap," she quipped in her little-girl voice, "a raise is forever."

"Don't hang up," Anton interjected. He took the receiver from Barrett, "Marla, be a sweetheart and call ahead to Dr. Morgan let her know we'll be…" he glanced at his wrist, "twenty maybe thirty minutes late."

"Yeah right. More like an hour," the receptionist replied. "What excuse would you like?"

"The truth, of course."

"An unexpected crisis at the clinic?" she suggested.

"Works for me."

Fielding hung up, "You ready?"

Barrett looked around her office, the voice mail button was blinking and her list of unread e-mails was a page and a half deep.

"There's always Monday," he said, intuiting her hesitation. "In my experience, if someone truly wants to get in touch, they call back."

She grabbed her briefcase and closed the door behind them. "So who's GF?" she asked as they headed to the underground garage.

"George Fitzsimmons," Anton replied, pushing the button for the automatic door opener on his midnight blue Jaguar XJR.

Barrett settled back into the tan leather and pushed away the hovering image of Ralph's bruised face, and the stench of the morgue. "So what did Mr. Fitzsimmons do?" she asked, trying to focus.

"Quite a bit. He's been bouncing in and out of Croton ever since he was in his teens. Before that it was Brighton Hall."

"What offenses?"

"There's a spread," Anton replied as he nosed the roadster up the ramp and onto First Avenue. As they dodged traffic on 34th, he sketched out the basics. "Fitzsimmons had problems from the get-go. Basically his temper coupled with schizophrenia and a bit of booze creates a volatile and unpredictable mix. Over the years I've seen him a number of times and it's always the same. The man we're going to see this afternoon will be an absolute angel. You'll ask yourself, 'Why wasn't he let out sooner?' He'll be polite, insightful; he'll talk about how he's benefited from treatment and how this time is going to be different."

"And?" she asked.

"And, he'll go out, have a drink or twenty, stop his medications because he knows not to mix pills and alcohol. Then the voices tell him that different celebrities are carrying the devil's children; he gets paranoid and if we don't catch him he'll do something very bad."

"So why are we here?" she asked.

"Why else—they want to release him."

"But…"

"Good lawyers through the consumer advocacy office and a persistent family," Anton answered. "The only problem is they're not real interested in helping George. Once he gets out; he's not the nicest person to live with, especially when he drinks. So it's up to us to put together the half-million dollar plan that could keep him in the community."

"Group home plus, plus, plus," Barrett replied.

"That about covers it, except he's already been through all the group homes in greater Manhattan. Once George has lived someplace, they don't want him back. Plus, he's set some fires and is a convicted felon, so public housing is out."

Barrett stared through her window at the lush greenery as they headed north on the Saw Mill. "I guess Jimmy Martin never had that problem."

Anton cut her a sideways glance. "How's that going?" he asked. "You seemed pretty freaked the other day."

"It's under control," she lied. "Now, you must have been involved when they put together his release."

"I was."

"As far as I can tell he's got the perfect discharge plan," she offered, choosing her words carefully. "A townhouse in Gramercy Park, all meals delivered, everything that money can buy. No skanky group home in the South Bronx for Jimmy."

"Money was not an issue in that case."

"So you've met him."

"Oh yeah, same kind of gig as this, only the first time I was in your seat and George Housmann was the clinic director."

"First time?"

"You know how it goes. No one gets out on the first try. Even with all his money."

"How long did it take him?"

"Years. People had a lot of concerns about him returning to Manhattan. The victims' parents put up quite a fuss, as did some of the neighbors. But his family had significant money and brought in big lawyers; they finally pushed the right buttons."

"They? His parents, you mean?"

"No, I never met them. It was his sister."

"You've met Ellen?"

"Yes. Nice lady, the complete opposite of her brother. But clearly, she cares a great deal for him. He would never have been released without her intervention...So what happened with your concerns about his overpayment and the bloodwork?"

"It worked out," she replied, noting how even talking about Jimmy cranked up her anxiety.

"Listen, I hope you're not still upset with me for not getting worked up about your phone conversation the other day. If we violated everyone who skips a couple doses of medication, we'd be out of a job. So how many times have you seen him now?"

"Twice," she said, wondering at the shift in Anton's attitude.

"Is he what you'd expected?"

"Not really. For one, he lost over a hundred pounds. Said that he'd gained it as a way of trying to avoid the unwanted attention of some of the Croton residents. I think he's got quite a bit of PTSD. And I'm not certain that the voice he says he hears is compatible with either schizophrenia or manic depression."

"But you do think he hears voices?"

"I do. But more along a dissociative spectrum."

"Please don't tell me you're going down the Ted Bundy route with him. Everyone's getting diagnosed with multiple personality disorder. *It wasn't me, Judge, it was my other me that hacked my wife into tiny little pieces."*

"I don't care what you call it, but he does flip between very different presentations. There's an almost sweet childlike Jimmy, and a split second later you have the feeling that he'd like to reach across the table and do something *very* nasty. And then there's this distant look he gets, as though he's looking through his body, but isn't really inside of it."

"You don't think he's schizophrenic?"

"I don't."

"So maybe it doesn't matter if he takes the meds."

"I think that's what he thinks. And to be fair, they give him a lot of problems. Did you know that he was a concert cellist, could have been a great one?"

"I'm sure I read that somewhere."

"Lithium and fine-motor control aren't the best of friends."

"He still plays?"

"Incredibly well. Apparently that's how he used to spend his sessions with Morris Kravitz."

Anton chuckled, "Morris was a character, but his monthly reports were on my desk when they were supposed to be. And I don't know how or when I turned into such a bureaucrat, but sometimes all I care about is getting the paperwork done and handed in on time."

"His reports don't say much," Barrett commented, "just when they met, how long each session was, and that the patient appeared to be stable and not engaged in any illegal activities."

"Do you doubt it?"

"I don't know what to think. At this point I'm just trying to figure out what makes him tick. I'd love to have interviewed Mason Carter…the guy who actually killed Nicole Foster and Stephen Guthrie."

"I knew Mason," Anton remarked, "he was a classic sexual sadist."

"You met him?"

"I did part of his prison evaluation. At the time I thought he was trying to manipulate a transfer into the forensic system. You know, follow Jimmy's lead. It didn't work though."

"He hung himself," Barrett said.

Anton nodded, keeping his eyes on the road. "In hindsight, I wonder if maybe he was telling the truth. But that's water under the bridge."

"Did he talk about Jimmy?"

"Some, did a pretty good job of implicating him. Said he'd been hired to kill Foster's fiancé. Of course, with his history he had zero credibility. The only real evidence was the cash found on Carter."

"Speculation?"

"Tons, but it's still a mystery."

Barrett sensed Anton holding back. She gently pushed. "Right, somehow Jimmy just happens to be in the apartment of a woman, who he's been obsessed with for years, who just broke his eighteen-year-old heart by telling him she's engaged."

"With no hard evidence to link him to the actual crime," Anton added.

"So why was he there? How did he get in?"

Anton turned off at the Croton exit. As the sports car climbed the gently sloped hill toward the red brick administration building he said, "I guess all of that is academic at this point. No one doubts that Jimmy was stalking her. Maybe he followed Carter, had some kind of rescue fantasy about stepping in after the boyfriend's killed. You know, like the knight in shining armor. Maybe he even intended to kill Carter. Which, if he'd actually hired him, would have been a good way to cover his tracks…plus, he'd come out looking like the hero."

Barrett looked across at her boss as he parked. She was torn—it felt good being able to discuss Jimmy's case, and to have a halfway decent conversation with Anton; on the other hand, she had the strong feeling that he was hiding things. She also knew that to call him on it would backfire. She thought about a saying that Sifu Li had taught her years ago, *"A lie is like a mole. When you try to dig it out, it will only burrow three times deeper."*

"You ready?" he asked, popping the release for the tiny trunk that just barely held their briefcases.

"Sure."

———

A Croton escort waited for Barrett and Anton, as they checked all sharp objects, beepers, and cellular phones at the guard desk.

Barrett wryly observed how careful the guards were, imagining that there had been hell to pay for the lapse that had resulted in the Charlie Rohr mess.

The first electronic steel door slid back while a guard walked them through a metal detector. Satisfied that they weren't carrying contraband or weapons, the second, and final, door opened.

"They're waiting for you," the escort informed them. "I was told you were going to be here half an hour ago."

"Traffic," Anton replied dully.

Barrett made an "mmm" noise and nodded her agreement.

They followed silently as their guide brought them to the locked elevators and then down two flights to the underground conference room.

How politically correct, Barrett thought, as she looked at the people seated around the scarred oak table. Even the furniture was arranged so that there was no definite head—just like the round table. All the players had assembled for George Fitzsimmons' case conference, including the man himself, who sat between his attorney and his silver-haired mother.

They'd duded him up in a tan leisure suit, a lawyer's ploy designed to make the six-foot-five redhead appear less threatening. Tan leisure suits were about as low as you could go on the apparel food chain. If you wanted someone to seem powerful you put them in black—like the judge—if you wanted them to appear weak and ineffectual—wouldn't hurt a fly—stick them in a tan leisure suit.

She looked at all the doctors, social workers, consumer advocates, and administrators, most of whom she knew from other such conferences.

She took a seat and sipped from a styrofoam cup of coffee that had been handed to her. A plate of dry chocolate-filled cookies landed in front of her, she selected from the meager offerings and passed them to Anton, as though they were so many communion wafers being dispensed to the faithful. In front of her was a thick stack of documents that contained information on the patient, as well as a blank treatment plan onto which they were encouraged to "brainstorm."

She found it hard not to be cynical as she counted thirty-two people in the room and quickly calculated the meeting's cost to the taxpayers. Thirty-two professionals at an average of seventy dollars an hour; it would be at least two hours, plus travel time—around ten grand. And there'd be more meetings and...

Her thoughts drifted while Felicia Morgan, Croton's medical director, called the meeting to order.

Anton nudged her and slid across a piece of paper.

She looked down at his hastily scrawled note, "Five bucks says Felicia is going to recommend a group home, everyone will agree, and then they won't be able to find one willing to take him."

Barrett grinned, grabbed the paper and wrote back, "Duh."

Dr. Felicia Morgan—an intense rail-thin woman in her forties, with black-rimmed glasses and dark hair that appeared to have been slicked back with brilliantine—turned to the patient/prisoner. "Mr. Fitzsimmons, what do you think you'll need to make it this time? We don't want to see you have to come back."

Barrett bit the inside of her mouth, while the medical transcriptionist hurriedly typed every word.

"Supervision," George Fitzsimmons mumbled.

"Say more," Dr. Morgan urged.

"I know that if I'm off by myself I get into stuff. I need to stay on my medications, and I want to...but if I'm not supervised...I might forget or something."

"Do you know what kind of supervised setting you'd want?" Dr. Morgan asked.

Barrett felt like joining in.

216

"A group home," he replied on cue. "I think a group home would be best."

For the next hour and a half the assembled congratulated George on his "courage and creativity." They then set about identifying potential group homes, all of which had sent representatives to the meeting. They had all reviewed George's records and one by one they politely declined to have him come live with them.

As Anton had predicted, the meeting went nowhere. Dr. Morgan closed the session by gushing, "This is all part of the process. I think we made real progress today. George, don't be discouraged."

"I'm not," he mumbled, while staring down at his size-fourteen loafers.

His previously silent mother roared to life. She glared at Dr. Morgan.

"I'm calling the commissioner and the governor!"

"This is unacceptable!" George's legal aide added. "He needs to go to a least-restrictive setting!"

"You can't keep him here forever," his mother said, "it's not fair."

Barrett tuned out the brewing fight. She knew that Dr. Morgan would try to appease everyone while doing absolutely nothing. The truth was, George would remain at Croton for years. Unlike Jimmy, he wouldn't be able to buy his way out.

The meeting broke up and Barrett and Anton edged for the door. It was best to get away before getting tagged for some kind of pointless task or subcommittee. The first time she'd attended one of these Anton had advised, "Say little and keep your head low."

Those were words to live by. The first time she'd spoken up at the release hearing of another patient, she was immediately sucked into a several-months project looking at the availability of supervised apartments in the greater Manhattan area. Only after they'd finished the task did she discover that the same study had been done four times before, and nothing had been done to improve the housing situation.

"Anton," she whispered as they made their getaway, "are you in a hurry?"

"Why?"

"I want to grab a look at Jimmy Martin's old chart."

He looked at his watch. "It's going to be on microfiche."

"I know, but I'm curious about a few things. And besides, we're not going to make it back in time to do anything anyway."

Reluctantly, he agreed. They got into his Jag and drove across the grounds to Gunther Hall. They showed their badges to the security guard, emptied their pockets into plastic baskets, and ran their briefcases through the metal detector.

In the climate-controlled basement library, Barrett pulled up Jimmy's file on a microfilm viewer. At the top of the screen it indicated that over ten thousand pages of information had been scanned on James Cyrus Martin IV. She scrolled through the index to the section labeled, "disciplinary."

"Ouch," Anton remarked, reading over her shoulder.

"What was he up to?" Barrett commented as the screen filled with over a dozen separate incidents, for which he'd received disciplinary tickets.

She clicked on the first selection. Three months after Jimmy's incarceration, he'd been caught having sex with another patient—Jackson Osborn.

She thought back through her last session with Jimmy, but the archived report led her to believe that the sex was consensual. It involved the two men being discovered by a night-duty nurse in the bathroom.

She punched in Jackson Osborn's name. An equally large file appeared for the man who'd successfully pled not guilty by reason of insanity for numerous pedophilic offenses. But unlike Jimmy's file, his final entry read "deceased."

She clicked on it.

"He hung himself," Anton remarked, looking at the screen.

"Seems so," she answered dully, as she back-clicked to the report of the disciplinary hearing. "Just a month after this."

"Interesting," Anton said, "what else is there?"

She looked at the second entry in Jimmy's disciplinary file. This time the infraction centered around one of the guards, caught giving Jimmy a CD player. In the investigation that followed the guard was transferred when it was discovered that he'd received money from Jimmy's sister—a clear violation of hospital rules.

Next case was again a sexual infraction. This time with a guard— Otto Beardsley. The guard alleged that Jimmy had made advances to him and that in a moment of weakness he'd acquiesced. Mr. Beardsley was terminated. Barrett scribbled the guard's name and employee identification number onto a piece of paper.

As she went down the list, the cases broke down along two lines, bribes and sex. The sex part, at least, somewhat jibed with Jimmy's story. In some of the reports he stated that he was an unwilling, or at least unenthusiastic, participant; in others he said nothing. The bribes were something else. Most were small, but there were obvious attempts to cover them up.

"Jesus," she muttered as she read through the fourth sex offense. Similar to the others, it involved Jimmy and two other patients being found by a security guard in a supply closet. The report verified some of the brutality that Jimmy hinted at; in this instance it seemed clear that Jimmy had been raped.

Barrett scribbled down the names of the perpetrators—Carl Greer and Lars Nordstrand—and passed them to Anton. "Could you pull these two up?" she asked, while she read through the incident report.

Anton switched on the adjacent microfilm viewer. He stared at the screen and said nothing.

"What did you find?" Barrett asked.

"This isn't good," he remarked, his face illuminated by the glowing monitor.

"What?" Barrett asked, half listening while she read through the guard's account.

"Lars Nordstrand killed himself in solitary."

"How the hell do you do that?"

"Not easy, even back then." Anton scrolled down, "Somehow he managed to get hold of a sheet and he looped it around a nail head in the wall."

"What about the other one?" she asked, sensing with a sickening certainty what the answer would be.

"Greer...let's see...oh shit!"

"Dead?"

"Dead."

"How?" she asked, tightening her gut.

"Looks like he was shot."

"In here?"

"No, transitioning back to the community. Let's see, the handwriting is hard to read…on a scheduled leave back to his mother's house in the Bronx, and both he and his mother were shot on the street. She survived; he didn't."

"How long after the incident?"

"About four years."

"So Jimmy would have still been at Croton?"

"Looks like it."

"And Nordstrand?"

Anton flipped to the other record. "Six months after." He paged down to the death certificate on Lars Nordstrand. "This is interesting, too."

"Yes?"

"The coroner lists asphyxiation as a result of hanging as the cause of death on Nordstrand, but he also gives a secondary cause…hypoglycemia."

"Huh?"

"I'm just reading what's here. It says Nordstrand's blood sugar was 20 at the autopsy."

Barrett felt the walls of the underground library press in on her. She pictured Jimmy winking as he asked her if she had a sister, she thought about Morris Kravitz and his insulin. She saw Ralph lying in the drawer at the morgue, bits of gravel embedded in his cheek. Pushing back from the table, she looked over Anton's shoulder. "Go to his medical file." She was finding it hard to breathe.

The two psychiatrists stared at the screen as Lars Nordstrand's yearly physicals and volumes of laboratory test results passed before their eyes.

"He wasn't diabetic," Barrett said. "And if someone's blood sugar is that low, there's no way he could be with it enough to hang himself, especially in such a creative way."

"Maybe it was a lab error?" Anton suggested.

"Maybe," Barrett replied, a part of her wanting to divulge her suspicions about Kravitz's death. But she held her tongue. How was it that Anton didn't know all of this? If he'd been involved in Jimmy's release, why should any of this be a surprise?

She went back to her terminal and paged through the last half-dozen incidents—all minor infractions that involved gifts to various employees. "Well, for the last five years he was here it seems Jimmy kept his nose clean."

"He would have had to in order to get released."

She stared down at her notes and then glanced at Anton.

"What are you thinking?" he asked.

"Nothing good," she said, mentally tallying the shocking deaths that surrounded her patient. "I think I've seen enough. Let's get out of here?"

"Sure…Bad things happen to people in here, Barrett," he said.

"They do," she replied, convinced now that Anton was deliberately concealing stuff. But why?

As they got up to leave, her beeper chirped.

"I'll be right back," she walked across to a phone and dialed the number on the display.

"Barrett?" Hobbs' voice felt like a balm on her jangled nerves.

"What's up?"

"I thought you'd want to know, the results came back on Kravitz's insulin."

"And?"

"It's insulin all right, but the concentration is ten times higher than it should be. Kravitz was murdered. We've pulled Sheila Kravitz in for questioning…Where are you right now?"

"Croton," she said, "I've been going through Martin's records."

"Find anything?"

"I can't talk here," she glanced over at Anton who was waiting with briefcase in hand by the elevator. "I don't think Sheila killed her husband."

"That makes two of us, but the only fingerprints on the bottle belong to her and her husband."

"Are you going to be around later?" she asked.

"Sure."

"I'll call you. Too many things aren't adding up."

"And I bet our boy is in the middle of it."

"Yes."

"He wants something from you, Barrett. And it's not duets."

"Don't be jealous," she tried to tease, but her anxiety was too high to carry it off.

"I don't want to see you get hurt," his tone deadpan.

"I can handle myself."

"I know. But sometimes the best strategy is to pull back until you know what you're facing."

"I can't run, Ed. Even if I wanted to, and right now there's a part of me that's scared shitless…It's not an option."

"You say that, Barrett. But you've got to be smarter than that. What am I missing?"

Barrett knew exactly why she couldn't run. She could hear her father's drunken rage, her mother screaming for Barrett to go to her room, the bruises on her face. The long drive. The paralyzing fear when he'd tracked them down. Sophie's words to her mother, *"There's a time to run, and a time to stay and fight."* If Jimmy killed Ralph—and God knows who else—leaving town wouldn't help. Erotomaniacs weren't so easily dissuaded. Once she started to run, she'd never be able to stop.

There was a pause. "Maybe someday you'll tell me," Hobbs said softly.

"Maybe."

EIGHTEEN

LATER THAT NIGHT, HOLED up in her cave-like Manhattan office, Barrett tried to work. The phone rang. "Hello?" Who'd be calling this late? It was after eight, and aside from the guard in the lobby and the cleaning crew, she was the only one left. She'd stayed, ostensibly to edit a chapter in her book. But the truth was, she didn't want to go home.

"Dr. Conyors," a woman's muffled and frightened voice spoke.

"Yes."

"If you want to get Jimmy Martin, find Gordon Mayfield."

"Who is this?" A sliver of fear shot up her spine.

"Gordon Mayfield," she repeated and then hung up.

Still holding the phone, Barrett muttered, "What the hell?" She focused on the woman's voice; it could have been anyone, even a man pretending to be a woman—even Jimmy for that matter. But why call so late? Either this person was expecting to get put into her voice mail, or knew she was here; not a comforting thought. She glanced around and considered calling the security desk to make certain that no one else had entered the building. She opened the door and peered down the dark hallway. As she did, the motion detectors turned on the lights; she was alone. She went back into her office, locked the door and jiggled the handle.

Standing in the middle of the room, she strained to hear the noises of the building, the gurgle of hot water through the radiators, a soft and distant buzzing from a dying florescent bulb. "Gordon Mayfield...why do I know that name?" She opened her bottom drawer and pulled out the growing stack that she'd collected on Jimmy. She'd given Marla the task of cajoling the Croton librarian into printing out several hundred pages of Jimmy's records and faxing them over. It had taken the better part of the day, but finally Barrett could spend the time she needed to hunt through Jimmy's history and find the pieces that had been overlooked. The thing that made him tick.

She ran through her notes from the visit to Croton, wondering if Mayfield's name was there; it wasn't. Still, it was familiar, on the tip of her tongue. "Mayfield," she repeated aloud as she flipped through records.

She tapped her mouse, the computer emitted an electronic twang and the screen blinked on. She ran the cursor down, called up the database for the center, and typed in *Mayfield, Gordon*.

What came back was not what she'd expected. The screen filled with a full page of patient names, all of them connected to Gordon Mayfield—MD. And then she remembered; Gordon Mayfield had been a psychiatrist here, but before her time. She'd even worked with clients who'd been treated by him. But that wasn't what people mentioned on those rare occasions when his name came up; he was the psychiatrist who'd killed himself. Sad, but not earth-shattering.

Why Mayfield would occasionally surface had to do with the how, the why, and the where of his death.

The story had it that he'd been caught sleeping with a patient. Scheduled for a disciplinary hearing, he was most likely about to lose his job and possibly his license. The day before the hearing, he went up to the roof—a twelve-story structure—and jumped.

But what, she wondered, *did he have to do with Jimmy?*

Scrolling down the patient list, she looked for a line that connected Mayfield to James C. Martin IV; there was nothing. As she got to the last name she realized that the database only went back eleven years. Jimmy would have been at Croton. She glanced over the stack of Jimmy's records on her desk, it was over a foot thick and it was only a fraction of what existed.

Trilling her fingers on the edge of the desk, *what about?* She logged onto the Croton library's web site. She typed in her password and gained access to the on-line literature search. She put in Mayfield's name; seven references materialized. Apparently, he'd written a series of articles on the assessment of sexual deviants, published in the *Journal of Criminal Psychiatry.* She printed out the page and placed it beside the monitor.

"Okay," she muttered, "that's something, but what else?" With her tongue clicking against the roof of her mouth, she switched from the library to her favorite on-line search engine. She again typed in *"Gordon Mayfield"* and waited to see what, if anything, appeared from the interlaced strands of the electronic web. There were forty-seven hits with Mayfield's name. As she scrolled through she discarded most of them, but halfway through she came upon a hyperlink for a web site called *Sex Killer Klub.*

"You've got to be kidding." Feeling repulsed, she double-clicked on the blue hyperlink and headed into a sick corner of the Internet. She had a millisecond's hesitation, knowing that all the clinic's computers were routinely audited to determine where the employees had traveled on the Web. It was a standing joke that Barrett's was always filled with pornographic and fetish-based web sites—a part of her research. She'd often interview anonymous individuals in chat rooms, where they seemed eager and willing to discuss their most secret and potent fantasies.

She read through the options and clicked a box titled *Rogues Gallery*. As she went down the list of high-profile killers, Mayfield's name was nowhere. Returning to the home page, she hunted for the scrap of data that connected her original search to the web page. She found a single phrase that was a different color that said—*reference materials*—and clicked. And there they were—Mayfield's articles. She pressed *print*.

As her state-issue Hewlett Packard hummed to life, spitting out twelve pages per minute, she rolled back and stared at the screen, a cartoon image of a man with an erect penis holding an ax above his head chased a woman across the monitor—someone's idea of a joke. But what the hell did this have to do with Jimmy?

She pulled the warm pages off of the tray and focused on the small print. Mayfield's style was dry and academic. The first article was titled *"Childhood Antecedents of Sexual Sadism."* As she read through the introduction, what caught her attention was the promise of "several case studies will be presented to illustrate common patterns of deviant upbringing." Immediately, she thought of her last session with Jimmy. She'd pushed him hard and he'd begun to give her something useful about his parents. She'd been the first person he'd ever told, he'd said, but maybe, just maybe…She rifled through the pages, looking for the small indented paragraphs that contained the case studies. The first was about a man convicted of serial rape and murder. About a rural upbringing that involved frequent beatings and repeated sexual abuse. The next gave the story of a man who spent much of his childhood in the care of pornographers who'd used him as a "model" in their magazines. None of this was news to Barrett. Children who'd been abused, raped, and tortured were much more likely to go on and do the same to others. The third report was about a famous serial killer where there was no history of abuse, but from an early age the subject had engaged in sadistic activities with animals that culminated in his setting his grandmother's bed on fire—with her in it. He was subsequently sent off to a residential school for delinquent children and then released upon the general public at eighteen. In the paragraphs that followed, Mayfield discussed the classic triad of cruelty to animals, bedwetting, and fire setting that were once thought to be the hallmarks of early sociopathic behavior. The sexual behavior, he hypothesized, started with the development of masturbatory fantasies during puberty, where aggressive impulses that had been previously played out with weaker children on the playground and in the neighborhood, now focused on erotic themes.

Barrett rubbed her temples as she read through the rest of the case studies. None were Jimmy's.

The second article, "*Co-conspiracy among Sexual Deviants,*" was a study of cases that involved gangs and partners in crime. Again Mayfield illustrated his points with detailed case studies. Barrett scanned the unbound pages, homing in on the clinical reports.

"No shit!" she blinked and stared down at a longer case study that spilled onto two pages. "It couldn't be." She read it carefully:

Case 3: Patient is a 24-year-old Caucasian male currently incarcerated in a high-security forensic hospital for his involvement in the abduction, rape, torture, and murder of a 21-year-old woman and her 24-year-old boyfriend. Despite multiple clinical assessments, the nature of his relationship with the convicted murderer has never been elucidated. For the purposes of this study the patient consented to a series of three Amytal hypnotic interviews. As such, the clinical information must be viewed in that context. This writer was unable to corroborate much of the material as the actual murderer committed suicide by hanging. Similarly, no member of the patient's family was willing to be interviewed.

The patient described his early childhood as being one of extreme wealth, sexual victimization, and emotional deprivation. He reported that from an early age he was repeatedly sodomized by his father and witnessed infidelities with both of his parents. His only source of succor came in the form of a close bond with his twin sister. He stated that beginning around the age of twelve he masturbated, using rescue fantasies that often involved fairy-tale-like plot lines, with damsels in distress, sleeping princesses, etc. The fantasies are voyeuristic in that he becomes aroused from watching the object of his desire and repulsed from thoughts of actual physical contact.

Patient, who is an accomplished artist, attended a high school for gifted children. There he encountered, and devel-

oped an erotomanic fixation on, a young instructor. He be-
lieved that she was in love with him, and his records indi-
cate that he stalked her for at least the three years prior to her
murder. He stated that they were to be married, and that she
was carrying his child. When confronted about her intentions
to wed another man, he stated that she was "testing" him.

The crimes, for which the patient was arrested, occurred
over a three-day period where this woman and her fiancé
were tortured and eventually killed by a second individual
with a history of severe sexual sadism. The subject became
markedly agitated and disorganized during this portion of
the interview. At times he appeared to be dissociating and re-
peatedly begged his sister to, "make him stop."

At the time of his arrest he was discovered by the police in
the closet of the murdered woman. Much of this interview is
corroborated by circumstances of the arrest, which verify the
patient's story. He persistently stated that he never physically
harmed either murder victim. An interesting and unresolved
footnote from this crime is that, according to the autopsy of
the female victim, she was indeed pregnant, although the fa-
ther of the fetus was undetermined.

Barrett's heart raced; this was Jimmy, it couldn't be anyone else.
It was also the type of article that would no longer be allowed into
a journal, for the simple fact that anyone who knew the patients
would be able to identify them from reading it. It also explained
why Ellen, years ago, hadn't wanted Barrett to interview her brother;
Mayfield had crossed the line. At that moment, Barrett could have
cared less; this was new information—at least to her.

She looked at the date on the article and subtracted back. About halfway through Jimmy's time at Croton, his parents had still been alive.

She glanced at the clock, it was after midnight. "You need to go home," she whispered, but her thoughts were buzzing.

"Let's see…you get a crazy phone call. Interesting, and a little freaky. But, who was it? They know Jimmy, and also Mayfield."

The printer stopped and a blinking orange light flickered. A message appeared on the monitor letting Barrett know that the paper had run out. As she slit open a fresh ream, she envisioned the scenes described in the case study. A lot was hidden in Mayfield's prose. She shuddered at the thought of what Nicole Foster and Steve Guthrie had endured during those three days. And if Jimmy were to be believed, it made no sense. If he believed that Nicole had loved him, why would he have let her be killed? The fiancé kind of made sense, get him out of the way…but it didn't add up. And what if he hadn't been dissociating when he pleaded with Ellen to make Mason Carter stop; what if she'd actually been there?

She thought about the method that Mayfield had used to get the information—Amytal, a drug notorious for encouraging a mixture of fantasy and reality. On the plus side, it showed that Jimmy was a good hypnotic subject; not surprising considering his history of repeated childhood trauma. It was well documented that children who'd been severely abused often developed the ability to hypnotize themselves as a way to block out the pain. As adults, that ability often persisted, and was thought to be the underpinning behind a variety of personality disorders—including Dissociative Identity Disorder, a.k.a. Multiple Personality Disorder.

The printer hummed and spat out the last pages. She gathered them up and dropped them into her briefcase. She reached in and retrieved the one that contained Jimmy's case study; she stared at the title. Mayfield's hypothesis on *Co-conspirators* was that an individual deviant might not act alone, but in the company of a like-minded other, all bets were off. From Mayfield's perspective Jimmy and Mason Carter had a symbiotic relationship, and it was no coincidence that Jimmy was in that apartment.

There were answers here, but the article raised new questions, such as, how would a rich kid like Jimmy hook up with a low-life jailbird like Carter? And if Jimmy and his sister were so close, why didn't she intervene before things got out of hand? And if Jimmy's sexual fantasies were about rescuing damsels in distress, what went wrong? And more ominously, if this was a pattern—working with a partner—had there been other Mason Carters? Was there one now? "Oh, God," she cradled her head in her hands. "How could they have let him out?" And then in a whisper, "And how the hell are you going to get him back?"

Barrett scribbled down names. She started with Nicole Foster and her fiancé, and then added the Croton patients and the guard, who'd been involved with Jimmy and subsequently died, then came Morris Kravitz, and the phlebotomist who'd had her pelvis shattered while transporting Jimmy's blood to the lab. And what about Mayfield—it was a suicide, right? Jimmy would have been locked away…but maybe that was the point; Jimmy didn't work alone. He never did.

Barrett shuddered. Over the years she'd worked with hundreds of murderers; poking around in the psyche of sexual deviants was nothing new. So why was she so frightened? Everything about this case was wrong, starting with the simple fact that Jimmy Martin should never have been released. He was not in the category of those who can be rehabilitated. Erotomanic delusions don't go away, and they don't respond to therapy or drugs. She couldn't fathom what would have led the board to let him out.

"They didn't know," she told herself, logging off the computer. And now he was all hers.

She grabbed her briefcase and headed out. Her thoughts focused on a single theme—how to get him locked up.

She strode quickly through the night-lit Manhattan streets, racking her brain for something concrete to get him sent back. She replayed the mystery phone call in her head; she was missing something. The caller had tried to disguise her voice. Why bother…unless…unless it was someone whose voice Barrett might normally recognize. "Huh," she said aloud, pulling the attention of a man she passed on the sidewalk.

It had to be someone she knew and someone who knew Jimmy, or at least knew of him. She thought of Sheila Kravitz, who kept referring to Jimmy as the Croton patient.

Last night over dinner in Little Italy, she'd asked Hobbs about what had happened when they'd brought her in for questioning.

He'd seemed convinced that she had nothing to do with her husband's death, a view that Barrett shared. He'd also expressed concern at the coldness of the trail. Too much changes at a crime scene over the course of a couple weeks; vital evidence gets inadvertently destroyed.

He'd also obtained copies of monitoring logs on Jimmy. As expected, they showed that he rarely left his home, and whenever he did, there was always notation of a corresponding phone conversation where he'd asked for, and received, permission to go beyond his geographic boundaries.

But what was now clear, and she berated herself for not catching it earlier, was that Jimmy didn't need to go out. In fact, it all came back to the tag line he'd used over and over at the time of his arrest, *"I never touched her."*

Barrett crossed the street and glanced back. She had the creepy feeling of being watched. She angled across the intersection, keeping a sideways glance at the street, trying to judge whether any of the pedestrians altered their paths. There were couples out walking, probably heading back from dinner or a show. Lone men and women darted in and out of the all-night convenience stores. She stopped on the corner of 5th and 27th Street. For a split second she made eye contact with a dark-haired man in an expensive black leather coat as he rounded the opposite corner and then headed uptown.

"How did you miss this?" she mumbled, trying to calm herself with the sound of her voice. Jimmy had a pattern; he needed an accomplice. Barrett scanned the streets, her eyes in the wide-focus mode she used when sparring. Everything seemed like just another night in Chelsea. But someone was out there doing Jimmy's bidding. Money would be no object, and finding someone in Manhattan willing to do anything for the right price was wholly possible.

The part she hated thinking about was that she figured into Jimmy's delusions. The evidence was piling up; it had been no accident that he'd asked for her. And if she followed that thought, it was no accident that Kravitz was killed...or Ralph.

She thought about Hobbs and how he'd pleaded with her to drop the case, to give it to someone else. He was right, she should have no contact with Jimmy. But in her gut she knew it was more complicated. If Jimmy was an erotomaniac, and she was the object of his delusions, there'd be no stopping him. In his mind he believed that she loved him, and if Mayfield was right, his every action, in some twisted way, was an attempt to prove his worth. It was starting to make sense. Ralph's death was just a hurdle, as was Kravitz's. "Oh shit!" She thought of Hobbs and whipped out her cell. As the phone rang her mind raced over all the people in her life. *This can't be happening,* she thought, and as Hobbs picked up, she blurted, "Ed, we've got to talk, and it's worse than I thought. I'm so fucking frightened."

NINETEEN

"WHAT DO YOU KNOW about Gordon Mayfield?" Barrett asked Anton over eggs and bacon at the Athena Diner three doors down from the clinic. She kept her eyes averted, not wanting him to see how frazzled she'd become.

"Before my time," he answered in a lowered voice. "Although he's something of a legend."

"Because he jumped?"

"The whole thing was pretty sordid. And after a few years the story gets twisted and the truth is hard to separate from the…speculative additions. What brings him up?"

Barrett hesitated; in the past she'd considered Anton a friend. The fact that this was their first breakfast together in over two months—something they used to do once or twice a week—was a clear indication that things had changed. "I got a weird call last night," she finally said.

"The guard mentioned you were here pretty late. In fact, you don't look like you slept at all."

"Couldn't sleep," she admitted, not comfortable with the fact that he'd plainly been checking on her, and wishing that she'd bothered to at least put on some lipstick.

"Losing your husband can't be easy," he commented. "You really should take time off," he looked at her and then shook his head. "So what did your call have to do with the unfortunate Dr. Mayfield?"

"It was odd, a woman's voice, but like she was talking through a towel."

"What did she want?"

Barrett considered telling him about the connection with Jimmy Martin; in the past she wouldn't have thought twice. "She didn't say much, just some stuff about Gordon Mayfield—rambled for thirty seconds and then hung up."

Anton dipped a toast point into a swirl of ketchup and egg yolk. "That's it?"

"Pretty much," Barrett lied.

"Probably some borderline he treated, just calling to let people know she's still alive. Or maybe there's substance to these legends," Anton remarked.

"What do you mean?"

"Well, the whole psychiatrist gone bad. Supposedly, and I hate to gossip, but he was caught sleeping with a patient. I don't know the details, but it's the kind of thing that you'd lose your license over, at least today. Back then, it was looser. Maybe that's who called."

"Interesting. So who was the allegedly slept-with patient?"

"No clue. I don't even know how much of that is accurate."

"Who would?" Barrett asked.

Anton took a swig of his coffee. "You might give George Housmann a call."

Barrett's interest perked at the name of the legendary forensic psychiatrist, who had recruited her, and then retired. "I didn't know he was still around," Barrett replied.

"In a manner of speaking. They made him emeritus and put him out to pasture right before you came. But back then, if anyone was going to be disciplined, George would have been front and center holding the whip."

———

The second she was back in the office, she tracked down Housmann's number. Three hours later she stood outside his Upper East Side apartment and rapped on the door.

"Dr. Conyors," a slight, silver-haired man dressed in gray flannel slacks, white shirt, navy blazer, and red silk tie greeted her in the hallway. "It's so nice to see you." He cocked his head forward, as though he were examining her through the thick lenses of his black-rimmed glasses. "Oh, but I'm forgetting…come in." And as he turned to lead her into his apartment, he stopped. "Please wipe your feet." He motioned toward a textured rubber pad in front of his door. Barrett stepped onto the soft squishy surface.

"There's a fast-drying fluid that destroys anything alive on the bottom of your shoes." He explained. "People carry all sorts of disease on the bottoms of their feet; horrible things that can live as spores for decades, just waiting for their chance. I'd rather not have them in my home."

Barrett complied, and wondered if this man, who had been a trailblazer in the field, and whom she'd met only once before when she had interviewed for the fellowship at the clinic, would actually be of any use.

"I'm so sorry to hear about your husband," he offered.

It surprised her that he even knew, "Thank you."

"He was a musician, wasn't he?"

"Yes."

"With the symphony?"

"Yes," she wondered at his interest. Had she mentioned Ralph at the interview those many years back? And then the smell hit, an antiseptic odor she associated with hospitals and prison infirmaries. She glanced down a long hallway, its floors covered in freshly waxed linoleum. Not what she expected in a pre-war building where hardwood floors were featured prominently in every real estate ad.

"Tragic." He led her inside. As she trailed behind the stooped octogenarian, she stole glances inside seamlessly joined glass-fronted bookcases that lined both walls. It reminded her of Jimmy's magnificent library, only here the cases were made of steel and seemed more appropriate for an institution than someone's home. Dr. Housmann stopped and turned back to face Barrett. "I don't get many visitors these days, please forgive the mess." And he slid back the paneled pocket doors that led into his living room.

Barrett blinked as her pupils shrank to pinpoints under the assault of bright sun that spilled through eight floor-to-ceiling windows that faced east and south.

Housmann watched his guest's reaction, "It's something isn't it? My wife had the whole thing curtained off, but after she died, I did away with all that. Sunlight fights depression."

"You have amazing views," she commented, taking in the vista that included the Empire State Building and the East River.

"I've had this apartment for over fifty years," he said. "We got it when we were married. Please sit." He motioned toward a grouping of 1950s metal-framed leather chairs that had once been red and were now a sun-washed pink. "So, you had some questions about Dr. Mayfield?"

"Yes, you were the director of the forensic center when he was there."

"Correct," Housmann pursed his thin purplish lips together. "An unpleasant business."

"I'm working with one of the patients who I believe he interviewed for his studies on deviant sexual behavior."

"It's interesting how someone's research can mirror their own peculiarities," he replied.

"In what way?"

"You're quick. That's good. I hope we have a chance to talk about some of your papers. I have to tell you that I think they're quite good, but that there are areas where you've missed some fundamental causalities." He pushed a strand of long white hair back over his thinning pate and tucked the end under his collar. "But I know that you've come for other reasons…curious, that after all these years, you're the first to ask about Mayfield. I suppose that like myself, anyone who was around during that time would just as soon forget…Mayfield didn't think that the rules applied to him. That was his undoing. All in all, a messy business. If I weren't such a dinosaur I wouldn't even talk to you about it, but at this point," he clicked his tongue, "I can't see that it matters. It's ancient history. You said you're meeting with one of his test subjects, which one?"

Barrett hesitated.

"Good girl," Housmann remarked, "you're wondering if this is a breach of confidentiality or not. Don't worry, I'm still on faculty, we can look at this as supervision. What we say here goes no further, correct?"

"Yes, and thank you. I've been meeting with James Cyrus Martin."

Housmann perked, his watery blue eyes peered intently at her through the magnifying surface of his convex lenses. He shook his head, about to say one thing, but only commenting, "Morris Kravitz was one of my students…I was so sorry to hear about his death; he wasn't an old man."

"I've taken over the case," Barrett replied, but not wanting to divulge the emerging facts around Morris Kravitz's murder.

"Why did you take it?"

Housmann's question stopped Barrett. "It seemed like an interesting case."

"If you're going to lie to me, we should stop."

"The money."

"Thank you," he said. "After all, we're talking about one psychiatrist who went down a wrong road, and I have a sick feeling that before we're done today, we'll see that particular path is well traveled." Housmann looked at the floor and then back at Barrett. He tapped a finger against the polished-chrome arm of his chair. "The question that I have to answer is, can *you* be trusted? I'd like you to start by presenting the case and then tell me exactly what brought you here."

Barrett wondered if this wasn't a waste of time, and that all she was going to accomplish was filling a lonely old man's afternoon.

"Well?" he asked.

And for the next fifteen minutes she presented a detailed account of her work with Jimmy Martin, ending with the late-night phone call that set her on the path of Gordon Mayfield.

"That was very clear, and fascinating," he said, having interrupted her only twice for minor points of clarification. "What is your diagnostic impression of your patient?" he asked.

In spite of herself, Barrett warmed to Dr. Housmann. He reminded her of what she had most enjoyed about her training: the pursuit of knowledge for its own sake. "Jimmy's diagnostic picture is complex," she said. "From the time of his arrest through ten years at Croton he carried a diagnosis of schizophrenia and schizoaffective disorder—bipolar type."

Housmann snorted derisively. "What do you think?"

"I think our *DSMIV* has a hard time with people like Jimmy," she commented, citing the diagnostic manual used by all psychiatrists.

"Having survived *DSM* versions one through four, you have to forgive me for taking a jaundiced view of the Chinese menu school of diagnosis. It's fine for Egg Foo Young, but falls short when it comes to people. So tell me how *you* think about your patient, if you don't believe he has schizophrenia or that other garbage-pail label."

Barrett cracked a smile as she listened to Housmann's diatribe. "Jimmy has a core defect in his personality. As to whether it's a nature or nurture thing, it's impossible to separate, and purely academic in relevance. Both of his parents exhibited polymorphous perverse and antisocial behaviors. Did they teach him that or was he born that way?"

"As you say," Housmann commented, "it's academic."

"Anyway, this gets coupled with severe post-trauma fragmentation and a high IQ and what I'm seeing is an extremely clever and narcissistic sociopath, who has some psychotic features, as well."

"But not psychotic in the way you think a schizophrenic is psychotic."

"No, Jimmy's voices are much more in keeping with a type of almost-continuous flashback."

"And they don't respond to the medication," he offered.

"I don't think so."

"So you keep him on the pills because…"

"To try and decrease his aggressive urges. But there's more, too. Sitting with him I get this feeling of instability in his affect. His moods shift radically and are accompanied by significant changes in vocal pitch, body carriage, demeanor. I'm pretty certain that he dissociates, and if we were going with the *DSM* I'm certain he'd meet criteria for dissociative identity disorder—and trust me, I'm no fan of the multiple-personality quagmire."

"That makes two of us, but you can't ignore either your gut or the facts…Okay, so far I'm agreeing with your treatment and your assessment. But I still think you're overlooking something critically important. Or…" he peered at her intently, "you're holding back. Tell me the thing you don't want to say."

Barrett met Housmann's gaze, and sucked in a deep breath, "I think Jimmy has an erotomanic fixation on me."

"That's not good," Housmann replied.

"It gets worse."

"Tell me everything," he directed, "and if you think something doesn't matter, tell me anyway."

Casting aside any reticence, she gave him her suspicions, wondering if he'd think she was paranoid. She related the circumstances of Ralph's death, the similarity to the accident that maimed the phlebotomist, the finding that Kravitz's insulin had been tampered with, even the series of mysterious deaths that surrounded those who had interfered with Jimmy Martin at Croton.

Housmann listened intently, occasionally nodding, or asking for further detail.

When Barrett had unburdened herself fully, she paused, and looked up.

Housmann pursed his lips and exhaled on a sigh. "Oh, my…where to begin?…I've admired your work, and I know that you're a woman who looks for patterns. I'm similar. After fifty-odd years as a psychiatrist you realize that people, even very sick people, are more alike than they're different. In the man you've just described, who seems to function with another—what Mayfield called a co-conspirator—there are some old truths that might be helpful."

Barrett pushed back, "You're talking about anaclitic depression."

"Right, no one uses that term anymore, but essentially Jimmy Martin feels empty inside and he needs someone to complete him. I believe this role has been mostly filled by his sister, but apparently there may have been others, such as the woman who was killed…now he needs someone else."

"Not a comforting thought."

"Good. It shouldn't be, but let's push further. In a child who was as badly abused as your patient, it's common to see these sorts of aberrations. It's caused by a disruption and perversion of the attachment process. The child falls off the developmental curve in particular ways. What might those be?" he quizzed.

245

"I think what you're getting at has to do with trust."

"Keep going…how does the child fall behind?" he urged. "What patterns emerge from that early disruption?"

"Aggression and an inability to handle frustration…"

"Keep going."

Barrett looked out a window, and suddenly understood where Housmann was taking her, "Emptiness and an incredible desire to be completed, to not be abandoned."

"Yes," he said, "now combine that unending emptiness and potent fear of abandonment and rejection with a brilliant sociopath and what do you get?"

"He's looking for someone."

"Yes!" Housmann agreed. "Probably for all of his life, Jimmy is looking for his other half. It's the only way he knows to make himself feel alive, even if it's only for a limited time, like a borderline who cuts or burns herself. But the big payoff for him, at least in his own mind, is finding the perfect somebody who will complete him."

"I left out something," Barrett said, meeting Housmann's gaze.

"I know, I was hoping you'd give me the missing piece."

"When I was much younger, like Jimmy and his sister I was involved in competitive music programs. In fact, I even played in recitals with the Martin twins."

"You think he remembered you from that? I think it's more likely with his narcissism than it's your accomplishments as a psychiatrist that attracted him. You have a remarkable body of work for someone so young. And despite your attempts to downplay your physical attractiveness, you are a beautiful woman."

Barrett squirmed, never comfortable with these kinds of compliments. "There's more," she said. "The Martin twins were supposed to be the stars of the show. My first competition, I was nine, my teacher wanted me to play *Für Elise*—I thought it was too easy. I wanted to win."

"So what happened?"

"I did a last-minute substitution and played something I liked, something harder—a Chopin etude."

"Which one?"

"C minor."

Housmann snorted, "*The Revolutionary*…I imagine that raised a few eyebrows."

"I got a standing ovation."

He chuckled, "So Jimmy's not the only one with a bit of narcissism."

"No."

"Nothing wrong with that, you wouldn't have gotten as far as you had without it. Most physicians, as you're well aware, have a healthy dose of self-admiration. Which leads us back to why you've come. While we all may be somewhat grandiose and self-important, most of us adhere to a strong moral code. Those of us who go into psychiatry generally have some degree of empathy, as well. And the few of us who pursue forensics have the added responsibility to accept a higher moral standard—similar in some ways to what you want to see in a police officer and why when a cop goes bad that's such a violation of the public trust. Mayfield was morally unfit for his chosen career. You might find this harsh, but at the time I wasn't sorry that he jumped. It was a messy end to a very messy business."

"Tell me about that?"

"It's like an onion, there's always another layer. It doesn't surprise me that years after the fact you've come to ask these questions. As for his articles, I only saw them after they were published. Mayfield was no fool. I would never have given the go-ahead for research that was so clearly identifiable. Martin's sister was well within her rights to be upset."

"His sister?" she asked, flashing on that one curious line in the case study.

"Oh yes. I had several unhappy discussions with his sister. That's the part I most hated about being an administrator—all of the complaints. Ellen…yes that was her name. Ellen Martin had somehow gotten hold of Mayfield's articles. Anyone who knew the case would have recognized Jimmy…and her. If Mayfield hadn't jumped there could have been lawsuits."

"Do you think that's why he did it?"

"Hardly, at least not in full. Mayfield was slippery. Very glib, handsome, the kind of man who could get others to do the labor while he'd take the credit. Like a lot of our patients he believed the rules were made for other people."

"A sociopath?"

"That might be a bit harsh—accurate, but harsh." Housmann smiled wryly. "At the very least he was a malignant narcissist. No concept of other people's feelings. I couldn't blame her and I told her so."

"Who?"

"Martin's sister. The articles—at least the cases studies—were libelous."

"So you met Ellen Martin?"

"On a number of occasions, although mostly she called. A few times she did little more than scream at me over the telephone."

"What did she want you to do?"

"Punish Mayfield. Make certain he had no further contact with her brother."

"Did you?"

"I didn't have to, for Mayfield everything came to a head at the same time. There was the other, more pressing unpleasantness."

"Please, I need to know about that."

"Ethically, I shouldn't. After all, that is what we're talking about—a man who let his professional judgment erode, if in fact it was there in the first place."

Barrett opened her mouth.

"But…" Housmann said raising his hand in front of him. "You put your trust in me, and I'll do the same. What do you want to know?"

"Is it true that he had an affair with a patient?"

"Yes, at least one that we knew of."

"Was he going to lose his license?"

"Not likely, back then, although I would have seen to it that he was terminated from the clinic."

"Who was the woman?" she asked, wondering if it was someone she'd met, or at least knew of, in the forensic system.

Housmann pushed back. He looked hard at Barrett and said nothing.

"Did you know who the woman was?" Barrett repeated.

"I heard you the first time. Yes, I knew her," he admitted. "But now I am in a quandary. You see, everything to this point doesn't have much impact on the living; I don't even see how this relates to the James Martin case. But we've just moved into something trickier."

"Why's that?"

"Well for starters, the woman in question is very much alive. I doubt she'd want this to resurface."

"I thought she was in the system."

"Was…she *was* in the system. Before I tell you anything more, I need you to tell me why this is so important."

"I'm not certain," Barrett confessed. "This could be a dead end, but Gordon Mayfield, in his case study—however unethical it might have been—got further with Jimmy Martin than anyone else."

"Because he cheated and used Amytal," Housmann said.

"Yes."

"That was Gordon in a nutshell. The fastest line between two points—and if morals stood in the way he'd just go through them. But you were saying…"

"Mayfield not only discovered what Jimmy was doing in Nicole Foster's apartment, he also got to a good piece of the *why*."

"I still don't see what that has to do with knowing the name of the woman Mayfield was screwing."

"I think that Jimmy had something to do with Mayfield's death."

"You need to redo your math; Martin would have still been in Croton when Mayfield jumped. Unless…"

"Exactly," Barrett said, knowing that the elder psychiatrist had made the logical conclusion. "He had someone else do it for him. He's like a two-headed animal. The only problem is every time one of his heads gets cut off—like Mason Carter—he grows a new one."

"Like the hydra," Housmann commented. "And of course there was his sister. I thought she had the makings of a good slander case against Mayfield. But I also doubted whether she'd bring such a sordid piece of business into court. That was part of Mayfield's gift. He made these excursions into the world of the morally bereft, but he wasn't stupid. He knew that Jimmy Martin would be recognized by anyone familiar with the case. He also figured the family wouldn't do a thing about it, for fear of publicity. But maybe they had other resources. Ellen Martin struck me as a most capable young woman. And now that I think of it, her calls stopped the day that Mayfield jumped…" he was about to say something further and then stopped.

"Or was pushed," Barrett offered.

"As you say…"

"The woman who called me tried to disguise her voice. Which makes me think she had reason to believe that I'd recognize her."

"And you think this was the woman Mayfield was involved with?"

"It's possible."

"It is," he admitted. "What will you do if I give you her name?"

"Try to talk with her."

Housmann turned away from Barrett and stared out the windows. "I always thought it was a bad idea."

"What was?"

"Giving her the job."

"I'm not following."

"Of course not. Why do women end up at Croton?" he asked abruptly.

"Because they've committed a violent crime and for whatever reason are found either not competent to stand trial because of mental illness, or they go to court and are found not guilty by reason of…"

"Not that," he said dismissively. "What kinds of crimes land women in Croton?"

"Crimes of passion," she answered. "Is that what you mean?"

"Do better. What separates the men from the women?"

Barrett pictured the faces of women she'd interviewed over the years. "The victim," she finally answered. "They hurt the ones closest to them; typically their husbands, boyfriends, and occasionally their children and parents."

"Right. I often found the women to be far more the victim than the perpetrator."

"Please, Dr. Housmann, I need to know her name."

"Humor me," he said. "I just wanted to be certain that you'd be careful. The woman in question spent a number of years at Croton after *accidentally* killing her abusive husband. Mayfield worked very hard to have her released. In hindsight I should have known something was up. Gordon Mayfield was no altruist."

"You mentioned giving her a job," Barrett commented. "Where was that job?"

"I think you've figured it out," Housmann answered.

"At the center?"

"Right in one."

"Who is she?"

Housmann brought his hands together and touched his fingertips to his chin, "Marla Dean," he said.

"Marla?"

He nodded. "I knew it was a bad idea, but I couldn't see punishing her for Mayfield's doing, and then when he…died, I didn't have the heart to fire her. It would have been too complicated, and so…"

"How long was she at the clinic before Mayfield's death?" Barrett asked.

"A while, certainly more than a year."

"But she would have been at Croton when Jimmy was there?"

"Yes."

"And she would have known who Mayfield's test subjects were?"

"Probably." Housmann sighed, "I think she typed his papers for him, and as you've seen, the case studies were easy to figure out."

"Dr. Housmann," Barrett said, pulling her briefcase on to her lap. "I want to thank you for your time. But I think I should be going."

"Of course," he said, not moving from his chair.

"What is it?" she asked, sensing there was more.

"About a year after Mayfield's death. I got another call from Ellen Martin. She wanted me to try and get her brother released. She was very persuasive, and without coming straight out and offering me a bribe, she informed me that it would be very easy to underwrite my research through a foundation her family financed. A foundation that would never be traced back to her brother. Of course, I declined. Every year or so, I'd get a similar phone call, and my answer was always the same. A year after I retired and Anton had taken over as director, Jimmy Martin obtained his release."

"You think Anton took the offer?" she asked, feeling a pit form in her stomach.

"I couldn't say. I do know that Anton's time is running out; I don't think he'll get tenure. As far as his research goes, it's careful, but it's small in scope and lacks any spark—unlike yours. Ellen Martin's offer would have been difficult to resist."

Barrett said nothing as she took this in, and jagged bits of data clicked into place. It felt as though the floor were dropping out from under her. "I should get going."

"Dr. Conyors...Barrett?"

"Yes," she was halfway out of her seat.

"Do you have *any* hard evidence? Anything at all to take to the board?"

"I don't," she admitted.

"That's not good," he shook his head, his expression worried.

"Tell me something I don't know," she said, trying to make light, to not be so afraid.

"You need to drop this case," he said.

"I know...I can't."

"This could end very badly."

"I have to get him sent back," she replied, but knowing he was right.

"Is there anything I could say that would make you reconsider?"

She shook her head. "He needs to be locked up; he should never have been let out. If I don't do it..."

He stared at her through the thick, distorting lenses. "I suppose in your position, I'd do the same." He suddenly seemed tired, defeated. "I'll see you out," he raised out of his chair, wincing slightly from having sat so long. As he unlocked his front door, he commented, "I very much enjoyed our talk. If you ever want a sounding board, I hope you'll call."

"Thank you," she said, stepping back onto the liquid-filled mat.

"And Barrett…"

"Yes?"

"I know that I don't have to say this, but be very careful. And the minute you get the evidence you need, take it to the board and get far away from Jimmy Martin…and his sister."

TWENTY

"MARLA, COULD YOU COME in here?" Barrett asked over the telephone.

A breathy voice responded, "Give me a couple minutes, Dr. Conyors."

Barrett clasped her hands beneath her chin and waited. She wanted to call Hobbs, and share the information from Housmann. And yes, she admitted to herself, she wanted the reassurance of his physicality, his humor. But there was something else he had that she needed. It was a difference in logic that made him a brilliant detective. Prior to the catastrophe that had ruined his career, he'd rocketed through the bureau and achieved the rarely granted rank of Detective First Class. His promotion to deputy chief was based on years of superb work that ran the gamut from high-profile serial killers to overseeing the investigation in a white-collar investment scam that could have left thousands of city employees robbed of their pensions.

While Barrett spent her days working with criminals, the mentally ill, and the sociopathic, her job didn't require setting traps—Ed's did. Typically the folks she worked with had already been caught. Any traps were merely a clarification of the perpetrator's thought process and motive. Jimmy, however, needed to be caught. She needed something concrete that could override the obstacles Anton might now erect.

Her hand hovered over the telephone.

A tentative knock came.

"Yes?" Barrett called out.

"Dr. Conyors," the door cracked open and Marla Dean's little girl voice wafted across the office. "You wanted to see me?"

Barrett stared at the six inches of space in the doorway. All she could see of Marla were the tips of three nail-bitten fingers curled around the edge.

"Come in," Barrett said, not certain how to proceed with the skittish secretary. "If you could close the door and sit down."

Marla did as instructed; her long dark hair shadowed her face as she sat expectantly.

Barrett smiled and looked at Marla, as the painfully thin woman sat tentative, her collar bones sharply visible through the neckline of her gray polyester blouse. "You've done something different with your hair?"

"I got rid of the gray," she admitted.

"It's good…you've been here a long time," Barrett commented as she slowly opened her top desk drawer.

"Yes," the secretary looked around, as her hands struggled to find a position of comfort. They reminded Barrett of birds in search of a safe perch: should they land on her lap? The chair? Should they hold each other or would they continually flutter about at the end of her bony arms, never finding a place to rest?

"How long?" Barrett persisted as she pretended to hunt for a chart.

"Almost fourteen years," she whispered.

Barrett paused, "I bet you've seen a lot."

"We don't see much out there."

"Do you remember Dr. Housmann?" Barrett asked.

Marla nodded her head, "I think I should go back out and help Violet."

"I won't be much longer...you know I saw him recently."

"Dr. Housmann?"

"Yes, we talked about you."

"Why would you do that?" Marla gasped.

Barrett tried to make eye contact; the secretary looked away. "We talked about Gordon Mayfield, and your name came up."

Marla Dean stood abruptly, turned, and reached for the doorknob.

"Don't!" Barrett said.

Marla froze.

Barrett persisted, "I think you know why I'm bringing this up."

With her hand on the door and her back into the room Marla spoke, "It was a long time ago."

"I know. Now please sit down; I won't keep you long."

"I have work to do," the secretary pleaded.

"It won't take long." Barrett waited as Marla slowly turned around. She found herself guessing at the woman's age. An old forty or a young sixty? She wore an inexpensive gray blouse and dull-green cotton skirt, her synthetic-leather shoes looked as though they might have come from a 14th Street five-dollar bin. Marla clasped her hands together and with her eyes fixed on the floor, she waited.

"How long did you know Dr. Mayfield?" Barrett asked.

"Why do you have to bring this up?" Marla asked. "It was a long time ago."

"I know," Barrett said, "but it has bearing on a case I'm currently working on."

"Jimmy Martin," Marla whispered.

"Yes. So you know about the connection?" Barrett asked, while trying to reconcile Marla's wispy voice with that of her mystery caller. "Tell me what you know about that."

"I helped him."

"Who?"

"Gordon. He couldn't type." Marla dabbed at the corners of her down-turned eyes with the back of her sleeve.

"Are you okay?"

"I don't want to talk about this. I should have found another job after he…died. But it's like I was frozen here and Dr. Housmann told me that it wouldn't be necessary, that it wasn't my fault; so I stayed."

"So how did you know about Jimmy?"

"Gordon told me who they all were. I didn't know that was something he wasn't supposed to do. But Gordon didn't care a lot about other people's rules. If he had, he'd never have loved me."

Barrett reached across her desk and retrieved a mostly empty box of tissues. "Here," she handed them to Marla. "You loved him?"

"At first I thought he just wanted to have sex with me. He made so many promises, but then I guess he must have fallen in love with me." She said the last words slowly, testing them out like they were a piece of thin ice that might not hold her weight. "He told me that he loved me, but men say that."

"They do," Barrett agreed. "What made him different?"

"His actions. 'By their fruit you shall know them," Marla answered. "He got me out of that place, found me a job, never hit me, and if he was seeing other women I never found out about it."

Barrett listened as Marla laid out her criteria for a good man. "Did you love him?"

"I'm crying, aren't I?"

"Yes, but tears can mean different things."

"I don't know," she whispered letting her long hair fall forward, hiding her sharp features behind its curtain. "Everyone talks about love, but I don't know what it is. Maybe I loved Gordon, maybe I was just grateful. I cried when he died. After all these years I still cry when I think about him. So I try not to think about him."

"Do you know why he jumped?"

"He didn't jump!" Marla said, her voice taking on an uncharacteristic force.

"How can you know?" Barrett asked, wondering at the change.

"I knew Gordon; that's how I know. People kill themselves because they can't see a future; Gordon lived in his future. He had so many plans, so many things he was going to do. That's one thing about men, and a lot about Gordon, they talk about themselves. I thought he was so smart, I liked to listen to his plans. Sometimes I'd even tell myself that he'd marry me and I'd start to see a future too. But I knew *that* was never going to happen."

"How come?"

"Look at what happened when people found out about us. I didn't know it was so wrong."

"Maybe that's why he jumped?" Barrett offered, and immediately regretted her lack of tact.

"No," Marla stated.

"How can you be so certain?"

"He told me that it didn't matter, that they'd give him a slap on the wrist and as long as I kept my mouth shut, nothing would happen."

"He could have lost his job, maybe his license to practice."

Marla glanced up quickly. She shook her head, "I'm sure you know what you're talking about, but that's not how he saw it. I just figured he'd stop seeing me; I'd keep my mouth shut, I owed him that. I even started to look for another job, but it's not easy for me. Maybe now I could do it, but back then….How do you tell an employer why you were at Croton for four years? At least here it wasn't such a big deal. Only Gordon and Dr. Housmann knew."

"Why *were* you at Croton?"

"You don't know; Housmann didn't tell you?"

"A little, but I'd rather hear it from you."

"Why? It's ancient history, better to leave it alone."

Barrett wondered, was there a warning in her words? While this voice was different from her caller, the message sounded similar. "You don't have to tell me," Barrett offered, "but it could help me with my case."

"Jimmy Martin, again. I should have known. I told him not to use Jimmy's case."

"Really? How come?"

"You have to be careful with some people. In my case you have to be careful with everyone. Gordon never understood that. He thought that the things people did to end up at Croton couldn't touch him. He never took it seriously; he should have…and you should too."

Barrett startled as the secretary made fleeting eye contact; Marla was her mystery caller. "But why Jimmy? Did you warn him about other cases?"

"You ask so many questions…Jimmy had people looking out for him; the others didn't."

"Who?"

"His sister for a start. She made it clear to Gordon that he wasn't to publish Jimmy's story."

"How did she even know?"

"I'm not sure, probably Jimmy told her. Although, the way Gordon interviewed people wasn't like the rest of them. I think most of them didn't even remember what they'd told him."

"Why's that?"

"He'd give you a shot first, and then you'd still be awake, but not all the way. Almost like you were dreaming."

"He interviewed you that way?"

"Yes, but it wasn't a bad thing. I sometimes thought that's why he worked so hard to get me released."

"Because of the injection?"

"No, because of the truth. I could hear the words leaving my mouth; it was so easy to tell him everything. I wasn't ashamed; I didn't even cry. That used to be my problem; I had too many tears. They'd get so I couldn't speak. I couldn't stop myself. I got diagnosed as having a psychotic depression. I took a lot of pills for that but nothing stopped the tears. That is until Gordon came along."

"What was different with him?"

"I'm trying to tell you. I wasn't even his patient. He was writing an article about women who kill. Isn't it funny? That's how we met. I sometimes wondered what would happen if we did get married. What would we tell people, or our children, about how we first met? Isn't that something married couples do? 'Well,' I'd say, 'I was in the nut house after lighting my first husband on fire and Daddy wanted to interview me, because I'd killed the bastard.' Not exactly something you put on a greeting card."

"No," Barrett agreed, feeling badly that she'd never really noticed Marla after all these years. "You mentioned Jimmy's sister, what did you know about her?"

"Just that she called Gordon. He didn't tell me a lot about it, and then some lawyers came around, basically saying that there'd 'be problems' if he used Jimmy's case."

"How did he respond?"

"He didn't. He thought they'd get over it. 'Old news' he'd say. After a couple weeks he figured everyone would forget it. Plus, he couldn't see the Martin family wanting to bring a case."

"Because?"

"You read the article?"

"Yes."

"Too much negative publicity. Martin's family is big money. He didn't think they'd want to rehash the stories about Jimmy, and all of the other stuff. Jimmy was the one they locked up, but the entire family was sick."

"Did you know Jimmy?"

"I guess. Croton's a big place, but not that big. He wasn't on my unit, but I'd see him at assemblies. You could tell that he was having a hard time of it."

"How?"

"I don't know, maybe I didn't think about it at the time, but when I was writing up his case, I started to think about things," Marla glanced at Barrett. "Like he was by himself whenever I saw him, and some of the things that didn't make it into the article let you know that people were bothering him. I know what that's like. And then people talked."

"About?"

"That it wasn't a good idea to mess with Jimmy; stuff happened to people who messed with him...bad stuff. Like there was this guy who supposedly tried to pimp him, and he ended up getting killed in solitary."

"Killed or committed suicide?"

"There's lots of ways to make things appear different than how they are. The guy ended up with a sheet around his neck."

"Things like that sometimes happen," Barrett offered.

"I suppose, but you don't get sheets in solitary, just a rubber mattress."

"Good point."

"There were others, too; always with a good explanation, nothing that would get anyone to point fingers...like with Gordon."

"You don't think he jumped."

"No."

"Did you say anything?"

"What good would it do? He was dead, I wasn't. Would my saying anything change that? And I'm too much of a realist. I know what would have happened if I'd said something."

"What were you afraid of?"

Marla shook her head, "What wasn't I afraid of? One thing leads to another. I was seeing my parole officer twice a month and there were too many ways I could screw up and get sent back to Croton. Better to keep your head down and just hope no one notices you. Everyone assumed Gordon jumped because of his trouble about me. That's bad enough. If I'd lost my job that could have been a violation of my release agreement. Just like they thought he jumped, they also thought he'd taken advantage of me. That's a joke. If anything it would have been the other way around."

"You took advantage of him?"

"In a way. I did what I had to. I mean I liked him well enough in the beginning. And then when the tears stopped…I guess I felt grateful. Can I ask you a question?"

"Sure."

"Why are you interested in all of this? If Jimmy Martin is your patient, I'd leave this alone."

"Is that a warning?"

"I don't mean to be disrespectful, but yes. People who mess with Jimmy end up dead…even when he's nowhere near them."

"Is that why you called me the other night?"

Marla's dark eyes narrowed and she pushed back in the chair, "I don't want to see you get hurt." She stood up and wiped her eyes with the back of her hands. "I probably shouldn't have said anything."

"I'm glad you did," Barrett said. "And if you can think of anything else…anything, I'd appreciate it."

Marla reached for the door handle and then paused, "There was one other thing…"

"Yes."

"Not about Gordon, it's about Dr. Kravitz."

Barrett's ears perked, "What?"

Marla bit her lower lip, "I think there was something going on with him and Jimmy."

"What do you mean?"

"Not sexually…I think something happened right at the end."

"What makes you say that?"

"I got a phone call a couple weeks before Dr. Kravitz died; he was asking me how he would go about getting bloodwork on Jimmy. At first I didn't think too much about it because Dr. Kravitz doesn't usually work with our clients. But then I realized that he should already know how to use the lab service."

"Did he say anything else?"

"It's sometimes what people don't say. Dr. Kravitz was a pretty funny guy, he'd tell me stupid jokes on the phone; it was kind of cute. But this time he was all business, and if you ask me…he sounded scared."

TWENTY-ONE

WEARING HER GOLD-FLOWER wire on the lapel of a navy jacket, Barrett sat across from Jimmy for their third session. Prior to coming she'd contemplated a stiff drink; she needed something. The near-constant surges of adrenalin had made it impossible to sleep last night. She'd lain awake, heart racing, thoughts hammering. If it wasn't Jimmy, it was Ralph, the morgue, the bruises beneath his eyes. Years back when she had gone to a psychiatrist about her panic attacks and the anxiety that surrounded them, he'd tried to put her on Valium and an antidepressant. She'd declined, and she'd made it through. But now, if she'd had one of those blue heart-shaped pills in her purse, she would have gladly taken it.

It was Thursday; four o'clock, and she had a goal—she wasn't leaving without something tangible with which she could violate Jimmy back to Croton.

"How's your week been going?" she began, taking a mental inventory of her patient, while trying hard to keep her nerves in check.

He was neatly dressed in dark green khakis and an ivory turtleneck. He'd combed back his hair with some kind of shiny pomade and she caught the smell of a musky aftershave. In his lap, the blue-eyed kitten lay curled.

"One week is much like the next," he fixed her with a stare.

"You've been taking the medication?"

"Can't you tell?" holding out a trembling hand.

"Does it do anything to keep away the voice?" she asked.

"Not really, no."

"Is that the reason why Dr. Kravitz didn't make you take them?"

A smile slowly spread across Jimmy's lips, "Whatever would make you say that?"

"It's pretty clear that you weren't taking the medication, and I know that Dr. Kravitz knew that, and for whatever reason, allowed it."

"Dr. Kravitz was not as strong a believer in medication as you are."

"I see...And if they really don't do anything for the voices, perhaps he had a point. Do they do anything for you?"

"Not really, other than make me want to sleep all the time. Are you suggesting that I might not have to take them?"

"No, at least not now, but later, we might be able to convince the board that they're unnecessary." She dangled the possibility like a carrot, wanting him to relax, to trust her.

"I'd like that."

"Whose idea was it not to take them?" she asked.

"I told him how badly it affected my playing; he took the hint."

"That's understandable," she replied, hiding her disappointment at his answer. The review board, she realized, might accept his explanation, if in fact Kravitz had colluded. Switching tactics, she infused her voice with warmth. "I wonder if we could try something different today…"

"What's that?"

Barrett was about to head into ethically vague territory, but then again, this was all being recorded, which was illegal considering Jimmy didn't know and she hadn't obtained a warrant. "Because so many of your symptoms go all the way back to the traumas and torture you endured as a child and as an adult, it causes fundamental shifts in the way your mind works. These traumas can be the source for all kinds of painful experiences," Barrett modulated her voice to be soft, with the words coming at a slow, even cadence. "This is why you experience things like panic attacks and flashbacks. Even the kinds of voices you describe may have their origin in traumatic things you've had to endure."

"Yes," he said.

"You've had a hard life, Jimmy, and even as a child were forced into horrible situations that weren't your fault, were they?"

"No," his voice softened.

"Of course not," she continued, "what I want to do today is help you go back, and together we can look at some things, but always with the understanding that we can stop whenever you want, and that I won't let anyone hurt you. Do you think you'd be willing to try? I'll be right with you and I won't go away."

"Okay," sounding now like a little boy.

The cat stirred, looked up at Jimmy and then across at Barrett. He jumped off Jimmy's lap and rubbed up against Barrett's ankle.

"That's good," she said, patting a space on the chair beside her. Fred needed little encouragement to wedge his tiny body between Barrett and the leather arm of the chair. "I'll be right with you, but to get there I'm going to need you to start by closing your eyes and taking a nice deep breath through your nose, like you're sniffing in a beautiful flower."

Barrett watched as Jimmy slipped easily into a light hypnotic state. From there, she led him through an induction sequence that brought him to a deep trance state. She'd been correct in her hypothesis—Jimmy was a wonderful hypnotic subject, she almost didn't need to use a formal induction. But like Mayfield before her, this was questionable territory—at least she wasn't drugging him with Amytal.

"How do you feel, Jimmy?" she asked, observing that his respirations had slowed and that his body appeared relaxed.

"Good…floaty."

"That's wonderful. I want you to feel wonderful, and we're going to play a fun game. I'll ask you questions, and if you answer them completely, you'll feel more and more wonderful. Would you like to play?"

"Yes."

"Good, let's start with something fun."

"Okay."

"When Dr. Kravitz used to come, was that fun?"

"Yes. But he didn't play very well," Jimmy answered in his little boy voice. "Ellen was much better. You play much better. I wish you'd play with me."

"How do you know that I play?"

"I saw you. You wore a velvet dress with lace around your throat and at your wrists. You have such pretty hands."

"Where were you?" Barrett asked, shaken by the accuracy of his memory, down to the detail of the dress that her mother had made for the recital.

"Backstage with Ellen. She was mad."

"How come?"

"Waterfalls of notes. You were supposed to play *Für Elise*, but we heard giant waterfalls of notes. You played the *Revolutionary Étude*."

"That made Ellen mad?"

"Ellen had to be the best. She was so angry and you were so pretty. Do you still have the velvet dress?"

His question surprised her; people under hypnosis tended to be passive and not ask questions. "I don't," she said. "I want you to take another deep breath and as you let the air out, it will be like riding down an elevator that makes you more and more relaxed. And breathe in…and out…That's good. Are you relaxed?"

"Yes," he answered, still with the child's voice.

"I'd like you to picture Dr. Kravitz. Can you see him?"

"Yes."

"You had fun with him, didn't you?"

"Yes."

"But at the end he wasn't fun anymore, was he?"

"No."

"You'll find that by telling me about why it stopped being fun, you'll get a wonderful feeling inside. Would you like to try that?"

"Yes."

"So tell me, when did Dr. Kravitz stop being fun?"

271

Jimmy's eyes opened and he looked at Barrett with a soft expression. "I told him I didn't want to see him anymore."

"How come?" Barrett asked, feeling anxious that his eyes were open.

"I'd lost all of the weight, and had gotten good again on the cello. I was ready to see you."

"Did you tell him that?" she asked, shocked by the deliberateness of his answer.

"No...just that I didn't want to see him anymore."

"What did he say?"

Jimmy's lower lip curled downward, "He got mad."

"That's not fun," Barrett said, modulating her tone to be the kindergarten teacher to his eight-year-old boy.

"No," he shook his head. "He tried to trick me."

"That wasn't very nice of him, was it?"

"No."

"How did he try to trick you?"

"He sent Kelly and Hector and they made me give them blood."

"That wasn't nice at all. Especially since you hadn't been taking any pills, had you?"

"No. He wanted to trick me, because he was mad."

"So what did you do?"

Jimmy blinked. His pink tongue flicked between his lips, and his pupils narrowed. "Dr. Conyors, this isn't fun," his voice shifted lowering in pitch. "Just what is it we're trying to do here? Where's my wonderful feeling?" he said, aping her hypnotic suggestion.

The cat stirred, and looked warily at Jimmy.

"It's a light hypnosis," she answered, feeling a chill, and worrying that he'd pulled himself from the trance.

"Just a light one? Like a small martini or a touch of fine-Moroccan hash?"

"Something like that," she answered, leaving her school-marm voice behind while trying to gauge Jimmy's current persona.

"So you'd like Jimbo to tell you what happened to the good doctor, is that it?"

"Yes," she answered.

"Aren't you supposed to tell me how wonderful and relaxed it will make me feel, to divulge all of his nasty secrets?"

"That's not what you want," she replied. "You want something else, don't you?"

"Of course," he answered, "I want what everyone wants, what you want, what Dr. Kravitz wants."

"What's that?" she asked, noticing how on edge this other Jimmy made her feel.

"Love. Admiration. A good fuck now and then. There's nothing wrong with that."

"No," she agreed, as the cat squirmed out of the chair and bolted beneath a bookcase.

"Can you give me that? If you can give me that I'll tell you about Dr. Kravitz."

"You can give that to yourself," she said.

He laughed, "That was lame. But I like watching you, so maybe I'll tell you anyway. It was simple. Morris was upset because the gravy train was leaving the station—without him."

"So he ordered bloodwork. Why?"

"He wanted leverage. Even Jimbo could see that."

"The bloodwork never made it to the lab."

"No, there was an accident. Oops!"

"And Dr. Kravitz?"

Jimmy smiled, "Oops, oops. Diabetics have to be so very careful." He leaned forward in his chair, his movements sinuous, like a python sidling up to its prey. "What is that perfume you have on?" he asked. "Here, let me breathe it in deeply like a flower, and as I do, I may feel wonderfully relaxed."

Barrett tensed.

"You do this so well, doctor," he closed his eyes and sank back into his chair. "And you didn't even use a shot. So talented, so filled with fun and games. It's no wonder he likes you so much."

"Who?"

"Jimbo. I can't blame him. I think the boy may finally be growing some taste." He closed his eyes and his tongue lewdly circled his lips.

"Is Jimbo there?" she asked.

"He's hiding. He's such a little fool, never could come out and ask for what he wanted. Perhaps we should enroll him in some assertiveness training? We did a lot of that in the hospital."

"And who are you?"

"James Cyrus Martin, of course."

"Which one?"

"Yes...he did pick well. I can't tell if it was the velvet dress, your flawless skin, your lips, your exquisite eyes, or that hint of a Southern accent you try so hard to hide. Did he ever tell you about his first love?"

In spite of her fear, Barrett felt a surge of excitement. Was he about to tell her the truth of what happened to Nicole Foster? "No."

"It was his nanny, a dark-skinned woman from Georgia. So sad what happened," he leered at Barrett.

"Tell me."

Jimmy chortled, "She was terminated." A shudder passed through him, he blinked and started to tremble.

Jimmy feels the red-hot heat from the furnace on his face. He hears the crackle and hiss of black coal. And there's Maylene, but why does she have that look in her eyes? So frightened, and Father's hands around her throat as she kicks and claws at his fingers. Father smiles and clamps down harder making her eyes grow big, like a plastic squeeze toy.

"Jimmy, what's happening?" Barrett asked, noting a look of wall-eyed terror in him.

"He's doing it again," the voice shifted pitch, the tone was now gravel-tinged and adult.

"Who is?"

"Father."

Tears stream down Maylene's face, her legs kick spastically and her white nurse's shoe falls to the cement floor.

"Make him stop."

"What is he doing?" she asked.

"He's in the basement. Please, you said no one was going to hurt me."

"Tell me what he's doing."

"I don't want to watch."

Maylene's looking at Jimmy, her eyes much too big as blood vessels burst inside the whites. She loves him, even as her life slips away, he knows that she loves him.

If he could bite Father's big hands, but he can't move. He strains against the leather belts that hold him captive in the wooden chair. There's nothing he can do but watch.

"He's killing her!"

"Tell me what he's making you watch," Barrett urged, feeling something evil and dangerous in the room.

"He's killing Maylene."

"She was your nanny?"

"Yes."

"Tell me what he's doing in the basement."

"He's singing…"

"The hip bone's connected to the leg bone, the leg bone's connected to the ankle bone," Father laughs as he checks for a pulse. He waltzes across the cellar floor, dragging Maylene's limp body. Her other shoe falls off and her knee-high nylons snag and run. Giant shadows cast by the flaming furnace create phantom couples dancing on the walls.

"Tell me what you see," Barrett pleaded.

"The smell is horrible."

Feces stain the back of Maylene's dress and golden pearls of urine cling to her torn and bunched up nylons. He lays her down on a rubber mat, and raises her head so that her dead and bulged-out eyes stare back at Jimmy. "You're getting too old for a nanny, Jimbo," Father says, as he nods Maylene's lifeless head up and down, as though she's agreeing with his assessment. Father lifts up her thin flower-print skirt and pulls out a butcher cleaver. He raises it overhead and brings it down right below her knee, hacking through the bone and flesh.

Jimmy shrieked and jumped in his chair. "There's blood on the floor and there's sparks coming out of the furnace. It's so hot. He's throwing her into the furnace."

Father's white shirt is soaked in blood and perspiration. He takes it off, wipes his face and tosses it into the furnace. All that remains of Maylene is her head. "And the neck bone's connected to the…" Father swings it up by the hair and dangles it inches in front of Jimmy's face. Even in death he can see the love in her eyes. "Give her a kiss, Jimbo…And here's the word of the lord." Her flesh is still warm as Father mashes the dead woman's lips to his son's. "Say goodbye"…and Father backs away, still dangling the blood-dripping head in front of Jimmy. He swings it back and forth, back and forth, and then tosses it into the sizzling fire.

"It's so hot." Jimmy sobbed, like a child. "It's too hot." He wept and coughed, his throat filled with the choking smells of burning flesh and heating fuel.

"It's okay, Jimmy," Barrett soothed, "I need you to leave the basement and go someplace happy."

He blinked and stared at her, a sneer crept across his lips. "She had such soft skin, like yours…"

"What is it you want?" she asked, sensing a grim shift in him.

His lips curled back, revealing two rows of perfect white teeth, "You'll find out."

"What happened to the little boy?"

Jimmy started to sing, "The breast bone's connected to the neck bone. The neck bone's connected to the...Wheee! Everyone into the pool!"

The clock chimed, and as it did Barrett knew that she had not gotten what she needed. Jimmy was a good hypnotic subject, but there was still a degree of free will, along with whatever odd configuration of personalities moved inside of him that weren't giving up the goods. She made a final stab, "Tell me what you did to Dr. Kravitz."

He blinked again, looked at Barrett and then at the clock, "Why nothing, Dr. Conyors. Why would you ask? And look, our time is up. Now aren't you supposed to tell me that you'll clap your hands and I'll wake, feeling fresh as a spring morning?"

"That doesn't appear necessary."

"No," he agreed. "I never touched Dr. Kravitz."

"You never touched Nicole Foster," she added. "You didn't have to because someone else did it for you."

"So you say." He leaned forward, sniffing the air as though he might capture her scent. "Such a lovely brooch," he commented. "A present from Detective Hobbs, no doubt."

Barrett recoiled, realizing that Jimmy knew she was wired, that he'd known the entire time.

Mimicking his little-boy voice, he chanted. "Maylene...Maylene."

"Who's helping you, Jimmy?" she persisted.

"I don't know what you're getting at. There's just me and millions and millions of dollars. Did you ever wonder what it might be like to have all that money? It's amazing how many people fantasize about having what I have. Do you wonder about that, Dr. Conyors? Do you wonder what will happen to all that money when I'm gone? You can see that Ellen isn't about to pop out a kid. Even if she wanted, the Martin women go through the change early; it's too late for Chicky. We have no heir…not yet…of course, there is Fred. Where is that cat? I think he'd…I'd make an interesting father, don't you think? That's what we should focus on, finding me a bride. Then we could get to work on James Cyrus Martin, the Fifth. It has a certain ring, maybe twins or triplets; it's good to have playmates, a spare or two to keep things jumping. But we really must do something about strengthening the blood. Far too much inbreeding."

Torn between wanting to get the hell out, and needing something, her eyes fell on a stack of envelopes next to Jimmy's chair.

"Oh, I almost forgot," he said, following her gaze. "I need to give you yours." He handed her the fine linen envelope.

Not understanding, she opened it, and stared at the engraved invitation.

James Cyrus Martin, IV
invites you to an evening of romance and music.
Place: Carnegie Hall/Weill Recital Hall
Time: 8:00 p.m.
Date: Saturday, May 1
Cello: James Cyrus Martin, IV
Piano: To be announced

"What is this?" she asked. "This is two days from now. Who gave you permission?"

"Ellen spoke to the board; they thought it was a good idea."

Barrett found it hard to breathe, why hadn't anyone told her, and what the hell was Ellen doing going behind her back? And why did the invitation remind her of the ones that she and Ralph had sent out for their wedding?

A hard knock came at the library doors.

Barrett startled and turned her head.

"You seem jumpy, Dr. Conyors. I hope it's nothing I said. That's just your detective," Jimmy commented getting to his feet. "But he's not invited...You know, I *do* feel refreshed." Halfway to the door he stopped and turned, "But I don't think you got what you came for today...pity. Maybe next time you'll do better...or maybe I will."

TWENTY-TWO

JIMMY WATCHED AS THE door shut on Detective Hobbs and Barrett Conyors. His temples pounded and saliva flooded his mouth. He heard them on the other side, their voices lowered. His stomach ached and the image of Maylene's bleeding head swinging from father's hand still burned in his mind.

He peered through the peephole. She was flirting with Hobbs, he could see it in her hand as it whipped back through her short hair and in the way she tilted her chin on that wonderfully long neck. *"The head bone's connected to the neck bone,"* Father sang.

The bloody cleaver high in the air, catching the reflection of the orange flames and then it comes down, chop, chop, chop—three times. "Too old for nannies."

Jimmy blinked, struggling for control. Father was itching to come up, and then there were all the others, some with names and others who swam about in the soup of his insides, constantly reliving their bits and pieces of his past. And it appeared that Dr. Conyors knew this; why else would she have used hypnosis, or brought up why his medications didn't work? She knew.

"She wants to trick you, Jimbo," Father cackled.

"No, but at least she sees me for who I am, and not some schizophrenic."

"She'll send you back, Jimbo. And where's the fun in that?"

"I'm not going anywhere," he headed back into the library and picked up his cello.

Father continued to prattle as Jimmy tried to focus on the music. It was an easy Debussy, but his fingers seemed fat and slow and he couldn't control the lithium tremor. His intonation soured and jarred in his ear. The longer he played, the worse it got, missing notes by a blackboard-screeching eighth tone, and losing the delicacy of the passages with fingers robbed of their usual dexterity.

And Father wouldn't shut up, *"It was a happy day, wasn't it?"* father prattled. *"So many good things all at once. It was your eighth birthday."* He sang, *"Happy birthday to you. Happy birthday to you…"*

"Happy birthday to you. Happy birthday to you. Happy birthday, dear Jimmy. Happy birthday to you." Father was drunk and drinking more while Jimmy and Ellen played duets in the library. Usually they'd run upstairs when they heard him come in, but this time they were too caught up in the back-and-forth fun of the Beethoven duos.

Jimmy smells whiskey and knows that tonight he'll get a visit from Father. His stomach churns and he hears Ellen pull the keyboard closed on the Bösendorfer. He wants to hide, but knows that only makes things worse.

"Come on Jimmy," Ellen says, pretending that everything is fine. "Let's go upstairs."

"Yes, little doves," Father teases, "fly away, fly away. But I do have a present for Jimbo."

Jimmy looks at Ellen, she shrugs her shoulders and shakes her head. There's no escape. Father disappears and there's a clanging of doors and distant footsteps clomping down into the basement and the cellar below that. And then the steps reverse and with them come an inconsistent thumping, as though some hobbled creature is rising up from the bowels of the earth. The kitchen door closes and Father sings, his squeaky voice rattling through the walls, "Happy birthday to you. Happy birthday to you…"

Jimmy sees the black wooden case first, it's covered with colored stickers and custom's stamps, some in English some in other languages from places like La Scala, The Tchaikovsky Festival, and the London Philharmonic. Father places the cello case in the center of the Sarouk. "Want to see?" he asks.

Jimmy nods, and cautiously approaches.

Father's fingers work at the case's snaps, clicking them open one by one.

Jimmy feels a hand on his shoulder as Ellen stands beside him. There's no present for her, on this their shared birthday, just the black cello case for Jimmy.

Father opens the case and in the soft evening light Jimmy sees Allegra. Her dark body lies nestled in a bed of black velvet with two securing bands strapped across her graceful curves.

"She's over three hundred years old," Father says, taking out one of the two ivory-tipped bows and handing it to Jimmy. "I thought you'd like her."

Jimmy walks up to the cello, not even caring that Father is so close. His hand reaches out and strokes the gleaming surface.

Father smiles and shakes his head, "It's okay, she's yours. Take her out."

Reverentially Jimmy liberates the Amati from its cradle. He pulls out the endpin and holding it by the gracefully scrolled neck he turns the instrument in the light. It feels light, and makes his own instrument seem clumsy.

"They say he crushed rubies and diamonds and mixed them into the varnish," Father says. "There were big secrets as to what went into the varnish, it was all about blood, and magic and sex. She's been owned by some of the world's greatest cellists, son—her name is Allegra— and now she's yours."

Jimmy carries his prize back to his chair and plucks the A string. It was in perfect pitch. Running a bow across the strings, the room fills with Allegra's warm throaty song.

Ellen walks back to the piano and lays into the opening runs of the Chopin. The music flows, as he and Ellen fill the room with glorious sound, shutting out the world in a blissful sea.

They play straight through. He forgets that father is in the room, until a harsh clap reminds him.

"You like the cello, Jimbo?" Father asks.

Jimmy fears a trick; there's always a trick. "Yes," he answers, hoping that Father wouldn't rip Allegra from his hands.

"I'm glad, I have another gift for you," he says.

"What is it?" Jimmy asks.

Father smiles, "It's a surprise. You'll have to come with me; it's in the basement."

Ellen slides off the piano bench and stands at her brother's side.

"Not you, Chicky," Father says. "This is for, Jimbo. Because today he gets his grown-up cello. And grown-ups have to put away their childish things. Things that threaten to tell, things that don't mind their P's and Q's." He holds his hand out, and wiggles his fingers, "Come on."

Reluctantly, Jimmy lays the glistening cello on its side. He puts his hand into father's clammy grip. Father drags Jimmy back through the kitchen, down to the basement, and down the rickety stairs to the dirt-floor cellar.

It's hot and smells of mildew and burning oil. Cobwebs stick to his face and his neck and as they round the great black furnace he sees Maylene.

"And when I became a man," Father says, "it was time to put away my childish things."

Jimmy blinked and found himself back in the library frozen with Allegra in his lap, his left hand on her neck and his right poised with the bow. Instinctively he glanced at the clock to see how much time he'd lost. He remembered Barrett's visit, how pretty she'd looked.

"That's a lovely brooch you're wearing, Dr. Conyors," Father taunted. *"A gift no doubt…she's trying to trick you, Jimbo. Send you back. We don't want to go back, do we?"*

Jimmy blinked.

He feels the heat of the furnace. There's no more blood, just the smoky smell of burned flesh. *"If anyone asks,"* Father instructs, "you'll say she went back to Georgia."

He blinked, and felt his hand gripped tightly on Allegra's neck. A fury welled up and before he could stop himself he'd hurled the priceless instrument across the room. As the ancient wood leapt from his fingers, he tried to stop it. Time stretched as the Amati sailed through the air and hit the marble fireplace. For a moment he thought all would be okay, and then he heard the crack and saw the neck break away from the darkly lacquered body.

He sobbed as he assessed the damage. Kneeling by his broken instrument, he stroked the pieces as he might comfort an injured child. "Where is she?" he cried, holding Allegra's body in his lap and rocking. "Where is she?"

Jimmy listens as father's footsteps vanish up into the house. He's been left tied up in the cellar.

A hand with long fingers rests on his shoulder, "It's okay, Jimmy," Ellen says as she walks over to the furnace. She opens the grate, her face illuminated with flickers of gold. She bends down and picks up the long-handled cleaver and reaches it inside the burner. She struggles and manages to pull Maylene's head to the opening, it tumbles and drops onto the plastic tarp. She stamps out a burning ember and kneels. "Her hair's still good," she says, stroking their nanny's hair. "At least that's still good." She picks up the cleaver and working the blade into the charred flesh she peels back the scalp, "at least that's still good." Ellen's face glows as she takes off Maylene's hair and gently places her head back into the furnace. "Here, Jimmy," she hands him the scalped hair, "don't let Father ever see this."

The phone rang. Jimmy stifled his sobs, and reached for it.

"Jimmy?" Ellen's voice.

"Ellen."

"What's wrong, Jimmy? How did your session with Dr. Cony-ors go?"

"Father's here," he said. "He got me so mad I've broken Allegra. You have to get her fixed before the concert."

"I'll see to it. Did you tell her?"

"Yes, I know she wants to come, I know she wants to play. I can see it, but I haven't yet proved myself. There's another test...I need your help. There isn't much time."

There was a long silence, and then Ellen—as he knew she would—said, "Of course, dear."

TWENTY-THREE

JUSTINE CONYORS MOANED AND clutched the crunchy hospital pillow tighter. The clanging noise wouldn't stop. It was familiar and annoying and it pulled her from the arms of the well-muscled man who embraced her in the warm Caribbean waters of her dream.

She opened her eyes and reached up to the head of the bunk bed in the on-call room.

"Whose is it?" a sleepy-voiced resident called out from the other side of the room.

"It's mine," she said, swinging her scrub-clad legs over the side of the top bunk. She landed on sneakers that she'd been too tired to remove. She grabbed her wrinkled lab coat from the hook, being careful to hold it upright lest she spill out the pockets onto the floor.

"Hurray, it's not mine," someone murmured as Justine gently turned the doorknob and went out into the dimly lit hallway of the fourteenth floor on-call suite. She looked at the number in her pager—it was a hospital extension.

She dialed.

"Dr. Conyors?" a woman's gravelly voice picked up.

"Yes."

"You're needed in the emergency room. There's a trauma case they want you to evaluate."

"I'll be right down," she said, trying to muster something that approximated enthusiasm.

After she hung up, she realized that she'd forgotten to ask for the patient's name. Then again, the nurse hadn't offered it.

It doesn't matter, she thought, as she walked down the hallway toward the bank of elevators. She pictured her chief resident and mentor-of-the-month, Don Fitzgerald, and had a pleasant flashback to her dream, suddenly realizing whose muscular arms she'd been embraced by.

When she got to the elevators she was met by a sandwich-board style out-of-order sign and matching orange plastic tape that had been stretched across the doors. "You've got to be kidding," she groaned, retracing her steps and following the lit EXIT signs to the stairwell.

She opened the door and smiled at a scrub-clad orderly who was struggling with a laundry cart. If she thought she had it bad, just imagine trying to get up and down the stairs with something like that.

The dark-haired man smiled at her and let her pass. As he did, Justine felt something sharp jab into her shoulder. She turned back to see what it was, and saw that the orderly had stabbed her with a syringe. He smiled as she opened her mouth to scream. A crackling plastic-coated pillow clamped onto her face, and she struggled for air, but she was so tired, and maybe this was all part of the dream.

She felt a pair of strong arms wrap around her waist. She pictured Don and warm turquoise waters filled with kaleidoscope fish. She moaned a final time, and felt nothing as Jimmy Martin gently arranged her inside the laundry cart, covered her over with linens and then wheeled her back to the elevator.

He removed the tape and out-of-order sign, placed them on top of the cart and pushed the button for the service elevator. Inside his head, Father clamored to get out. *No*, he thought, Father was dead, and Jimmy's own life was about to start. The elevator opened and he pushed his cargo inside. His emotions bubbled with an almost unbearable anticipation, and with a fear that he struggled to quell. Nothing would go wrong, not this time. He glanced up nervously as the elevator descended. It stopped on the fifth floor and a security guard entered.

Jimmy's pulse accelerated as the dark-skinned man greeted him. "Hell of a night," he said, pressing the button for the lobby level.

Jimmy mumbled his agreement, wondering if this was another test. He felt inside his pocket for the syringe, as his eyes fell on a strand of Justine Conyor's auburn hair visible from beneath a sheet. He could hardly breathe, as Father whispered, *"They'll send you back Jimbo."*

He startled when the elevator stopped, and looked up at the lit letter "L."

"Have a good one," the guard said, getting out.

"You too," Jimmy answered, and held his breath until the doors closed.

He pushed the cart out into the basement, having earlier mapped out his route to the hospital's delivery bays. Getting the side door open, he glanced up at a security camera trained on the spot-lit garage style openings. Why hadn't he seen those before?

A dark van backed toward him. He jumped to the ground, and hurriedly opened the doors, then climbing the half set of stairs he reached into the laundry cart, and careful to keep his prize covered, loaded her into the van.

"I'll stay in back," he said, closing the doors behind.

"Anyone see you?" Ellen, her hair covered in a wig like her brother's and wearing tinted glasses, asked from the driver's seat.

"No," he said, not wanting to mention either the guard or the cameras.

"Good," and just like when they were children, Hansel and Gretel continued on their way.

TWENTY-FOUR

NEEDING TO CLEAR HER head, to not think that tomorrow was Ralph's funeral, Barrett, dressed for jogging, was heading out the door. The phone rang. It was seven o'clock on a Saturday morning, and even that ordinary sound sent her pulse racing, *who the hell could it be?* Playing it safe, she checked the caller ID and picked up.

"Barrett?" her mother's anxious voice greeted her.

"What's wrong?"

"Have you seen Justine?"

"No, why? What's going on?"

"I don't know," Ruth said. "I just got a call from her chief resident wanting to know if I'd heard from her. He said she didn't show up for morning report."

"Slow down, Mom. She was on call last night?"

"Yes."

"And she's not in the hospital this morning?" Barrett asked, not yet understanding.

"No, he said that she had an admission around midnight, and that someone remembered her getting paged at two or three in the morning, and that's the last anyone saw her."

"You called her apartment?"

"She didn't answer, I'm there right now; she hasn't been home. This isn't like her, Barrett. She wouldn't just leave the hospital."

"No," Barrett agreed, shunting away the nightmare stories of what can happen to a young female house officer late at night in an inner-city hospital. "What was the name of the resident that called you?" she asked, grabbing pencil and paper.

"It was something, Fitzgerald…where could she be?"

"I don't know, did he say anything else?"

"No…" Ruth Conyors started to cry. "He said that she was a wonderful resident, the best he'd ever had."

"It's going to be okay, Mom," Barrett said, not at all convinced of that. "Have they called the cops?"

"I don't think so. I don't know. He said he wanted to check around first and see if maybe she'd gone home sick in the middle of the night. But she would have told someone. She wouldn't just walk out."

"Mom, I'm going to hang up and call back the resident. If they haven't found her and she's not in her apartment, I'll call the police. I'll let you know whatever I find out."

"Barrett, I'm so scared."

"It's going to be okay, Mom. We'll find her."

Barrett hung up and immediately called the hospital where she had done her internship years earlier. She glanced at the clock as the operator paged Dr. Fitzgerald. It was just after seven and he'd be finishing rounds and morning report, getting set to go home.

She waited, and she prayed that Justine had fallen asleep in the wrong call room or had gotten tied up with some emergency room fiasco and lost track of time. Or maybe the battery had run down in her pager and…

"Hello?" a man's deep voice picked up.

"Hi, is this Dr. Fitzgerald?"

"Yes."

"This is Barrett Conyors, I'm Justine Conyors' sister."

"Have you seen her?" his voice hopeful.

Despair welled; he didn't know where she was, they hadn't found her. "No," she said.

"Your mother said that she was going to check her apartment."

"She did; Justine hasn't been there. And even if she'd left the hospital, she would have told somebody."

"I know," he said. "This seems unreal. She performed an emergency appendectomy last night."

"When was that?"

"We finished around nine. She told me she was going to the on-call room, and the other residents said she was on the top bunk. Somebody thought she got paged a few hours later, and that's the last anyone saw her. We always have breakfast as a team in the morning before report and rounds."

"When would that have been?"

"Five-thirty."

"And you paged her?"

"Not right away. I figured she could have another half-hour's sleep if she wanted."

"So about six?"

"Yeah, I didn't want her to miss morning report. Harrison doesn't forgive things like that."

"And then what?"

"She didn't answer her page, or call back, or show up. So we went into morning report and Harrison immediately saw that she wasn't there. For God's sake, she's about to be the first woman ever to make chief surgical resident and she's not at morning report…it didn't sit well. So I paged her again, and I started to get worried. And the other resident said that she wasn't in the on-call room when she came down and that she thought Justine had gotten an admission in the middle of the night. Only, we hadn't gotten any admissions in the middle of the night. And right around that time Harrison sent the resident back to the on-call suite and down to the emergency room, and he called hospital security. I tried her apartment and your mom and…"

"Did anyone see anything?" Barrett asked.

"Security is sweeping the hospital and the grounds. I haven't heard anything."

"Have the cops been called?"

"I don't think so."

"You need to," Barrett said. "I'm going to check out something else."

"Where she might be?"

Barrett pictured Jimmy's townhouse and the horrific ramblings of their last session, "I hope not." She gave him her pager and cell phone numbers and hung up.

She wiped back tears—she needed to focus. She glanced at her watch, it was just seven. It was hard to think. All she could see was Justine and the knowledge that something bad had happened, that someone had done something—was doing something—to her Justine. And the other image that kept flashing was Jimmy's face.

She dug her knapsack out of the closet and threw her pager, wallet, and cell phone inside. She considered changing out of her sweats, but somehow her all-black jogging outfit seemed right for the nightmare she was in.

———

"Where are you, Hobbs?" Barrett pleaded silently as the precinct's desk clerk informed her that he wasn't on duty. She stood on the corner of Park Avenue South and 21st Street, holding her cell phone and looking east into a partial view of Gramercy Park. The tall trees, gas lamps, and belle époque mansions and hotels seemed out of place in this bustling, horn-honking, exhaust-spewing heart of Manhattan.

"I could put you into his voice mail?" the clerk offered.

"There's no way you could page him?" Barrett asked, winded from her cross-town dash. She'd already tried his apartment, but had been met by another answering machine. He was probably out with his daughters doing some wonderful early Saturday morning, divorced-father thing.

"I can try."

"Please do" and Barrett gave her cell number. "Let me leave a message on his machine, as well."

"One moment."

The phone rang and then she heard his voice. Her spirits lifted briefly, perhaps he was in after all—he wasn't, it was just a recording.

"Ed," she began after the beep, "it's Barrett." Her words tumbled fast, "Justine is missing from the hospital. I've had them call the police, but you and I both know that a less-than-twenty-four-hour missing person report doesn't get jack. This is not like her and I'd bet my life Jimmy knows something. That's where I am now. I have both my cell and beeper, as soon as you get this call me."

She hung up and stared down 21st Street. From where she was, she couldn't see Jimmy's house, so she walked past the Calvary Church, just to the point where, through the park's lush greenery, she could glimpse the elaborate ironwork front of the Martin mansion.

What was he doing now? she wondered. What if she was wrong, what if none of this was connected to Jimmy? What if they'd already found Justine, and she'd just fallen asleep in the doctor's lounge or a patient's room? It was still early. It could happen. And how could Jimmy have anything to do with her sister? He couldn't leave…but that's not his way, she heard the Jimmy Martin tag line in her head, *"I never touched her."* But it was clear that someone else…others…could do lots of things for him, without his ever leaving his velvet cage. But maybe she was wrong. What if he did have a way to get out? With his kind of money, finding a way to slip off his bracelet without detection might not be that hard. As the idea percolated, she felt sure that was it. But then, how would he get by the neighbors? In rarified old Gramercy Park, there'd be enough neighbors who'd know his story. They'd know Jimmy and notice his coming and going—or anyone else entering the Martin mansion. He wouldn't risk it. She backed away and jogged in the opposite direction. She turned south on the avenue, bypassing Gramercy and then turned east on 19th Street.

She'd never been in the kitchen, but Hobbs had told her about the garden that ran out back. It had to end somewhere, what was on the other side? She crossed to the south side of 19th and looking in the uptown direction she jogged down the block trying to eyeball which building would be flush in-line with the mansion. Even early on a Saturday, 19th Street was active. A pair of waiters carrying clean white shirts hurried past her, as an after-hours club on Irving Place dislodged its mascara-smeared patrons into the bright spring sunlight. An impromptu parade of cabs zeroed in on the potential customers and took them off to their scattered beds in groupings of one, two, or more. Yet for all of the activity, it was anonymous. None would recognize who might be standing next to them, a perfect venue for Jimmy if he were stepping out.

Barrett walked up the stoop of an apartment building and peered over the rooftops of the opposing structures. Craning her neck she caught a glimpse of Jimmy's roof—another potential source of egress. How difficult would it be for him to go up to the roof and then come down and out through some other building?

Mentally she drew a straight line between Jimmy's roof and the matching building on the north side of 19th Street. The connection was suddenly obvious. There, between two metal-gated storefronts was a two-story carriage house covered in graffiti and posters, but under those she glimpsed the same weathered brownstone as the Martin mansion. She crossed the street and approached the building with its three bay doors and adjoining entryway three steps below the sidewalk.

"Isn't that perfect?" she muttered, walking down the steps, and noticing how the shadows surrounded her. The door had been outfitted with a fish-eye peephole and above her were positioned small cameras trained in either direction of the street. "Clever boy." It was clear that the arrangement allowed whoever was behind the door to get a panoramic view of the street.

Wishing that she'd worn gloves, she tried to turn the tarnished brass door knob. It was securely locked, and unlike her inadequate apartment security, Jimmy—or whoever—had installed two un-pickable Medeco cylinders. As she took her hand back, she felt a sticky resistance. She tapped her forefinger against the brass, and then rubbed her thumb against it. She looked at her fingers, and brought them to her nose. There were barely visible traces of a tacky chalk-white powder...resin...cello resin from his bow.

She thought about again calling Hobbs, but realized that ei-ther he'd get her messages or he wouldn't. She was alone. Justine needed her, and she had to do something.

She went back up to the sidewalk; it was eight o'clock. What occurred to her was risky, but she saw no choice. She walked back toward Irving Place and past the row of yellow cabs and tweaked-out revelers wearing club-kid black and clutching bottles of de-signer water used to rehydrate from the effects of designer drugs.

She turned onto Gramercy South and walked up the front steps of Jimmy's townhouse. She rang the bell and waited. Seconds passed into a minute; she pressed it again, and heard it resonate inside the cavernous foyer. She rang a third time. Stepping back, she stared up the front of the six-story mansion, peering through the open-ings in the lacy ironwork.

"Interesting," she pulled off her knapsack, looked up Jimmy's number in her Palm Pilot, and dialed. She waited, letting the phone ring. No answering machine cut in. After all, why would he need one? He wasn't going anywhere. But then, why wasn't he picking up? She let it ring for several minutes, then put her ear to the thick oak door to see if she could hear it coming from inside; she could.

She hung up and called the review board's twenty-four-hour hotline. Maybe Jimmy was on a scheduled outing.

She quickly introduced herself and asked if they could check to see where her patient was.

"At home," the woman told her.

"I'm at his home," Barrett informed her. "I've rung the bell three times and let the phone go for a good five minutes."

"I'm looking at his bracelet log," the woman told her. "He hasn't left his geographic zone in weeks. Are you sure you had the right number when you called?"

"Look," Barrett said tersely, "we have one of two possibilities here, either Jimmy Martin is AWOL and has figured out a way to deactivate his bracelet, or he's unable to get to his door or his phone—either way I want you to get the supervisor on call and have them page me now. And while you're doing that, I need an outreach team with cops, because if he's not in there, we've got a problem."

Barrett hung up, and pressed Jimmy's buzzer again. She stabbed it repeatedly with her forefinger. Hope surged through the fear; she was going to get him.

Her cell phone chirped to life. Barrett flipped it open and pulled out the antenna.

A familiar Boston-accent voice spoke; it was Anton and he sounded pissed. "I just got off the line with the monitoring center. They said you called and were saying something about Jimmy Martin going AWOL."

"I'm at his house right now, Anton. He's not answering the door or picking up the phone."

"What are you doing there? It's not even eight o'clock. This could be construed as harassment."

"Really?" she said. "I find your response interesting. Anton. If this was anyone other than Jimmy Martin, you wouldn't be giving me this crap."

"Don't push me, Barrett. It's clear that you've lost your perspective with this case. On Monday morning you and I are going to have a talk and transfer his care to someone else."

"He wouldn't like that," she said.

"What are you saying?"

"Look Anton, if anyone's ass is going in a sling it's yours. You neglected to tell me that Jimmy asked for me by name. This wasn't some throw-Barrett-a-bone favor. And you know what? I think that's just the tip of the iceberg."

"What are you talking about?"

"Stay out of my way," she warned. "And do whatever you have to do to get a Croton bed ready for him, because when I get through that door, either he's sick and dying, or else he's somewhere he shouldn't be. And swear to God—if he is—he'll be back in Croton before nightfall."

"Don't do this. Barrett."

"Goodbye, Anton." And she hung up.

Ten minutes later a team of case managers from the forensic evaluation center and a patrol car—with lights, no siren—appeared at the Martin residence. Barrett rang the buzzer as they approached.

"That's really strange," the young Latino case manager commented. "Jimmy doesn't go anywhere."

"You know him?" Barrett asked.

"I'm Hector. Most of the time I'm the one who brings him his meds." He smiled sheepishly, "And his coffee."

A uniformed patrolwoman came up beside Barrett. "So what's the deal?" she asked.

Barrett quickly sketched the details, while Hector produced a set of keys. The officer gripped the fox-head doorknocker and rapped harshly. "Police, we'd like you to open the door."

An older couple out walking their Welsh corgi stopped and watched. The silver-haired man shook his head, said something to his wife, and then they disappeared around the corner.

"I'd better do that," the officer told Hector, taking the keys from him. "Stay down and away at the bottom of the stairs." Her partner stood behind her, and unsnapped his holster.

The female officer turned the bottom lock, and was placing the key into the top one when the door opened.

The patrolman tensed, one hand on his firearm.

Jimmy, with his blond hair crumpled and dressed in a velour bathrobe and no slippers looked out over the assemblage on his front stoop. "What's going on?" he asked, looking directly at Barrett.

She walked up the stairs, her eye catching on the flash of red on his ankle bracelet. "Why didn't you answer your phone?"

"I didn't hear it," he replied. "The medications make me so tired. I didn't hear a thing."

The patrolwoman turned to Barrett. "Everything okay?" she asked.

Barrett knew that it was anything but okay, but couldn't argue with Jimmy being right where he was supposed to be.

"Your doc was worried," Hector interjected, coming up the stairs.

"I can see that," Jimmy said. "Her concern is…admirable. But as you see I'm just fine." He looked across the park and spied the elderly couple who were again watching, only now from behind the iron fence. "Quite the show for the neighbors," he commented, waving in the direction of the couple and their dog.

As he did, his sleeve slid back, revealing the soiled cuff of a white shirt.

"You sleep in your clothes?" Barrett asked.

"Is that a crime?" he replied.

"No, just curious."

"Do you need us for anything else?" the female officer asked.

"No," Barrett said, racking her brain for anything that could give them probable cause to enter the house.

Jimmy said nothing as the uniformed officers got back into their squad car and drove away.

"I should have brought your meds," Hector commented. "So I guess I'll see you in a little while," and he and his partner walked off, leaving Barrett alone with Jimmy.

"So, Dr. Conyors, what brought you ringing my doorbell at such an early hour? And this isn't our day, is it?"

"I think you know."

"Do I? And where's your lovely brooch? And for that matter, what happened to Detective Hobbs?"

Barrett seethed; she felt him toying with her, trying to get her to break down, but even more than her anger was a paralyzing fear that kept her rooted to the ground, as she stared into the glittering blue of his eyes.

"Black suits you," he continued. "Could I offer you some coffee? I find that I can't get started without some."

"I know you've been going out, Jimmy."

"Prove it. Or is that what you were trying to do? And here I am, just where I'm supposed to be. You must be disappointed. But I don't want to stand out here; I've given the neighbors enough for the week. You sure I can't offer you anything? Oh, but that's right, you don't like to meet with me alone, and I don't see Officer—I mean Detective—Hobbs and his sidekick," he stepped back into his doorway, shadows curtained his face.

Barrett knew that Anton would skewer her with the morning's events, but that's not what drove her up the last step and across the threshold. All she could think about was Justine, and the awful possibility that Jimmy knew what had happened to her.

"Coffee would be nice," she said, breathing Jimmy's acrid sweaty scent, and realizing that he'd been exerting himself.

"I'm glad," he shut the door behind her and turned the locks, "there's so much we have to discuss."

TWENTY-FIVE

"Do you smoke?" Barrett asked, tensing as Jimmy bolted the door.

"No, why? Would you like to?" he straightened to his full height, his body not three feet from hers.

Barrett thought about her mother, waiting up for a teenage Barrett to come home from a party. *"Have you been drinking?"* she'd ask. "Have you been drinking, Jimmy?"

"Of course not," he answered. "I'm not allowed. But let's have that coffee." He disappeared through a doorway to the right; Barrett followed. She felt like a frightened Alice following the rabbit down the hole, only instead of opium-smoking caterpillars, she had a murderous cellist.

He led her through a serving room off the banquet-sized dining room and from there into the kitchen. She took in her surroundings, realizing that his kitchen was larger than her entire co-op. "You have a beautiful house," she commented, struggling to keep her fear in check and trying to find some topic for conversation that wouldn't set him off.

"Thanks, not that I had anything to do with it."

An odd thought occurred to her, "How do you keep it clean? I never see any servants."

"I do it myself…I don't like having strangers in my house, and besides, I've got plenty of time."

"You must get lonely."

"Strangely enough, I don't. I think that's the only thing that holds me together; I don't have to be around people…present company excluded, of course. And there is Fred."

"Where is he?" she asked, wondering what had happened to the small Siamese.

He looked down at the floor. "That's odd…he's probably in the library. I hope…"

"What?"

Jimmy walked back the way he came, calling to his cat, "Fred…Fred…"

Barrett listened as his voice reverberated through the walls. She heard his feet pounding up the stairs as he searched for his kitten. Then she heard something else, a faint mewling sound coming from the other side of the kitchen door.

Barrett got up from the table and looked out through a window onto the courtyard filled with full-grown trees, tangled beds of weeds and a dense thicket in the distance. If she hadn't known about the carriage house on 19th Street she'd have missed the tiny glimpses of weathered brownstone. Fred meowed loudly from the middle of a bluestone path that ended in an elaborate, but nonfunctioning, fountain. She opened the door and stepped out into the cool morning. Her head spun as she drank in the clean air and approached the cat.

"You found him," Jimmy said coming up behind her.

She swallowed, trying to find some saliva in her mouth. She could hear Sifu Li's advise, *"Fear is the enemy. Conquer fear and you cannot be defeated."*

The cat sniffed at her extended hand and then butted his head against it. She picked him up, glad for the warmth and softness of his tiny body.

"He likes you," Jimmy said.

"I'm surprised you let him out," she commented.

"He doesn't go far," Jimmy said "… like me."

"But this is nice," she replied, looking up at the flowering trees. "At least you can get some fresh air."

"It's not fresh," he replied.

"Because of New York?"

"No…what do you see in this courtyard?"

"Old trees—I think that one's a London plane tree," she commented noting the multi-colored bark. "And that looks like a ginkgo."

"Very good, have you been reading the signs on the park trees?"

"Yes," she admitted.

"Don't feel bad, I used to do it all the time when I was a kid. I can tell you what each and every tree is in English and Latin, both around the park and inside it. The same goes for Stuyvesant Park. But what else do you see?"

"It used to be a formal garden."

"Yes, it was Mother's. She had roses, and she had a gardener…actually a string of them, mostly El Salvadorians." He looked apprehensively toward the thicket and the carriage house beyond.

She followed his gaze, wondering what it was that frightened him, yet somehow too scared to ask.

"I'm cold. I want to go back inside," he finally said, turning around.

"They were her lovers," Barrett commented, as she followed him back into the kitchen, still clutching the kitten to her chest.

"She had sex with them," he pulled the half-filled carafe out of the coffeemaker and poured the steaming liquid into mugs. "I wouldn't call them lovers." He shook his head. "Now how did we get on to this? Morning coffee…what do you take?"

"Just black."

"That is best, isn't it?" He handed her the mug, his hands perfectly steady. For a moment longer than necessary, they both held the cup. "Careful," he said, looking her straight in the eye, "it's hot."

"Thank you," she pulled it back from him, and for a fleeting moment wondered if he might try to drug her. But as though he sensed her hesitation, he raised his cup and took a sip. "So is your mother's sexual activity under the heading of things you don't talk about?" she asked, trying to maintain a professional façade.

"I think I'm beyond that. But if you must know, Ellen and I used to watch," he told her. "I think that's one of the many reasons I'm as messed up as I am."

"What would you see?" She needed to figure out who he was today, not the frightened child, not the hissing man, but someone almost rational with a kind of detachment, like a reporter reading the news.

"Different things on different days, but mostly men who'd left family and children behind in South America, who found themselves the object of Mother's desires. I don't think they had much choice. Looking back, I think they were all illegals, which made it easier for her to play her games."

"You're being vague."

"Mother liked to humiliate and hurt them. Ellen and I would watch through peepholes in her bedroom wall. And the sickest part…"

"Yes?"

"I'm pretty certain she knew that we were there." He blinked and turned. "But I've already told you this, haven't I?"

"Yes," she said, "Sometimes, I think you forget things."

"That's not it, not entirely…" He gestured toward the window, "So that was Mother's rose garden. Ellen cut down all the roses after their accident."

"Your parents both died while you were in the hospital," Barrett commented.

"Yes, a terrible accident," his tone sarcastic. "I was allowed out for the funeral."

"Were they alive when Gordon Mayfield's article was published?" she lobbed the question like a grenade into the middle of the room.

"They saw it," he said, seemingly unflustered. "Ellen told me that they didn't think anyone would read it and that she was making too much fuss; they were probably right."

"Do you remember Mayfield?"

"Of course. He tricked me. It was the start of a very bad time for me, and I blame him for a great deal of it."

"Because?"

"Because, Dr. Conyors—and I wish you'd let me call you Barrett—I sometimes struggle with what goes on between my ears. And after my sessions with Dr. Mayfield I found myself losing great big chunks of time, and then waking up with something horrible happening."

"You dissociate," she said.

"No shit."

"So you know?"

"Of course, I didn't always, just thought that I had blackouts. I'd be sitting having a conversation with somebody and the next thing you know I'd be getting raped in the laundry room and not remember how I got from point A to point B."

"Does that still happen?"

"The rapes?" he asked with a twisted grin.

"No, the memory lapses?"

"Not for a while, we all seem to be sticking together."

"We?"

"Yes, I know…but I don't know how else to describe it. That's why everyone thought I was schizophrenic, because I do hear voices. But that doesn't make me schizophrenic, does it?"

"No."

"Let's go into the library," he said, without waiting for her reply.

Putting the cat down and carrying her mug, she followed him back toward their usual meeting place. As he turned to open the doors, Fred attacked his ankle, pushing up his pant leg. She looked down and noticed something askew with his monitoring bracelet; it wasn't latched.

"So you have been out."

He froze, and then pushed open the doors. "You're mistaken," he commented.

"You've tampered with your bracelet."

He sank into a leather club chair and crossed his ankle over his knee. "Oh dear, I'm coming undone," he smiled and squeezed the sides of his electronic tether until they clicked firmly into place.

"So, where are you going, Jimmy?" she asked, taking the opposing chair.

"I think you've jumped a couple steps, Dr. Conyors. Perhaps if you'd play a little music with Jimmy, I might come up with some better answers; help connect the dots." His blue eyes focused on her face, his expression filled with longing, yet his voice carried something dark and threatening. "I'll make it worth your while."

"I don't want your money," she replied.

"That's not the offer." He blinked and his tongue flicked out and ran across the tip of an incisor. "Whom do you love, Barrett?" he asked.

"Where is she?"

"Patience…I once knew a woman named Patience…not a pilgrim at all, but a just and righteous woman. Shall we play?" he stood up and extended a hand across the space between them. "It would mean so much to Jimbo."

"What have you done with her? Where is she?"

"I'm sure I don't know what you're talking about," he answered, "but music has a way of jogging the memory. One duet, Dr. Conyors, what could it hurt?"

Barrett stood, her thoughts swam. She'd been right, and that knowledge did little to comfort her. She should have pushed sooner, tried harder, found something to get Jimmy sent back, but now…."I'm leaving," she said, knowing that she had to get out of there, to find Hobbs.

"Do you think that's wise?" he asked. "Life is so fragile, so delicate, so fleeting. We have to be careful with the ones we love; there aren't all that many, are there?"

"If you do anything…"

He put a finger to his lips, "Sshhh, this is not a time for hollow threats and paper tigers. All we ask is for a little music. Is that so much?"

She glared back at him.

"Well?" he glanced back at the Bösendorfer. "It's your move."

"Yes," she said.

He exhaled. "I thought we could play Brahms." His voice light and excited as he led her to the piano, where the score for the E Minor Sonata lay open on the lyre.

"That's a different cello," she remarked, noting the flame-varnished instrument that had replaced the darker one.

"I had an accident. This was my first cello," he answered, picking it up and settling down in his chair. He took his bow from the stand and tightened the nut, bringing the pale horsehair taut. He picked up a cake of well-used black resin and ran it across the bow. "It's still quite good, eighteenth-century French."

Barrett said nothing as she pulled back the intricately inlaid rosewood piano bench and settled behind the keyboard. She knew that this had been orchestrated, that since her first visit he'd been waiting for this moment. She stared up at the black notes covering the page.

"You start," he commented.

She nodded and, taking a quick look at the key signature, she raised her hands, letting her long fingers fall onto the ivory. The first chords filled the room with a lush sound. Barrett couldn't help but admire the piano's responsive action, making her own beloved Mason and Hamlin seem like a vapid imitation of what a piano could do.

And then Jimmy began. A haunting run of notes rose up from his cello, they hung in the air and mingled with the steady advances of her accompaniment.

The music wasn't difficult for Barrett, and she found herself wanting to match Jimmy's virtuosity, and finding moments of exquisite beauty as they progressed through the movements written in a minor key. Time vanished and she struggled to not think about the powerful sadness and longing that infused his playing. And always in her thoughts was Justine, that she was doing this for her. That she'd play this music, and so what if she enjoyed it, or felt like she was rediscovering a limb that had been removed. The music soared, filling the cavernous space, filling her, filling him.

Tears streamed down her face as she turned the last page—a part of her didn't want the music to end, but it did. The final chords resonated through the room. Neither she nor Jimmy spoke as they stayed perfectly still, letting the last harmonics melt into the dark wood and priceless carpets.

She looked at him.

He gazed back at her and nodded his head slowly, "Do you know how amazing you are?" he finally asked.

"You play beautifully," she replied, sincere in her response.

"Why did you stop playing?" He seemed on the verge of tears. "You could have gone and done anything."

"Maybe another time, we can talk about that. I kept my end of the bargain, Jimmy. You need to tell me whatever you know about my sister."

His eyes shut tightly, and then he opened them. He glared at her and abruptly stood, holding the cello roughly by its neck, almost as if he were strangling it.

"Why do you spoil things?" he walked across to the cello stand and clumsily replaced the instrument in its padded cradle. "Wasn't it beautiful enough for you?"

"It was," she replied, as the traces of the music coursing through her fingers and through her body were replaced by the sickening tingle of fear. "But we made a deal."

"Yes, it's time to play, Let's Make a Deal. Okay, so the lovely Dr. Conyors has played the lovely Brahms and now she'd like a bit of information about the lovely Justine. I can see by your outfit that you've come without your wire today. So, perhaps we can chat and do a little tit for tat…and what lovely tits she has."

Barrett shot up, sending the piano bench toppling behind her.

Jimmy laughed, "Careful, Dr. Conyors. I don't think that kind of physical display is necessary, although I can tell by the look in your eyes all the things you'd like to do. But let's face it; Jimbo is no stranger to a good thrashing. In fact," and he lowered his voice to a conspiratorial whisper, "I think he likes it. Must have been all those afternoons watching Mommy and the gardener. Now my little Chicky, she was always more of a hitter than a catcher. Like father, like daughter, I guess. Though you'd think his years in the nuthouse might have changed him. Because you know what they say," he asked rhetorically. "Today's catcher is tomorrow's pitcher."

"Where is my sister? What have you done with her?"

"Me? I haven't touched her," he winked and walked across the room. He leaned over the mahogany secretary and flipped down the top. "Let's see. I know I've got a little something here for you." He picked up a thick manila envelope, carried it back to her and dangled it in front of her face. "I can see what you're thinking," he said. "At this very minute you're just itching to get to your Detective Hobbs and figure out how you can trap little Jimbo. Well, we're not heading down that road. Let's be clear on that. If you ever want to see your sister…at least in a breathing state…there will be no police. Do you understand?"

"Yes."

"Good, and this," he said, releasing his hold on the envelope, "is a little present."

Barrett felt the thick packet in her hand.

"Open it. See what's inside."

She tore the top of the package open, revealing a stack of newspaper clippings and articles that had been downloaded from the Internet.

As she pulled them out she was met by a series of stories involving police corruption.

"Didn't you ever wonder," he began, "how it is that your detective Hobbs went from being a Deputy Chief to…to little more than a babysitter. Somehow I have a hard time reconciling your forgiving and forgetting his past trespasses. Unless…no, that couldn't be," he chuckled. "Unless he never told you. Or maybe he told you something that was a little less than the truth, the whole truth and nothing but the truth, so help him God. Men can be such crafty little devils. Such dirty little pigs."

Barrett stared at the articles, flipping through them and feeling sickened as she read headline after headline that spoke of bribes and corruption. Yes, he'd told her about that, but there was more.

"But you already knew that, didn't you," Jimmy persisted. "You don't have the best track record with men. I think you're too trusting. At least with Jimbo, what you see is what you get...Is something wrong, Dr. Conyors?"

"No," she lied, wondering how she would have reacted if Ed had told her everything. Would she have kissed him? Would she be hoping, even now, that she'd hear his knock at Jimmy's door?

"Are you sure? Are you quite sure that you're not standing there feeling the sweet birdie of love up and fly away? Because somehow I don't think he told you everything. That it wasn't just gambling and prostitution; it was mountains and mountains of kiddy porn, and little bitty children being used in unspeakable ways." Jimmy moved closer to Barrett, leaving barely a foot between them. "And at the top of it all, there's your boyfriend...There's a couple things I don't quite understand, and from the rather sour look on your face, I imagine you're having similar thoughts."

"Where's my sister?"

"That's not where I was going," he replied, a look of mock disappointment on his lips. "The thing, actually two things, I don't understand are, how did he get to keep his job? And, of course, the thing that has Jimbo's panties all twisted up is what the hell do you see in him?" Jimmy shut his eyes and when he opened them his shoulders sagged and he stepped back slightly. "He doesn't love you," his voice soft. "He's not good enough for you," he looked down at his feet and then back at her, "but I am."

Barrett's stomach lurched.

"It's true," he persisted, "there's a way out for both of us. It's the only answer." He awkwardly dropped to one knee and grabbed her hand, "Marry me, Barrett; everything will work out. Marry me."

She dropped back, easily twisting her hand from his grip, while clamping the other to her mouth.

He gasped at the force of her rejection and stared slack-jawed up at her.

Neither one spoke.

Jimmy blinked, and sprang to his feet. "Get out!"

"Shit," she'd misplayed her hand, why hadn't she seen this coming? "You surprised me, that's all," she tried to hide her revulsion.

"I'm sure he did."

"Look," she said, standing her ground, "the deal was I play music in exchange for my sister."

"No," he snarled, "That wasn't the deal. I'm not certain I know anything about a Justine."

"Please, don't hurt her. Just tell me what it is that you want."

"There you go, I thought we'd finally make our way to tit for tat. It all comes down to family, doesn't it?"

"What do you mean?"

"In the end, it's family that matters. They can fuck you in the ass, and beat you till there's blood coming out of your eyes. They can chop you up and stick you in the furnace, but when push comes to shoving down the stairs, it's family that's there for you. Don't ya find?"

"I just want my sister. Tell me what you want."

"Always looking for the simple answer, aren't you? What do they call that…Occam's razor? That cheap disposable doesn't work in this house. I would have thought you'd have figured that out by now. Don't let's start playing stupid; it's not attractive. It's not you."

"Was he…you're serious. Is that what it is? You want to marry me?"

"You sound surprised. Jimbo's getting to be that certain age. He's certainly eligible. I can think of a couple dozen society cunts that would love to wrap their creamy thighs around Jimbo's money. I don't think they'd care too much about his…dubious past. After all, with our kind of money, a little touch of eccentricity is expected; it's the norm. No telling how many nannies have gone into the fire."

"So let me get this straight. I marry you and Justine goes free, nothing's done to her. No games…she's free."

Jimmy stepped in close to Barrett, a sliver of air separated them.

She held her ground.

"There's so much more," he whispered. "Think of the music, you have to admit that was wonderful."

"It was."

"Relationships have grown from lesser things. You and Jimbo can make something of extraordinary beauty. How many couples can say that? So, he's got a few quirks, a little extra baggage. At heart, he's a good boy."

"If I marry you…him, you'll let her go?" she repeated, feeling his breath on her face, wondering if he was going to try and kiss her, and would she be able to stand her ground?

"Tit for tat," he whispered, bringing a finger up to the side of her face, and coming a hair's breadth away from touching her. "Shall he try again…last chance…last dance…last stab for a little romance."

"Yes," she said.

He blinked. Tears welled in his eyes. "Marry me," he gasped, reaching out his hand and then pulling it back, as though fearing a second rejection.

"Yes," she said. "But you can't let anything happen to her. You have to keep my sister safe. Do you understand, Jimmy? If you want me, you have to keep her safe. Now I need you to take me to her."

His eyes shut tightly and stayed that way for several seconds. His expression twisted and his teeth ground noisily.

Barrett watched, tensed and prepared for anything.

When he opened his eyes he said nothing as he stared at her. He clicked his tongue against the roof of his mouth. "We have a problem," he said.

"What?"

"It's sad to say, especially for two people about to embark on a lifetime of marital bliss," he smiled. "We have some trust issues. Nothing that can't be overcome. It's just…"

The doorbell rang.

Jimmy blinked, as the grandfather clock started to chime, "It's Hector," he said, "it's ten o'clock. You mustn't say anything," he warned. "If you tell anyone, we'll know. Do you understand?"

"Yes."

"If you tell Detective Hobbs, I have no doubt that your sister will die, and it won't be an easy death."

"Is she safe?"

"For now…Here's the deal. Come tonight and come alone," he walked over to a mahogany hutch and picked up a thick cream colored envelope. He handed it to her. "Open it."

And for the second time, she stared at the engraved invitation to Jimmy's Carnegie Hall recital. Only on this one, there was a single change:

James Cyrus Martin, IV
invites you to an evening of romance and music.
Place: Carnegie Hall/Weill Recital Hall
Time: 8:00 p.m.
Date: Saturday, May 1
Cello: James Cyrus Martin, IV
Piano: Barrett Conyors

"Any deviation, any altering of the plan and your sister will be nothing but a memory. And as clever as you are, Dr. Conyors, we've been at this a much longer time. I'll know if we're being followed. I'll know if you're wearing a wire. I know all of your reindeer games." He laughed, "Perhaps one day as we're chatting to our grandchildren you'll understand how very old we really are."

The doorbell rang again. Jimmy blinked and went to answer it.

She followed and watched as Hector entered the foyer.

"Hey doc," he called to her. "You're still here."

"She was just leaving," Jimmy said, as he took the plastic medication box from the aide.

"You feeling okay?" the aide asked her.

"I'm fine," she mumbled.

"You look kind of green," he said.

"I must be coming down with something," she answered as her toe caught on the library threshold and she stumbled.

"You want me to call you a cab?"

"No, I'm fine," she straightened and looked through the open door at the park's shadowy canopy.

"Goodbye, Dr. Conyors," Jimmy said in the tone a child uses when responding to a teacher.

She looked back at him, his features arranged in a neutral and pleasant expression. For an instant she had the illusion that he was wearing a mask, and that beneath it she could see a different face, one with eyes that burned. "Goodbye, Jimmy," she turned on shaky legs, and grabbing the iron handrail, walked away.

TWENTY-SIX

Fifty feet from the house, she stopped and stood weak-kneed on the sidewalk. She looked back at the park, as joggers looped around the carefully tended paths. Children played, and nannies, Russian au pairs, and parents chatted on gracefully scrolled iron-work benches.

"Barrett," a man's voice intruded into her thoughts.

She saw Hobbs coming toward her, dressed in jeans and a flannel shirt.

"I just got your message, I was out with my girls," he blurted, "I came as fast as I…"

She nearly screamed at the sound of a second voice—Jimmy's.

"Oh, Dr. Conyors," he sang out, from the top of his stoop. "You forgot your bag. Why, look who's here…it's Detective Hobbs." He clicked his tongue against the roof of his mouth. He shook his head. "Not getting off to a very good start, are we?"

She felt trapped, wanting to tell Hobbs everything. To have him pull out his service revolver right there and take Jimmy in or….

But even as that fantasy sparked, it was answered by the horrible knowledge that if she did that, Justine would die. It was Jimmy's way. And just because he might be taken into custody, it wouldn't alter the outcome.

Jimmy bounded down the steps with her black bag and the manila envelope filled with newspaper clippings, "and I believe these are yours, as well," he said handing them over. He looked up and down the block and then back at Hector who was peeking out of the front door holding a protesting kitten in his arms. "It's such a beautiful day. I wonder if I might get permission to go for a walk."

"I could take you," Hector said, "we could do some shopping."

"That would be great," Jimmy replied. "I could use a few things. What is it they say?" he smiled at Barrett. "Today is the first day of the rest of our lives," and he scampered back up the stairs.

Hobbs stared up at the house and watched as the aide followed Jimmy back inside and closed the door. "What the hell was that?"

"Don't say anything," she whispered. And then loud enough to be heard, "Here!" she thrust the envelope filled with clippings at him. "You forgot to tell me a few things," feigning anger.

Bewildered, Hobbs opened it. His expression darkened as he viewed the contents. "Look," he started.

She grabbed it from him, and with her back to the Martin house, she slipped in the announcement of the recital. "I don't ever want to see you again!" and she threw the envelope to the ground, turned and began to jog and then to run.

"Barrett, wait!" he shouted, the envelope on the sidewalk. "Wait!" He ran after her; he didn't catch her.

TWENTY-SEVEN

"*Always a bridesmaid, never a bride, Jimbo*," Father cackled.

"You're wrong," Jimmy argued, struggling against the fear and the doubt that Father brought, like crows to a roadside kill.

"*We'll see. Awfully convenient the way her cock-of-the-walk stud just happens to be here. Like Prince Fucking Charming.*"

"Stop it!"

"*Can't ignore the facts, Jimbo. He wants her. She's a fine piece of ass. Tell me, did you think about throwing her to the floor and peeling off those luscious tight pants. We'd like to know. Didn't think you had it in you.*"

"Shut up."

"*That's right, you have a thing about not touching them. I wonder where that came from. But now you'll have years and years of free therapy.*"

"She said yes," Jimmy muttered, no longer interested in Father's twisted input.

"*Was it really a yes, Jimbo? Let's not get too excited. You've got her arm twisted behind her back. What was she going to say? She might even have let you sneak a hand inside those tight little britches. That would have been tasty. But now…missed opportunity.*"

"That's not what I want and you know it."

"*You don't know what you want,*" Father spat back. "*You're just a pissant little punk who never grew up.*"

"Whose fault is that?"

"*Fine, this is where the parents get blamed for everything. If your mother were only here…although I bet you could dredge her up. Wouldn't that be fun? So you told her about the peepholes and Mommy's games. And now she's going to marry you. I don't think so, Jimbo.*"

"She loves me!" Jimmy said.

"*No she doesn't. Right now she's out there thinking of ways to trick you.*"

"No!"

"*She's sharing all your secrets with her big-dicked stud.*"

"She won't do that," he stuck the tip of his thumb into his mouth. "She loves me."

"*But what about…*"

Jimmy imagined a wall coming down inside his head, thick cement with tight seams and steel rebar, nothing could get through, not Father, not the vague and shadowy others that hung out well beyond the reaches of his probing thoughts. The important thing was she had said "Yes." She said "Yes." Proof that she loved him. There was so much that needed to be done, and chitchatting with Father was no help. They had a concert to give. He felt Father banging against the cement, wanting to make him doubt.

"No...no," that wouldn't happen. She would come...the past three weeks preparing...so much work, but worth it, all worth it. And then he remembered something critical he'd forgotten.

He ran upstairs to Mother's room, walked into her closet, and opened the wall safe. He sat cross-legged on the floor and piled jewelry boxes in a wall around him. One by one he opened them.

Father pushed through a chink in the wall, *"Something old."*

"Go away!" Jimmy muttered. Father was such a corny old bugger. He picked out all of the ring boxes. One by one he went through them, trying to find something suitable. He knew that he was down to the last hurdles, the tests of love.

He stared at great-great grandmother's sapphire and diamond art deco cocktail ring. He picked up the jewel and held it in the dull light. The diamonds that surrounded the four-carat sapphire were water blue, large and flawless. There was a coldness about them, but just on the outside, as light sparkled and burst in rainbows from their depths. He remembered seeing Barrett's wedding picture and the flapper-style dress that she'd worn; she'd like this ring. He put it back in its satin-lined box, popped the lid closed, and dropped it into his pocket.

Next he opened a large Cartier box and stared at the glorious diamond and platinum set that included the swan-tear necklace. The stones blue-white, large and perfect. The earrings would dangle and glitter around her long, graceful neck. The necklace—that even fifty years ago had cost in the mid six figures—was fit for his princess, his queen. "Yes," they were beautiful, she was beautiful. And Father was wrong, she did love him; even Ellen could see that. And most importantly, she had said, "Yes."

Sitting cross-legged in Mother's climate-controlled closet, surrounded by couture gowns and chiffoniers filled with lingerie, he drifted into a world of possibility—a future with a beautiful wife, children, and music, glorious music. And in the center of it all, there he'd be, happy, free, and loved.

Father chortled and hissed through his vision, *"Little Jimbo, happy at last."*

TWENTY-EIGHT

BARRETT STOOD ON THE corner of 7th Avenue and 57th; it was 7:30, and she could barely move. She felt numb and not real, as the city whizzed by on a beautiful May night, where the sun was just now setting, turning the clouds purple and smearing the sky with vivid arcs of pink.

Since meeting with Jimmy and his insane proposal, she'd struggled, trying to find the loophole that would end the nightmare. Every time she'd seen the shimmer of a possibility, she'd pictured Justine, and hope fled.

She'd taken frantic calls from her mother, and had even spoken to a patrolman who'd reluctantly agreed to look into Justine's disappearance. She'd told him nothing; she had no choice.

"Where is she?" her mother had cried. "Someone's done something to my baby. Why?"

Barrett had tried to reassure her. To let her know that Justine would be okay, that somehow everything would work out fine.

And she almost believed that—the truth far stranger than the easy fiction of, "No word."

The minutes and hours had ticked by.

And now, staring across at the performer's entrance to Carnegie Hall, she felt a vortex sucking her down. With every step, as she crossed the street, she felt its pull, Jimmy's pull, dragging her in, closer and closer. He wanted her to be there; she was. He wanted her alone; she was. He wanted her to play music, and she had. And now, they were going to give a concert. But to whom? And why?

Halfway across the street, the absurdity hit. A murderous cellist—her patient—was in love with her, and if she didn't come up with something fast, he intended to blackmail her into marriage...or kill her sister...or both.

She remembered Sifu Li's sign, *"Fear doesn't live in the present, it resides in the past and the future."*

At least now, as bizarre as it was, she knew what Jimmy wanted. He wanted to marry her. He wanted to play music with her. She almost laughed at the simplicity of it. What was it Hobbs had said, *"He's got a crush."*

But there was more, Jimmy's psyche was made of quicksilver, with an unstable personality that shifted with the breezes of suggestion and frustration. He was like a minefield, constructed through decades of torture and, she suspected, generations of twisted doings at the mansion. A wrong word, an uncareful gesture, a misperceived glance, they could all set him off. Even despite the heart-stopping agony of Justine's kidnapping, Barrett felt something for Jimmy. Not the romantic thrall that he imagined, but there was something endearing that, in a certain light, at certain times, gave her glimpses of the unhappy child in his past and the brilliant man he might have been. But then she thought about Justine and about the ever-expanding list of victims. Yes, she would do as he told her, but she had to find a way to save Justine and bring this to an end.

———

Hobbs fought to keep his emotions in check as he viewed Barrett through a pair of polarized binoculars. The poisonous manila envelope lay next to him on the seat of his anonymous navy blue Impala parked at the western side of 7th Avenue. He'd tried to phone her after she'd run from him. He knew that she was screening her calls, because she wouldn't pick up and then ten minutes later he'd call again and her line would be busy.

He should have told her the whole truth. But how do you do that? How do you tell someone that because of your stupidity a child-pornography ring was allowed to operate? Even though he eventually brought it down and was the whistle blower on fellow detectives, it didn't matter. If he'd even known for just a day, what did that equate to in the suffering of a child? That a man he'd considered a good friend had lied to him didn't matter. That detail never found its way into the papers. It was his fault and he accepted that. He'd wanted to believe his men, to give them that one chance to pull their act together. But if he'd known…it was a familiar game and one that he wished he could stop. If he'd known, he would have acted and none of this would have happened.

"But then you wouldn't be here," he reminded himself. *You'd still be with Margaret* and that was a mixed bag. He wouldn't have admitted that to himself a year ago, but the truth was that while he loved his two daughters—life with his ex hadn't been good. He had never cheated and knew that he never would, but the passion had fled their marriage years earlier, and their only point of connection was their children.

Somewhere after his eighth attempt to call Barrett, he'd noticed the concert invitation stuffed in the bottom of the envelope. When he saw Barrett's name on it, he immediately understood. She was in trouble and had sent him a message.

So rather than continue his fruitless calls, he'd staked out her apartment and then trailed her.

———

Ellen Martin gazed down from the fourteenth floor of her company's Carnegie Towers Suite as Barrett crossed the street. The risk of what they were doing was massive, and the presence of the detective in the unmarked car was bad news. He'd need to be taken care of—a contingency she was prepared for—but at the moment, she had more pressing matters.

She gathered her bags and headed toward the elevators. She tried not to think about how much was at stake, and how things could go wrong. It was a crazy plan, Jimmy was certifiable, but if they could pull this off, none of that would matter. She knew how to handle him and all of the swirling others that lived inside of him.

As the elevator brought her down to the basement that connected the towers to the historic concert hall, she thought about Jimmy's obsession with fairy tales, and their childhood games of Hansel and Gretel, where the storyline would wander for hours, as they'd conquer endless foes, with the inevitable climax of each of their enemies being fed into the massive furnace. Just as Father, during that horrible night of their eighth birthday, had killed Maylene and incinerated her—a memory that had only recently returned.

While she would never tell Jimmy, Ellen knew why he did it. Jimmy had confided in Maylene, and she had naively confronted Father, had even threatened to go to the authorities if the abuse didn't stop; she never saw it coming.

Tonight would be different. More like one of Maylene's fairy tales. The gown nestled in tissue paper, and the antique jewels from Cartier and Tiffany, fit for a princess. The detective, like one of their childhood villains, would be vanquished, and the concert, while a bit over the top for her taste, was Jimmy's Cinderella ball. A magical night for him to shine, to prove his love…to take a bride.

All of which was good for him, but for Ellen—who Father had always called the practical one—the goal was less about the bride and all about the making of an heir to continue the Martin dynasty. But more too…there was a hunger inside of Ellen…a need for this child, Jimmy's child, a chance to get it right and unmake all the horrors of their past. The elevator doors opened, and shouldering her precious burden, she mouthed, "And they all lived happily ever after."

TWENTY-NINE

Old memories flooded Barrett as the red-jacketed doorman led her back to the dressing rooms for the Weill—the smallest performance space in Andrew Carnegie's 1891 gift to New York City. As a child and teenager she'd performed in all three halls. The Weill, with its classical arches, graceful woodwork, and massive crystal chandelier, was her favorite. This felt like stepping back in time.

But now, each footfall caused her gut to tighten. The doorman stopped and unlocked a dressing room door, "The other performer is already here, you want me to tell him you've arrived?"

"No," Barrett said, wanting to grab the doorman and tell him that the other performer was a homicidal maniac, and would he please call the police. "I'm sure he'll find me," she said, looking in at a brightly lit room that reeked of roses. The bouquet was massive, dozens of blood-red blooms surrounded by plumes of angel's breath; it took up half the counter along the mirrored wall. Propped in front of the vase was an envelope.

"Will you need anything else?" the man asked.

Many things came to mind—more bullets for the gun that lay heavy in her bag, the whereabouts of her sister, a large and heavy object to fall on Jimmy. "No, I'm all set."

He looked at her, glanced questioningly at her back pack, and then at an empty clothes rack—like the ones that get wheeled up and down the fashion district. "Are you expecting your wardrobe?"

She glimpsed her reflection through the baby's breath—she was still in the black sweats she'd worn that morning—so long ago—sitting across from Jimmy and watching as all the different voices spilled out of him. She'd thought of changing, had even stared into her closet, unable to decide what to wear. Her mind struggling against the other piece of things—he'd proposed...and she'd accepted. She'd thought of Ralph, and their wedding day—her ivory satin dress now carefully boxed and folded in tissue paper. Tomorrow was supposed to be his funeral. Throughout the afternoon she'd been on and off the phone with her mother, not able to tell her—or anyone—the awful truth.

A knock at the door, and the rustle of plastic and paper and then Ellen Martin, dressed in a midnight-blue watered-silk gown, her blond hair lacquered into an elegant upsweep, diamonds glittering from her ears and around her bare throat, pushed into the space.

The doorman excused himself, "Looks like your stuff arrived."

Ellen glanced at him, and then at Barrett. She smiled as she hung a bulky garment bag on the clothes rack, and deposited a small rectangular makeup box on the counter. She fished a bill out of a dainty purse, the same color as her dress, and handed it to the worker, "Thanks so much."

"Will you ladies be needing anything else?"

"Barrett, honey?" Ellen asked.

"No," stunned by Ellen's involvement, and realizing that she had made a serious miscalculation. She'd overlooked the obvious—Jimmy's accomplice was his sister.

"You know," Ellen said, checking in the mirror, "I'm a little parched. Be a dear," reaching into her purse and peeling off a couple of C notes, "get us a bottle of Crystal…and keep the change."

"Thanks," and he was gone.

"Well," Ellen turned to look at Barrett, "we do have our work cut out for us, don't we? Just sit yourself down, and I'll start in on hair and makeup."

"Why are you here?" Barrett asked through clenched teeth, wondering at the near-feverish enthusiasm of Jimmy's sister. "Why are you doing this to me?"

"Don't be silly," Ellen replied, "miss my brother's wedding, not on your life," and the smile vanished. "Now sit down, and stop asking questions…you need to focus on your performance, you need to think about your sister, and you need to think about the honor of marrying into our family."

Barrett thought how easy it would be to overpower Ellen, and wondered if that was a way out; Jimmy's sister in exchange for Justine.

As though reading her mind, Ellen clicked her tongue against the roof of her mouth, "And dear, I'd be very careful about any attempts to change the course of events. Your sister's life hangs by a thread. Should anything happen to either my brother, or me, she will not survive. Do we understand each other?" staring Barrett in the eye.

It would have felt so good, to take her down, but the risk… Defeated, she said, "Yes."

"Good, now in the chair—we don't have much time."

As Barrett complied, Ellen grabbed Barrett's bag from the floor, unzipped the main compartment and spilled its contents across the counter by the roses. The small firearm—an unregistered snub-nosed pistol—landed heavily, alongside her cell phone, pager, and PDA.

"Oh, my," Ellen commented, with mock exasperation as she removed the batteries from the cell phone and pager, "what will we do with you?" And the firearm and electronics disappeared into a slit pocket in the voluminous skirt of her gown. "Now," pulling a brush from the makeup case, "turn around, and let's see what we can do."

Barrett faced forward, and seethed as Ellen worked a brush through her hair, combing it straight back with assured strokes, making it smooth and shiny.

"I'd always wanted a sister," Ellen remarked, as she twisted and pinned Barrett's short hair back, augmenting it with matched human-hair pieces that she worked into a tidy French knot.

"Why are you doing this?" Barrett asked, trying to keep her anger in check, not wanting to give in to the paralyzing fear that simmered a hair beneath the surface.

"Soon," Ellen said—then, to a knock at the door. "It's open."

The bellman wheeled in a cart with iced champagne and two crystal flutes.

"Thanks so much," Ellen flashed a smile.

"Will you ladies need anything else?"

She met Barrett's eye in the mirror. "No, everything's just about set."

Once he'd gone, Ellen, not turning her back, opened the garment bag.

Despite herself, Barrett stared into the zippered opening. At first she thought the dress was black, but as Ellen lifted out the rustling garment, it caught the light, flashing a deep green. "Vintage Dior," she said. "I hope you appreciate what I went through to get this. I had it remade just for you."

Barrett said nothing, as Ellen hung the gown. "It's a perfect length for playing," she commented, stepping back from the rack. "Now, let's get changed…don't be shy. It's nothing I haven't seen before."

A thought came to Barrett, something Hobbs had mentioned about the locks on her apartment. "You've been in my condo," she stated.

"Of course, how else could I get your size right? Now move. I promise not to peek. You get changed, and I'll pour the bubbly."

Barrett got up, glanced at Ellen, and then at the gorgeous dress.

"Go on," Ellen urged. "It won't bite. We don't have much time."

Using the hanging garment bag as a partial screen, Barrett disrobed down to her underwear, while keeping an eye on Ellen. She knew that if she were going to survive and save Justine, she needed to stay sharp. Now was not the time to fight, but it would come; it would have to come. She unhooked and unzipped the back of the dress, noting the elaborate sewn-in corset. As she stepped into the dress and pulled it up, Ellen glanced at her, two champagne flutes in her hands.

"You're going to have to take off your bra…it's strapless, but trust me, you look fabulous."

Holding the shimmering satin in front of her breasts, Barrett reached back and unhooked her bra.

"Here," Ellen glided across the tight space, handing her a glass of champagne, "I'll do the back."

Barrett stiffened as Ellen's strong fingers worked the tiny hooks that cinched the garment in tight around her belly, and ribs. As Barrett watched her reflection, she realized that this dress had indeed been custom fitted…for her. The elegantly draped front revealed the tops of her breasts, her waist corseted in tight and the ankle-length skirt flowed out like the petals of some fantastic flower. As she slipped on perfectly fitting black-velvet pumps, new doubts crept in. She felt her throat tighten.

Ellen stepped back and looked at her, "See if you can sit," she said. "And you better have some of that champagne; you look like you're about to jump out of your skin…go on." Ellen picked her glass off the counter, and raised it in Barrett's direction. "To new beginnings," she offered, and sipped the cold bubbly.

Barrett felt the walls close around her, sweat beaded her forehead. Everything had been planned; there was no way out; it was hard to think.

"Just drink," Ellen urged, "you need something to calm down."

Barrett hesitated. She'd not seen Ellen pour the champagne, and wondered if it had been drugged.

"Drink it," Ellen ordered. "Or I could just as easily give you a shot; I'm sure I've got something in my bag." She smiled, "But Crystal is better, a glass or two shouldn't hurt your performance."

Barrett saw no choice and carefully took a sip, tasting it with her tongue. It was cool and it seemed to dissolve upon contact, the bubbles flying up her nostrils.

"Now sit, and we can get on to makeup, and…Jimmy brought you presents."

Still holding the sweating glass, Barrett got back in the chair, as Ellen deftly spread a plastic apron around her shoulders and over the gown. "I understand you're a fantastic sight reader," she remarked as she pumped a mascara brush into its tube and proceeded to work on Barrett's lashes. "Good thing, the Chopin is tricky—especially the opening—but I understand you've already been through the Brahms."

Barrett said nothing, as she watched her transformation in the mirror. Occasionally, she'd sip at her drink, even letting Ellen refill it for her. It helped a little, the alcohol a tiny balm against her surging panic.

"Voilá!" Ellen announced, ripping off the makeup apron.

Barrett stared at the beautiful woman with flawless skin in a spectacular shimmering green-black dress. From her ears dangled tear-shaped blue-white diamonds—Ellen had said something about the jewels having belonged to her great-great grandmother. Around her throat was the matching necklace with large stones drawing attention to the sweep of her neck and the full curve of her breasts that were molded by the dress's intricate, but invisible, architecture.

"Come," Ellen said, offering her hand.

Barrett stood, and felt the blood leave her head. The room swayed, and she immediately thought of the champagne, but no, she'd only had a couple glasses. Unless…her head pivoted, she looked at the satisfied smiled on Ellen's lips, and then at her own reflection. Her eyes, there was something wrong, why were her pupils so tiny? And there was a strange warmth in her belly—not unpleasant—kind of floaty. She glanced at the floor, her feet hidden by the glimmering fabric. She stuck out a foot and admired the pointy tip of her velvet slipper. And the gown was so pretty, the way it caught the dull light of the dressing room, and shot sparkles of the most-beautiful green.

"Yes," Ellen mused. "You're finally ready."

THIRTY

It was all Jimmy could do to stay in control. Father howled wanting to come out, but that would be catastrophe. From behind the velvet curtain, he peeked into the packed recital hall. While he'd not seen most of those in attendance in nearly two decades—at least not in person—he easily put names to many of the faces. The invitations had only gone out a week ago, yet from the bubbling noise that filtered back, it sounded like a packed house. If Father came out…Father couldn't play, only Jimmy could. He balled his fingers into fists and then relaxed them, repeating the exercise several times, slowing his breath, trying to keep his excitement in check. He was so close. "And they lived happily ever after," he mouthed under his breath, catching a glimpse of his cello, nestled in the curve of the gleaming concert grand.

The chandelier dimmed. The murmur of voices swelled, and then settled, growing softer with the fading light. A single spot shone on center stage, and he watched—still hidden—as Ellen appeared. She looked lovely in her midnight blue silk, her hair done up special. So much of this night was her doing, the invitations to Manhattan's old money, her idea. The shame of his youth about to be redeemed, the Martin name being cleared.

"Ladies and gentleman," Ellen's husky voice carried through the perfectly balanced acoustics, each of the two hundred fifty attendees able to catch every word. "I wanted to thank each and every one of you for coming. Tonight is a very special night for my brother...and for me. It's a celebration. Tonight," she paused, and scanned the room, "not only will my brother return to the concert stage, but more importantly..." She smiled, and scanned the room looking at the faces. "I don't want to ruin the surprise, but tonight will end with an important announcement."

The silence was total.

"So without further ado, I give you my brother, James Cyrus Martin IV, and on piano, Dr. Barrett Conyors."

———

From her vantage point in the wings, Barrett watched Ellen's announcement. She stared at the black piano, and the gleaming cello in front of it. Her body felt light, and while she knew she should be terrified, that Justine was in mortal danger, and that she was about to be married to a psychotic murderer, she somehow could not feel afraid. *I've been drugged*, she thought, *something hallucinogenic*. As she turned her head, rainbow halos clung to the outlines of the furniture and to the dimming lights.

"I think that's your cue," a woman in a red-and-black usher's outfit whispered.

"Thank you," Barrett said, and as though gliding on magic shoes, she stepped onto the stage.

From the opposite wing, Jimmy emerged; his hair slicked back, the lapel of his tuxedo, made of the same greenish-black satin as her dress. *We match*, she thought.

In center stage Ellen stood looking at her, and then at her Jimmy. "Come," she mouthed to Barrett, holding out her left hand. With her right she motioned toward Jimmy. She grasped Barrett's fingers, and her brother's. She joined them together, and faced the audience.

Barrett looked at Jimmy, he seemed so young. And then she realized, in a deeper way than before, that Jimmy was not a single person. That the diagnosis she'd resisted was in fact the correct one. Jimmy had distinct and separate personalities inside of him. The thirty-five-year-old man, whose hand she was holding, and whose expression seemed so young and innocent, was actually Jimmy the child, the virtuoso, and the victim.

He met her gaze, his eyes filled with longing. "Thank you," he grasped her hand tight.

The moment hung, as she looked at him. There was no doubt, the eyes that gazed back with such sweetness were those of a little boy. "Jimmy," she whispered, knowing that Ellen could also hear. "I'll do this, but nothing must ever happen to my sister. You have to swear, you all have to swear. I know you're not in there alone."

A sliver of fear sliced through her drug-induced euphoria, as the planes of his face shifted. A harsh appraisal shone through his pale eyes. Something dark and dangerous peered back, like the gaze of a serpent.

"Swear," she repeated.

"Of course," he said, his tongue clicked wetly against the roof of his mouth. "A deal's a deal."

"And you," she looked at Ellen, their hands all still entwined. "Swear it, and I'll do this."

"You have my word," she whispered, through clenched teeth. Her gaze outward toward the audience. "Do as you're told, and all will be well." Leaving Barrett's hand in Jimmy's, Ellen stepped back. "And now," she addressed the room, "I give you a night of romance and magic."

———

Ed Hobbs flashed his shield and showed the lobby usher the parchment concert invitation.

"Where is this?" he asked.

"Third floor."

He bypassed the elevator and ran up the marble stairs. He arrived as the audience funneled into the recital hall. Dressed in jeans, work boots, and a flannel shirt he felt exposed in the excited crowd of perfectly groomed men—some in tuxedoes—and women in couture gowns and diamonds.

Hanging back, as though he were a member of the maintenance staff, he caught snippets.

"Could have knocked me over with a feather," a woman in a black cocktail dress commented, "after all these years; I thought they'd locked him away for life. I hate to say it," she said, casting her eyes, and passing over Ed, as though he were invisible, "I wouldn't have missed this just for the freak value."

A thirty-something man, his eyes bright with champagne, agreed, "Of course, but think about the money. Neither one with an heir, she's…at that age…and he, well, I always thought he was a bit light in the loafers."

"They say the father was," a second woman in pale pink added, sipping her drink.

"And she was no better," the woman in black replied, "had a thing for the help…can you imagine?"

"To be fair," the man offered, "Ellen Martin pulled the company out of the fire. God, if I'd only kept that stock."

"She never married," pink lady replied. "And she's not bad looking. Lezzie?"

"Maybe," he said, "I know Harold Anderson made the attempt."

"Good family, what happened?" Pinky asked.

"Well," he leaned toward her as they moved into the auditorium, "the way I heard it…"

And no matter how Ed strained, he couldn't catch the outcome of Ellen Martin's involvement with the eligible son. Keeping to the periphery, as the crowd streamed through the gracious double doors, Ed searched for a hiding place in the elegant, but intimate, concert hall. Barrett's message, while hazy, had been clear on one point. She was deathly afraid, and didn't want Jimmy—or anyone he was working with—to know that she'd gone to the cops. And the absurdity…she was going to play a Carnegie Hall concert with her patient, a man Ed was convinced lay at the center of a decade's-long blood bath. Up until a couple of hours ago, it still hadn't made sense, and then, while flipping through the day's roster of cases—an old habit from his days as deputy chief—he'd come upon a just-opened case that sucked the breath from his chest. A young doctor had gone missing from the Harlem hospital where she was in training. Staring at the report of Justine Conyors' disappearance, the pieces had clicked horribly into place.

Needing to hide before the curious audience took their seats, he aimed for a curtained alcove to the left of the doors.

Behind the red velvet was a small room with a dimly lit balding man in front of an expansive control panel. He glanced up, "No one's allowed in…"

Ed flashed his shield. "Please," he said, "I need to be here, and tell no one."

"What's going on?" the man swallowed, glancing from Ed's shield to his face. "Am I in trouble?"

"No, I just need an observation point where no one can see me."

"Okay," he said, looking from Ed down to a series of three monitors on the table.

Ed joined him behind his equipment, and was afforded a view of the empty stage.

"Okay if I get started?" the man asked.

"Sure, just do everything the way you were told, nothing different."

The sound-and-light technician glanced at the clock as the second hand kissed the twelve; exactly eight. His right hand eased back on a lever; the chandelier dimmed. The crowd settled and Ed, shifting his attention between the monitors, watched as Ellen took the stage.

"Here," the technician passed a pair of headphones across the table. "You want to hear better; it comes straight from the mike."

"Thanks," Ed put them on, and listened to Ellen Martin's cryptic announcement.

It was all he could do to not bolt out of there and get Barrett the hell away. She should have listened to him, should have given up this damn case, but now…his failure to act, to save her, was tearing him up. And he knew that to call for reinforcements might bring down Jimmy and his sister, but without his knowing exactly what leverage they had to get Barrett into that dress and onto that stage, the risk was too high. She was in deadly peril, the same probably for her sister; that's the only thing that would have gotten her here.

As he watched and listened, the technician zoomed in on the three figures holding hands in center stage. He tapped Ed on the shoulder.

Ed pulled up one earpiece.

"Concert's being filmed," the techie offered. "I've done a lot of these, but I think this is the first combo recital and engagement…surprised they didn't get the whole damn thing done and haul in a minister."

"What? What did you just say?"

The techie looked up, and then back at his complicated equipment. "That's the big surprise. The cello player is gonna propose to the accompanist."

"Oh, shit!" Ed stared at the image on the screen, and what struck him hardest was the expression on Barrett's face. She wasn't frightened, or if she was, she was giving one hell of a performance. But more than that, Ed was jolted by her beauty. As he looked at Jimmy in his tuxedo, Ed startled as he named the powerful feeling coursing through him—jealousy.

The camera panned back, framing the piano and cello. Ellen followed Barrett to the piano, and sat in a chair slightly behind and to the left of the bench, as the technician manipulated two spots to frame Jimmy and Barrett in separate circles of soft amber light.

347

The effect made their faces glow, and as Barrett, her back straight, lifted her bare arms, and brought her hands down onto the keys, Ed was unprepared for what followed. How was it that he could have known her for all of these years and not known that she could make this magic?

He gasped as the first dizzying run of Chopin spilled from the piano, the timing impossibly difficult, the subtlety amazing. And then Jimmy lifted his bow, his head cocked slightly in her direction, and started to play.

THIRTY-ONE

BARRETT GASPED AS THE first notes from Jimmy's cello blossomed into the most exquisite music she'd ever heard. The painfully tragic melody floated in the air, mixing with the furious off-kilter runs that spilled from her fingers. She recognized what she was playing, having often heard—but never played—Chopin's Cello Sonata in G Minor. It was his last work, written on Capri, and the only thing he had ever written for the cello. He was dying there, his lungs collapsing, overcome by the tuberculosis that had plagued him from childhood. Chopin, Polish like Sophie, had been a constant of Barrett's life. She remembered her first competition, at nine, her fingers flying over the *Revolutionary Étude*, a piece that seasoned performers could barely handle.

Tonight, her playing felt effortless, and she barely noticed when Ellen would lean forward, wait for her nod, and turn the page. The music was glorious. The cello's dreamy song, her assured reply, the joined effort of two people, two instruments, becoming one. They flew through the movements, the soulful allegro moderato, the rapid back and forth of the scherzo, the longing ache of the largo, and the spectacular finale—Chopin's last musical statement.

Her fingers lifted slightly as the intense chords resonated through the darkened hall.

She lifted her head and looked at Jimmy, his arm still raised from the final sweeping arc of the bow. He turned to her, sweat dripping from his brow. In the amber light, his face glowed and she saw the brilliant child from all those years back.

"I love you," he mouthed. "I will always love you."

Frozen in time, she wanted to respond. The music had transcended all, how could she have given this up?

Ellen whispered into her ear, "Take a bow."

Barrett tried to remember where she was…a thunderous applause surrounded them, as the house lights raised slightly on the well-dressed audience.

She watched as Jimmy placed his instrument on the floor and came toward her. He took her hand and led her toward the front of the stage. "That was incredible," he gushed. "You were incredible."

"So were you," she said, as she felt the heat of his hand in hers, its warmth traveling up her arm, she shuddered; something wasn't right. "You played beautifully," she answered truthfully, her tongue thick in her mouth.

As the traces of their playing vanished, and they took their bows, Barrett struggled against a dense fog-like curtain that made it hard to think. What was she doing on stage? And who was this man who'd just told her that he loved her? He played beautifully, but hadn't she given up music, or had that been a dream? Perhaps this was a dream, and that's why it didn't make sense. This had to be a dream. She looked over the audience and saw that many of them were holding champagne flutes—a clear violation of Carnegie Hall rules—no food or drink allowed in the performance spaces; this was definitely a dream, and soon she'd wake to some other reality. She took a third bow.

"One more?" Jimmy asked, as the audience continued with unrelenting applause.

"Yes," she answered, feeling the glow of adoration, remembering what it had felt like, and thinking that if this were a dream, it wasn't so bad.

———

Ellen watched as Jimmy and Barrett took their bows. Hanging back by the piano, she scanned the audience. They'd all come; she knew they would. Like some dying breed of rare bird—Manhattan's old money. Here were no flash-in-the-pan real estate moguls or hotshot brokers; her guests had families with roots that ran deep. These had been the supposed playmates of her childhood, all running under the watchful eyes of dark-skinned nannies and governesses at the Bailey Beach Club, while the parents got stoned on martinis and Manhattans. They'd all come; all wanting to see what had become of the Martin twins. Keeping a pleasant smile fixed on her face, she ran over the names, all of the families with debutante daughters and iron-clad trust funds. All of the eligible men from eligible families that Mother and Father had tried to interest her in. To please them, she'd endured a series of uncomfortable outings with shallow boys who spoke endlessly of their own pathetic accomplishments, who fumbled for kisses, and who lacked any spark of talent.

As she watched her brother and the woman he loved, she felt a surge of jealousy. How ironic, she thought, that the one man of true genius was the one man she could not have. And the woman, drugged and her memory clouded by the potent amnestic she'd placed in her champagne, was undeniably beautiful, and grudgingly Ellen had to admit that her playing was better than anything she had ever done. But she did not love Jimmy; it was just an illusion that would vanish in the morning. She had so much that needed to be done; it caused a shiver of panic. "One step at a time," she mouthed. The concert, a wedding gift to her brother and his bride, served an important purpose, and it was the only reason she would have taken such a risk, because here tonight, in front of 250 descendants of robber barons, Jimmy's engagement was about to be announced. Not one of the attendees would forget this evening, and the beautiful woman in dark-green satin who'd held her brother's hand, who'd glowed in the spotlight. There would be no more questions, no awkward accusations; after all they'd all seen them together. A beautiful couple, so talented, so well-matched, so in love.

No, she mused, as Jimmy led Barrett back to the piano for their second and final sonata—the Brahms E Minor. There'd be no questions, the child—maybe twins if they were lucky—would be born. And the mother, who would be remembered at her most beautiful and her most brilliant, would meet with a tragic end in childbirth.

She leaned forward and centered the music on the lyre. She glanced at Barrett, with her creamy complexion, high cheekbones, and gray-green eyes. The child would be beautiful. For the briefest of moments Ellen allowed herself to fantasize that Barrett was actually Jimmy's willing bride. But Ellen—as her father had always reminded her—was the practical one. Barrett Conyors was merely a vessel, a means to a critical end.

Jimmy glanced back, catching her eye, and then Barrett's. He nodded in her direction, raised his bow, and touching it down to the strings, began a performance that would be remembered by many in the audience as the single most glorious piece of music they had ever heard.

THIRTY-TWO

THE AUDIENCE WAS ON their feet, the applause thunderous. From his hiding place, Ed strained to see the stage. Jimmy and Barrett were taking their bows.

Ellen Martin stepped from behind the piano and approached the footlights. She raised her arms to quiet the audience. She smiled and put a finger to her lips. She nodded to her brother and stepped to the side.

To Ed, as Jimmy came down on one bent knee and produced a ring box, it felt as though the air had been sucked from the room. He reached for Barrett's hand and through the microphone Hobbs clearly heard, "Barrett Conyors, will you marry me?"

Even from this distance he caught the flash of the ring as Barrett, quietly responded, "Yes Jimmy, I will marry you."

The room exploded with fresh applause, as Jimmy slipped the jewel on her finger, and rising, gave her a chaste kiss on the lips, and taking her hand, led her offstage.

The clapping didn't stop. He waited—along with the rest—for the performers to return. Shouts erupted, "Bravo! Encore! Encore!" It turned into a chant.

"Encore! Encore! Encore!"

He waited, not certain of what he'd just seen, just heard. With the passing seconds, apprehension grew, and then, with a sickening certainty, he knew they weren't returning.

"Shit," he bolted from his cover, and ran toward the front of the auditorium. His previous caution, replaced by urgency, Barrett was in mortal danger, and his moment to act was racing away.

He flew up the stage steps and ran in the direction he'd seen them leave. An usher stood back in the wings, looking out at the room.

"Where did they go?" Ed asked.

"Gone," the usher replied. "You think I should go out and tell them?"

Ignoring his question, "Which way?"

"Out, I guess. They really should have played an encore. They just bolted."

"Which door?"

"There," he said.

Ed sprinted through the side door and hurtled down a tight stairwell. As he went, passing exits to the second and first floors, he knew they'd gone. At the base of the steps he pushed the red handle of an emergency door that led out to 7th Avenue.

A blast of cool night air rushed in. He scanned north and south, looking for any trace of the Martins and Barrett. A cab pulled away from the sidewalk, at first he passed over it, but something pulled his attention. The driver was a blond, and as it accelerated down-town, he caught a glimpse of Jimmy Martin staring back through the rear window.

"Shit!" Ed's heart sank.

He bolted across the street toward his parked, unmarked car, trying to hang on to a couple distinguishable features of the yellow cab, like the cracked taillight and crumpled right-rear fender. He yanked open the door, jammed the key in the ignition, and in the split-second his brain registered that his car door shouldn't have been unlocked, he saw a flash of blue flame, the tank exploded and his world went black.

———

The euphoria from whatever drug Ellen had given her had vanished. Now she felt only panic, and fear. Barrett, her hands cuffed, searched for the handle of the cab door, all the time her eyes fixed on Jimmy, who stared back through the window. In the front seat Ellen sat rigid, her hands on the wheel, her eyes occasionally visible in the rear-view mirror, watching her.

"The door's locked," she said, observing Barrett's attempts. "Just remember that if you try anything funny, your sister will die."

"Why?" Barrett managed, her head pounding, her tongue thick in her mouth.

"Because he loves you," she said, and the cab lurched to the left, as a loud explosion sounded behind them.

"What was that?" Barrett asked.

"Jimmy?" Ellen asked, "Did you see?"

"Yes," he settled back in his seat, his eyes on Barrett. "No more detective Hobbs."

"What?" Barrett shuddered, "Ed…what have you done?"

"You're very popular," Ellen commented. "What with the husband, the detective…any more suitors we should know about?"

"Your detective Hobbs," Jimmy commented in his wheezy old-man voice, "just blew up. So sad, and I believe he had children, too."

"No," Barrett gasped, "Oh God, no."

"We can't be having other roosters in Jimbo's hen house," he cackled, his voice dripping with the sarcasm Barrett had learned to associate with the personality that claimed to be his father.

"And Barrett," Ellen said, making eye contact through the rear-view mirror, "you need to know that from this moment forward your actions have consequence. Should you attempt to escape or to contact your mother, or any friends or coworkers, they'll meet with fates similar to your detective and your poor, dead husband. Ralph, wasn't it? By now, your mother will have received a letter from you, apologizing for this shameful behavior, but you've fallen in love and for the time being desperately need to be alone with your fiancé. In fact, you won't be able to show your face at your husband's funeral tomorrow."

"She'll never believe that," Barrett said, her fear growing by the second.

"For her sake," Ellen said flatly, "let's hope she does. If not, how sad, and a bit of a cliché, the female bartender walking home late at night. So many bad things can happen in such a big city. And if you're wondering about your colleagues and the good Dr.

Fielding, by this time tomorrow he'll have explained to the clinic the seriousness of your behavior. You will become an example of the most serious of ethical breaches—falling in love with a patient. They will be cautioned against having anything to do with you."

"Anton would never believe…" but even as she spoke, she began to understand. "How did you get to him?"

"It's not important," Ellen said, "suffice it to say that Dr. Fielding is finally on the way to the tenure he so desperately desires."

Barrett found it hard to catch her breath. Through the mirror she saw the faintest of smiles on Ellen's painted lips. She thought about the board that oversaw Jimmy's release from the hospital, and wondered how they'd respond to this bizarre piece of news. Certainly they'd investigate. But that thought was immediately followed by the realization that Anton, as a key member of the review board and the director of the forensic clinic, could easily sway the discussion in whichever direction suited his needs.

"So now, Chicky," Jimmy's wheezing father asked, "what's on the menu?"

"Her," Ellen replied, her voice tense.

"I assume you've worked through the indelicate details."

"Of course," she said. "Mother told me the two of you never had sex and that Dr. Jenson did the actual insemination. As for Little Jimmy, I don't think he's quite up to the task, and we've come too far to take the chance."

"Very good, and will Dr. Jenson be officiating at tonight's festivities?"

Ellen pressed a remote-control button on the dash as she turned onto 19th Street. "That won't be necessary." She eased the cab into the last bay door of the carriage house. "I've got everything under control." And hitting the button again, the door shut behind them.

THIRTY-THREE

BARRETT LAY FLAT ON her back, her hands manacled over her head, and her feet stretched to the corners of the bed. She was alone in a dark room. "Help me!" she screamed. But her ears, trained from an early age, recognized how her voice seemed encapsulated. It bounced from the ceiling and the walls; the room was soundproof. She thought that she was in the carriage house, but she couldn't be certain. She didn't know what had happened with Jimmy or Ellen; they'd left some time ago. At least it felt that way. She felt the soreness in her right shoulder, and remembered how they'd drugged her a second time…or maybe it had been more than that.

Think Barrett; how long have you been here?

She strained against padded leather cuffs, the same kind used in psychiatric hospitals. She tensed the muscles of her forearm and twisted her fingers in tight, feeling for any play. She pictured the straps and the locks; she slowed her breath, and fought against the panic. *Where's Justine?* Her ears strained into the silence, wondering when they'd come back. "Justine? Are you there?"

Only silence. Time passed, as she tensed and relaxed her wrists, making tiny movements, and slowly creating give in the tight cuffs. "Come on," she whispered, feeling her right wrist slip further back. "Come on."

A door clicked; she froze. Then came a blinding light.

"So how are we doing?" Ellen asked.

Barrett peered through narrowed slits. What she saw was completely disorienting; it wasn't possible. "Where? This can't…"

"Nice, isn't it?" Ellen remarked.

Barrett's immediate thought was that this had to be a dream. Ellen Martin was dressed in a nurse's uniform, and Barrett was manacled to her own bed in her own condo. The sheets were ones she'd picked out with Ralph, the Ikea furniture was hers, the books, the medical journals, a stack of annotated musical scores on Ralph's bedside table. *This has to be a dream.*

"You must be getting tired of laying flat for so long," Ellen commented. She reached down and checked the restraints.

Barrett couldn't breathe, as Ellen inspected the tightness, and felt pulses in her wrists and ankles to ensure that the blood flow wasn't being cut off.

"Not much longer," Ellen said, as she pulled a syringe from a patch pocket on the front of her starched-white uniform.

"What is that?" Barrett managed, realizing this was no dream.

"Hormones," Ellen replied, as she uncapped the syringe and tapped the tip with an elegantly manicured nail. "Want to get you off to a good start."

Barrett felt a cool alcohol wipe over her throbbing shoulder.

"Just a little prick," Ellen smiled, as the needle sank into her flesh. "There we go, and now it's best for you to rest up. We've got quite a day ahead of us."

"Where's Justine?" Barrett managed, as she watched Ellen pull out a second loaded syringe.

"She's safe…nearby. In fact, if you're very good, I might let the two of you stay together. We'll have to see. I think it might be nice, get you through those difficult months."

As she spoke, Barrett noted inconsistencies in her carefully constructed cage. This wasn't her condo, and the grand piano that she glimpsed through the opening into the living room was not hers. The bedspread that had fallen to the floor was the right pattern, but the parts that were supposed to be green were peach and vice versa. This wasn't her condo, but a carefully constructed approximation.

"You've gone to a lot of trouble," she managed, through a throat that was parched.

"No trouble at all," Ellen answered, "now just one more shot."

"Why?"

"To help you sleep."

"No," Barrett was trying to remember. "Why? Why are you doing this?"

"It's not so strange," Ellen said, gazing at Barrett. "Many couples have trouble conceiving."

"God, no!"

"Best not to worry yourself. Stress is bad for the baby."

"Please let me see my sister," tears streamed down her face. Frustration welled, and then she felt the needle jab into her flesh.

"In time," Ellen said. "Now rest, we've got a big night ahead of us."

"Night?" Barrett croaked. "What day is it?"

"Monday," Ellen said standing by the bed. "You've been sleeping, and soon…I'm so glad he picked you." And with that, she leaned over and kissed Barrett on the forehead. "It's going to be all right. You'll see."

Barrett struggled. As Ellen leaned over, she thought of her mother, tucking her and Justine into bed at night. The kiss, the feel of her lips, soft and maternal. A familiar feeling of weightlessness came over her, as the room darkened. It was okay, she was safe at home in her own bed, and this was all a dream. It wasn't so bad, it was a dream about having a baby. She and Ralph had talked a lot about starting a family. It was time to do it, the clock was ticking. She felt the pull of sleep, the soothing languor and calming forgetfulness of whatever drug Ellen had just given her.

"No," Barrett said into the darkness, the sound of her voice an anchor to something real. "Not a dream," she managed. "Come on, it's Monday. I've been asleep. Wake up. Please wake up." She thought of Sifu. "Focus, Barrett. Don't fall asleep." She forced her eyes wide and stared into the darkness. "Come on." She felt her hands and the restraints around her wrists and ankles. Ellen had missed the slack that she'd developed. The right wrist, "Come on, Barrett." Pushing through the lull of the narcotic, she twisted her wrist, folding her fingers in tight. "Come on." She visualized the tiny bones in her hand, and drew them in tight. The restraint scraped the skin of her hand as she drew it back, she felt the flesh slowly rip; she didn't care. "Come on." She pulled harder, and felt pain and blood. "Come on," the cuff was all the way to the knuckle. Drawing back from her wrist, she pulled hard. The pain, even dulled by the drugs, sent a sheering jolt to her brain. She gasped, and yanked back hard. A scream flew from her lips as her hand, lubricated with blood, came free of the shackle.

She lay there, breathing hard. "Good," she reached across her chest, twisting in the sheets, feeling for her left hand. She stretched with her cramped and bleeding hand, feeling down her left arm, her shoulder twisting painfully. Her fingers felt for the restraint, the tips moving over the leather, feeling for the buckle. Her heart sank when she realized that it was the type that required a key to open, and not the sort that just buckled. "No." She sobbed, as she again tried to work away at her wrist, feeling for any play. Desperation welled, "No." With every ounce of strength, she pushed through the pain as her fingers cramped, and her skin tore. She felt the cuff start to slip, as millimeter by millimeter she pulled back. And with a final painful tug, her left hand was free. She sat up in bed, her feet still bound. Her fingers throbbed, the knuckles wet with blood. She listened into the darkness, and heard the dull absence of sound, like being in a recording studio. She reached down to her ankles, and felt the straps. "Yes," a surge of thankfulness as she realized that these buckled without a key. In a matter of seconds she'd removed the right and then the left.

As she swung her legs over the side of the bed, she didn't want to think about what had been done to her—about what might have happened in those hours she couldn't remember. She felt the sheer silky fabric that covered her, like a slip. They'd undressed her. And then a fierce cramping hit hard in her belly. She gasped and doubled over. She pictured Ellen in her nurse's uniform, "God, no." Barrett cried. They were giving her hormones, wanting to get her pregnant...or maybe....It was Monday, at least a day had passed. A fresh wave of pain hit hard in her middle. She wrapped her belly in her arms and leaned over, waiting for it to pass. On shaky legs she touched her feet down on the floor. She felt the rug underfoot, and stood. Her head swam as the pain receded. Her eyes discerned the outlines of her furniture. "No, it's not mine," she whispered, "none of this is real." A rumbling aftershock grabbed at her gut. That was real, and Barrett wondered what the hell Ellen and Jimmy had done to her as she'd slept. Had they raped her? And where exactly was she. This had to be the mansion, or had they taken her someplace else, someplace where no one would look for her. She thought of Hobbs, and then remembered—they'd done something to him. And Ralph, her sweet Ralph. And Justine. What would they do to her if they knew Barrett had gotten out of bed? They thought nothing of killing. Justine was just a pawn.

She staggered toward where her living room was supposed to be. That's where Ellen had come from. With every step she stopped and listened. It was dead quiet. She headed toward the front door, and twisted the knob; it was locked. She felt the light switches to the right, her fingers lingered. If she turned on the lights would they see? Were they watching her now, maybe having some kind of night vision cameras trained on her? She felt for the deadbolt and turned, feeling it slide back. She tried the knob again...nothing. She was trapped. "Don't panic." She tried to calm herself, "she said she was coming back...but when." She realized that they wouldn't expect to find her out of bed, so maybe there was a chance. She'd need a weapon; she'd need to make them let her go, make them take her to Justine, to free them both.

She stared into the darkness, trying to inventory what in her apartment—or her pseudo apartment—could make a weapon. Feeling along the furniture, she walked into the galley kitchen and opened the drawer where the knives were kept. She felt in the plastic bins, but where she should have found steel, her fingers came upon plastic cutlery. She reached up into the cupboards, wanting her heavy enamel cookware, but that too was gone. Even the books were all paperbacks, the lamps bolted to the tables, and Barrett, weakened by the drugs, doubted her physical strength. She needed to find something. Stumbling back to the living room, her hip banged into the piano. Her hands felt over its hard surface. "Yes." She lifted up the lid, and gingerly placed the brace in its groove. Her fingers reached inside and gently moved over the surface of the tautly stretched steel strings. She pictured the yards of cable in varying lengths and widths, which created the different notes. As a child, Sophie had instructed her in the importance of learning how to tune her own piano. It was an exercise meant to create perfect pitch, but now another pearl from that lesson remained.

"In older pianos," Sophie had told her, "it's common to find a tuning key hidden underneath." Sophie kept hers in the lift-up compartment of the bench.

Barrett felt over the surface of the piano, her fingers ran around the distant curve, and felt a patch of scarred wood. It was hers—inherited from Sophie. She cautiously edged back toward the keyboard. Her knee bumped up against the bench. She bent down, and opened it, feeling familiar volumes of Chopin, Czerny, Brahms, and Beethoven. The smell of it stopped her, the faint whiff of Jasmine—Sophie's perfume. This was her piano. "Jesus," she muttered, wondering what her neighbors would have said as movers had taken it away. Shouldn't someone have asked where she was? As she stood, she remembered snippets of the concert with Jimmy. Jimmy had proposed—and she'd accepted—in front of a couple hundred people.

But what about her mother…and Justine…but Justine was gone, missing. And Ralph…dead. Hobbs, wasn't there an explosion? "Your detective Hobbs is dead." They're all dead. She pictured Anton—he was involved in this. Jimmy should never have gotten out, yet Anton opened the cage. She remembered her conversation with Housmann. Jimmy was erotomanic. Beyond that, he had multiple personalities—at least three: the little boy who played cello and was Hansel to his sister's Gretel, the scary father who'd done awful things, and a third adult Jimmy, who she'd only glimpsed for moments, who seemed a kind of ghost—the Jimmy that might have been, but never had the chance.

As she felt in the corner of the piano bench, her fingers found the L-shaped steel tuning wrench. Her mind flew over other cases where men had stalked and captured women. The ones she knew about, the ones where she'd evaluated the men after the fact, had all gone bad. The women—usually raped and murdered—spent their last days, and in one particular case, two-and-half years, in carefully constructed prisons. The preparation that had gone into their prisons often stretched over years. Sometimes the victims were random. But more often, as in her case, they'd been selected, carefully watched, and then….

She took the key gingerly and moved the wrench side over a tuning peg for one of the razor-thin strings in the upper register. *If this were a case?* She thought, *What are the facts? What are the patterns in Jimmy's…and Ellen's behavior?* Careful to make no noise, she unwound the string, feeling the tension release. *Jimmy is classic,* she realized. *He selected his victim—me—and then got rid of all competition*. The horror of what had happened to Ralph and to Hobbs sank in. She fought back tears. But there was more, Ellen was as bad—possibly worse. She had to be the driving force, because the personalities that Barrett had glimpsed in Jimmy seemed too mercurial to sustain this kind of planning and effort.

As the string came free in her hands, she thought too about Nicole Foster—the young violinist, who like herself was a transplant from the south—had there been a similar prison constructed for her, or had all those years in Croton given Jimmy—and Ellen—the time to plan?

She twisted the steel string in her hands, feeling it bite into the bruised and bleeding flesh of her knuckles. The pain was a tonic, helping her to push past the drugs. She gripped the string hard and pictured it around Jimmy's throat—or better still—Ellen's. With her prize, she padded toward the front door, and standing motionless by the frame, she waited.

———

Little Jimmy wondered if he should tell Ellen. As he'd done since Barrett's arrival, he sat transfixed in front of the row of monitors that let him view every inch of Barrett's apartment. He'd watched as she'd struggled to free herself from the restraints, he could see her pain and determination, and with each forward movement he could feel her triumph. He knew that if he told Ellen, she'd be right back in there tying her down. But he didn't want that. His princess needed to be free, to be happy, to have the run of her kingdom that Jimmy had made for her. He didn't understand why she was taking apart the piano, but Father pushed past little Jimmy, and with a triumphant surge took control.

"*Jimbo*," father hissed. [*I think our bride wants to trick us. She's a naughty girl, but we know how to take care of naughty girls, don't we?*"

Not interested in Jimmy's response, James Cyrus Martin knew that he and Ellen would have to be more careful. Barrett's antics couldn't continue for another nine months. They needed to ensure a healthy heir. After that, well, poor little Jimbo would find himself both a father and a widower.

THIRTY-FOUR

ELLEN—WHO'D BEEN RELAXING in the library with a scotch, and Mahler's Fifth cranked to the point of near pain—fumed as Jimmy spoke in the lisping voice she associated with Father.

"*Chicky,*" he cautioned, battling the music. "*She's stronger than she looks.*"

"That's the least of our concerns," Ellen replied, clicking off the stereo and plunging the room into silence.

No longer in her nurse's outfit, a show she put on for the benefit of little Jimmy, Ellen moved quickly through the mansion to the kitchen. "She can be up as much as she wants in another day," she muttered, as she rifled through the pantry looking for the right vials and syringes.

With Father at her side, she jogged back through the courtyard and toward Barrett's cage on the second floor. This kind of foolishness would not do.

At the top of the stairs, she pulled a gun from her shoulder bag. She unclasped the safety and handed it to her brother, "Don't shoot anyone. We don't want to go through this another time."

"*No,*" he agreed, savoring the feel of the cold compact weapon. "*This one is perfect. Much better than the first one. We'll have a beautiful baby.*"

A dread shiver passed through Ellen. Father's personality would have to be dealt with in the future. There was no way she'd ever let him lay a finger on Jimmy's baby. How she'd manage that hadn't been fully worked out, but right now she needed him.

"*Maybe,*" Father continued, as Ellen punched in the electronic door code that let them into the small control room constructed outside of Barrett's cage, "*we could keep her around for another kid, just like you and Jimbo.*"

Ellen froze, as she realized that Father knew exactly what she'd intended. "What are you talking about?"

"*Come now, Chicky. Fooling Jimbo is one thing, but you're talking with the old man. I'm not much for fairy tales. Jimbo won't be getting his happily ever after with the good doctor.*"

"Have you told him?"

"*Why would I do that? We're on the same side. Let's go in and settle down our lovely doctor. It's a pity I never liked girls. I think she'd be fun.*"

Ellen held her tongue, as she flipped the lights and looked at the monitors. She spotted Barrett next to the door, the infrared cameras showing that she had something in her hands that was difficult to see.

"*She took something out of the piano,*" Father remarked.

Ellen pressed the zoom control on the camera. She wondered how Barrett had gotten out of the restraints, and how was it possible for her to be so awake after the large doses of tranquilizers? But what really worried her was that Barrett's stressed state jeopardized the success of the fertilization. If it failed, it would take another month to get her ovulating again, and Ellen had few illusions that every day Barrett Conyors was in captivity was a day of grave peril for her and Jimmy. This new complication—that Father had figured out her end game—was also worrisome. Ellen never fully understood how such very different people came to live inside her brother, but at times she'd seen the boundaries between Father, little Jimmy, and the others shift. She wasn't certain that Father could keep the secret, and if he didn't, it would break little Jimmy's heart. She pressed a button on the panel and spoke into the microphone. "Dr. Conyors, you need to get back into bed. We need you to do it now, and if you don't we'll begin cutting off your sister's fingers."

"*That was good,*" Father commented, his eyes ablaze, his breathing fast. "*Very good. Look at how frightened she is. Oh…she's so lovely, looking around, knowing she's being watched. Wondering where we are, wondering if she can get to us…*" He clapped his hands in excitement.

Ignoring him, Ellen pressed the button again, "You have fifteen seconds to put down whatever you have in your hands, and get back into bed, or else we'll be bringing you her fingers. One, two three…"

———

Barrett froze, the steel piano wire coiled around her wrists. She heard Ellen's counting through hidden speakers. She had no doubt they'd make good on the threat. Defeated, she returned to bed, but held onto a length of piano string, a single razor-thin strand.

"Now lie down," Ellen's voice, boomed overhead. "I'm sorry if you find it uncomfortable, but you have one more day of bed rest and then you can be up and about as much as you like…now lie back…close your eyes…and don't try anything."

Seething and scared, Barrett did as told. She'd never had a chance. All the time she'd been struggling out of the restraints, she'd been watched. Despair crashed down, threatening to break her will. Sifu's admonition of *"fear nothing"* rang in her head. With her right hand she worked the piano wire under the sheet between the mattress and the metal bed frame. She let her fingers play over its tip, taking comfort in the needle sharpness, as light flooded the room.

Jimmy entered first, a gun in his hand, grinning wildly. *"Someone's been very naughty,"* he commented, keeping his distance, the tip of the gun trained on Barrett's forehead.

Then Ellen, dressed in black slacks and sweater, came into the room. She looked at Barrett with an expression of exasperation and concern. "Lie back," she instructed. "And put your hands and feet by the cuffs the way they were. I'm sorry if it's uncomfortable, but we need to make certain that everything takes, and bed rest for forty-eight hours is the only way."

With Jimmy at her side, the gun cocked and loaded, Ellen approached. "I'm going to give you a little sedative to get you through, but after that I promise you'll be up and about, and I think we'll even let you and your sister stay here together. Now won't that be nice?"

Ellen uncapped the syringe, and met Barrett's gaze. "I promise," she said, "things are going to work out…you'll see."

Barrett flinched as the cold wet alcohol pad touched down on her bare shoulder. She saw Ellen's profile, her expression intent as she brought the needle close. *Now*, she thought. And forcing her body into action she yanked the piano wire from under the mattress and with a single sweeping movement pushed up, grabbing Ellen and twisting her around as she lost balance. With a single lightning movement Barrett wrapped the wire tight around her neck; she twisted, pulling it in harder.

———

Father blinked, shocked by Barrett's rebellion. She was crouched in bed, a piano wire tight around Chicky's throat. Chicky's eyes were bulging, and he could see the bite of the wire, as her fingers clawed at her neck, trying to free herself.

Barrett yanked tighter, and Chicky stopped struggling.

"Put down the gun, Jimmy," Barrett barked, "or swear to God, I'll kill her."

"*Interesting,*" Father hissed, the gun pointed at Barrett's head. Chicky was staring at him, fear in her eyes. Little Jimmy stirred in the background, trying to break through. "*What to do? What to do?*" With his gaze fixed on Ellen's, he hissed, "*Sorry Chicky,*" backed out of the room, and bolted.

THIRTY-FIVE

BARRETT'S THOUGHTS RACED AS Jimmy ran. With her fingers twisted in piano wire, and Ellen's hands clawing at her own, her options weren't great. The minute Jimmy—or whoever the fuck he was—made it to the other side, she'd be back where she'd started, locked in her cage, and not one step closer to freedom, or to finding Justine. But if she ran after him, and left Ellen, that was bad too. Or the third choice—all options flashing through her mind at once—*kill her*. She willed herself numb, as her hands pulled the wire tighter; the sinews in Ellen's neck bulged. The hands waved frantically, her body bucked, arcing back. Barrett went for the kill, Ellen Martin's body sagged heavily. Barrett thought briefly to check a pulse, to make sure she was dead, but Jimmy was moving fast. Already at the door, he'd flipped open a hidden panel above the knob and was punching in a code. She sprinted across the living room.

With a heave he jerked the door open.

She was too late. She pictured the closing door and leapt over the couch, landing in a forward roll, her entire being focused on the handle. She grabbed it tight, her body in a crouch, her hands slick with blood.

She pulled back…nothing…but then she felt a tiny bit of play, and realized Jimmy was still on the other side; he hadn't gotten it fully closed. Hanging on to the knob she sank down to the floor, braced her legs on either side of the door, and pulled for her life.

Through the thick door, she heard Jimmy's lisping persona, swearing. If she let go—if he got the door latched—she'd be lost. The muscles of her calves and hamstrings strained, her forearms corded and sweat popped on her brow. It was all about focus—*get the door open, just get the door open.*

Time warped and stretched; it seemed eternity that she lay back, straining, and then, in a cartoonish moment Jimmy let go, and Barrett fell back hard, her grip off the knob, her head landing with a crack on the tiled floor. Winded, dizzy, she struggled to upright herself. Terrified, she focused on the crack of space between the door and whatever lay on the other side. She grabbed for the handle, ignoring the blinding pain in her head. She pulled, expecting Jimmy on the other side; he wasn't. The door opened into a semi-dark hallway, with filtered light that spilled in from frosted windows on either end.

Trying to calm her breath, she stood still and listened. Whereas her condo/prison had been devoid of outside sounds, the hallway was filled with many. Traffic noises to her right, and much less on her left…she heard a door bang in the distance. She moved cautiously toward the window away from the traffic noises. The frosting on the glass was impenetrable; she reached up and found the catch. She pushed, at first it held tight, but as she jammed the bony parts of her hands hard against the painted wood frame, it shuddered and moved up. She hit it again, pushing past the pain as splinters of wood bit into her flesh. Through the four-inch opening, she stared down, on a tangled mass of greenery. And in the distance she caught glimpses of the Martin mansion.

The smart thing would be to get the hell out, to jump out the window on the other side if need be. To run in her slip and bare feet to find help, but that would take time and explanations, and maybe a search warrant, and by then...*no.*

Moving toward an open door, which let out onto a stairwell, her entire awareness tuned outward, listening for every creak, the chirp of a bird, the acceleration of cars and trucks that seemed so close. As she came to the landing she was in a hallway that mirrored the one above. Security monitors lay at one end, their black and white screens providing multiple views of 19th Street. There were two doors, one that had a glass top that provided a view of darkly glimmering vehicles, four of them—a yellow cab, a panel truck, and two others she couldn't make out. She put her hand on the knob of the second door. She again thought of going for help, but thinking of Jimmy with Justine made her turn the knob.

———

James Cyrus Martin's strength was slipping. It wasn't just physical, as he pulled back, trying to latch and lock the damn door, with Conyors to the other side. Inside his head a war raged. Little Jimmy howled for Chicky, screaming at Father to let him out. Jimbo cried and yelled, and clawed for control.

With a malicious shove on the door, James Cyrus reversed direction and pushed in. It was a horrible risk, but the result bought him time. He didn't stop to hear her fall; he was down the stairs, and running, pumping his legs wildly across the garden path and into the main house. He twisted the kitchen lock shut, and slammed the door behind. It was all a series of horrible risks, but he was a betting man, and he bet that she'd come after him. The lock on the door wouldn't hold her long, just enough for him to be ready. As he unlatched the door that led down to the basement, he tried to placate little Jimmy—this was not the time for Jimbo to come out and play—this called for an adult—there was too much at risk. *"It's going to be okay, Jimbo. Everything's going to be okay."*

He heard his son sobbing, his grief palpable. Maybe Chicky was okay, he pictured the ferocity of that woman as she strangled his daughter. Chicky was gone, and now it was just him and Jimbo. But that would be okay, he'd stay in control, just like before. Maybe Jimbo would never come out again. A not unpleasant thought as he turned on the basement lights, felt the heat from the furnace, and saw the outline of the metal cage in which Justine Conyors was trapped.

———

Ellen Martin's eyes stared at the ceiling, the whites growing dry; she did not move. Then, a sea of white shot through her optic nerve and into the back of her brain. She blinked, and wondered briefly if she were dead, and then pain, unlike anything she'd ever known, like a circle of fire around her neck, told her she was very much alive—or in hell. She gasped for breath, the subtle movement of the air through her bruised and bloodied throat almost too much to bear.

Her hands reached back to the bed, pushing up. She looked into the living room, past the piano and at the open door. Barrett Conyors was gone, and Jimmy too was nowhere in sight.

She swore as she got to her feet, her head swam, and the searing pain doubled her over. A sticky sweat popped on her brow and along her back. She thought of her brother, and of all she'd built with the company; it gave her strength. She was going to fight; she always did. She steadied herself against a bureau, caught her reflection in the mirror, the bright band of raw red like a bloody necklace. *Damn her!* And then she remembered father's betrayal. *Damn them both,* and retrieving her gun from under the bed, she staggered toward the door.

THIRTY-SIX

BAREFOOT AND DRESSED IN a green satin nightgown that snagged and tore on thorns, Barrett pushed through the thicket and raced across the courtyard. The kitchen door was locked. She grabbed a rock, shattered the glass, and let herself in. From below she heard a door slam and the sound of footsteps moving deep into the bowels of the house; he wanted her to follow him, and she didn't see a choice. At least with Ellen out of the way the odds were better.

She glanced around, and saw the open door that led down a darkened stairway. With each passing second she knew that he was plotting, thinking of ways to trap her, to get her back into her cage. The door was a trap, but she could hear something down there, the sound of creaking metal, and the stirring of water through pipes. Torn between catching him and running away, she heard a woman's scream. "Justine," she gasped, and not able to stop herself, she moved through the door. With each step down the darkness became more complete, wrapping her in an eerie shell. Cobwebs wisped against her face, and warm waves of dusty air washed over her.

She heard her sister sob, and as her eyes slowly adjusted she saw a distant glow of fiery orange. The heat grew and as she moved toward the source of the light, she made out the outlines of an ancient furnace, like a giant iron oven. At first she didn't see Jimmy, just the cage, and her sister, dressed in scrubs, inside what appeared to be a kennel, with metal bars, and just enough room to stand. Justine's eyes were wide and her back was pressed tight against her cage. Tears glistened down her cheek, and then Barrett saw him, hidden behind Justine, his hands holding a cord tight around her throat.

She felt him watching her, smiling.

"Now this is fun, isn't it?" he lisped.

"Let her go," Barrett said. "I'll do whatever you want if you just let her go."

"Oh, dear," James Cyrus replied. *"If only I believed you. Trust is so hard to come by, and once trust is gone, well…there's only the strangling of relatives to keep true love on course…don't you find? Isn't this a perfect symmetry?"*

She heard his anger, and knew that it was just a matter of a few pounds of pressure to end Justine's life…just as she'd ended Ellen Martin's. "What do you want me to do?" she asked.

"That's better. Get into the cage and close the door behind yourself."

She looked at the opening to her sister's prison, a simple door with a latch, and a heavy padlock that lay open. So how would he manage putting the lock back on once she was inside? He'd need to let go of Justine.

"Get in!" he shouted. *"Do it now."*

"Okay," she said, with the sickening certainty that he intended to kill Justine once she'd complied. She stepped through the opening, having to duck her head, and noting the bare mattress and plastic bucket that Justine had been forced to use as a toilet. But it was the stark fear in her sister's eyes, the desperation that mirrored her own, that held her. "I'm so sorry," she whispered, reaching toward her.

"Don't touch her," James Cyrus ordered. *"Close the door, and then reach through the bars and put on the lock."*

Of course, she thought, he had no intention of letting go of Justine. He'd wait until the lock was in place, and just as she'd strangled Ellen, he'd do the same to Justine.

A shuffling noise, and the sound of the door banging open at the top of the stairs, made Barrett turn, and James Cyrus inhale. Footsteps, coming closer, and for Barrett the surge of hope, that someone had come to her rescue. Into the light, blood glinting around her neck, Ellen Martin appeared, gun in hand.

"Good," she croaked, assessing the vignette.

"Chicky, so good to see you. I hope you understand; I didn't have a choice."

Ellen Martin approached the cage, her gun fixed on Barrett. "Don't even think of moving," she whispered hoarsely, as she reached for the lock.

"If you hurt her," Barrett said, "I'll never give you what you want. Do you hear me?"

Ellen paused. "What are you saying?"

"If you harm my sister, I swear to God, I'll abort, I'll puncture my uterus. I'll make sure you never get your heir. Do you hear me Jimmy?" she was shouting.

"*There are other bitches in the sea,*" James Cyrus hissed back.

"Not you!" Barrett said. "I'm not talking to you! Jimmy. I want to talk to Jimmy, little Jimmy. I want little Jimmy now! Come out now!"

"*So sorry, but little Jimmy can't come out to…Barrett,*" Jimmy Martin's voice shifted, softer, younger. "Barrett."

"Jimmy," Barrett said, her eyes fixed on Ellen Martin, not yet hearing the click of the lock, "you have to let go of my sister."

"You hurt Ellen, I saw you hurt Ellen. You tried to kill her."

Ellen smiled, as she closed the lock.

"Jimmy, if you hurt Justine, I'll kill myself."

"No! You can't."

"I will, Jimmy. But that's what's going to happen to me anyway after I give Ellen and your father what they want. They're planning to kill me."

"No! That's a lie."

"Shut up!" Ellen said, pointing the barrel of the gun from Barrett to Justine.

"It's true," Barrett said, positioning her body between Justine and the gun. She had no way of knowing how far Ellen had gotten with her homegrown artificial insemination, but she did know that her only bargaining chip was her womb, its viability, and what might—or might not—be growing in it. "Ask your sister—she was planning to kill me right after I gave birth. Isn't that right, Ellen?"

"She's lying, Jimmy."

"I'm not," Barrett persisted, "even your father can tell you that. He and Ellen were in this together. Let go of Justine, Jimmy. Do it now. Do it for me."

"Okay."

And Justine crumpled to the ground.

It was the tiniest of victories and short-lived, as Ellen circled the cage.

"Hurt her, and I will kill myself," Barrett repeated. "You won't get your heir, and eventually, even with all of your money, they'll come looking for me. Remember, with Jimmy under board supervision, they don't even need a search warrant to come in here."

"They can look all they want," Ellen said, "it's a pity things have to be like this." She looked at Justine, barely moving on the floor, and then back at Barrett.

"What do you mean?" Jimmy asked, bewildered. "Ellen? She's my wife. You can't kill her."

"That's what she's going to do, Jimmy," Barrett said. "She'll take the baby, and then I'll go into the oven. It's just another game of Hansel and Gretel."

"Noooo."

"It's not true, Jimmy," Ellen's voice was soothing—the big sister—the strong one.

"Ask your father," Barrett persisted, shielding Justine's body as Ellen circled. It was a stalemate that couldn't last, she'd pushed Jimmy, but Ellen was as steady as the lock on the metal bars. Barrett frantically scanned the meager furnishings of Justine's prison—the bare mattress, the slop bucket, the remnants of a meal tray, complete with the same plastic cutlery used in the hospital. She grabbed for the tray and retrieved the white-plastic knife.

"What are you doing?" Ellen asked.

Barrett met her gaze, as she squatted next to Justine and showed the knife. "You're going to kill us both anyway, and I'll be damned if I'm going to be your brood mare." She moved the knife under the hem of her slip.

"Jimmy!" Ellen shouted at her brother. "Run up to the pantry and get me the syringes."

"Don't hurt her," Jimmy pleaded.

"She's hurting herself, do it now! Hurry!"

Barrett remembered years back in training, she'd had a horrific experience of a psychotic woman who'd punctured her uterus out of the delusional belief that she was carrying the devil's child. If in fact Ellen had succeeded with the insemination, this didn't seem all that different. She felt the scraping of the plastic against her naked flesh, and heard Justine's sobs, her body shivering. She thought of her mother, and of Ed Hobbs. She pictured her last night with Ralph, as Jimmy's footsteps came bounding back down the stairs.

"Don't hurt her," he pleaded with his sister, as he handed her the capped syringes.

"Jimmy," Ellen said, "I need Father, now. Tell him to come out."

"No. You're going to hurt her."

"I need Father, now!"

"No…I won't…you can't…*Hi Chicky*."

"Thank God," Ellen said, and handed the gun to James Cyrus. "If you fuck up again…"

Barrett's body tensed as Ellen approached the cage.

"Stay away from me," Barrett shouted, when in fact she was praying for Ellen to unlock the door and give her one last chance. "Stay away," she made a show of moving her elbow around as the knife moved harmlessly against her inner thigh.

The key went into the lock, the shank came free, and with James Cyrus aiming the gun at Barrett and Justine, Ellen entered the cage.

Barrett was through with caution; no one was coming to their rescue. She lunged, toppling Ellen back, as James Cyrus, excitedly shouted. *"Stop! Leave her alone."*

Barrett slammed Ellen's head back hard against the cement floor and with the palm of her hand, shattered the bridge of her nose, sending fragments of bone and fat up into the tiny vessels of her brain; it was a killing blow, one that Sifu had shown her late at night many years back after several shots of his favorite whiskey.

With cat-like precision Barrett was on her feet and explosively lunged at the cage door, just as James Cyrus was struggling to replace the lock. The metal door swung out and caught him in the side of the face and shoulder. He stumbled back, his gun raised. Barrett dove for the ground as the first shot hit the floor behind her. She tried not to think about her semiconscious sister, as she tucked into a somersault and tackled him. A second shot rang overhead. Her fingers clamped down on Jimmy's wrist, and she struggled to get him to drop the gun. He kicked and spit in her face. *"Bitch, cunt!"*

She kneed him in the groin, and shot her elbow hard into his solar plexus. The air flew out of him, and the gun came free. She pushed off of the gasping man, and pointed the gun at his head. "Move and you're dead."

James Cyrus struggled to get his breath; flat on his back, he stared up at her; he blinked. "I'm sorry," Jimmy said, in his little boy's voice. "I love you. I'm sorry."

She felt her finger tighten on the trigger; it would be so easy. "Justine," she called out, "get away from the cage…You…in it. Now!"

Jimmy cowered, his eyes wide and innocent, "I love you. You love me. I'm sorry."

"Get in the cage Jimmy or I pull the trigger."

He blinked; his tongue licked lewdly across his upper lip, "*I don't think you would, Doctor.*"

Repulsed, her grip tightened. "You have until three. One …two …"

"*This isn't over,*" he said, crawling toward the cage, while keeping his eyes fixed on the gun. "*You married the boy, and a wife must perform certain duties. You have a responsibility to the community. To the family…*"

She tuned out his prattle, watching for the moment he was fully inside. She moved fast, slammed the door and clicked the lock.

"Justine, go upstairs and call for help. Then get yourself out of here…Go to mom's. I'll meet you there."

"I'm not leaving without you," her sister replied, as Jimmy's father persona continued to ramble.

"Please don't argue," Barrett said, keeping her eyes on Jimmy as she knelt next to Ellen's unmoving body. With two fingers she felt for a pulse; there was nothing. "Good, go Justine…I'll be fine." She sat cross-legged in front of Jimmy's locked cage, holding the gun steady, and listening to the sound of her sister running up the stairs. Help would come soon. And this time there'd be no slip-ups; she'd stay until the cops arrived; she'd make sure that everything was done by the book, and that Jimmy Martin would get locked away—and never, ever come out.

THIRTY-SEVEN

FOUR WEEKS LATER, BARRETT was back in her office, trying to get through her work, but unable to focus. She was pregnant. She'd done a home pregnancy test immediately after her escape, and was shocked to see it was positive. Of course, as her gynecologist told her, that could have been from the fertility drugs they'd been giving her. What complicated matters was that, if in fact she was pregnant, it could quite possibly have happened that last night she was with Ralph. She'd been ready to have a baby, they'd not used protection, but now...she was waiting for the results of the DNA test. Was the fetus inside her Ralph's or Jimmy's? And depending on how that got answered, she either would—or wouldn't have—some hard options to consider. In her entire life Barrett had never contemplated abortion. She firmly believed in a woman's right to choose, but that was other women; it had never been this personal, this immediate. It was hard to breathe, and she wished the damn call would come. Her doctor had said it would take at least a week—the week was up.

The phone rang, her stomach lurched and she picked up.

"Hey Barrett," it was Hobbs, calling from his hospital room.

"How's it going?" she asked, glad for the intrusion, and remembering how relieved she'd been to discover he was alive, but shocked when she'd gone to visit him that first day in the hospital. He'd been heavily sedated and lucky to be alive. He'd been covered in gauze, and what exposed skin she could see was red and slick with antibiotic dressing—more than 30 percent of his body had second- and third-degree burns. Ed was facing months in the unit, and had tried to crack jokes about the mind-numbing series of skin grafts he was facing.

"It's going. Although I just got word that Jimbo's attorneys are going to shoot for the not guilty by reason of mental defect crap."

"No surprise there," she said.

"You think he'll get it?"

She pondered the complexities of the case, and of Jimmy, "Hard to know. It could go either way."

"Yeah," he admitted, "they'll try and pin the actual murders on Ellen, and make him out as some crazy-assed accomplice. Either way, he ain't ever coming out."

"You sure of that?" she said.

These calls with Hobbs helped. Even with the burns that covered his face, hands, scalp, and torso, he'd insisted on following the case, and keeping Barrett up-to-date. The Martin mansion was sealed off and thoroughly searched, as was the carriage house and the elaborate reproduction of Barrett's condo. Each day had revealed fresh horrors that stretched back through decades.

In the dirt-floored basement of the mansion, bone fragments and ancient blood-spatter were discovered in the area of the coal-burning furnace. Jimmy's story about the nanny was probably accurate, although the exact identity of the nanny, Maylene, wasn't known. When they brought in a small excavator and dug up the courtyard they found additional bone fragments, the DNA matching that of James Cyrus Martin and Vivian Alfort Martin.

He also told her how the investigating team had been besieged with calls from distant Martin relatives, all wanting to know what would happen with the Martin fortunes.

"They have two detectives and a forensic accountant working on just that," he'd told her. "You can't imagine how rich these people were."

"So have you heard?" he asked.

"Not yet," she admitted, glad that Hobbs knew everything, and she didn't have to explain how she might be pregnant with Jimmy Martin's child.

"Can I make a horrible joke?" he asked.

"Yes, but only you at this point."

"You know if it is his kid...and don't shoot me...but he'd be the natural heir to all of that money."

"I know," she admitted. "And don't think I haven't thought about that, and don't think I hate myself for even mulling it over."

"It's human, Barrett. Don't beat yourself up over it. Whatever decisions you have to make, you'll do the right thing."

"I wish I was so sure, she said, feeling the tears that were never far off. "I wish I had the fucking test results...Ed?"

"What?"

"There's something else...when Jimmy showed me all that crap about you, I shouldn't have listened. I should have trusted that you would have told me—or not—I should have just trusted."

"Water under the bridge, considering what you've been through…what we've both been through…all that seems kind of small. Any chance I'll be seeing you? I could use the company. This place is boring as hell."

"Sure…I'll pick up Chinese. Although, if I get the results, I could be a total basket case."

"Is that the clinical name for it?"

"Yeah, that or head case." And after she hung up, she was surprised to see she was actually smiling.

Hobbs had that effect on her, unlike work, and this new job, which she wasn't certain she wanted. Anton had hastily resigned; his last interaction with Barrett an embarrassing and disturbing encounter.

"You can ruin me," he'd told her, knowing that the trail of his research funding could be easily traced back to Ellen Martin. "I'm begging you not to."

She'd said little, her rage too close to the surface. "It'll all come out; I'm not going to stop that."

"But you could…"

"I won't," she'd said. "You let Jimmy out." She'd wanted to say more, but the meaning was clear.

"I didn't know."

She'd glared at him, realizing that all of this could have been prevented if he'd done his job, and resisted the money. "Get out, Anton," were her final words. She'd tried to remember how they had ever been friends.

The day he handed in his resignation, she got a call from Housmann.

"They're pulling me out of mothballs to head up a search committee. I don't know why, seeing as they didn't take my advice the last time," the retired psychiatrist had told her. "I told them that you were the only internal candidate I'd consider. What do you think?"

"I don't know. Right now I'm just trying to keep one foot in front of the other."

"I just read your article in the *American Journal*. They'd be foolish not to give you the job. It can be whatever you want it to be. You get to take the best cases, the best students. And I'll see to it that they don't try to stiff you on the salary..."

"It's not that," she'd said, picturing the bespectacled man in his sun-flooded living room.

"I know; we're still human. You can't go through something like what you've been through without being changed by it. The only people who wouldn't be affected are sociopaths. That's why I think they're better adapted for survival. Stuff like this doesn't faze them... So what are your symptoms? Flashbacks? Nightmares? Jumping every time the phone rings?"

"All of the above, and always feeling like I'm two steps away from a panic attack."

"Are you seeing anyone?" he'd asked.

"No."

He'd chuckled, "Spoken like a true doctor...You could see me. We wouldn't call it therapy, more like supervision."

"I'd like that," she'd said, knowing that there were few others who'd be able to understand.

"And you'll think about taking the job?"

"If you throw yourself in as a supervisor, not just about this, but I don't know a thing about being an administrator, and you do."

"Deal," he'd said, and then pushed further. "So I'll tell the board that you'll fill in as the acting director with the expectation that after a brief and cursory search we'll offer you the job."

"If I don't like it, or can't do it?"

He had laughed, "I don't think your competency is in question, but we'll talk about how you survive being the boss. If you think Martin was a pain in the ass, just try telling forty whining employees that they can't *all* have Christmas week off."

Still, there was more. Daily encounters with reporters and photographers who waited outside her co-op and the clinic, trying to get her photograph and gruesome details of the millionaire murderers. The tabloids and even *The Times* devoted pages of ink to the ongoing investigation and the titillating discoveries in the Gramercy Park mansion.

The forensic center which was, she discovered, part of the reason Housmann was recruited to play white knight, received less favorable mention in the press. A great deal was made of the fact that Jimmy had a deviant history and had been released into the community without adequate supervision. Editorials about releasing known sex offenders back into the community popped up in every newspaper. Television reporters left messages with her secretary asking for interviews, and even national programs were looking to do exposés about releasing violent patients.

But now, all she could think about was the damn phone. When it rang again, she half expected it to be Hobbs again; it wasn't.

"This is Dr. Harrison's office for Barrett Conyors."

"Yes," her mouth dry, heart in her throat.

"The doctor has your test results, and wanted to set up a time…possibly later this afternoon, to review them with you."

"Of course," she said, unable to breathe. "I could be there any time."

"He has a cancellation at four, is that too soon?"

"No, I'll be there."

THE END

ABOUT THE AUTHOR

Charles Atkins, MD, is a board-certified psychiatrist, author, and professional speaker. He is on the clinical faculty at Yale University and is an attending psychiatrist at Waterbury (Connecticut) Hospital. In addition to thrillers and a book on bipolar disorder, he has written hundreds of articles, columns, and short stories for both professional and popular magazines, newspapers, and journals.

His web site is www.charlesatkins.com

http://www.charlesatkins.com